Johann Caspar Lavater

Essays on physiognomy

For the promotion of the knowledge and the love of mankind

Johann Caspar Lavater

Essays on physiognomy
For the promotion of the knowledge and the love of mankind

ISBN/EAN: 9783337257965

Printed in Europe, USA, Canada, Australia, Japan

Cover: Foto ©Andreas Hilbeck / pixelio.de

More available books at **www.hansebooks.com**

on

PHYSIOGNOMY;

for the Promotion of the

K: NOWLEDGE and the LOVE

OF MANKIND;

Written in the German Language

By J. C. LAVATER,

Abridged from. M.ʳ Holcroft's. Translation

Lavater Contemplating a Bust

BOSTON,
Printed for William Spotswood, &
David West.

Advertiſement.

[Annexed to the MOST APPROVED LONDON EDITION *of this work, from which this* FIRST AMERICAN EDITION *has been reprinted.]*

THE Eſſays on Phyſiognomy of M. Lavater, are now ſo univerſally known and celebrated, that it is unneceſſary to attempt their eulogium ; even thoſe who conſider the ſcience they are written to ſupport as viſionary, cannot but admire the lively force of imagination, and animated argument, with which the author has explained and defended his favourite hypotheſis. The reception the work has met with from the public, has encouraged certain literary pirates to ſeize almoſt the whole of it, and appropriate it to themſelves, by the aid of a pair of ſciſſars ; but in their eagerneſs to graſp their reward, they have in ſome places ſo mangled and disfigured it by abſurd errors, in copying or of the preſs, that the author or tranſlator (of whoſe labour they have availed themſelves, verbatim, with the utmoſt effrontery and without any acknowledgment) would ſcarcely be able to diſcover the meaning, without having recourſe to the work they have ſo diſgraced, by their mutilated and inaccurate copy. In ſome places whole ſentences abſolutely neceſſary to the ſenſe have been omitted, and in others, words altered to a meaning diametrically oppoſite. A liſt of all the errors, which totally deſtroy or change the ſenſe of the paſſage, without enumerating common typographical miſtakes, would fill more than a page. The publiſhers and proprietors, therefore, of the work thus impudently ſtolen, and wretchedly mutilated, now preſent to the public an abridgment carefully reviſed, correctly printed, and containing, in addition to all that is to be found in the other, nearly a whole ſheet of letter preſs, and two additional copper-plates, containing twelve heads.

A

PHYSIOGNOMY.

CHAPTER I.

INTRODUCTION.

*Physiognomy a Science.—The Truth of Physiognomy.—
—The Advantages of Physiognomy.—Its Disadvan-
tages.—The Ease and Difficulty of studying Physiognomy.—A Word concerning the Author.*

IT has been afferted by thoufands, that " though
" there may be fome truth in phyfiognomy,
" ftill it never can be a fcience." Thefe affertions will be repeated, how clearly foever their objections may be anfwered, and however little they
may have to reply. Phyfiognomy is as capable of
becoming a fcience as any one of the fciences,
mathematics excepted. It is a branch of the phyfical art, and includes theology ·and the belles
lettres. Like thefe, it may, to a certain extent,
be reduced to rule, and acquire an appropriate
character, by which it may be taught.

Whenever truth or knowledge is explained by

B

fixed principles, it becomes fcientific, fo far as it
can be imparted by words, lines, rules, and definitions. The queftion will ftand fimply thus : Whether it be poflible to explain the undeniable ftriking
differences which exift between human faces and
forms, not by obfcure and confufed conceptions,
but by certain characters, figns and expreflions ?
Whether thefe figns can communicate the ftrength
and weaknefs, health and ficknefs of the body ; the
folly and wifdom, the magnanimity and meannefs,
the virtue and vice of the mind ? This is the only
thing to be decided ; and he who, inftead of invef-
tigating the queftion, fhould continue to declaim
againft it, muft either be deficient in the love of
truth, or in logical reafoning.

The experimental philofopher can only proceed
with his difcoveries to a certain extent ; only can
communicate them by words ; can only fay,
" Such and fuch are my experiments, fuch my
" remarks, fuch is the number of them, and fuch
" are the inferences I draw : purfue the track that
" I have explored." Yet, will he not be unable,
fometimes, to fay thus much ? Will not his active
mind make a thoufand remarks, which he will
want the power to communicate ? Will not his eye
penetrate receffes, which he fhall be unable to difcover to that feebler vifion that cannot difcover for
itfelf ? Is any fcience brought to perfection at the
moment of its birth ? Does not genius continually,
with eagle-eye and flight, anticipate centuries ?
How long did the world wait for Wolf ? Who,
among the moderns, is more fcientific than Bonnet ?
Who more accurately diftinguifhes falfehood from
truth ? Yet to whom would he be able to communicate his fudden perception of the truth ; the refult or refources of thofe numerous, fmall, inde-
fcribable, rapid, profound remarks ? To whom
could he impart thefe by figns, tones, images and
rules ? Is it not the fame with phyfic, theology, and
all the arts and fciences ? Is it not the fame with

painting, at once the mother and daughter of phyſiognomy?

How infinitely does he, who is painter or poet born, ſoar beyond all written rule! But muſt he, who poſſeſſes feelings and power which are not to be reduced to rule, be pronounced unſcientiſic? So, phyſiognomonical truth may, to a certain degree, be deſined, communicated by ſigns and words, as a ſcience. This is the look of contempt, this of innocence. Where ſuch ſigns are, ſuch and ſuch properties reſide.

There can be no doubt of the truth of phyſiognomy. All countenances, all forms, all created beings, are not only different from each other in their claſſes, races, and kinds, but are alſo individually diſtinct. Each being differs from every other being of its ſpecies. However generally known, it is a truth the moſt important to our purpoſe, and neceſſary to repeat, that " there is no roſe perfectly " ſimilar to another roſe, no egg to an egg, no eel " to an eel, no lion to a lion, no eagle to an eagle, " no man to a man."

Confining this propoſition to man only, it is the ſirſt, the moſt profound, moſt ſecure and unſhaken foundation-ſtone of phyſiognomy, that however intimate the analogy and ſimilarity of the innumerable forms of men, no two men can be found, who, brought together, and accurately compared, will not appear to be very remarkably different. Nor is it leſs incontrovertible, that it is equally impoſſible to find two minds, as two countenances, which perfectly reſemble each other.

Conſiderations like theſe will be ſufficient to make it received as a truth, not requiring farther demonſtration, that there muſt be a certain native analogy between the external varieties of the countenance and form, and the internal varieties of the mind. Anger renders the muſcles protuberant; and ſhall not therefore an angry mind and protuberant muſcles be conſidered as cauſe and effect?

B

After repeated obfervation, that an active and vivid eye, and an active and acute wit, are frequently found in the fame perfon, fhall it be fuppofed that there is no relation between the active eye and the active mind ? Is this the effect of accident ? Ought it not rather to be confidered as fympathy, an interchangeable and inftantaneous effect, when we perceive that, at the very moment the underftanding is moft acute and penetrating, and the wit the moft lively, the motion and fire of the eye undergo, at that moment, the moft vifible alteration ?

But all this is denied by thofe who oppofe the truth of the fcience of phyfiognomy. Truth, according to them, is ever at variance with herfelf : Eternal order is degraded to a juggler, whofe purpofe it is to deceive.

Calm reafon revolts when it is afferted, that the ftrong man may appear perfectly like the weak, the man in full health like another in the laft ftage of a confumption, or that the rafh and irafcible refemble the cold and phlegmatic. It revolts to hear it affirmed, that joy and grief, pleafure and pain, love and hatred, all exhibit themfelves under the fame traits, that is to fay, under no traits whatever, on the exterior of man. Yet fuch are the affertions of thofe who maintain that phyfiognomy is a chimerical fcience. They overturn all that order and combination by which Eternal wifdom fo highly aftonifhes and delights the underftanding. It cannot be too emphatically repeated, that blind hance and arbitrary diforder conftitute the philofophy of fools, and that they are the bane of natural knowledge, philofophy, and religion. Entirely to banifh fuch a fyftem, is the duty of the true inquirer, the fage, and the divine.

It is indifputable that all men, abfolutely all men, eftimate all things whatever by their phyfiognomy, their exterior temporary fuperficies. By viewing thefe on every occafion, they draw their conclufions concerning their internal properties.

What merchant, if he be unacquainted with the perfon of whom he purchafes, does not eftimate his wares by the phyfiognomy or appearance of thofe wares? If he purchafed of a diftant correfpondent, what other means does he ufe in judging whether they are or are not equal to his expectation? Is not his judgment determined by the colour, the finenefs, the fuperficies, the exterior, the phyfiognomy? Does he not judge money by its phyfiognomy? Why does he take one guinea, and reject another? Why weigh a third in his hand? Does he not determine according to its colour, or impreffion, its outfide, its phyfiognomy? If a ftranger enter his fhop, as a buyer or feller, will he not obferve him? Will he not draw conclufions from his countenance? Will he not, almoft before he is out of hearing, pronounce fome opinion of him? and fay, " This man has an honeft " look—this man has a pleafing or forbidding " countenance." What is it to the purpofe whether his judgment be right or wrong? He judges, and, though not wholly, he depends, in part, upon the exterior form, and thence draws inferences concerning the mind.

The farmer, walking through his grounds, regulates his future expectations by the colour, the fize, the growth, the exterior; that is to fay, by the phyfiognomy of the bloom, the ftalk or the ear of his corn, the ftem and fhoots of his vine-tree.— " This ear of corn is blighted—that wood is full " of fap—this will grow, that not," affirms he at the firft or fecond glance.—" Though thefe vine- " fhoots look well, they will bear but few grapes." And wherefore? He remarks in their appearance, as the phyfiognomift in the countenances of fhallow men, the want of native energy. Does he not judge by the exterior?

Does not the phyfician pay more attention to the phyfiognomy of the fick, than to all the accounts

that are brought him concerning his patient?
Zimmermann, among the living, may be brought
as a proof of the great perfection at which this
kind of judgment is arrived; and, among the dead,
Kemp, whofe fon has written a treatife on temperament.

I will fay nothing of the painter, as his art too
evidently reproves the childifh and arrogant preju-
dices of thofe who pretend to difbelieve phyfiognomy. The traveller, the philanthropift, the mi-
fanthropift, the lover, (and who not?) all act according to their feelings and decifions, true or
falfe, confufed or clear, concerning phyfiognomy.
Thefe feelings, thefe decifions, excite compaflion,
difguft, joy, love, hatred fufpicion, confidence,
referve, or benevolence.

By what rule do we judge of the fky, but by its
phyfiognomy? No food, not a glafs of wine or
beer, nor a cup of coffee or tea comes to table,
which is not judged by its phyfiognomy, its exterior, and of which we do not then deduce fome
conclufion refpecting its interior good or bad properties. Is not all nature phyfiognomy, fuperficies
and contents, body and fpirit, exterior effect and
internal power, invifible beginning and vifible end-
ing?

Phyfiognomy, whether underftood in its moft extenfive or confined fignification, is the origin of all
human decifions, efforts, actions, expectations, fears
and hopes; of all pleafing and unpleafing fenfations, which are occafioned by external objects.
From the cradle to the grave, in all conditions and
ages, throughout all nations, from Adam to the laft
exifting man, from the worm we tread on to the
moft fublime of philofophers, phyfiognomy is the
origin of all we do and fuffer.

Every infect is acquainted with its friend and its
foe; each child loves and fears, although it knows
not why. Phyfiognomy is the caufe: nor is there

enced by phyfiognomy ; not a man who cannot figure to himfelf a countenance, which fhall to him appear exceedingly lovely, or exceedingly hateful ; not a man who does not, more or lefs, the firft time he is in company with a ftranger, obferve, eftimate, compare, and judge of him according to appearances, although he might never have heard of the word or thing called phyfiognomy ; not a man who does not judge of all things that pafs through his hands by their phyfiognomy, that is, their internal worth by their external appearance.

The act of diffimulation itfelf, which is adduced as fo infuperable an objection to the truth of phyfiognomy, is founded upon phyfiognomy. Why does the hypocrite affume the appearance of an honeft man, but becaufe that he is convinced, though not perhaps from any fyftematic reflexion, that all eyes are acquainted with the characteriftic mark of honefty ?

What judge, wife or unwife, whether the criminal, confefs or deny the fact, does not fometimes in this fenfe decide from appearances ? Who can, is, or ought to be abfolutely indifferent to the exterior of perfons brought before him to be judged ? What king would choofe a minifter without examining his exterior, fecretly at leaft, and to a certain extent ? An officer will not enlift a foldier without thus examining his appearance, putting his height out of the queftion. What mafter or miftrefs of a family will choofe a fervant without confidering the exterior ? No matter that their judgment may or may not be juft, or that it may be exercifed unconfcioufly.

I am weary of citing fuch numerous inftances, which are fo continually before our eyes, to prove that men, tacitly and unanimoufly, confefs the influence which phyfiognomy has over their fenfations and actions. I feel difguft at being obliged to write thus, in order to convince the learned of truths which lie within the reach of every child.

Let him fee who has eyes to fee ; but fhould the light by being brought too clofe to his eyes, produce phrenfy, he may burn himfelf by endeavouring to extinguifh the torch of truth. I am not fond of ufing fuch expreffions ; but I dare to do my duty, and my duty is boldly to declare, that I believe myfelf certain of what I now and hereafter fhall affirm ; and that I think myfelf capable of convincing all lovers of truth, by principles which are in themfelves incontrovertible. It is alfo neceffary to confute the pretenfions of certain literary defpots, and to compel them to be more cautious in their decifions. It is therefore proved, it being an eternal and manifeft truth, that, whether they are or are not fenfible of it, all men are daily influenced by phyfiognomy ; nay, there is not a living being, which does not, at leaft after its manner, draw fome inferences from the external to the internal ; which does not judge concerning that which is not, by that which is apparent to the fenfes.

This univerfal though tacit confeffion, that the exterior, the vifible, the fuperficies of objects, indicate their nature, their properties, and that every outward fign is the fymbol of fome inherent quality, I hold to be equally certain and important to the fcience of phyfiognomy.

When each apple, each apricot, has a phyfiognomy peculiar to itfelf ; fhall man, the lord of earth, have none ? The moft fimple and inanimate object has its characteriftic exterior, by which it is not only diftinguifhed as a fpecies, but individually ; and fhall the firft, nobleft, beft harmonifed, and moft beautiful being, be denied all characteriftic ?

Whatever may be objected againft the truth and certainty of the fcience of phyfiognomy, by the moft illiterate or the moft learned ; how much foever he, who openly profeffes faith in this fcience, may be fubject to ridicule, to philofophis pity and contempt ; it ftill cannot be contefted, that there is no fubject, thus confidered, more important, more worthy of obfervation, more interefting than man ; nor any occupation fuperior to that of difclofing the beauties and perfections of human nature.

I fhall now proceed to inquire into the *Advantages* of phyfiognomy. Whether a more certain, more accurate, more extenfive, and thereby a more perfect knowledge of man, be, or be not profitable ; whether it be, or be not, advantageous to gain a knowledge of internal qualities from external form and feature ? is a queftion moft deferving of inquiry. This may be claffed firft as a general queftion, Whether knowledge, its extenfion, and increafe, be of confequence to man ?

Certain it is, that if a man has the power, faculties and will to obtain wifdom, that he fhould exercife thofe faculties for the attainment of wifdom. How paradoxical are thofe proofs, that fcience and knowledge are detrimental to man, and that a rude ftate of ignorance is to be preferred to all that wifdom can teach ! I here dare affert, that phyfiognomy has at leaft as many claims of effential advantage, as are granted by men, in general, to other fciences.

With how much juftice may we not grant precedency to that fcience which teaches the knowledge of men ? What object is fo important to man, as man himfelf ? What knowledge can more influence his happinefs, than the knowledge of himfelf ? This advantageous knowledge is the peculiar province of phyfiognomy.

Whoever would wifh perfect conviction of the advantages of phyfiogromy, let him imagine but for a moment, that all phyfiognomical knowledge and fenfation were loft to the world. What confufion, what uncertainty and abfurdity muft take place in millions of inftances, among the actions of men ! How perpetual muft be the vexation of the eternal

uncertainty in all which we fhould have to tranfact
with each other! and how infinitely would probability, which depends upon a multitude of circumftances, more or lefs diftinctly perceived, be weak-
ened by this privation! From how vaft a number
of actions, by which men are honoured and benefit-
ed, muft they then defift!

Mutual intercourfe is the thing of moft confequence to mankind, who are deftined to live in fociety. The knowledge of man is the foul of this
intercourfe, that which imparts animation to it,
pleafure and profit. Let the phyfiognomift obferve varieties, make minute diftinctions, eftablifh
figns, and invent words, to exprefs thefe his remarks; form general abftract propofitions; extend
and improve phyfiognomical knowledge, language,.
and fenfation; and thus will the ufes and advantages of phyfiognomy progreffively increafe.

Phyfiognomy is a fource of the pureft, the moft
exalted fenfations; an additional eye, wherewith
to view the manifold proofs of Divine wifdom and
goodnefs in the creation, and, while thus viewing
unfpeakable harmony and truth, to excite more
ecftatic love for their adorable Author. Where
the dark, inattentive fight of the unexperienced
perceives nothing, there the practical view of the
phyfiognomift difcovers inexhauftible fountains of
delight—endearing, moral, and fpiritual. With
fecret delight, the philanthropic phyfiognomift dif-
cerns thofe internal motives which would otherwife be firft revealed in the world to come. He
diftinguifhes what is permanent in the character
from what is habitual, and what is habitual from
what is accidental. He, thererefore, who reads
man in this language, reads him moft accurately.

To enumerate all the advantages of phfiogno-
my, would require a large treatife. The moft indifputable, though the moft important of thefe its
advantages, are thofe the painter acquires, who, if
he be not a phyfiognomift, is nothing. The great-

eft is that of forming, conducting, and improving the human heart.

I fhall now fay fomething with refpect to the *Difadvantages* of phyfiognomy.

Methinks I hear fome worthy man exclaim : " O thou, who haft ever hitherto lived the friend " of religion and virtue ! what is thy prefent pur- " pofe ? What mifchief fhall not be wrought by " this thy phyfiognomy ? Wilt thou teach man the " unbleffed art of judging his brother by the am- " biguous expreffions of his countenance ? Are " there not already fufficient of cenforioufnefs, " fcandal, and infpection into the failings of " others ? Wilt thou teach man to read the fe- " crets of the heart, the latent feelings, and the " various errors of thought ?

" Thou dwelleft upon the advantages of the " fcience ; fayeft thou fhalt teach men to con- " template the beauty of virtue, the hatefulnefs " of vice, and, by thefe means, make them vir- " tuous ; and that thou infpireft us with an ab- " horrence of vice, by obliging us to feel its ex- " ternal deformity. And what fhall be the con- " fequence ? Shall it not be, that for the appear- " ance, and not the reality of goodnefs, man " fhall wifh to be good ? that, vain as he al- " ready is, acting from the defire of praife, and " wifhing only to appear what he ought determi- " nately to be, he will yet become more vain, " and will court the praife of men, not by words " and deeds alone, but by affumed looks and coun- " terfeited forms ? Oughteft thou not rather to " weaken this already too powerful motive for " human actions, and to ftrengthen a better ; to " turn the eyes inward, to teach actual improve- " ment and filent innocence, inftead of indu- " cing him to reafon on the outward fair ex- " preffions of goodnefs, or the hateful ones of " wickednefs ?"

This is a heavy accufation, and with great appearance of truth. Yet how eafy is defence to me, and how pleafant, when my opponent accufes me from motives of philanthropy, and not of fplenetic difpute ! The charge is twofold, Cenforioufnefs and Vanity. I will anfwer thefe charges feparately ; and now proceed to reply to the firft objection.

I teach no black art ; no noftrum, the fecret of which I might have concealed, which is a thoufand times injurious for once that it is profitable, the difcovery of which is therefore fo difficult. I do but teach a fcience, the moft general, the moft palpable, with which all men are acquainted ; and ftate my feelings, obfervations, and their confequences.

It ought never to be forgotten, that the very purport of outward expreffion is to teach what paffes in the mind, and that to deprive man of this fource of knowledge were to reduce him to utter ignorance ; that every man is born with a certain portion of phyfiognomical fenfation, as certainly as that every man, who is not deformed, is born with two eyes ; that all men, in their intercourfe with each other, form phyfiognomical decifions, according as their judgment is more or lefs clear ; that it is well known, though phyfiognomy were never to be reduced to a fcience, moft men, in proportion as they have mingled with the world, derive fome profit from their knowledge of mankind, even at the firft glance, and that the fame effects were produced long before this queftion was in agitation. Whether, therefore, to teach men to decide with more perfpicuity, and certainty, inftead of confufedly ; to judge clearly with refined fenfations, inftead of rudely and erroneoufly with fenfations more grofs ; and, inftead of fuffering them to wander in the dark, and venture abortive and injurious judgments, to learn them by phyfiognomical experiments, by the rules of prudence and caution, and the fublime voice of philanthropy, to miftruft, to be diffident and flow to pronounce, where they imagine they difcover evil: whether this, I fay, can be injurious, I leave the world to determine.

I think I may venture to affirm, that very few perfons will, in confequence of this work, begin to judge ill of others, who had not before been guilty of the practice.

The fecond objection to phyfiognomy is, that " it renders men vain, and teaches them to affume " a plaufible appearance." The men thou wouldft reform are not children, who are good, and know that they are fo ; but men who muft, from expe-rience, learn to diftinguifh between good and evil ; men who, to become perfect, muft neceffarily be taught their own various, and confequently their own beneficent qualities. Let therefore, the defire of obtaining approbation from the good, act in concert with the impulfe to goodnefs. Let this be the ladder, or, if you pleafe, the crutch to fup-port tottering virtue. Suffer men to feel that God has ever branded vice with deformity, and adorned virtue with inimitable beauty. Allow man to rejoice when he perceives that his countenance improves in proportion as his heart is ennobled. Inform him only, that to be good from vain mo-tives, is not actual good, but vanity ; that the or-naments of vanity will ever be inferior and ignoble ; and that the dignified mien of virtue never can be truly attained, but by the actual poffeffion of virtue, unfullied by the leven of vanity.

Let me now fay a word or two as to the *Eafe* and *Difficulties* attending the ftudy of phyfiogno ny. To learn the loweft, the leaft difficult of fciences, at firft appears an arduous undertaking, when taught by words or books, and not reduced to actual practice. What numerous dangers and dif-ficulties might be ftarted againft all the daily enter-prifes of men, were it not undeniable that they are

C

performed with facility ! How might not the poſſibility of making a watch, and ſtill more a watch
worn in a ring, or of ſailing over the vaſt ocean,
and of numberleſs other arts and inventions, be
diſputed, did we not behold them conſtantly practi-
ſed ! How many arguments might be urged
againſt the practice of phyſic ! and, though ſome
of them be unanſwerable, how many are the reverſe !

It is not juſt, too haſtily to decide on the poſſible
eaſe or difficulty of any ſubject which we have not
yet examined.   The ſimpleſt may abound with difficulties to him who has not made frequent experiments, and, by frequent experiments, the moſt difficult may become eaſy.

Whoever poſſeſſes the ſlighteſt capacity for, and
has once acquired the habit of, obſervation and
compariſon, ſhould he ſee himſelf daily and inceſ-
ſantly ſurrounded by hoſts of difficulties, yet he
will certainly be able to make a progreſs.   There
is no ſtudy, however difficult, which may not be
attained by perſeverance and reſolution.

We have men conſtantly before us.   In the
very ſmalleſt towns there is a continual influx and
reflux of perſons, of various and oppoſite characters : among theſe many are known to us without
conſulting phyſiognomy ; and that they are patient or choloric, credulous or ſuſpicious, wiſe or
fooliſh, of moderate or weak capacity, we are convinced paſt contradiction.   Their countenances
are as widely various as their characters, and theſe
variety of countenances may each be as accurately
drawn as their varieties of character may be de-
ſcribed.

There are men, with whom we have daily intercourſe, and whoſe intereſt and ours are connected.
Be their diſſimulation what it may, paſſion will frequently for a moment, ſnatch off the maſk, and give
us a glance, at leaſt a ſide-view, of their true form.

Has Nature beſtowed on man the eye and car,

and yet made her language fo difficult, or fo entirely unintelligible ? and not the eye and ear alone, but feeling, nerves, internal fenfations, and yet has rendered the language of the fuperficies fo confufed, fo obfcure ? She who has adapted found to the ear, and the ear to found ; fhe who has created light for the eye, and the eye for light ; fhe who has taught man fo foon to fpeak, and to underftand fpeech ; fhall fhe have imparted innumerable traits and marks of fecret inclinations, powers, and paffions, accompanied by perception, fenfation, and an impulfe to interpret them to his advantage ; and, after beftowing fuch ftrong incitements, fhall fhe have denied him the poffibility of quenching this his thirft of knowledge ? She who has given him penetration to difcover fciences ftill more profound, though of much inferior utility ; who has taught him to trace out the paths, and meafure the curves of comets ; who has put a telefcope into his hand, that he may view the fatellites of the planets, and has endowed him with the capability of calculating their eclipfes through revolving ages ; fhall fo kind a mother have denied her children (her truth-feeking pupils, her noble philanthropic offfpring, who are fo willing to admire and rejoice in the majefty of the Moft High, viewing man his mafter-piece) the power of reading the ever prefent, ever open book of the human countenance ; of reading man, the moft beautiful of all her works, the compendium of all things, the mirror of the Deity ?

Awake ! view man in all his infinite forms ! Look, for thou mayeft eternally learn ; fhake off thy floth, and behold. Meditate on its importance ; take refolution to thyfelf, and the moft difficult fhall become eafy.

Let me now mention the *Difficulties* attending this ftudy. There is a peculiar circumftance attending the ftarting of difficulties. There are fome who poffefs the particular gift of difcovering and inventing difficulties, without number or limits, on the moſt common and eaſy ſubjects. I ſhall be brief on the innumerable difficulties of phyſiog-nomy ; becauſe, it not being my intention to cite them all in this place, the moſt important will oc-caſionally be noticed and anſwered in the courſe of the work. I have an additional motive to be brief, which is, that moſt of theſe difficulties are included in the indeſcribable minuteneſs of innumerable traits of character, or the impoſſibility of ſeizing, expreſſing, and analyſing certain ſenſations and obſervations.

Nothing can be more certain than that the ſmalleſt ſhades, which are ſcarcely diſcernible to an unexperienced eye, frequently denote total oppoſi-tion of character. How wonderfully may the expreſſion of countenance and character be altered by a ſmall inflexion or diminiſhing, lengthening or ſharpening, even though but of a hair's breadth !

How difficult, how impoſſible, muſt this variety of the ſame countenance, even in the moſt accurate of the arts of imitation, render preciſion ! How often does it happen, that the ſeat of character is ſo hidden, ſo enveloped, ſo maſked, that it can only be caught in certain, and perhaps uncommon poſitions of the countenance ; which will again be changed, and the ſigns all diſappear, before they have made any durable impreſſion ! or, ſuppoſing the impreſſion made, theſe diſtinguiſhing traits may be ſo difficult to ſeize, that it ſhall be impoſſible to paint, much leſs to engrave, or deſcribe them by language.

It is with phyſiognomy as with all other objects of taſte, literal or figurative, of ſenſe, or of ſpirit. How many thouſand accidents, great and ſmall, phyſical and moral ; how many ſecret incidents, alterations, paſſions ; how often will dreſs, poſiti-on, light and ſhade ; and innumerable diſcordant circumſtances, ſhow the countenance ſo diſadvanta-geouſly, or, to ſpeak more properly, betray the

phyſiognomiſt into a falſe judgment on the true
qualities of the countenance and character ! How
eaſily may theſe occaſion him to overlook the eſſential traits of character, and form his judgment on
what is wholly accidental ! How ſurpriſingly may
the ſmall-pox, during life, disfigure the countenance ! How may it deſtroy, confuſe, or render
the moſt deciſive traits imperceptible !

We will therefore grant the oppoſer of phyſiognomy all he can aſk, although we do not live without hope, that many of the difficulties ſhall be re-
ſolved, which, at firſt, appeared to the reader and
to the author inexplicable*.

It is highly incumbent upon me that I ſhould
not lead my readers to expect more from me than
I am able to perform. Whoever publiſhes a con-
ſiderable work on phyſiognomy, gives his readers
apparently to underſtand, that he is much better
acquainted with the ſubject than any of his cotemporaries. Should an error eſcape him, he expoſes
himſelf to the ſevereſt ridicule ; he is contemned,
at leaſt by thoſe who do not read him, for pretenſions which probably they ſuppoſe him to make,
but which in reality he does not make.

The God of truth, 'and all who know me, will
bear teſtimony, that from my whole ſoul I deſpiſe
deceit, as I do all ſilly claims to ſuperior wiſdom
and infallibility, which ſo many writers, by a thouſand artifices, endeavour to make their readers
imagine they poſſeſs.

Firſt, therefore, I declare, what I have uniformly
declared on all occaſions, although the perſons who
ſpeak of me and my works endeavour to conceal it
from themſelves and others, that I underſtand but
little of phyſiognomy ; that I have been, and continue daily to be, miſtaken in my judgment : but
theſe errors are the moſt natural and moſt certain

* The following lines, to the end of the Introduction, contain M.
Lavater's own remarks on himſelf.

means of correcting, confirming, and extending my knowledge.

It will probably not be difagreeable to many of my readers, to be informed, in part, of the progrefs of my mind in this ftudy.

Before I reached the twenty-fifth year of my age, there was nothing I fhould have fuppofed more improbable, than that I fhould make the fmalleft inquiries concerning, much lefs that I fhould write a book on, phyfiognomy. I was neither inclined to read nor make the flighteft obfervations on the fubject. The extreme fenfibility of my nerves occafioned me, however, to feel certain emotions at beholding certain countenances. I fometimes inftinctively formed a judgment according to thefe firft impreffions, and was laughed at, afhamed, and became cautious. Years paffed away before I again dared, impelled by fimilar impreffions, to venture fimilar opinions. In the mean time, I occafionally fketched the countenance of a friend, whom by chance I had lately been obferving. I had, from my earlieft youth, a propenfity to drawing, and efpecially to drawing of portraits, although I had but little genius or perfeverance. By this practice my latent feelings began partly to unfold themfelves. The various proportions, fimilitudes, and varieties of the human countenance became more apparent. It has happened that, on two fucceffive days, I have drawn two faces, the features of which had a remarkable refemblance. This awakened my attention ; and my aftonifhment increafed when I received certain proofs that thefe perfons were as fimilar in character as in feature.

I was afterwards induced by M. Zimmermann, phyfician to the court of Hanover to write my thoughts on this fubject. I met with many opponents ; and this oppofition obliged me to make deeper and more laborious refearches, till at length the prefent work on phyfiognomy was produced.

Here I muft repeat the full conviction I feel,

that my whole life would be infufficient to form any approach towards a perfect and confiftent whole. It is a field too vaft for me fingly to till. I fhall find various opportunities of confeffing my deficiency in various branches of fcience, without which it is impoffible to ftudy phyfiognomy with that firmnefs and certainty which are requifite. I fhall conclude by declaring, with unreferved candour, and wholly committing myfelf to the reader who is the friend of truth,

That I have heard, from the weakeft men, remarks on the human countenance, more acute than thofe I had made; remarks which made mine appear trifling.

That I believe, were various other people to sketch countenances, and write their obfervations, thofe I have hitherto made would foon become of little importance.

That I daily meet an hundred faces, concerning which I am unable to pronounce any certain opinion.

That no man has any thing to fear from my infpection, as it is my endeavour to find good in man, nor are there any men in whom good is not to be found.

That fince I have begun thus to obferve mankind, my philanthropy is not diminifhed, but, I will venture to fay, increafed.

And that now (January 1783), after ten years daily ftudy, I am not more convinced of the certainty of my own exiftence, than of the truth of the fcience of phyfiognomy, or than that this truth may be demonftrated: and that I hold him to be a weak and fimple perfon, who fhall affirm, that the effects of the impreffions made upon him by all poffible human countenances are equal.

CHAPTER II.

On the Nature of Man, which is the Foundation of the Science of Physiognomy—Difference between Physiognomy and Pathognomy.

MAN is the moſt perfeƈt of all earthly creatures, the moſt imbued with the principles of life. Each particle of matter is an immenſity, each leaf a world, each inſeƈt an inexplicable compendium. Who, then, ſhall enumerate the gradations between inſeƈt and man ? In him all the powers of nature are united. He is the eſſence of creation. The ſon of earth, he is the earth's lord : the ſummary and central point of all exiſtence, of all powers, and of all life, on that earth which he inhabits.

There are no organiſed beings with which we are acquainted, man alone excepted, in which are ſo wonderfully united theſe different kinds of life, the animal, the intelleƈtual, and the moral. Each of theſe lives is the compendium of various faculties, moſt wonderfully compounded and harmoniſed.

To know, to deſire, to aƈt, or accurately to obſerve and mediate, to perceive and to wiſh, to poſſeſs the power of motion and reſiſtance—theſe combined, conſtitute man an animal, intelleƈtual, and moral being.

Endowed with theſe faculties, and with this triple life, man is in himſelf the moſt worthy ſubjeƈt of obſervation, as he likewiſe is himſelf the moſt worthy obſerver. In him each ſpecies of life is conſpicuous ; yet never can his properties be wholly known, except by the aid of his external form, his body, his ſuperficies. How ſpiritual, how incorporeal ſoever his internal eſſence may be, ſtill is he only viſible and conceivable from the harmony of

his conftituent parts.   From thefe he is infeparable.
He exifts and moves in the body he inhabits, as in
his element.   This threefold life which man cannot
be denied to poffefs, neceffarily firft becomes the
fubject of difquifition and refearch, as it prefents
itfelf in the form of body, and in fuch of his faculties as are apparent to fenfe.

By fuch external appearances as affect the fenfes,
all things are characterifed ; they are the founda-
tions of all human knowledge.   Man muft wander
in the darkeft ignorance, equally with refpect to
himfelf and the objects that furround him, did he
not become acquainted with their properties and
powers by the aid of their externals ; and had not
each object a character peculiar to its nature and
effence, which acquaints us with what it is, and
enables us to diftinguifh it from what it is not.

We furvey all bodies that appear to fight under
a certain form and fuperficies ; we behold thofe
outlines traced which are the refult of their organifation.   I hope I fhall be pardoned the repetition
of common-place truths, fince on thefe is built
the fcience of phyfiognomy, or the proper ftudy
of man.

The organifation of man peculiarly diftinguifhes
him from all other earthly beings ; and his phyfiognomy, that is to fay, his fuperficies, and outlines
of this organifation, fhow him to be infinitely fuperior to all thofe vifible beings by which he is furrounded.   We are unacquainted with any form
equally noble, equally majeftic with that of man ;
and in which fo many kinds of life, fo many powers, fo many virtues of action and motion unite as
in a central point.   With firm ftep he advances
over the earth's furface, and with erect body raifes
his head to heaven.   He looks forward to infini-
tude ; he acts with facility and fwiftnefs inconceivable, and his motions are the moft immediate and
the moft varied.   By whom may their varieties be
enumerated ?   He can at once both fuffer and per-

form infinitely more than any other creature. He
unites flexibility and fortitude, strength and dexte-
rity, activity and rest. Of all creatures he can the
soonest yield, and the longest resist. None resemble him in the variety and harmony of his powers.
His faculties, like his form, are peculiar to himself.

The make and proportion of man, his superior
height, capable of so many changes, and such variety of motion, prove to the unprejudiced obferver
his superior eminent strength, and aftonishing facility of action. The high excellence and physiological unity of human nature are visible at the first
glance. The head, especially the face, and the
formation of the firm parts, compared to the firm
parts of other animals, convince the accurate obferver, who is capable of investigating truth, of the
greatness and superiority of his intellectual qualities. The eye, the look, the cheeks, the mouth,
the forehead, whether considered in a state of entire rest, or during their innumerable varieties of
motion,—in fine, whatever is understood by physiognomy—are the most expressive, the most convincing picture of interior sensation, desires, passions, will, and of all those properties which so
much exalt moral above animal life.

Although the physiological, intellectual, and moral life of man, with all their subordinate powers,
and their constituent parts, so eminently unite in
one being ; although these three kinds of life do
not, like three distinct families, reside in separate
parts or stories of the body, but co-exist in one
point, and by their combination form one whole ;
yet it is plain, that each of these powers of life has
its peculiar station, where it more especially unfolds
itself and acts.

It is beyond contradiction evident, that, though
physiological or animal life displays itself through
all the body and especially through all the animal
parts, yet it acts more conspicuously in the arm,
from the shoulder to the ends of the fingers.

It is not lefs evident, that intellectual life, or the
power of the underftanding and the mind, make
themfelves moft apparent in the circumference and
form of the folid parts of the head, efpecially the
forehead ; though they will difcover themfelves, to
an attentive and accurate eye, in every part and
point of the human body, by the congeniality and
harmony of the various parts. Is there any occafion to prove, that the power of thinking refides
neither in the foot, in the hand, nor in the back,
but in the head, and in its internal parts ?

The moral life of man particularly reveals itfelf*
in the lines, marks and tranfitions of the countenance. His moral powers and defires ; his irritability, fympathy, and antipathy ; his facility of attracting or repelling the objects that furround him :
thefe are all fummed up in, and painted upon his
countenance when at reft. When any paffion is
called into action, fuch paffion is depicted by the
motion of the mufcles, and thefe motions are accompanied by a ftrong palpitation of the heart. If
the countenance be tranquil, it always denotes tranquillity in the region of the heart and breaft.

This threefold life of man, fo intimately interwoven through his frame, is ftill capable of being
ftudied in its different appropriate parts ; and, did
we live in a lefs depraved world, we fhould find
fufficient data for the fcience of phyfiognomy.

The animal life, the loweft and moft earthly,
would difcover itfelf from the rim of the belly to
the organs of generation, which would become its
central or focal point. The middle or moral life
would be feated in the breaft, and the heart would
be its central point. The intellectual life, which
of the three is fupreme, would refide in the head,
and have the eye for its centre. If we take the
countenance as the reprefentative and epitome of
the three divifions, then will the forehead to the
eyebrows be the mirror or image of the underftanding ; the nofe and cheeks, the image of the moral

and fenfitive life ; and the mouth and chin, the image of the animal life ; while the eye will be to the whole as its fummary and centre.

All that has been hitherto advanced is fo clear, fo well known, fo univerfal, that we fhould blufh to infift upon fuch common-place truths, were they not firft the foundation on which we muft build all we have to propofe ; and, again, had not thefe truths (can it be believed by futurity ?) in this our age been fo many thoufand times miftaken and con-tefted with the moft inconceivable affectation.

• The fcience of phyfiognomy, whether underftood in the moft enlarged or moft confined fenfe, indu-bitably depends on thefe general and incontrover-tible principles; yet, incontrovertible as they are, they have not been without their opponents. Men pretend to doubt of the moft ftriking, the moft convincing, the moft felf-evident truths ; although, were thefe deftroyed, neither truth nor knowledge would remain. They do not profefs to doubt con-cerning the phyfiognomy of other natural objects; yet do they doubt the phyfiognomy of human na-ture—the firft object, the moft worthy of contem-plation, and the moft animated the realms of na-ture contain.

We have already hinted to our readers, that they are to expect only fragments on phyfiognomy from us, and not a perfect fyftem. However, what has been faid, may ferve as a fketch for fuch a fyftem. We fhall conclude this chapter with fhow-ing the difference between *Phyfiognomy* and *Pathog-nomy*.

Phyfiognomy is the fcience or knowledge of the correfpondence between the external and internal man, the vifible fuperficies and the invifible con-tents. Phyfiognomy, oppofed to pathognomy, is the knowledge of the figns of the power and in-clinations of men-- Pathognomy is the knowledge of the figns of the paffions. Phyfiognomy there-fore teaches the knowledge of character at reft, and pathognomy of character in motion. Character at reft is taught by the form of the folid and the appearance of the moveable parts while at reft. Character impaffioned is manifefted by the moveable parts in motion.

Phyfiognomy may be compared to the fum-total of the mind; pathognomy, to the intereft which is the product of this fum-total. The former fhows what man is in general, the latter what he becomes at particular moments; or, the one what he might be, the other what he is. The firft is the root and ftem of the fecond, the foil in which it is planted. Whoever believes the latter and not the former, believes in fruit without a tree, in corn without land.

CHAPTER III.

Signs of Bodily Strength and Weaknefs—Of Health and Sicknefs.

WE call that human body ftrong, which can eafily alter other bodies, without being eafily altered itfelf. The more immediate it can act, and the lefs immediately it can be acted upon, the greater is its ftrength; and the weaker, the lefs it can act, or withftand the action of others. There is a tranquil ftrength, the effence of which is immobility; and there is an active ftrength, the effence of which is motion. The one has motion, the other ftability, in an extraordinary degree. There is the ftrength of the rock, and the elafticity of the fpring.

There is the Herculean ftrength of bones and

D

finews ; thick, firm, compact, and immoveable as
a pillar.

There are heroes lefs Herculean, lefs firm, fi-
newy, large ; lefs fet, lefs rocky ; who yet, when
roufed, when oppofed in their activity, will meet
oppreffion with fo much ftrength, will refift weight
with fuch elaftic force, as fcarcely to be equalled
by the moft mufcular ftrength.

The elephant has native, bony ftrength. Irritated or not, he bears prodigious burdens, and
crufhes all on which he treads. An irritated wafp
has ftrength of a totally different kind : but both
have compactnefs for their foundation, and efpecially the firmnefs of conftruction. All porofity
deftroys ftrength.

The ftrength, like the underftanding of a man,
is difcovered by its being more or lefs compact. The
elafticity of a body has figns fo remarkable, that
they will not permit us to confound fuch body with
one that is not elaftic. How manifeft are the varieties of ftrength between the foot of an elephant
and a ftag, a wafp and a fly !

Tranquil, firm ftrength is fhown in the proportions of the form, which ought rather to be fhort
than long. In the thick neck, the broad fhoulders,
and the countenance, which, in a ftate of health,
is rather bony than flefhy. In the fhort, compact,
the knotty forehead ; and efpecially when the *finus
frontales* are vifible, but not too far projecting ; flat
in the middle, or fuddenly indented, but not in
fmooth cavities. In horizontal eyebrows, fituated
near the eye. Deep eyes, and ftedfaft look. In
the broad, firm nofe, bony near the forehead, efpecially in its ftraight, angular outlines. In fhort,
thick, curly hair of the head and beard. In fhort,
broad teeth, ftanding clofe to each other. In compact lips, of which the under rather projects than
retreats. In the ftrong, prominent, broad chin.

In the ftrong, projecting *os occipitis.* In the bafs voice, the firm ftep, and in fitting ftill.

Elaftic ftrength, the living power of irritability, muft be difcovered in the moment of action; and the firm figns muft afterwards be abftracted, when the irritated power is once more at reft. " This " body, therefore, which at reft was capable of " fo little, acted and refifted fo weakly, can, thus " irritated, and with this degree of tenfion, be- " come thus powerful." We fhall find on inquiry, that this ftrength, awakened by irritation, gene rally refides in thin, tall, but not very tall, and bony, rather than mufcular bodies; in bodies of dark or pale complexions; of rapid motion, join- ed with a certain kind of ftiffnefs; of hafty and firm walk; of fixed penetrating look; and with open lips, but eafily and accurately to be clofed.

Signs of weaknefs are, difproportionate length of body; much flefh; little bone; extenfion; a tottering frame; a loofe fkin; round, obtufe, and particularly hollow outlines of the forehead and nofe; fmallnefs of nofe and chin; little noftrils; the retreating chin; long, cylindrical neck; the walk very hafty or languid, without firmnefs of ftep; the timid afpect; clofing eyelids; open mouth; long teeth; the jaw-bone long, but bent towards the ear; whitenefs of complexion; teeth inclined to be yellow or green; fair, long, and tender hair; fhrill voice.

I fhall now proceed to confider Medicinal Semei- otics, or the Signs of *Health* and *Sicknefs.*—Not I, but an experienced phyfician ought to write on the phyfiognomonical and pathognomonical femeiotica of health and ficknefs, and defcribe the phyfiolo- gical character of the body, and its propenfities to this or that diforder. I am beyond defcription ignorant with refpect to the nature of diforders and their figns; ftill may I, in confequence of the

few obfervations I have made, declare, with fome
certainty, by repeatedly examining the firm parts
and outlines of the bodies and countenances of
the fick, that it is not difficult to predict what
are the difeafes to which the man in health is moft
liable.

Of what infinite importance would fuch phyfiognomonical femeiotics, or prognoftics of poffible
or probable diforders, be, founded on the nature
and form of the body ! How effential were it, could
the phyfician fay to the healthy, "You naturally
have, fome time in your life, to expect this or
" that diforder. Take the neceffary precautions
" againft fuch or fuch a difeafe. The virus of the
" fmall-pox flumbers in your body, and may thus
" or thus be put in motion : thus the hectic, thus
" the intermittent, and thus the putrid fever."
Oh, how worthy, Zimmermann, would a treatife on phyfiognomonical *Diætetice* (or regimen) be
of thee !

Whoever fhall read this author's work on *Experience*, will fee fee how characteriftically he de-
fcribes various difeafes which originate in the paffions. Some quotations from this work, which
will juftify my wifh, and contain the moft valuable
femeiotical remarks, cannot be unacceptable to the
reader.

" The obferving mind examines the phyfiogno-
" my of the fick, the figns of which extend over
" the whole body; but the progrefs and change
" of the difeafe is principally to be found in the
" countenance and its parts. Sometimes the pa-
" tient carries the marks of his difeafe : in burn-
" ing, bilious, and hectic fevers ; in the chlorofis;
" the common and black jaundice ; in worm ca-
" fes."—I, who know fo little of phyfic, have feveral times difcovered the difeafe of the tape-worm
in the countenance.

" In the *furor uterinus*, the leaft obfervant can

" read the difease. The more the countenance
" is changed, in burning fevers, the greater is the
" danger. A man whose natural aspect is mild
" and calm, but who stares at me, with a florid
" complexion, and wildness in his eyes, prognos-
" ticates an approaching delirium. I have like-
" wise seen a look indescribably wild, accompa-
" nied by palenefs, when nature, in an inflam-
" mation of the lungs, was coming to a crisis,
" and the patient was becoming excessively cold
" and frantic. The countenance relaxed, the
" lips pale and hanging, in burning fevers, are
" bad symptoms, as they denote great debility ;
" and if the change and decay of the counte-
" nance be sudden, the danger is great. When
" the nose is pointed, the face of a lead colour,
" and the lips livid, inflammation has produced
" gangrene.

" There is frequently something dangerous to
" be observed in the countenance, which cannot
" be known from other symptoms, and which yet
" is very significant. Much is to be observed in the
" eyes. Boerhaave examined the eyes of the pa-
" tient with a magnifying glass, that he might see
" if the blood entered the smaller vessels. Hippo-
" crates held, that the avoiding of light, involunta-
" ry tears, squinting, one eye less than the other,
" the white of the eye inflamed, the small veins
" inclined to be black, too much swelled, or too
" much sunken, were each and all bad symptoms.

" The motion of the patient, and his position in
" bed, ought likewise to be enumerated among the
" particular symptoms of disease. The hand car-
" ried to the forehead, waved or groping in the
" air, scratching on the wall, and pulling up the
" bed-clothes, are of this kind. The position in
" bed is a very significant sign of the internal situa-
" tion of the patient, and therefore deserves every

" attention. The more unufual the pofition is, in
" any inflammatory difeafe, the more certainly may
" we conclude that the anguifh is great, and con-
" fequently the danger. Hippocrates has defcri-
" bed the pofition of the fick, in fuch cafes, with
" an accuracy that leaves nothing to be defined.
" The beft pofition in ficknefs is the ufual pofition
" in health."

I fhall add fome other remarks from this phyfician and phyfiognomift, whofe abilities are fuperi-
or to envy, ignorance and quackery. " Swift was
" lean while he was the prey of ambition, chagrin,
" and ill-temper ; but, after the lofs of his under-
" ftanding, he became fat." His defcription of
Envy, and its effects on the body, is incomparable.
" The effects of Envy are vifible, even in children.
" They become thin, and eafily fall into confump-
" tions. Envy takes away the appetite and fleep,
" and caufes feverifh motion ; it produces gloom,
" fhortnefs of breath, impatience, reftleffnefs, and
" a narrow cheft. The good name of others, on
" which it feeks to avenge itfelf by flander, and
" feigned but not real contempt, hangs like the
" fword fufpended by a hair over the head of En-
" vy, that continually wifhes to torture others,
" and is itfelf continually on the rack. The
" laughing fimpleton becomes difturbed as foon as
" Envy, that worft of fiends, takes poffeffion of
" him, and he perceives that he vainly labours
" to debafe that merit which he cannot rival. His
" eyes roll, he knits his forehead, he becomes
" morofe, peevifh, and hangs his lips. There is,
" it is true, a kind of envy that arrives at old
" age. Envy in her dark cave, poffeffed by tooth-
" lefs furies, there hoards her poifon, which,
" with infernal wickednefs, fhe endeavours, to
" eject over each worthy perfon and honourable act.
" She defends the caufe of vice, endeavours to

" confound right and wrong, and vitally wounds
" the pureſt innocence."

CHAPTER IV.

Of the Congeniality of the Human Form.

THE ſame vital powers that make the heart
beat, give motion to the finger ; that which
roofs the ſkull, arches the finger-nail. Art is at
varience with herſelf: not ſo Nature. Her creation is progreſſive. From the head to the back,
from the ſhoulder to the arm, from the arm to the
hand, and from the hand to the finger ; from the
root to the ſtem, the ſtem to the branch, the branch
to the twig, the twig to the bloſſom and fruit, each
depends on the other, and all on the root : each is
ſimilar in nature and form. There is a determinate effect of a determinate power. Through all
nature each determinate power is productive only
of ſuch and ſuch determinate effects. The finger
of one body is not adapted to the hand of another
body. Each part of an organized body is an image
of the whole. The blood in the extremity of the
finger, has the character of the blood in the heart.
The ſame congeniality is found in the nerves, in
the bones. One ſpirit lives in all. Each member
of the body is in proportion to that whole of which
it is a part. As from the length of the ſmalleſt
member, the ſmalleſt joint of the finger, the proportion of the whole, the length and breadth of
the body may be found ; ſo alſo may the form of
the whole from the form of each ſingle part.
When the head is long, all is long, or round when
the head is round, or ſquare when it is ſquare.

One form, one mind, one root appertain to all: therefore is each organized body fo much a whole, that, without difcord, deftruction, or deformity, nothing can be added or diminifhed.

Every thing in man is progreffive; every thing congenial; form, ftature, complexion, hair, fkin, veins, nerves, bones, voice, walk, manner, ftyle, paffion, love, hatred. One and the fame fpirit is manifeft in all. He has a determinate fphere, in which his powers and fenfations are allowed, within which they may be freely exercifed, but beyond which he cannot pafs. Each countenance is, indeed, fubject to momentary change, though not perceptible, even in its folid parts; but thefe changes are all proportionate: each is meafured, each proper and peculiar to the countenance in which it takes place. The capability of change is limited. Even that which is affected, affumed, imitated, heterogeneous, ftill has the properties of the individual, originating in the nature of the whole, and is fo definite, that it is only poffible in this, but in no other being.

I almoft blufh to repeat this in the prefent age. What, Pofterity! wilt thou fuppofe, thus to fee me fo often obliged to demonftrate to pretended fages, that nature makes no emendation? She labours from one to all. Her's is not disjointed organization, not mofaic work. The more there is of the mofaic in the works of artifts, orators, or poets, the lefs are they natural; the lefs do they refemble the copious ftreams of the fountain; the ftem extending itfelf to the remoteft branch.

The more there is of progreffion, the more there is of truth, power, and nature; the more extenfive, general, durable, and noble is the effect. The defigns of nature are the defigns of a moment; one form, one fpirit, appear through the whole. Thus nature forms her leaft plant, and thus her moft exalted man. I fhall have effected nothing by

my phyfiognomical labours, if I am not able to
deftroy that opinion, fo taftelefs, fo unworthy of
the age, fo oppofite to all found philofophy, that
nature patches up the features of various countenances, in order to make one perfect countenance ;
and I fhall think them well rewarded, if the congeniality, uniformity, and agreement of human
organization be fo demonftrated, that he who fhall
deny it, will be declared to deny the light of the
fun at noon-day.

The human body is a plant, each part of which
has the character of the ftem. Suffer me to repeat
this continually, fince this moft evident of all
things is continually controverted, among all ranks
of men, in words, deeds, books, and works of art.
I therefore find the greateft incongruities in the
heads of the greateft mafters. I know no painter,
of whom I can fay he has thoroughly ftudied the
harmony of the human outline, not even Pouffin,
no not even Raphael himfelf. Let any one clafs
the forms of their countenances, and compare
them with the forms of nature. Let him, for in-
ftance, draw the outlines of their foreheads, and
endeavour to find fimilar outlines in nature, and he
will find incongruities, which could not have been
expected in fuch great mafters.

Chodowiecki, excepting the too great length and
extent, particularly of his human figures, perhaps
had the moft exact feeling of congeniality in caricature, that is to fay, of the relative propriety of
the deformed, the humorous, or other character-
iftical members and features. For as there is conformity and congeniality in the beautiful, fo is
there alfo in the deformed. Every cripple has the
diftortion peculiar to himfelf, the effects of which
are extended to his whole body. In like manner,
the evil actions of the evil, and the good actions of
the good, have a conformity of character ; at

leaft, they are all tinged with this conformity of character.

Little as this feems to be remarked by poets and painters, ftill is it the foundation of their art ; for wherever emendation is vifible, there admiration is at an end. Why has no painter yet been pleafed to place the blue eye befide the brown one ? Yet, abfurd as this would be, no lefs abfurd are the incongruities continually encountered by the phyfiognomical eye—The nofe of Venus on the head of Madona.—I have been affured by a man of fafhion, that, at a mafquerade, with only the aid of an artificial nofe, he entirely concealed himfelf from the knowledge of all his acquaintance. So much does nature reject what does not appertain to herfelf.

I have never yet met with one Roman nofe among an hundred circular foreheads in profile. In an hundred other fquare foreheads, I have fcarcely found one in which there were not cavities and prominences. I never yet faw a perpendicular forehead with ftrongly arched features in the lower part of the countenance, the double chin excepted.

I meet no ftrong-bowed eye-brows combined with bony perpendicular countenances.

Wherever the forehead is projecting, fo in general are the under lips, children excepted.

I have never feen gently arched, yet much retreating foreheads, combined with a fhort fnub nofe, which, in profile, is fharp and funken.

A vifible nearnefs of the nofe to the eye, is always attended by a vifible widenefs between the nofe and mouth.

A long covering of the teeth, or, in other words a long fpace between the nofe and mouth, always indicates fmall upper lips. Length of form and face is generally attended by well drawn flefhy lips.

I fhall at prefent produce but one more example, which will convince all who poffefs acute phyfiognomical fenfation, how great is the harmony of all nature's forms, and how much fhe hates the incongruous.

Take two, three, or four fhades of men remarkable for underftanding ; join the features fo artificially that no defect fhall appear, as far as relates to the act of joining ; that is, take the forehead of one, add the nofe of a fecond, the mouth of a third, the chin of a fourth, and the refult of this combination of the figns of wifdom fhall be folly. Folly is perhaps nothing more than the emendation of fome heterogeneous addition. " But let thefe four wife countenances be fuppofed " congruous." Let them fo be fuppofed, or as nearly fo as poffible, ftill their combination will produce the figns of folly.

Thofe therefore who maintain that conclufion cannot be drawn from a part, from a fingle fection of the profile, to the whole, would be perfectly right, if unarbitrary Nature patched up countenances like arbitrary Art ; but fo fhe does not. Indeed, when a man, being born with underftanding, becomes a fool, there expreffion of heterogeneoufnefs is the confequence. Either the lower part of the countenance extends itfelf, or the eyes acquire a direction not conformable to the forehead, the mouth cannot remain clofed, or the features of the countenance, in fome other manner, lofe their confiftency : all becomes difcord; and folly, in fuch a countenance, is very manifeft. Let him who would ftudy phyfiognomy, ftudy the relation of the conftituent parts of the countenance : not having ftudied thefe, he has ftudied nothing.

He only is an accurate phyfiognomift, and has the true fpirit of phyfiognomy, who poffeffes fenfe, feeling, and fympathetic proportion of the congeniality and harmony of nature ; and who hath a fimilar fenfe and feeling for all emendations and

additions of art and conſtraint. He is no phyſiognomiſt who doubts of the propriety, ſimplicity,
and harmony of nature, or who has not this phyſiognomical eſſential ; who ſuppoſes nature ſelects
members to form a whole, as a compoſitor in a
printing-houſe does letters to make up a word ;
who can ſuppoſe the works of nature are the
patch-work of a harlequin jacket. Not the moſt
inſignificant of inſects is ſo compounded, much
leſs man, the moſt perfect of organized beings.
He reſpires not the breath of wiſdom, who doubts
of this progreſſion, continuity, and ſimplicity of
the ſtructure of nature. He wants a general feeling for the works of nature ; conſequently of art,
the imitator of nature. I ſhall be pardoned this
warmth. It is neceſſary. The conſequences are
infinite, and extend to all things. He has the
maſter-key of truth, who has this ſenſation of the
congeniality of nature, and, by neceſſary induction,
of the human form.

   All imperfection in works of art, productions of
the mind, moral actions, errors in judgment ; all
ſcepticiſm, infidelity, and ridicule of religion, naturally originate in the want of this knowledge and
ſenſation. He ſoars above all doubt of the Divinity and Chriſt, who hath them, and who is conſcious of this congeniality. He alſo who, at firſt
ſight, thoroughly underſtands and feels the congeniality of the human form, and that from the
want of this congeniality ariſes the difference obſerved between the works of nature and of art, is
ſuperior to all doubt concerning the truth and divinity of the human countenance.

   Thoſe who have this ſenſe, this feeling, call it
which you pleaſe, will attribute that only, and nothing more, to each countenance, which it is capable of receiving. They will conſider each according to its kind, and will as little ſeek to add a
heterogeneous character, as a heterogeneous noſe

to the face. Such will only unfold what nature is defirous of unfolding, give what nature is capable of receiving, and take away that with which nature would not be incumbered. They will perceive in the child, pupil, friend, or wife, when any difcordant trait of character makes its appearance; and will endeavour to reftore the original congeniality, the equilibrium of character and impulfe, by acting upon the ftill remaining harmony, by cooperating with the yet unimpaired effential powers. They will confider each fin, each vice, as deftructive of this harmony; will feel how much each departure from truth, in the human form, at leaft to eyes more penetrating than human eyes are, muft be manifeft, muft diftort, and muft become difpleafing to the Creator, by rendering it unlike his image. Who, therefore, can judge better of the works and actions of man, who lefs offend or be offended, who more clearly develop caufe and effect, than the phyfiognomift, poffeffed of a full portion of this knowledge and fenfation?

CHAPTER V.

Defcription of Plates I. *and* II.

WE fhall occafionally introduce fome figures, in order to fupport and elucidate thofe opinions and propofitions which may be advanced. Thefe plates refer to objects that have been already alluded to in the preceding pages.

E

Defcription of Plate I. *Number* 1. *See the Frontif-*
piece.
This is a boldly fketched portrait of ALBERT
DURER. Whoever examines this countenance,
cannot but perceive in it the traits of fortitude,
deep penetration, determined perfeverance, and
inventive genius. At leaft, every one will acknowledge the truth of thefe obfervations, when
made.

Number 2. MONCRIEF.
There are few men capable of obfervation, who
will clafs this vifage with the ftupid. In the afpect,
the eye, the nofe efpecially, and the mouth, are
proofs, not to be miftaken, of the accomplifhed
gentleman, and the man of tafte.

Number 3. JOHNSON.
The moft unpractifed eye will eafily difcover, in
this fketch of Johnfon, the acute, the comprehenfive, the capacious mind, not eafily deceived, and
rather inclined to fufpicion than credulity.

Number 4. SHAKESPEARE.
How deficient muft all outlines be! Among ten
thoufand can one be found that is exact? Where
is the outline that can pourtray genius? Yet who
does not read, in this outline, imperfect as it is,
from pure phyfiognomonical fenfation, the clear,
the capacious, the rapid mind, all conceiving, all
embracing, that, with equal fwiftnefs and facility,
imagines, creates, produces?

Number 5. STERNE.
The moft unpractifed reader in phyfiognomy will
not deny to this countenance all the keen, the
fearching penetration of wit, the moft original
fancy, full of fire, and the powers of invention.

Plate II.

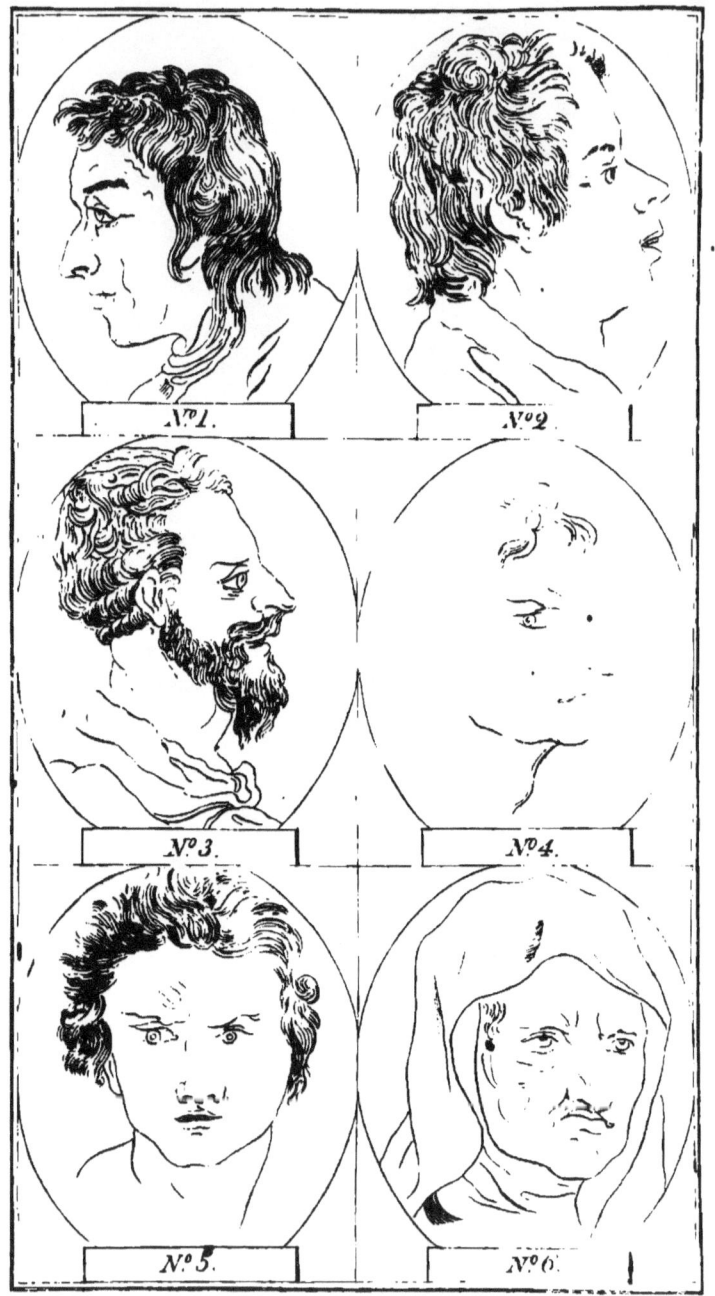

Who is fo dull as not to view, in this countenance, fomewhat of the fpirit of poor Yorick?

Number 6. S. CLARKE.

Perfpicuity, benevolence, dignity, ferenity, difpaffionate meditation, the powers of conception and perfeverance, are the moft apparent characteriftics of this countenance. He who can hate fuch a face, muft laborioufly counteract all thofe phyfiognomonical fenfations with which he was born.

Defcription of Plate II.

Hitherto we have beheld nature in the moft perfect of her productions; we muft now view the reverfe : we muft proceed to contemplate her in her deformity. In this aifo n w i   ! '' '
fhe fpeak to t ie eyes of all, t t'   . t   .

Number 1.

Who does not here rea ie n de
pidity almoft funken to b ut   y I .
wrinkles of a lovering f rel.ad. ,
mouth, the whole pofition of the head, do they not all denote manifeft dulnefs and debility?

Number 2. A fool.

From the fmall eyes in this figure, the open mouth, particularly from the under part of the countenance, no man whatever will expect penetration, reafoning, or wifdom.

Number 3.

True or falfe, nature or caricature, this countenance will, to the common fenfations of all men, depict an inhuman and brutal character. It is impoffible that brutality fhould be overlooked in the

nofe and mouth, or in the eye, though ftill it deferves to be called a human eye.

Number 4.

Let us proceed to the characters of paffion, which
are intelligible to every child; fo that concerning
thefe there can be no difpute, if we are in any degree acquainted with their language. The more
violent the paffion is, the more apparent are its
figns. The effect of the ftiller paffions is to contract, and of the violent to diftend the mufcles.
Every one will perceive, in this countenance, fear
mingled with abhorrence.

Number 5.

No man will expect cheerfulnefs, tranquillity,
..., ftrength of mind, and magnanimity, from
. countenance. Fear and terror **are here ftrongly**
r' ..'.

Number 6.

r r .eighte.ed by native indocility of cha-
.., ... ftrongly marked.

Such examples might be produced without end;
but to adduce fome of the moft decifive of the various claffes is fufficient We fhall give fome farther fpecimens hereafter.

CHAPTER VI.

The Univerfal Excellence of the Form of Man.

EACH creature is indifpenfable in the immen-
fity of God's creation; but each creature does

not know it is thus indifpenfable. Of all earth's creatures, man alone rejoices in his indifpenfability. No man can render any other man difpenfable. The place of no man can be fupplied by another.

This belief of the indifpenfability and individuality of all men, and in our own metaphyfical indifpenfability and individuality, is one of the unacknowledged, the noble fruits of phyfiognomy ; a fruit pregnant with moft precious feed, whence fhall fpring lenity and love. Oh, may pofterity behold them flourifh ! may future ages repofe under their fhade ! The moft deformed, the moft corrupt of men is ftill indifpenfable in this world of God, and is more or lefs capable of knowing his own individuality and unfuppliable indifpenfability. The wickedeft, the moft deformed of men, is ftill more noble than the moft beauteous and perfect animal. Contemplate, O man ! what thy nature is, not what it might be, not what is wanting. Humanity, amid all its diftortions, will ever remain wondrous humanity !

Inceffantly might I repeat doctrines like this: Art thou better, more beauteous, nobler, than many others of thy fellow-creatures ? If fo, rejoice, and afcribe it not to thyfelf, but to Him who, from the fame clay, formed one veffel for honour, another for difhonour ; to Him who, without thy advice, without thy prayer, without any defert of thine, caufed thee to be what thou art.

Yea, to Him ! " for what haft thou, O man ! " that thou didft not receive ? Now, if thou didft " receive, why doft thou glory as if thou hadft " not received ?"—" Can the eye fay to the hand, " I have no need of thee ?"—" He that oppreffeth " the poor, reproacheth his Maker."—" God " hath made of one blood all nations of men."— Who more deeply, more internally, feels all thefe divine truths than the phyſiognomiſt ? the true phyſiognomiſt, who is not merely a man of literature, a reader, a reviewer, an author, but—a man !

I am ready to acknowledge, that the moſt humane phyſiognomiſt, he who ſo eagerly ſearches whatever is good, beautiful, and noble in nature; who delights in the *ideal;* who duly exerciſes, nouriſhes, refines his taſte, with humanity more improved, more perfect, more holy ; even he is in frequent danger, at leaſt is frequently tempted to turn from the common herd of depraved men; from the deformed, the fooliſh, the apes, the hypocrites, the vulgar of mankind ; in danger of forgetting that theſe miſhapen forms, theſe apes, theſe hypocrites, alſo are men ; and that notwithſtanding all his imagined or his real excellence, all his noble feelings, the purity of his views (and who has cauſe to boaſt of theſe ?) all the firmneſs, the ſoundneſs of his reaſon, the feelings of his heart, the powers with which he is endowed, ſtill he is, very probably from his own moral defects, in the eyes of his ſuperior beings, in the eyes of his much more righteous brother, as diſtorted as the moſt ridiculous, moſt depraved moral or phyſical monſter appears to be in his eyes.

Liable as we are to forget this, reminding is neceſſary both to the writer and reader of this work. Forget not, that even the wiſeſt of men are men. Forget not how much poſitive good may be found even in the worſt, and that they are as neceſſary, as good in their place as thou art. Are they not, equally indiſpenſable, equally unſuppliable ? They poſſeſs not, either in mind or body, the ſmalleſt thing exactly as thou doſt. Each is wholly, and in every part, as individual as thou art. Conſider each as if he were ſingle in the univerſe ; then wilt thou diſcover powers and excellencies in him, which, abſtractedly of compariſon, deſerve all attention and admiration. Compare him afterwards with others, his fimilarity, his diffimilarity to fo many of his fellow-creatures. How mult this incite thy amazement ! How wilt thou value the individuality, the indifpenfability of his being ! How wilt thou wonder at the harmony of his parts, each contributing to form one whole ; at their relation, the relation of his million-fold individuality, to fuch multitudes of other individuals ! Yes, we wonder at and adore the fo fimple, yet fo infinitely varied expreffion of Almighty power inconceivable, fo efpecially and fo glorioufly revealed in the nature of man.

No man ceafes to be a man, how low foever he may fink beneath the dignity of human nature. Not being beaft, he ftill is capable of amendment, of approaching perfection. The worft of faces ftill is a human face. Humanity ever continues the honour and ornament of man.

It is as impoffible for a brute animal to become man, although he may in many actions approach, or almoft furpafs him, as for man to become a brute, although many men indulge themfelves in actions which we cannot view in brutes without abhorrence.

But the very capacity of voluntarily debafing himfelf, in appearance even below brutality, is the honour and privilege of man. This very capacity of imitating all things by an act of his will, and the powers of his underftanding, this very capacity man only has, beafts have not. The countenances of beafts are not fufceptible of any remarkable deterioration, nor are they capable of any remarkable amelioration or beautifying. The worft of the countenances of men may be ftill more debafed ; but they may alfo, to a certain degree be improved and ennobled.

The degree of perfection, or degradation, of which man is capable, cannot be defcribed. For this reafon, the worft countenance has a well-founded claim to the notice, efteem, and hope of all good men. Again, in every human counte-nance, however debafed, humanity is ftill vifible, that is, the image of the Deity.

I have feen the worft of men, in their worft of moments, yet could not all their vice, blafphemy, and oppreffion of guilt, extinguifh the light of good that fhone in their countenances, the fpirit of hu-manity, the ineffaceable traits of internal, external perfectibility. The finner we would exterminate, the man we muft embrace. O phyfiognomy, what a pledge art thou of the everlafting clemency of God towards man ! O man, rejoice with what-ever rejoices in its exiftence, and contemn no be-ing whom God doth not contemn !

CHAPTER VII.

Of the Forehead.

I SHALL appropriate this and fome of the fol-lowing chapters to remarks on certain individu-al parts of the human body. The following are my own remarks on foreheads.

The form, height, arching, proportion, obli-quity, and pofition of the fkull, or bone of the forehead, fhow the propenfity, degree of power, thought and fenfibility of man. The covering or fkin of the forehead, its pofition, colour, wrinkles, and tenfion, denote the paffions and prefent ftate of the mind. The bones give the internal quanti-ty, and their covering the application of power.

Though the fkin be wrinkled, the forehead bones remain unaltered; but this wrinkling varies according to the various forms of the bones. A certain degree of flatnefs produces certain wrinkles ; a certain arching is attended by certain other wrinkles ; fo that the wrinkles, feparately confidered, will give the arching ; and this, vice verfa, will give the wrinkles. Certain foreheads can only have perpendicular, others horizontal, others curved, and others mixed and confufed wrinkles. Cup-formed (fmooth) cornerlefs foreheads, when they are in motion, commonly have the fimpleft and leaft perplexed wrinkles.

I confider the peculiar delineation of the outline and pofition of the forehead, which has been left unattempted by ancient and modern phyfiognomifts, to be the moft important of all the things prefented to phyfiognomical obfervation. We may divide foreheads, confidered in profile, into three principal claffes, the retreating, the perpendicular, and the projecting. Each of thefe claffes has a multitude of variations, which may eafily again be claffed, and the chief of which are rectilinear ; half round, half rectilinear, flowing into each other ; half round, half rectilinear, interrupted ; curve lined, fimple ; the curve lined, double and triple.

I fhall add fome more particular remarks, which I apprehend will not be unacceptable to my readers :

1. The longer the forehead, the more comprehenfion, and lefs activity.

2. The more compreffed, fhort, and firm the forehead, the more compreffion, firmnefs, and lefs volatility in the man.

3. The more curved and cornerlefs the outline, the more tender and flexible the character ; the more rectilinear, the more pertinacity and feverity.

4. Perfect perpendicularity, from the hair to the eye-brows, want of underftanding.

5. Perfect perpendicularity, gently arched at the

top, denotes excellent propenſities of cold, tranquil, profound thinking.

6. Projecting—imbecility, immaturity, weakneſs, ſtupididity.

7. Retreating, in general, denotes ſuperiority of
imagination, wit, and acuteneſs.

8. The round and prominent forehead above,
ſtraight lined below, and on the whole perpendicular, ſhows much underſtanding, life, ſenſibility,
ardour, and icy coldneſs.

9. The oblique, rectilinear forehead, is alſo
very ardent and vigorous.

10. Arched foreheads appear properly to be
feminine.

11. A happy union of ſtraight and curved lines,
with a happy poſition of the forehead, expreſs the
moſt perfect character of wiſdom. By happy union, I mean, when the lines inſenſibly flow into
each other ; and by happy poſition, when the
forehead is neither too perpendicular, nor too retreating.

12. I might almoſt eſtabliſh it as an axiom, that
right lines, conſidered as ſuch, and curves, conſidered as ſuch, are related as power and weakneſs,
obſtinacy and flexibility, underſtanding and ſenſation.

13. I have hitherto ſeen no man with ſharp projecting eye-bones, who had not great propenſity
to an acute exerciſe of the underſtanding, and to
wiſe plans.

14. Yet there are many excellent heads which
have not this ſharpneſs, and which have the more
ſolidity, if the forehead, like a perpendicular wall,
ſink upon the horizontal eyebrows, and be greatly
rounded on each ſide towards the temples.

15. Perpendicular foreheads, projecting ſo as not
immediately to reſt upon the noſe, which are ſmall,
wrinkly, ſhort and ſhining, are certain ſigns of

weaknefs, little underftanding, little imagination, little fenfation.

16. Foreheads with many angular, knotty protuberances, ever denote much vigorous, firm, harfh, oppreffive, ardent activity, and perfeverance.

17. It is a fure fign of a clear, found underftanding, and a good temperament, when the profile of the forehead has two proportionate arches, the lower of which projects.

18. Eyebones with defined, marking, eafily delineated, firm arches, I never faw but in noble and in great men. All the ideal antiques have thefe arches.

19. Square foreheads, that is to fay, with extenfive temples and firm eyebones, fhow circumfpection and certainty of character.

20. Perpendicular wrinkles, if natural to the forehead, denote application and power ; horizontal wrinkles, and thofe broken in the middle, or at the extremities, in general negligence, or want of power.

21. Perpendicular, deep indentings, in the bones of the forehead, between the eyebrows, I never met with but in men of found underftanding, and free and noble minds, unlefs there were fome pofitively contradictory feature.

22. A blue vena frontalis, in the form of a Y, when in an open, fmooth, well-arched forehead, I have only found in men of extraordinary talents, and of an ardent and generous character.

23. The following are the moft indubitable figns of an excellent, a perfectly beautiful and fignificant, intelligent, and noble forehead.

An exact proportion to the other parts of the countenance. It muft equal the nofe or the under part of the face in length, that is, one-third.

In breadth, it muft be either oval at the top

(like the foreheads of moft of the great men of England) or nearly fquare.

A freedom from unevennefs and wrinkles, yet with the power of wrinkling when deep in thought, afflicted by pain, or from juft indignation.

Above it muft retreat, project beneath.

The eyebones muft be fimple, horizontal, and, if feen from above, muft prefent a pure curve.

There fhould be a fmall cavity in the centre, from above to below, and traverfing the forehead fo as to feparate into four divifions, which can only be perceptible by a clear defcending light.

The fkin muft be more clear in the forehead than in the other parts of the countenance.

The forehead muft every where be compofed of fuch outlines as, if the fection of one third only be viewed, it can fcarcely be determined whether the lines are ftraight or circular.

24. Short, wrinkled, knotty, regular, preffed in one fide, and fawcut foreheads, with interefting wrinkles, are incapable of durable friendfhip.

25. Be not difcouraged fo long as a friend, an enemy, a child, or a brother, though a transgreffor, has a good, well proportioned, open forehead : there is ftill much certainty of improvement, much caufe of hope.

C H A P T E R   VIII.

Of the Eyes and Eyebrows.

BLUE Eyes are generally more fignificant of weaknefs, effeminacy, and yielding, than brown and black. True it is, there are many powerful men with blue eyes ; but I find more ftrength, manhood, and thought, combined with brown than with blue. Wherefore does it happen, that the Chinese, or the people of the Philippine Iflands, are very feldom blue-eyed ; and that Europeans only, or the defcendants of Europeans, have blue eyes in thofe countries ? This is the more worthy inquiry, becaufe there are no people more effeminate, luxurious, peaceable or indolent than the Chinefe.

Choleric men have eyes of every colour, but more brown, and inclined to green, than blue. This propenfity to green is almoft a decifive token of ardour, fire, and courage.

I have never met with clear blue eyes in the melancholic, feldom in the choloric ; but moft in the phlegmatic temperament, which, however, had much activity.

When the under arch defcribed by the upper eyelid is perfectly circular, it always denotes goodnefs and tendernefs, but alfo fear, timidity, and weaknefs.

The open eye, not compreffed, forming a long acute angle with the nofe, I have but feldom feen, except in acute and underftanding perfons.

Hitherto I have feen no eye, where the eyelid formed a horizontal line over the pupil, that did not appertain to a very acute, able, fubtle man ; but be it underftood, that I have met with this eye in very worthy men, but men of great penetration and fimulation.

Wide, open eyes, with the white feen under the apple, I have often obferved in the timid and phlegmatic, and alfo in the courageous and rafh. When compared, however, the fiery and the feeble, the determined and the undetermined, will eafily be diftinguifhed. The former are more firm, more ftrongly delineated, have lefs obliquity, have thicker, better cut, but lefs fkinny eyelids.

F

ADDITION,

From the Gotha Court Calendar, 1771, *or rather from Buffon.*

" The colours moſt common to the eyes are, the orange, yellow, green, blue, grey, and grey mixed with white. The blue and orange are moſt predominant, and are often found in the ſame eye. Eyes ſuppoſed to be black are only yellow, brown, or a deep orange; to convince ourſelves of which, we need but look at them cloſely; for when ſeen at a diſtance, or turned towards the light, they appear to be black; becauſe the yellow-brown colour is ſo contraſted to the white of the eye, that the oppoſition makes it ſuppoſed black. Eyes alſo of a leſs dark colour paſs for black eyes, but are not eſteemed ſo fine as the other, becauſe the contraſt is not ſo great. There are alſo yellow and light yellow eyes, which do not appear black, becauſe the colours are not deep enough to be overpowered by the ſhade.

" It is not uncommon to perceive ſhades of orange, yellow, grey, and blue, in the ſame eye; and whenever blue appears, however ſmall the tinĉture, it becomes the predominant colour, and appears in ſtreaks over the whole iris. The orange is in flakes, round, and at ſome little diſtance from the pupil; but it is ſo ſtrongly effaced by the blue, that the eye appears wholly blue, and the mixture of orange is only perceived when cloſely inſpected.

" The fineſt eyes are thoſe which we imagine to be black or blue. Vivacity and fire, which are the principal characteriſtics of the eyes, are the more emitted when the colours are deep and contraſted, rather than when ſlightly ſhaded. Black eyes have moſt ſtrengh of expreſſion, and moſt vivacity;

but the blue have moſt mildneſs, and perhaps are more arch. In the former there is an ardour uninterruptedly bright, becauſe the colour, which appears to us uniform, every way emits ſimilar re-flexions. But modifications are diſtinguiſhed in the light which animates blue eyes, becauſe there are various tints of colour, which produce various reflexions.

" There are eyes which are remarkable for hav-ing what may be ſaid to be no colour. They ap-pear to be differently conſtituted from others. The iris has only ſome ſhades of blue, or grey, ſo feeble, that they are, in ſome parts, almoſt white ; and the ſhades of orange which intervene are ſo ſmall that they ſcarcely can be diſtinguiſhed from grey or white, notwithſtanding the contraſt of theſe colours. The black of the pupil is then too mark-ing, becauſe the colour of the iris is not deep enough, and, as I may ſay, we ſee only the pupil in the centre of the eye. Theſe eyes are unmean-ing, and appear to be fixed and aghaſt.

" There are alſo eyes, the colour of the iris of which is almoſt green ; but theſe are more uncom-mon than the blue, the grey, the yellow, and the yellow-brown. There are alſo people whoſe eyes are not both of the ſame colour.

" The images of our ſecret agitations are parti-cularly painted in the eyes. The eye appertains more to the ſoul than any other organ ; ſeems af-fected by, and to participate in, all its motions ; expreſſes ſenſations the moſt lively, paſſions the moſt tumultuous, feelings the moſt delightful, and ſentiments the moſt delicate. It explains them in all their force, in all their purity, as they take birth ; and tranſmits them by traits ſo rapid, as to infuſe into other minds the fire, the activity, the very image with which themſelves are inſpired.

The eye at once receives and reflects the intelligence of thought, and the warmth of fenfibility. It is the fenfe of the mind, the tongue of the underftanding."

Again, " As in nature, fo in art, the eyes are differently formed in the ftatues of the gods, and in heads of ideal beauty, fo that the eye itfelf is the diftinguifhing token. Jupiter, Juno, and Apollo, have large, round, well arched eyes, fhortened in length, in order that the arch may be the higher. Pallas, in like manner, has large eyes ; but the upper eyelid, which is drawn up, is expreffive of attraction and languifhment. Such an eye diftinguifhes the heavenly Venus Urania from Juno ; yet the ftatue of this Venus bearing a diadem, has for that reafon often been miftaken, by thofe who have not made this obfervation, for the ftatue of Juno. Many of the modern artifts appear to have been defirous of excelling the ancients, and to give what Homer calls the ox-eye, by making the pupil project, and feem to ftart from the focket. Such an eye has the modern head of the erroneoufly fuppofed Cleopatra, in the Medicean villa, and which prefents the idea of a perfon ftrangled. The fame kind of eye a young artift has given to the ftatue of the Holy Virgin in the church St. Carlo al Torfo."

I fhall quote one more paffage from Paracelfus, who, though an aftrological enthufiaft, was a man of prodigious genius :

" To come to the practical part, and give proper figns, with fome of their fignifications, it is to be remarked, that blacknefs in the eyes generally denotes health, a firm mind not wavering, but courageous, true, and honourable. Grey eyes generally denote deceit, inftability, and indecifion. Short fight denotes an able projector, crafty and intriguing in action. The fquinting, or falfefighted, who fee on both fides, or over and under, certainly denotes a deceitful, crafty perfon, not eafily deceived, miftruftful, and not always to be trufted ; one who willingly avoids labour where he can, indulging in idlenefs, play, ufury, and pilfering. Small and deep funken eyes are bold in oppofition ; not difcouraged, intriguing, and active in wickednefs ; capable of fuffering much. Large eyes denote a covetous greedy man, and efpecially when they are prominent. Eyes in continual motion, fignify fhort or weak fight, fear and care. The winking eye denotes an amorous difpofition, forefight, and quicknefs in projecting. The downcaft eye fhows fhame and modefty. Red eyes fignify courage and ftrength. Bright eyes, flow of motion, befpeak the hero, great acts, audacious, cheerful, one feared by his enemies."

It will not be expected I fhould fubfcribe to all thefe opinions, they being moft of them ill founded, at leaft ill defined.

The Eyebrows.

Eyebrows regularly arched are characteriftic of feminine youth ; rectilinear and horizontal, are mafculine ; arched and the horizontal combined, denote mafculine underftanding, and feminine kindnefs.

Wild and perplexed, denote a correfponding mind, unlefs the hair be foft, and they then fignify gentle ardour.

Compreffed, firm, with the hairs running parallel, as if cut, are one of the moft decifive figns of a firm, manly, mature underftanding, profound wifdom, and a true and unerring perception.

Meeting eyebrows, held fo beautiful by the Arabs, and by the old phyfiognomifts fuppofed to be the mark of craft, I can neither believe to be beautiful, nor characteriftic of fuch a quality.

They are found in the most open, honest, and worthy countenances. It is true, they give the face a gloomy appearance, and perhaps denote trouble of mind and heart.

Sunken eyebrows, says Winkelmann, impart something of the severe and melancholy to the head of Antinous.

I never yet saw a profound thinker, or even a man of fortitude and prudence, with weak, high eyebrows, which in some measure equally divide the forehead.

Weak eyebrows denote phlegm and debility, though there are choloric and powerful men who have them ; but this weakness of eyebrows is always a deduction from power and ardour.

Angular, strong, interrupted eyebrows, ever denote fire and productive activity.

The nearer the eyebrows are to the eyes, the more earnest, deep and firm the character.

The more remote from the eyes, the more volatile, easily moved, and less enterprising.

Remote from each other, warm, open, quick sensation.

White eyebrows signify weakness ; and dark brown, firmness

The motion of the eyebrows contains numerous expressions, especially of ignoble passions, pride, anger, and contempt.

C H A P T E R IX.

Of the Nose.

I HAVE generally considered the Nose as the foundation or abutment of the brain. Whoever

is acquainted with the Gothic arch will perfectly
underſtand what I mean by this abutment: for
upon this the whole power of the arch of the forehead reſts, and without it the mouth and cheeks
would be oppreſſed by miſerable ruins.

A beautiful noſe will never be found accompany-
ing an ugly countenance. An ugly perſon may
have fine eyes, but not a handſome noſe. I meet
with thouſands of beautiful eyes before one ſuch
noſe ; and wherever I find the latter, it denotes an
extraordinary character. The following is requi-
ſite to the perfectly beautiful noſe :

Its length ſhould equal the length of the forehead. At the top ſhould be a gentle indenting.
Viewed in front, the back ſhould be broad, and
nearly parallel, yet above the centre ſomething
broader. The button, or end of the noſe, muſt
be neither hard nor fleſhy, and its under outline
muſt be remarkably definite, well delineated, neither pointed nor very broad. The ſides ſeen in
front muſt be well defined, and the deſcending
noſtrils gently ſhortened. Viewed in profile, the
bottom of the noſe ſhould not have more than one
third of its length. The noſtrils above muſt be
pointed ; below, round, and have in general a
gentle curve, and be divided into two equal parts,
by the profile of the upper lip. The ſides, or arch
of the noſe, muſt be a kind of wall. Above, it
muſt cloſe well with the arch of the eyebone, and
near the eye muſt be at leaſt half an inch in
breadth. Such a noſe is of more worth than a
kingdom. There are, indeed, innumerable excellent men with defective noſes, but their excellence is of a very different kind. I have ſeen the
pureſt, moſt capable, and nobleſt perſons, with
ſmall noſes, and hollow in profile ; but their worth
moſt conſiſted in ſuffering, liſtening, learning, and
enjoying the beautiful influences of imagination ;

provided the other parts of the form were well organized. Nofes, on the contrary, which are
arched near the forehead, are capable of command,
can rule, act, overcome, deftroy. Rectilinear
nofes may be called the key-ftone between the two
extremes. They equally act and fuffer with power
and tranquillity.

Boerhaave, Socrates, Laireffe, had, more or lefs,
ugly nofes, and yet were great men ; but their
character was that of gentlenefs and patience.

I have never yet feen a nofe with a broad back,
whether arched or rectilinear, that did not appertain to an extraordinary man. We may examine
thoufands of countenances, and numbers of portraits, of fuperior men, before we find fuch a one.

Thefe nofes were poffeffed, more or lefs, by
Raynal, Fauftus Socinus, Swift, Cæfar Borgia,
Clepzecker, Anthony Pagi, John Charles von
Enkenberg (a man of Herculean ftrength), Paul
Sarpi, Peter de Medices, Francis Caracci, Caffini,
Lucas van Leyden, Titian.

There are alfo nofes that are not broad backed,
but fmall near the forehead, of extraordinary power ; but their power is rather elaftic and momentary than productive.

The Tartars generally have flat indented nofes ;
the negroes broad, and the Jews hawk nofes. The
nofes of Englifhmen are feldom pointed, but generally round. The Dutch, if we may judge from
their portraits, feldom have handfome or fignificant nofes. The nofe of the Italian is large and
energetic. The great men of France, in my opinion, have the characteriftic of their greatnefs
generally in the nofe : to prove which, examine
the collection of portraits by Perrault and Morin.

Small noftrils are ufually an indubitable fign of
unenterprifing timidity. The open, breathing nof-

tril, is as certain a token of fenfibility, which may eafily degenerate into fenfuality.

CHAPTER X.

Of the Mouth and Lips.

THE contents of the mind are communicated to the mouth. How full of character is the mouth, whether at reft or fpeaking, by its infinite powers !

Whoever internally feels the worth of this member, fo different from every other member, fo infeparable, fo not to be defined, fo fimple, yet fo various ; whoever, I fay, knows and feels this worth, will fpeak and act with divine wifdom. Oh ! wherefore can I only imperfectly and tremblingly declare all the honours of the mouth—the chief feat of wifdom and folly, power and debility, virtue and vice, beauty and deformity, of the human mind—the feat of all love, all hatred, all fincerity, all falfehood, all humility, all pride, all diffimulation and all truth ?

Oh ! with what adoration would I fpeak, and be filent, were I a more perfect man ! Oh ! difcordant, degraded humanity ! Oh ! mournful fecret of my mifinformed youth ! When, Omnifcience, fhalt thou ftand revealed ? Unworthy as I am, yet do I adore. Yet worthy I fhall be ; worthy as the nature of man will permit : for he who created me, gave me a mouth to glorify him !

Painters and defigners, what fhall I fay that may induce you to ftudy this facred organ in all its

beauteous expreffions, all its harmony and proportion ?

Take plafter impreffions of characteriftic mouths,
of the living and the dead ; draw after, pore over
them ; learn, obferve, continue day after day to-
ftudy one only ; and, having perfectly ftudied that,
you will have ftudied many. Oh ! pardon me ;
my heart is oppreffed. Among ten or twenty
draughtfmen, to whom for three years I have
preached, whom I have inftructed, have drawn
examples for, not one have I found who felt as
he ought to feel, faw what was to be feen, or
could reprefent that which was evident. What
can I hope ?

Every thing may be expected from a collection
of characteriftic plafter impreffions, which might
fo eafily be made, were fuch a collection only once
formed. But who can fay whether fuch obfervations might not declare too much ? The human
machine may be incapable of fuffering to be thus
analyfed. Man, perhaps, might not endure fuch
clofe infpection ; and, therefore, having eyes, he
fees not.—I fpeak it with tears ; and why I weep,
thou knoweft, who with me inquireft into the
worth of man. And you, weaker, yet candid,
though on this occafion unfeeling readers, pardon me !

Obferve the following rules : Diftinguifh in each
mouth the upper lip fingly ; the under lip the
fame ; the line formed by the union of both when
tranquilly clofed, if they can be clofed without
conftraint ; the middle of the upper lip, in particular ; and of the under lip ; the bottom of the
middle line at each end ; and, laftly, the extending of the middle line on both fides. For, unlefs
you thus diftinguifh, you will not be able to delineate the mouth accurately.

As are the lips, fo is the character. Firm lips,

firm character ; weak lips, and quick in motion, weak and wavering character.

Well defined, large, and proportionate lips, the middle line of which is equally ſerpentine on both ſides, and eaſy to be drawn, though they may denote an inclination to pleaſure, are never ſeen in a bad, mean, common, falſe, crouching, vicious countenance.

A lipleſs mouth, reſembling a ſingle line, denotes coldneſs, induſtry, a love of order, preciſion, houſewifery ; and if it be drawn upwards at the two ends, affectation, pretenſion, vanity, and, which may ever be the production of cool vanity, malice.

Very fleſhy lips muſt ever have to contend with ſenſuality and indolence : the cut-through, ſharp-drawn lip, with anxiety and avarice.

Calm lips, well cloſed, without conſtraint, and well delineated, certainly betoken conſideration, diſcretion, and firmneſs.

A mild overhanging upper lip generally ſignifies goodneſs. There are innumerable good perſons alſo with projecting under lips : but the goodneſs of the latter is rather cold fidelity, and well-meaning, than warm active friendſhip.

The under lip, hollowed in the middle, denotes a fanciful character. Let the moment be remarked, when the conceit of the jocular man deſcends to the lip, and it will be ſeen to be a little hollow in the middle.

A cloſed mouth, not ſharpened, not affected, always denotes courage and fortitude ; and the open mouth always cloſes where courage is indiſpenſible. Openneſs of mouth ſpeaks complaint ; and cloſeneſs, endurance.

Though Phyſiognomiſts have as yet but little noticed, yet much might be ſaid concerning the lip improper, or the fleſhy covering of the upper teeth, on which anatomifts have not, to my knowledge, yet beftowed any name, and which may be called the curtain, or pallium, extending from the beginning of the nofe to the red upper lip proper.

If the upper lip improper be long, the proper is alwas fhort; if it be fhort and hollow, the proper will be large and curved—another certain demonftration of the conformity of the human countenance. Hollow upper lips are much lefs common than flat and perpendicular: the character they denote is equally uncommon.

CHAPTER XI.

Of the Teeth and Chin.

NOTHING is more ftriking, or continually vifible, than the characteriftics of the teeth, and the manner in which they difplay themfelves. The following are the obfervations I have made thereon:

Small, fhort teeth, which have generally been held by the old phyfiognomifts to denote weaknefs, I have remarked in adults of extraordinary ftrength; but they feldom were of a pure white.

Long teeth are certain figns of weaknefs and pufillanimity. White, clean, well-arranged teeth, vifible as foon as the mouth opens, but not projecting, nor always entirely feen, I have never met with in adults, except in good, acute, honeft, candid faithful men.

I have alfo met foul, uneven, and ugly teeth, in perfons of the above good character; but it was always either ficknefs, or fome mental imperfection, which gave this deformity.

Whoever leaves his teeth foul, and does not attempt to clean them, certainly betrays much of the negligence of his character, which does him no honour.

As are the teeth of man, that is to fay, their form, pofition, and cleanlinefs (fo far as the latter depends on himfelf), fo is his tafte.

Wherever the upper gum is very vifible at the firft opening of the lips, there generally much cold and phlegm.

Much, indeed, might be written upon the teeth, though they are generally neglected in all hiftorical paintings. To be convinced of this, we need but obferve the teeth of an individual during the courfe of a fingle day, or contemplate an apartment crowded with fools. We fhould not then, for a moment, deny that the teeth, in conjunction with the lips, are very characteriftic ; or that phyfiognomy has gained another token, which triumphs over all the arts of diffimulation.

The Chin.

I am, from numerous experiments, convinced that the projecting chin ever denotes fomething pofitive, and the retreating fomething negative. The prefence or abfence of ftrength in man is often fignified by the chin.

I have never feen fharp indentings in the middle of the chin but in men of cool underftanding, unlefs when fomething evidently contradictory appeared in the countenance.

The pointed chin is generally held to be a fign of acutenefs and craft, though I know very worthy perfons with fuch chins. Their craft is the craft of the beft dramatic poetry.

The foft, fat, double chin, generally points out

G

the epicure ; and the angular chin is feldom found
but in difcreet, well difpofed, firm men.

Flatnefs of chin fpeaks the cold and dry ; fmallnefs, fear ; and roundnefs, with a dimple, benevolence.

————————   ⸱

C H A P T E R   XII.

Of Sculls.

HOW much may the anatomift fee in the mere
fcull of man ! How much more the phyfiognomift! And how much the moft the anatomift
who is a phyfiognomift ! I blufh when I think how
much I ought to know, and of how much I am
ignorant, while writing on a part of the body of
man which is fo fuperior to all that fcience has yet
difcovered—to all belief, to all conception !

I confider the fyftem of the bones as the great
outline of man, and the fcull as the principal part
of that fyftem. I pay more attention to the form
and arching of the fcull, as far as I am acquainted
with it, than all my predeceffors ; and I have confidered this moft firm, leaft changeable, and far
beft defined part of the human body, as the foundation of the fcience of phyfiognomy. I fhall
therefore be permitted to be particular in my obfervations on this member of the human body.

I confefs that I fcarcely know where to begin,
where to end, what to fay, or what to omit. I
think it advifeable to premife a few words concerning the generation and formation of human bones.

The whole of the human fœtus is at firft fuppofed to be only a foft mucilaginous fubftance, homo-

geneous in all its parts ; and that the bones themfelves are but a kind of coagulated fluid, which
afterwards becomes membraneous, then cartilaginous, and at laft hard bone.

As this vifcous congelation, originally fo tranf-
parent and tender, increafes, it becomes thicker
and more opaque, and a dark point makes its appearance different from the cartilage, and of the
nature of bone, but not yet perfectly hard. This
point may be called the kernel of the future bone,
the centre round which the offification extended.

We muft, however, confider the coagulation
attached to the cartilage as a mafs without fhape,
and only with a proper propenfity for affuming its
future form. In its earlieft, tendereft ftate, the
traces of it are expreffed upon the cartilage,
though very imperfectly.

With refpect to the bony kernels, we find differences which feem to determine the form of the
future bones. The fimple and fmaller bones have
each only one kernel ; but, in the more grofs,
thick, and angular, there are feveral, in different
parts of the original cartilage ; and it muft be remarked, that the number of the joining bones is
equivalent to the number of the kernels.

In the bones of the fcull, the round kernel firft
is apparent, in the centre of each piece ; and the
offification extends itfelf, like radii from the centre,
in filaments, which increafe in length, thicknefs,
and folidity, and are interwoven with each other
like net-work. Hence thefe delicate, indented
features of the fcull, when its various parts are at
length joined.

We have hitherto only fpoken of the firft ftage
of offification. The fecond begins about the
fourth or fifth month, when the bones, together
with the reft of the parts, are more perfectly form-

G 2.

ed, and, in the progrefs of offification, include the whole cartilage, according to the more or lefs life of the creature, and the original different impulfe and power of motion in the being.

Agreeable to their original formation through each fucceeding period of age, they will continue to increafe in thicknefs and hardnefs. But on this fubject anatomifts difagree—So let them. Future phyfiognomifts may confider this more at large. I retreat from conteft, and will travel in the high road of certainty, and confine myfelf to what is vifible.

Thus much is certain, that the activity of the mufcles, veffels, and other parts which furround the bones, contribute much to their formation, and gradual increafe in hardnefs.

The remains of the cartilaginous in the young bones, will, in the fixth and feventh month, decreafe in quantity, harden, and whiten, as the bony parts approach perfection. Some bones obtain a certain degree of firmnefs in much lefs time than others ; as, for example, the fcull bones, and the fmall bones within the ear. Not only whole bones, but parts of a fingle bone, are of various degrees of hardnefs. They will be hardeft at the place where the kernel of offification began, and the parts adjacent ; and the rigidity increafes more flowly and infenfibly, the harder the bones are, and the older the man is. What was cartilage will become bone ; parts that were feparate will grow together, and the whole bones be deprived of moifture.

Anatomifts divide the form into the natural or the effential, which is generally the fame in all bones in the human body, how different foever it may be to other bodies ; and into the accidental, which is fubject to various changes in the fame individual, according to the influence of external objects, or, especially, of the gradations of age.

The first is founded in the universality of the nature of parents, and the circumstances which naturally and invariably attend propagation. Anatomists consider only the designation of the bones individually; on this, at least, is grounded the agreement of what they call the essential form, in distinct subjects. This, therefore, only speaks to the agreement of human countenances, so far as they have each two eyes, one nose, one mouth, and other features thus or thus disposed.

This natural formation is certainly as different as human countenances afterwards are; which difference is the work of Nature, the original destination of the Lord and Creator of all things. The physiognomist distinguishes between original form and deviations.

Each bone hath its its original form, its individual capacity of form. It may, it does continually alter; but it never acquires the peculiar form of another bone, which was originally different. The accidental changes of bones, however great, or different from the original form, are yet ever governed by the nature of this original individual form; nor can any power of pressure ever so change the original form, but that, if compared to another system of bones that has suffered an equal pressure, it will be perfectly distinct. As little as the Ethiopian can change his skin, or the leopard his spots, whatever be the changes to which they may be subject, as little can the original form of any bone be changed into the original form of any other bone.

Vessels every where penetrate the bones, supplying them with juices and marrow. The younger the bone is, the more are there of these vessels—

confequently the more porous and flexible are the
bones, and the reverfe. The period when fuch or
fuch changes take place in the bones cannot eafily
be defined ; it differs according to the nature of
men and accidental circumftances.

Large and long and multiform bones, in order
to facilitate their offification and growth, at firft
confift of feveral pieces, the fmaller of which are
called fupplemental. The bone remains imperfect
till thefe become incorporated. Hence their poffible diftortion in children, by the rickets, and other
difeafes.

CHAPTER XIII.

Suggeftions to the Phyfiognomift concerning the Scull.

THE fcientific phyfiognomift ought to direct his
attention to the diftortion of the bones, efpecially thofe of the head. He ought to learn accurately to remark, compare and define the firft
form of children, and the numerous relative deviations. He ought to have attained that precifion
that fhould enable him to fay, at beholding the
head of a new-born infant, of half a year, a year,
or two years old, " Such and fuch will be the
" form of the fyftem of the bones, under fuch and
" fuch limitations ;" and on viewing the fcull at
ten, twelve, twenty, or twenty-four years of age,
" Such or fuch was the form, eight, ten, or twenty
" years ago ; and fuch or fuch will be the form,
" eight, ten, or twenty years hence, violence excepted." He ought to be able to fee the youth
in the boy, and the man in the youth ; and, on

the reverfe, the youth in the man, the boy in the youth, the infant in the boy, and, laftly, the embryo in its proper individual form.

Let us, O ye who adore that Wifdom which has framed all things! contemplate, a moment longer, the human fcull. There are, in the bare fcull of man, the fame varieties as are to be found in the whole external form of the living man.

As the infinite varieties of the external form of man is one of the indiftruftible pillars of phyfiognomy, no lefs fo, in my opinion, muft the infinite varieties of the fcull itfelf be. What I have hereafter to remark will, in part, fhow that we ought particulary to begin by that, if, inftead of a fubjeft of curiofity or amufement, we would wifh to make the fcience of phyfiognomy univerfally ufeful.

I fhall fhow that from the ftrufture, form, outline, and properties of the bones, not all, indeed, but much may be difcovered, and probably more than from all the other parts.

Objeftion and Anfwer.

What anfwer fhall I make to that objeftion, with which a certain anti-phyfiognomift has made himfelf fo merry ?

" In the catacombs near Rome (fays he) a number of fkeleton's were found, which were fuppofed to be the relics of faints, and, as fuch, were honoured. After fome time, feveral learned men began to doubt whether thefe had really been the fepulchres of the firft chriftians and martyrs, and even to fufpeft that malefaftors and banditti might have been buried there. The piety of the faithful was thus much puzzled ; but if the fcience of phyfiognomy be fo certain, they might have removed all their doubts by fending for Lavater, who with very little trouble, by merely examining and touching them, might have diftinguifhed the bones of the faints from the bones of the banditti, and thus have reftored the true relics to their juft and original pre-eminence."

" The conceit is whimfical enough (anfwers a cold and phlegmatic friend of phyfiognomy); but, having tired ourfelves with laughing, let us examine what would have been the confequence had this ftory been fact? According to our opinion, the phyfiognomift would have remarked great differences in a number of bones, particularly in the fculls, which, to the ignorant, would have appeared perfectly fimilar ; and, having claffed his heads, and fhown their immediate gradations, and the contraft of the two extremes, we may prefume, the attentive fpectator would have been inclined to pay fome refpect to his conjectures on the qualities and activity of brain which each formerly contained.

" Befides, when we reflect how certain it is that many malefactors have been poffeffed of extraordinary abilities and energy, and how uncertain it is whether many of the faints who are honoured with, red-letter days in the calendar, ever poffeffed fuch qualities, we find the queftion fo intricate that we fhould be inclined to pardon the poor phyfiognomift were he to refufe an anfwer, and leave the decifion. to the great infallible judge."

Further Reply.

Let us endeavour farther to inveftigate the queftion ; for, though this anfwer is good, it is infufficient. Who ever yet pretended abfolutely to diftinguifh faints from banditti, by infpecting only the fcull?

To me it appears, that justice requires we should in all our decisions concerning books, men, and opinions, judge each according to their pretensions, and not ascribe pretensions which have not been made to any man.

I have heard of no physiognomist who has had, and I am certain that I myself never have had, any such presumption. Notwithstanding which I maintain as a truth most demonstrable, that, by the mere form, proportion, hardness, or weakness of the scull, the strength or weakness of the general character may be known with the greatest certainty. But, as hath been often repeated, strength and weakness are neither virtue nor vice, saint nor malefactor.

Power, like riches, may be employed to the advantage or detriment of society, the same as wealth may be in the possession of a saint or a demon ; and as it is with wealth, or arbitrary positive power, so is it with natural innate power. As in an hundred rich men there are ninety-nine who are not saints, so will there scarcely be one saint among an hundred men born with this power.

When, therefore, we remark in a scull great original and percussive power, we cannot indeed say this man was a malefactor ; but we may affirm there was this excess of power, which, if it were not qualified and tempered during life, there is the highest probability it would have been agitated by the spirit of conquest, would have become a general, a conqueror, a Cæsar, a Cartouch. Under certain circumstances he would probably have acted in a certain manner, and his actions would have varied according to the variation of circumstances ; but he would always have acted with ardour, tempestuously, always as a ruler and a conqueror.

Thus, also, we may affirm of certain other sculls,

which, in their whole ſtructure and form, diſcover
tenderneſs, and a reſemblance to parchment, that
they denote weakneſs ; a mere capability of perceptive, without percuſſive, without creative power.
Therefore, under certain circumſtances, ſuch perſons would have acted weakly.   They would not
have had the native power of withſtanding this or
that temptation, of engaging in this or that enterpriſe.   In the faſhionable world, they would have
acted the fop, the libertine in a more confined circle, and the enthuſiaſtic ſaint in a convent.

Oh ! how differently may the ſame power, the
ſame ſenſibility, the ſame capacity, act, feel, and
conceive, under different circumſtances !   And
hence we may, in part, comprehend the poſſibility
of predeſtination and liberty in one and the ſame
ſubject.

Take a man of the commoneſt underſtanding to
a charnel-houſe, and make him attentive to the differences of ſculls ; in a ſhort time he will either
perceive of himſelf, or underſtand when told, here
is ſtrength, there weakneſs ; here obſtinacy, and
there indeciſion.

If ſhown the bald head of Cæſar, as painted by
Rubens or Titian, or that of Michael Angelo, what
man would be dull enough not to diſcover that
impulſive power, that rocky comprehenſion, by
which they were peculiarly characteriſed ; and that
more ardour, more action muſt be expected, than
from a ſmooth, round, flat head ?

How characteriſtic is the ſcull of Charles XII !
How different from the ſcull of his biographer
Voltaire ! Compare the ſcull of Judas with the
ſcull of Chriſt, after Holbein, diſcarding the muſ-
cular parts, and I doubt, if aſked which was the
wicked betrayer, which the innocent betrayed,
whether any ony one would heſitate.

I will acknowledge, that when two determinate.

heads are prefented to us, with fuch ftriking differences, and the one of which is known to be that of a malefactor, the other that of a faint, it is infinitely more eafy to decide ; but he who can diftinguifh between them, fhould not therefore affirm he can diftinguifh the fculls of faints from the fculls of malefactors.

To conclude this chapter. Who is unacquainted with the anecdote in Herodotus, that it was poffible, many years afterwards, on the field of battle, to diftinguifh the fculls of the effeminate Medes from thofe of the manly Perfians ? I think I have heard the fame remark made of the Swifs and the Burgundians. This at leaft proves it is granted that we may perceive, in the fcull only, a difference of ftrength and manners, as well as of nations.

CHAPTER XIV.

Of the Difference of Sculls, as they relate to Sex, and particularly to Nations.—Of the Sculls of Children.

AN effay on the difference of bones, as they relate to fex, and particularly to nations, has been publifhed by M. Fifcher, which is well deferving of attention. The following are fome thoughts on the fubject, concerning which nothing will be expected from me, but very much from M. Kamper.

Confideration and comparifon of the external and internal make of the body, in male and female, teaches us, that the one is deftined for labour and ftrength, and the other for beauty and

propagation. The bones particularly denote maſ-
culine ſtrength in the former ; and, ſo far as the
ſtronger and the prominent are more eaſy to deſcribe than the leſs prominent and the weaker, ſo
far is the male ſkeleton and the ſcull the eaſieſt to
define.

The general ſtructure of the bones in the male,
and of the ſcull in particular, is evidently of ſtronger formation than in the female. The body of
the male increaſes, from the hip to the ſhoulder,
in breadth and thickneſs ; hence the broad ſhoul-
ders and ſquare form of the ſtrong : whereas the
female ſkeleton gradually grows thinner and weaker
from the hip upwards, and by degrees appears as
if it were rounded.

Even ſingle bones in the female are more tender,
ſmooth, and round ; have fewer ſharp edges, cut-
ing and prominent corners.

We may here properly cite the remark of San-
torinus, concerning the diﬀerence of ſculls, as they
relate to ſex. " The aperture of the mouth, the
palate, and in general the parts which. form the
voice, are leſs in the female ; and the more ſmall
and round chin, conſequently the under part of
the mouth correſpond."

The round or angular form of the ſcull may be
very powerfully and eſſentially turned to the advantage of the phyſiognomiſt, and becomes a ſource
of innumerable individual judgments. Of this the
whole work abounds with proofs and examples.

No man is perfectly like another, either in external conſtruction or internal parts, whether great
or ſmall, or in the ſyſtem of the bones. I find this
diﬀerence, not only between nations, but between
perſons of the neareſt kindred ; but not ſo great
between theſe, and between perſons of the ſame
nation, as between nations remote from each other,
whoſe manners and food are very diﬀerent. The

more confidently men converfe with, the more
they refemble each other, as well in the formation
of the parts of the body, as in language, manners,
and food; that is, fo far as the formation of the
body can be influenced by external accidents.
Thofe nations, in a certain degree, will refemble
each other, that have commercial intercourfe, they
being acted upon by the effect of climate, imita-
tation and habit, which have fo great an influence in forming the body and mind; that is to
fay, the vifible and invifible powers of man; although national character ftill remains, and which
character in reality, is much eafier to remark than
to defcribe.

We fhall leave more extenfive inquiries and obfervations concerning this fubject to fome fuch
perfon as Kamper, and refrain as becomes us ;
not having obtained fufficient knowledge of the
fubject to make remarks of our own of fufficient
importance.

Differences with refpect to ftrength, firmnefs,
ftructure, and proportion of the parts, are certainly vifible in all the bones of the fkeletons of
different nations; but moft in the formation of the
countenance, which every where contains the peculiar expreffion of nature, of the mind.

The fcull of a Dutchman, for example, is in general rounder, with broader bones, curved, and
arched in all its parts, and with the fides lefs flat
and comprefied.

A Calmuc fcull will be more rude and grofs ;
flat on the top, prominent at the fides; the parts
firm and comprefied, the face broad and flat.

The fcull of the Ethiopian is fteep, fuddenly
elevated ; as fuddenly fmall, fharp, above the eyes ;
beneath ftrongly projecting ; circular, and high
behind.

II

In proportion as the forehead of the Calmuc is flat and low, that of the Ethiopean is high and narrow ; while the back part of an European head has a much more protuberant arch, and spherical form behind, than that of a negro.

Of the Sculls of Children.

The scull, or head, of a child, drawn upon paper without additional circumstance, will be generally known, and seldom confounded with the head of an adult. But, to keep them distinct, it is necessary the painter should not be too hasty and incorrect in his observations of what is peculiar, or so frequently generalize the particular, which is the eternal error of painters, and of so many pretended physiognomists.

Notwithstanding individual variety, there are certain constant signs proper to the head of a child, which as much consist in the combination and form of the whole as in the single parts.

It is well known that the head is larger in proportion to the rest of the body, the younger the person is ; and seems to me, from comparing the scull of the embryo, the child, and the man, that the part of scull which contains the brain is proportionably larger than the parts that compose the jaw and the countenance. Hence it happens that the forehead in children, especially the upper part, is generally so prominent.

The bones of the upper and under jaw, with the teeth they contain, are later in their growth, and more slowly attain perfect formation. The under part of the head generally increases more than the upper, till it has attained full growth. Several processes of the bones, as the *processus mamillares*, which lie behind and under the ears, form themselves after the birth ; as do also, in a great mea-

fure, various hidden finuffes, or cavities, in thefe
bones. The quill-form of thefe bones, with their
various points, ends and protuberances, and the
numerous mufcles which are annexed to them, and
continually in action, make the greater increafe
and change more poffible and eafy than can happen
in the fpherical bony covering of the brain, when
once the futures are entirely become folid.

This unequal growth of the two principal parts
of the fcull muft neceffarily produce an effential
difference in the whole, without enumerating the
obtufe extremities, the edges, fharp corners, and
fingle protuberances, which are chiefly occafioned
by the action of the mufcles.

As the man grows, the countenance below the
forehead becomes more protuberant ; and as the
fides of the face, that is to fay, the temple-bones, .
which are alfo flow in coming to perfection, continually remove farther from each other, the fcull
gradually lofes that pear form which it appears to
me to have had in embryo.

The *finus frontales* firft form themfelves after
birth. The prominence at the bottom of the forehead, between the eyebrows, is likewife wanting
in children. The forehead joins the nofe without
any remarkable curve. This latter circumftance
may alfo be obferved in fome grown perfons, when
the *finus frontales* are either wanting or very fmall ;
for thefe cavities are found very different in different fubjects.

The nofe, during growth, alters exceedingly ;
but I am unable to explain in what manner the
bones contribute to this alteration, it being chiefly
cartilaginous. Accurately to determine this, many
experiments on the heads and fculls of children,
and grown perfons, would be neceffary ; or, rather, if we could compare the fame head with

itſelf at different ages, which might be done by the means of ſhades, ſuch gradation of the head or heads would be of great utility to the phyſiognomiſt.

CHAPTER XV.

Deſcription of Plate III.

Number 1.

THIS outline, from a buſt of Cicero, appears to me an almoſt perfect model of congeniality. The whole has the character of penetrating acuteneſs, an extraordinary, though not great profile. All is acute; all is ſharp : diſcerning, ſearching, leſs benevolent than ſatirical, elegant, conſpicuous, ſubtle.

Number 2.

Another congenial countenance. Too evidently nature, for it to be miſtaken for ideal, or the invention and emendation of art. Such a forehead does not betoken the rectilinear, but the noſe thus bent. Such an upper lip, ſuch an open, eloquent mouth. The forehead does not lead us to expect high poetical genius; but acute punctuality, and the ſtability of retentive memory. It is impoſſible to ſuppoſe this a common countenance.

Number 3.

The forehead and noſe not congenial. The noſe ſhows the very acute thinker. The lower part of the forehead, on the contrary, eſpecially the diſ-

Plate III.

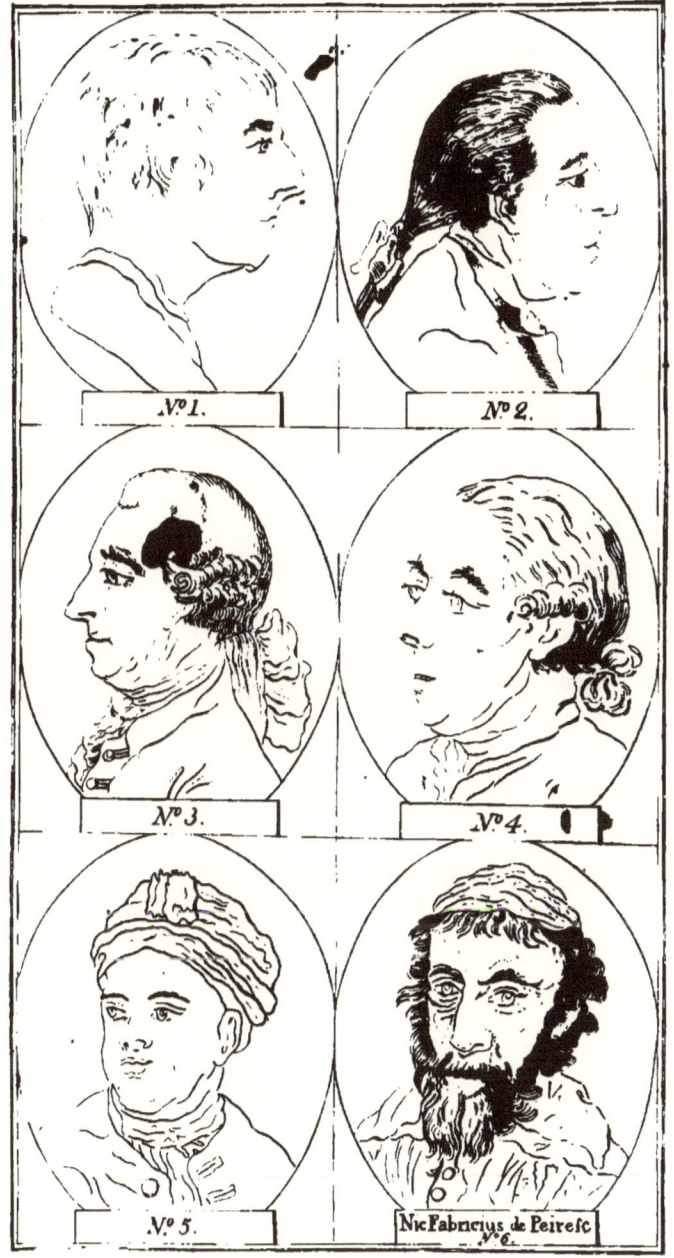

No 1.

No 2.

No 3.

No 4.

No 5.

Nic Fabricius de Peiresc
No 6.

tance between the eyebrow and eye, do not betoken this high degree of mental power. The ftiff
pofition of the whole is much at variance with the
eye and mouth, but particularly with the nofe.
The whole, the eyebrow excepted, fpeaks a calm,
peaceable, mild character.

Number 4.

The harmony of the mouth and nofe is felf-
evident. The forehead is too good, too comprehenfive, for this very limited under part of the
countenance. The whole befpeaks a harmlefs character ; nothing delicate, nor fevere.

Number 5.

We have here a high bold forehead, with a fhort-
feeming blunt nofe, and a fat double chin. How
do thefe harmonife ! It is almoft a general law of
nature, that, where the eyes are ftrong drawn, and
the eyebrows near, the eyebrows muft alfo be ftrong.
This countenance, merely by its harmony, its prominent congenial traits, is expreffive of found, clear
underftanding : the countenance of reafon.

Number 6.

The perfect countenance of a politician. Faces
which are thus pointed from the eyes to the chin,
always have lengthened nofes, and never poffefs
large, open, powerful, and piercing eyes. Their
firmnefs partakes of obftinacy, and they rather
follow intricate plans than the dictates of common
fenfe.

CHAPTER XVI.

The Physiognomist.

ALL men have talents for all things ; yet we may venture to affert, that very few have the determinate and effential talents. All men have talents for drawing : they can all learn to write, well or ill ; yet not an excellent draftfman will be produced in ten thoufand. The fame may be affirmed of eloquence, poetry, and phyfiognomy. All men who have eyes and ears, have talents to become phyfiognomifts ; yet not one in ten thoufand can become an excellent phyfiognomift.

It may, therefore be of ufe to fketch·the character of the true phyfiognomift, that thofe who are deficient of the requifite talents may be deter-ed from the ftudy of phyfiognomy. The pretended phyfiognomift, with a foolifh head and a wicked heart, is certainly one of the moft contemptible and mifchievous creatures that crawls on the face of the earth.

No one whofe perfon is not well formed, can become a good phyfiognomift. Thofe painters were the beft, whofe perfons were the handfomeft. Reubens, Vandyke, and Raphael, poffeffing three gradations of beauty, poffeffed three gradations of the genius of painting. The phyfiognomifts of the greateft fymmetry are the beft. As the moft virtuous can the beft determine on virtue, and the juft on juftice ; fo can the moft handfome countenances on the goodnefs, beauty, and noble traits of the human countenance, and confequently on its defects and ignoble properties. The fcarcity of human beauty is the reafon why phyfiognomy is fo much decried, and finds fo many opponents.

No perfon, therefore, ought to enter the fanctuary of phyfiognomy, who has a debafed mind, an
ill-formed forehead, a blinking eye, or a diftorted
mouth. " The light of the body is the eye : if,
therefore, thine eye be fingle, thy whole body fhall
be full of light ; but if thine eye be evil, thy whole
body fhall be full of darknefs : if, therefore, that
light that is in thee be darknefs, how great is that
darknefs !"

Any one who would become a phyfiognomift,
cannot meditate too much on this text. O fingle
eye ! that beholdeft all things as they are, feeft nothing falfely, with glance oblique nothing over-
lookeft ! O moft perfect image of reafon and wifdom !—Why do I fay image ? Thou art reafon
and wifdom themfelves ! Without thy refplendent
light, would all that appertains to phyfiognomy become dark !

Whoever does not, at the firft afpect of any man,
feel a certain motion of affection or diflike, attraction or repulfion, never can become a phyfiognomift.

Whoever ftudies art more than nature, and pre-
fers what the painters call manner to the truth of
drawing ; whoever does not feel himfelf moved
almoft to tears, at beholding the ancient ideal beauty, and the prefent depravity of men and imitative
art ; he who views antique gems, and does not
difcover enlarged intelligence in Cicero, enterprifing refolution in Cæfar, profound thought in So-
lon, invincible fortitude in Brutus, in Plato godlike wifdom ; or, in modern medals, the height of
human fagacity in Montefquieu, in Haller the energetic contemplative look and moft refined tafte,
the deep reafoner in Locke, and the witty fatirift
in Voltaire, even at the firft glance ; never can become a phyfiognomift.

Whoever does not dwell with fixed rapture on

the afpect of benevolence in action, fuppofing itfelf
unobferved ; whoever remains unmoved by the
voice of innocence, the guilelefs look of unviolated
chaftity, the mother contemplating her beauteous
fleeping infant, the warm preffure of the hand of
a friend, or his eye fwimming in tears ; whoever
can lightly tear himfelf from fcenes like thefe, and
turn them to ridicule, might much eafier commit
the crime of parricide than become a phyfiognomift.

If fuch be the cafe, what then is required of the
phyfiognomift ? What fhould his inclination, talents, qualities, and capabilities be ?

In the firft place, as hath been in part already
remarked, his firft of requifites fhould be a body
well proportioned, and finely organized; accuracy of fenfation, capable of receiving the moft
minute outward impreffions, and eafily tranfmit-
ing them faithfully to memory ; or, as I ought
rather to fay, impreffing them upon the imagination, and the fibres of the brain.   His eye, in particular, muft be excellent, clear, acute, rapid, and
firm.

Precifion in obfervation is the very foul of phyfiognomy.   The phyfiognomift muft poffefs a moft
delicate, fwift, certain, moft extenfive fpirit of
obfervation.   To obferve is to be attentive, fo as
to fix the mind on a particular object, which it fe-
lects, or may felect, for confideration, from a number of furrounding objects.   To be attentive, is to
confider fome one particular object, exclufively of
all others ; and to analyze, confequently to diftinguifh what is fimilar, what diffimilar, to difcover
proportion and difproportion, is the office of the
underftanding.

If the phyfiognomift has not an accurate, fuperior, and extended underftanding, he will neither
be able rightly to obferve, nor to compare and clafs

his obfervations, much lefs to draw the neceffary conclufions. Phyfiognomy is the higheft exercife of the underftanding, the logic of corporeal varieties.

To the cleareft and profoundeft underftanding, the true phyfiognomift unites the moft lively, ftrong, comprehenfive imagination, and a fine and rapid wit. Imagination is neceffary to imprefs the traits with exactnefs, fo that they may be renewed at pleafure ; and to range the pictures in the mind as perfectly as if they ftill were vifible, and with all poffible order.

A keen penetration is indifpenfable to the phyfiognomift, that he may eafily perceive the refemblance that exifts between objects. Thus, for example, he fees a head or forehead poffeffed of certain characteriftic marks : thefe marks prefent themfelves to his imagination, and a keen penetration difcovers to what they are fimilar. Hence greater precifion, certainty, and expreffion, are imparted to his images. He muft have the capacity of uniting the approximation of each trait that he remarks, and be able to define the degree of this approximation. No one who is not inexhauftibly copious in language, can become a phyfiognomift ; and the higheft poffible copioufnefs is poor, comparatively with the wants of phyfiognomy. All that language can exprefs, the phyfiognomift muft be able to exprefs. He muft be the creator of a new language, which muft be equally precife and alluring, natural and intelligible.

Every production of art, tafte, and mind ; all vocabularies of all nations, all the kingdoms of nature muft obey his command, muft fupply his neceffities.

The art of drawing is indifpenfable, if he would be precife in his definitions, and accurate in his decifions. Drawing is the firft, moft natural, and

unequivocal language of phyfiognomy ; the beft
aid of the imagination, the only means of preferving and communicating numberlefs peculiarities,
fhades, and expreffions, which are not by words,
or any other mode, to be defcribed. The phyfiognomift, who cannot draw haftily, accurately, and
charaçteriftically, will be unable to make, much
lefs to retain, or communicate, innumerable obfervations.

The knowledge of anatomy is indifpenfable to
him ; as alfo is phyfiology, or the fcience of the
human body in health ; not only that he may be
able to remark any difproportion, as well in the
folids as in the mufcular parts, but that he may
likewife be capable of naming thefe parts in his
phyfiognomical language. He muft alfo be acquainted with the temperament of the human body : not only its different colours and appearances,
occafioned by the mixture of the blood ; but alfo
the conftituent parts of the blood itfelf, and their
different proportions. Still more efpecially muft
be underftood the external fymptoms of the confti-
tution, relative to the nervous fyftem ; for on
this depends more than even on the knowledge of
the blood.

What an extenfive knowledge ought he to have
of the human heart, and the manners of the world!
How thoroughly ought he to infpeçt, to feel himfelf ! That moft effential, yet moft difficult of all
knowledge to the phyfiognomift, ought to be poffeffed by him in all poffible perfeçtion. In proportion only as he knows himfelf, will he be enabled
to know others.

Not only is this felf-knowledge, this ftudying of
man by the ftudy of his own heart, with the gene-
alogy and confanguinity of inclinations and paffions, their various fymptoms and changes, necef-

fary to the phyfiognomift, for the foregoing caufes, but allo for an additional reafon.

" The peculiar fhades (I here cite the words of
one of the critics on my firft effay), the peculiar
fhades of feeling which moft affect the obferver of
any object, frequently have relation to his own
mind, and will be fooneft remarked by him in proportion as they fympathize with his own powers.
They will affect him moft according to the manner in which he is accuftomed to furvey the phyfical and moral world. Many, therefore, of his
obfervations are applicable only to the obferver
himfelf; and, however ftrongly they may be conceived by him, he cannot eafily impart them to
others. Yet thefe minute obfervations influence
his judgment. For this reafon, the phyfiognomift
muft, if he knows himfelf, which he in juftice
ought to do before he attempts to know others,
once more compare his remarks with his own peculiar mode of thinking, and feparate thofe which
are general from thofe which are individual and
appertain to himfelf." I fhall make no commentary on this important precept. I fhall here only repeat, that an accurate and profound knowledge of
his own heart, is one of the moft effential qualities
in the character of the phyfiognomift.

Reader, if thou haft not often blufhed at thyfelf, even though thou fhouldeft be the beft of
men, for the beft of men is but man ; if thou haft
not often ftood with downcaft eyes, in prefence of
thyfelf and others ; if thou haft not dared to confefs to thyfelf, and to confide to thy friend, that
thou art confcious the feeds of every vice are latent
in thy heart ; if, in the gloomy calm of folitude,
having no witnefs but God and thy own confci-
ence, thou haft not a thoufand times fighed and
forrowed for thyfelf ; if thou wanteft the power to
obferve the progrefs of the paffions from their

very commencement, to examine what the impulfe was which determined thee to good or ill, and to avow the motive to God and thy friend, to whom thou mayeft thus confefs thyfelf, and who alfo may difclofe the recefies of his foul to thee ; a friend who fhall ftand before thee the reprefentative of man and God, and in whofe eftimation thou alfo fhalt be invefted with the fame facred character ; a friend, in whom thou mayeft fee thy very foul, and who fhall reciprocally behold himfelf in thee : if, in a word, thou art not a man of worth, thou never canft learn to obferve or know men well ; thou never canft be, never wilt be, worthy of being a good phyfiognomift. If thou wifheft not that the talent of obfervation fhould be a torment to thyfelf, and an evil to thy brother, how good, how pure, how affectionate, how expanded ought thy heart to be ! How mayeft thou ever difcover the marks of benevolence and mild forgivenefs, if thou thyfelf art deftitute of fuch gifts ? How, if philanthropy does rot make thine eye active, how mayeft thou difcern the impreffions of virtue, and the marks of the fublimeft fenfations ? How often wilt thou overlook them in a countenance disfigured by accident ! Surrounded thyfelf by mean paffions, how often will fuch falfe obfervers bring falfe intelligence ! Put far from thee felf-intereft, pride and envy, otherwife " thine eye " will be evil, and thy whole body full of dark- " nefs." Thou wilt read vices on the forehead whereon virtue is written, and wilt accufe others of thofe errors and failings of which thine own heart accufes thee. Whoever bears any refemblance to thine enemy, will by thee be accufed of all thofe failings and vices with which thy enemy is loaded by thy own partiality and felf-love. Thine eye will overlook the beauteous traits, and magnify the difcordant. Thou wilt behold nothing but caricature and difproportion.

But, to draw to a conclufion, the phyfiognomi t fhould know the world; he fhould have intercourfe with all manner of men, in all various ranks and conditions; he fhould have travelled, fhould pof-fefs extenfive knowledge, a thorough acquaintance with artifts, mankind, vice, and virtue, the wife and the foolifh, and particularly with children; together with a love of literature, and a tafte for painting, and the other imitative arts I fay, can it need demonftration, that all thofe, and much more, are to him indifpenfable? To fum up the whole: to a well formed, well organized body, the perfect phyfiognomift muft unite an acute fpirit of obfervation, a lively fancy, an excellent judgment, and, with numerous propenfities to the arts and fciences, a ftrong, benevolent, enthufiaftic, inno-cent heart; a heart confident in itfelf, and free from the paffions inimical to man. No one, cer-tainly, can read the traits of magnanimity, and the high qualities of the mind, who is not himfelf ca-pable of magnanimity, honourable thoughts, and fublime actions.

I have pronounced judgment againft myfelf in writing thefe characteriftics of the phyfiognomift. Not falfe modefty, but confcious feeling, impels me to fay, that I am as diftant from the true phyfi-ognomift as heaven is from earth. I am but the fragment of a phyfiognomift, as this work is but the fragment of a fyftem of phyfiognomy.

CHAPTER XVII.

Lavater's own Remarks on National Physiognomy.

IT is undeniable, that there is national phyſiognomy, as well as national character. Whoever
doubts of this can never have obſerved men of different nations, nor have compared the inhabitants
of the extreme confines of any two. Compare a
Negro and an Engliſhman, a native of Lapland
and an Italian, a Frenchman and an inhabitant of
Terra del Fuego. Examine their forms, countenances, characters, and minds. Their difference
will be eaſily ſeen, though it will ſometimes be very
difficult to deſcribe it ſcientifically.

It ſeems to me probable, that we ſhall diſcover
what is national in the countenance, better from
the ſight of an individal at firſt, than of a whole
people ; at leaſt ſo it appears to me, from my own
experience. Individual countenances diſcover
more the characteriſtic of a whole nation, than a
whole nation does that which is national in individuals. The following, infinitely little, is what I have
hitherto obſerved from the foreigners with whom
I have converſed, and whom I have noticed, concerning national character.

The French I am leaſt able to characteriſe.
They have no traits ſo bold as the Engliſh, nor ſo
minute as the Germans. I know them chiefly by
their teeth and their laugh. The Italians I diſcover by the noſe, ſmall eyes, and projecting chin.
The Engliſh by their foreheads and eyebrows.
The Dutch by the rotundity of the head, and the
weakneſs of the hair. The Germans by the angles
and wrinkles round the eyes and in the cheeks.

The Ruffians by the fnub nofe, and their light-coloured or black hair.

I fhall now fay a word concerning Englifhmen in particular. Englifhmen have the fhorteft and beft arched foreheads ; that is to fay, they are arched only upwards, and, towards the eyebrows, either gently decline, or are rectilinear. They very feldom have pointed, but often round, full, me-dullary nofes ; the Quakers and Moravians ex-cepted, who, wherever they are found, are gene-rally thin lipped. Englifhmen have large, well defined, beautifully curved lips. They have alfo a round full chin ; but they are peculiarly diftinguifh-ed by the eyebrows and eyes, which are ftrong, open, liberal, and ftedfaft. The outline of their countenance is, in general, great ; and they never have thofe numerous, infinitely minute traits, an-gles, and wrinkles, by which the Germans are fo efpecially diftinguifhed. Their complexion is fair-er than that of the Germans.

All Englifh women whom I have known perfo-nally or by portrait, appear to be compofed of mar-row and nerve. They are inclined to be tall, flen-der, foft, and as diftant from all that is harfh, rigo-rous, or ftubborn, as heaven is from earth.

The Swifs have generally no common phyfiog-nomy or national character, the afpect of fidelity excepted. They are as different from each other as nations the moft remote. The French Swifs peafant is as diftinct as poffible from the peafant of Appenzel. It may be that the eye of a foreigner would better difcover the general character of the nation, and in what it differs from the French or German than that of a native.

In each canton of Switzerland I find character-iftic varieties. The inhabitants of Zurich, for in-ftance, are middle fized, more frequently meagre than corpulent, but ufually one or the other. They feldom have ardent eyes, and the outline is not often grand or minute. The men are feldom handfome, though the youth are incomparably fo ; but they it on after. The people of Bern are tall, ſtraight, fair, pliable, and firm, and are moſt diſtinguiſhed by their upper teeth, which are white, regular, and eaſily to be feen. The inhabitants of Baſle (or Baſil) are more round, full, and tenſe of countenance, the complexion tinged with yellow, and the lips open and fluccid. Thoſe of Schafhauſen are hard boned. Their eyes are feldom funken, but generally prominent. The fides of the forehead diverge over the temples, the cheeks fleſhy, and the mouth wide and open. They are commonly ſtronger built than the people of Zurich, though in the canton of Zurich there is fcarcely a village in which the inhabitants do not differ from thoſe of the neighbouring village, without attending to dreſs, which, notwithſtanding, is alfo phyſiognomical.

Round Wadenſchweil and Oberreid I have feen many handſome, broad-fhouldered, ſtrong, burden bearing men. At Weiningen, two leagues from Zurich, I met a company of well formed men, who were diſtinguiſhable for their cleanlineſs, circumfpection, and gravity of deportment.

An extremely intereſting and inſtructive book might be written on the phyſiognomical character of the peaſants of Switzerland. There are confiderable diſtricts where the countenances, the noſe not excepted, are moſt of them broad, as if preſſed flat with a board. This difagreeable form, wherever found, is confiſtent with the character of the people. What could be more inſtructive than a phyſiognomical and characteriſtic defcription of fuch villages, their mode of living, food, and occupation ?

CHAPTER XVIII.

Extracts from Buffon on National Physiognomy.

TRAVERSING the furface of the earth, and beginning in the north, we find, in Lapland, and on the northern coaft of Tartary, a race of men fmall of ftature, fingular of form, and with countenances as favage as their manners.

Thefe people have large flat faces, the nofe broad, the pupil of the eye of a yellow brown inclining to a black, the eyelids retiring towards the temples, the cheeks extremely high, the mouth very large, the lower part of the face narrow, the lips full and high, the voice fhrill, the head large, the hair black and fleek, and the complexion brown or tanned. They are very fmall, and fquat, though meagre. Moft of them are not above four feet, and hardly any exceed four feet and an half. The Borandians are ftill fmaller than the Laplanders. The Samoiedes more fquat, with large heads and nofes, and darker complexions. Their legs are fhorter, their knees more turned outwards ; their hair is longer, and they have lefs beard. The complexion of the Greenlanders is darker ftill, and of a deep olive colour.

The women, among all thefe nations, are as ugly as the men ; and not only do thefe people refemble each other in uglinefs, fize, and the colour of their eyes and hair, but they have fimilar inclinations and manners, and are all equally grofs, fuperftitious, and ftupid. Moft of them are idolaters ; they are more rude than favage, wanting courage, felf-refpect, and modefty.

I 3

If we examine the neighbouring people of the long flip of land which the Laplanders inhabit, we shall find they have no relation whatever with that race, excepting that of the Oftiacks and Tongufians. The Samoiedes and the Borandians have no refemblance with the Ruffians, nor have the Laplanders with the Finlanders, the Goths, Danes, or Norwegians. The Greenlanders are alike different from the favages of Canada. The latter are tall and well made; and though they differ very much from each other, yet they are still more infinitely different from the Laplanders. The Oftiacks feem to be Samoiedes, fomething lefs ugly, and dwarfifh, for they are fmall and ill formed.

All the Tartars have the upper part of the countenance very large and wrinkled, even in youth; the nofe fhort and grofs, the eyes fmall and funken, the cheeks very high, the lower part of the face narrow, the chin long and prominent, the upper jaw funken, the teeth long and feparated, the eyebrows large, covering the eyes, the eyelids thick, the face flat, their fkin of an olive colour, and their hair black. They are of a middle ftature, but very ftrong and robuft; have little beard, which grows in fmall tufts, like that of the Chinefe; thick thighs, and fhort legs.

The Little or Nogais Tartars have loft a part of their uglinefs, by having intermingled with the Circaffians. As we proceed eaftward, into free or independent Tartary, the features of the Tartars become fomething lefs hard, but the effential characteriftics of their race ever remain. The Mogul Tartars, who conquered China, and who were the moft polifhed of thefe nations, are, at prefent, the leaft ugly and ill made; yet have they, like the others, fmall eyes, the face large and flat, little beard, but always black or red, and the nofe fhort and comprefled.

Among the Kergifi and Tcheremifi Tartars there
is a whole nation, or tribe, among whom are very
fingularly beautiful men and women. The manners
of the Chinefe and Tartars are wholly oppofite,
more fo than are their countenances and forms.
The limbs of the Chinefe are well proportioned,
large, and fat. Their faces are round and capacious, their eyes fmall, their eyebrows large, their
eyelids raifed, and their nofes little and comprefled.
They only have feven or eight tufts of black hair
on each lip, and very little on the chin.

The natives of the coaft of New Holland, which
lies in fixteen degrees fifteen minutes of fouth latitude, and to the fouth of the ifle of Timor, are
perhaps the moft miferable people on earth, and of
all the human race moft approach the brute animal. They are tall, upright and flender. Their
limbs are long and fupple, their heads great, their
forehead round, their eyebrows thick, and their
eyelids half flut. This they acquire by habit in
their infancy, to preferve their eyes from the gnats,
by which they are greatly incommoded ; and as
they never much open their eyes, they cannot fee
at a diftance, at leaft not unlefs they raife the
head as if they wifhed to look at fomething above
them. They have large nofes, thick lips, and
wide mouths. It fhould feem that they draw the
two upper fore teeth, for neither man nor woman,
young nor old, have thefe teeth. They have no
beard ; their faces are long, and very difagreeable,
without a fingle pleafing feature ; their hair not
long and fleek, like that of moft of the Indians,
but fhort, black, and curly, like the hair of the
Negroes. Their fkin is black, and refembles that
of the Indians of the coaft of Guinea.

If we now examine the nations inhabiting a more
temperate climate, we fhall find, that the people
of the northern provinces, of the Mogul empire,

Perfia, the Armenians, Turks, Georgians, Mingrelians, Circaffians, Greeks, and all the inhabitants of Europe, are the handfomeft, wifeft, and beft formed of any on earth ; and that, though the diftance between the Cachemire and Spain, or Circaffia and France, is very great, there is ftill a very fingular refemblance between people fo far from each other, but fituated in nearly the fame latitude. The people of Cachemire are renowned for beauty, are as well formed as the Europeans, and have nothing of the Tartar countenance, the flat nofe, and the fmall pig's eyes, which are fo univerfal among their neighbours.

The complexion of the Georgians is ftill more beautiful than that of Cachemire ; no ugly face is found in the country, and nature has endowed moft of the women with graces which are no where elfe to be difcovered. The men alfo are very handfome, have natural underftanding, and would be capable of arts and fciences, did not their bad education render them exceedingly ignorant and vicious ; yet, with all their vices, the Georgians are civil, humane, grave, and moderate ; they feldom are under the influence of anger, though they become irreconcileable enemies having once entertained hatred.

The Circaffians and Mingrelians are equally beautiful and well formed. The lame and the crooked are feldom feen among the Turks. The Spaniards are meagre, and rather fmall ; they are well fhaped, have fine heads, regular features, good eyes, and well arranged teeth ; but their complexions are dark, and inclined to yellow. It has been remarked, that in fome provinces of Spain as near the banks of the river Bidaffoa, the people have exceedingly large ears.

M. Lavater here makes this digreffion : Can large ears hear better than fmall ? I know one perfon with large, rude ears, whofe fenfe of hearing is acute, and who has a good underftanding; but, him excepted, I have particularly remarked large ears to betoken folly; and that, on the contrary ears inordinately fmall appertain to very weak, effeminate characters, or perfons of too great fenfibility.—Thus far Lavater: let us now return to Buffon.

· Men with black or dark-brown hair begin to be rather uncommon in England, Flanders, Holland, and the northern provinces of Germany; and few fuch are to be found in Denmark, Sweden, and Poland. According to Linnæus, the Goths are very tall, have fleek, light-coloured filver hair, and blue eyes. The Finlanders are mufcular and flefhy, with long and light yellow hair, the iris of the eye a deep yellow.

If we collect the accounts of travellers, it will appear, that there are as many varieties among the race of Negroes as the Whites. They alfo have their Tartars and their Circaffians. The Blacks on the coaft of Guinea are extremely ugly, and emit an infufferable fcent. Thofe of Sofala and Mozambique are handfome, and have no ill fmell. Thefe two fpecies of Negroes refemble each other rather in colour than features. Their hair, fkin, the odour of their bodies, their manners and propenfities, are exceedingly different. Thofe of Cape de Verd have by no means fo difagreeable a fmell as the natives of Angola. Their fkin alfo is more fmooth and black, their body better made, their features lefs hard, their tempers more mild, and their fhape better.

The Negroes of Senegal are the beft formed, and beft receive inftruction. The Nagos are the moft humane, the Mondongos the moft cruel, the Mimes the moft refolute, capricious, and fubject to defpair.

The Guinea Negroes are extremely limited in their capacities. Many of them appear to be wholly ftupid ; or, never capable of counting more than three, remain in a thoughtlefs ftate if not aĉted upon, and have no memory ; yet, bounded as is their underftanding, they have much feeling, have good hearts, and the feeds of all virtue.

The Hottentots have all very flat and broad nofes ; but thefe they would not have, did not their mothers fuppofe it their duty to flatten the nofe fhortly after birth. They have alfo very thick lips, efpecially the upper ; the teeth white, the eyebrows thick, the head heavy, the body meagre, and the limbs flender.

The inhabitants of Canada, and all thefe confines, are rather tall, robuft, ftrong, and tolerably well made ; have black hair and eyes, very white teeth, tawny complexions, little beard, and no hair, or almoft none, on any other part of the body. They are hardy and indefatigable in marching, fwift of foot, alike fupport the extremes of hunger, or excefs in feeding ; are daring, courageous, haughty, grave and moderate. So ftrongly do they refemble the eaftern Tartars in complexion, hair, eyes, the almoft want of beard, and hair, as well as in their inclinations and manners, that we fhould fuppofe fhem the defcendants of that nation, did we not fee the two people feparated from each other by a vaft ocean. They alfo are under the fame latitude, which is an additional proof of the influence of climate on the colour, and even on the form of man.

CHAPTER XIX.

Some of the moſt remarkable Paſſages from an excellent Eſſay on National Phyſiognomy, by Profeſſor Kant of Konigſberg.

THE ſuppoſition of Maupertuis, that a race of men might be eſtabliſhed in any province, in whom underſtanding, probity, and ſtrength, ſhould be hereditary, could only be realized by the poſſibility of ſeparating the degenerate from the conformable births ; a projeƈt which, in my opinion, might be praƈticable, but which, in the preſent order of things, is prevented by the wiſer diſpoſitions of nature, according to which the wicked and the good are intermingled, that by the irregularities and vices of the former, the latent powers of the latter may be put in motion, and impelled to approach perfeƈtion. If nature, without tranſplantation or foreign mixture, be left undiſturbed, ſhe will after many generations, produce a laſting race that ſhall ever remain diſtinƈt.

If we divide the human race into four principal claſſes it is probable that the intermediate ones, however perpetuating and conſpicuous, may be immediately reduced to one of theſe. 1. The race of Whites. 2. The Negroes. 3. The Huns, (Monguls, or Calmucs). 4. The Hindoos or people of Hindoſtan.

External things may well be the accidental, but not the primary cauſes of what is inherited or aſſimilated. As little as chance, or phyſico-mechanical cauſes, can produce an organized body, as little can they add any thing to its power of propagation ; that is to ſay, produce a thing which ſhall propagate itself by having a peculiar form or proportion of parts.

Man was undoubtedly intended to be the inhabitant of all climates, and all soils. Hence the seeds of many internal propensities must be latent in him, which shall remain inactive, or be put in motion, according to his situation on the earth. So that, in progressive generations, he shall appear as if born for that particular soil in which he seems planted.

The air and the sun appear to be the causes which most influence the powers of propagation, and effect a durable developement of germ and propensities ; that is to say, the air and the sun may be the origin of a distinct race. The variations which food may produce, must soon disappear on transplantation. That which affects the propagating powers, must not act upon the support of life, but upon its original source, its first principle, animal conformation, and motion.

A man transplanted to the frigid zone must decrease in stature, since, if the power or momentum of the heart continues the same, the circulation tion must be performed in a shorter time, the pulse become more rapid, and the heat of the blood increased. Thus Crantz found the Greenlanders not only inferior in stature to the Europeans, but also that they had a remarkably greater heat of body. The very disproportion between the length of the body and the shortness of the legs, in the northern people, is suitable to their climate ; since the extremes of the body, by their distance from the heart; are more subject to the attacks of cold.

The prominent parts of the countenance, which can less be guarded from cold, by the care of nature for their preservation, have a propensity to become more flat. The rising cheek-bone, the half-closed, blinking eyes, appear to be intended for the prefervation of fight againft the dry, cold air, and the effufions of light from the fnow (to guard againft which the Efquimaux fnow-fpectacles), though they may be the natural effect of the climate, fince they are found only in a fmaller degree in milder latitudes. Thus gradually are produced the beardlefs chin, the flatted nofe, thin lips, blinking eyes, flat countenances, red-brown complexion, black hair, and, in a word, the face of the Calmuc. Such properties, by continued propagation, at length form a diftant race, which continues to remain diftinct, even when tranfplanted into warmer climates.

The red-brown or copper colour appears to be as natural an effect of the acidity of the air in cold climates, as the olive-brown of the alcaline and bilious quality of the juices in warm; without taking the native difpofition of the American into the eftimate, who appears to have loft half the powers of life which may be regarded as the effect of cold.

The growth of the porous parts of the body muft increafe in the hot and moift climates. Hence the thick fhort nofe and projecting lips. The fkin muft be oiled, not only to prevent exceffive perfpiration, but alfo the imbibing the putrefcent particles of the moift air. The furplus of the ferruginous or iron particles, which have lately been difcovered to exift in the blood of man, and which, by the evaporation of the phofphoric acidities, of which all Negroes fmell fo ftrong, being caft upon the retiform membrane, occafions the blacknefs which appears through the cuticle; and this ftrong retention of the ferruginous particles feems to be neceffary, in order to prevent the general relaxation of the parts. Moift warmth is peculiarly favourable to the growth of animals, and produces the Negro, who, by the providence of nature, perfect-

K

ly adapted to his climate, is ftrong, mufcular, agile ; but dirty, indolent, and trifling.

The trunk, or ftem of the root may degenerate ; but this having once taken root, and ftifled other germs, refifts any future change of form, the chaٰra̅cter of the race having once gained a preponderance in the propagating powers.

CHAPTER XX.

Extracts from other Writers on National Phyſiogneٰmy.—From Winkelmann's Hiſto·y of Art.—From the Recherches Philoſophiques ſur les Americains, by M. de Pauw.—Obſervations by Lintz.—From a Letter written by M. Fueſsli.—From a Letter written by Profeſſor Camper.

From Winkelmann's Hiſtory of Art.

OUR eyes convince us, with refpect to the form of man, that the character of nation, as well as of mind, is vifible in the countenance. As nature has feparated large diftricts by mountains and waters, fo likewife has fhe diftinguifhed the inhabitants by peculiarity of features. In countries far diftant from each other, the difference is likewife vifible in other parts of the body, and in ftature. Animals are not more varied, according to the properties of the countries they inhabit, than men are ; and fome have pretended to remark, that animals even partake of the propenfities of the men.

The formation of the countenance is as various as languages, nay, indeed, as dialects, which are thus or thus various in confequence of the organs of fpeech. In cold countries, the fibres of the tongue muſt be leſs flexible and rapid than in warm. The natives of Greenland, and certain tribes of America, are obſerved to want ſome letters of the alphabet, which muſt originate in the ſame cauſe. Hence it happens, that the northern languages have more monoſyllables, and are more clogged with conſonants, the connecting and pronouncing of which is difficult, and ſometimes impoſſible, to other nations.

A celebrated writer has endeavoured to account for the varieties of the Italian dialects, from the formation of the organs of ſpeech. " For this reaſon (ſays he) the people of Lombardy, inhabiting a cold country, have a more rough and conciſe pronunciation. The inhabitants of Florence and Rome ſpeak in a more meaſured tone ; and the Neapolitans, under ſtill warmer ſky, pronounce the vowels more open, and ſpeak with more fulneſs."

Perſons well acquainted with various nations, can diſtinguiſh them as juſtly from the form of their countenance, as from their ſpeech. Therefore, ſince man has ever been the object of art and artiſts, the latter have conſtantly given the forms of face of their repective nations ; and that art, among the ancients, gave the form and countenance of man, is proved by the ſame effect having taken place among the moderns. German, Dutch, or French, when the artiſts neither travel nor ſtudy foreign forms, can be known by their pictures as perfectly as Chineſe or Tartars. After reſiding many years in Italy, Rubens continued to draw his figures as if he had never left his native land.

Another Paſſage from Winkelmann.

The projecting mouths of the Negroes, which they have in common with their monkies, is an excefs of growth, a fwelling, occafioned by the heat of the climate ; like as our lips are fwelled by heat or fharp faline moifture, and alfo, in fome men, by violent paffion. The fmall eyes of the diftant northern and eaftern nations are in confequence of the imperfection·of their growth. They are fhort and flender. Nature produces fuch forms the more fhe approaches extremes, where fhe has to encounter heat or cold. In the one fhe is prompter and exhaufted, and in the other crude, never arriving at maturity. The flower withers in exceffive heat, and, deprived of fun, is deprived of colour. All plants degenerate in dark and confined places.

Nature forms with greater regularity the more fhe approaches her center, and in more moderate climates. Hence the Grecian and our own idea of beauty, being derived from more perfect fymmetry, muft be more accurate than the idea of thofe, in whom to ufe the expreffion of a modern poet, the image of the Creator is half defaced.

From the Recherches Philofophiques fur les Americaines, by M. de Pauw.

The Americans are moft remarkable, becaufe that many of them have no eyebrows, and none have beards ; yet we muft not infer that they are enfeebled in the organs of generation, fince the Tartars and Chinefe have almoft the fame characteriftics. They are far, however, from being very fruitful, or much addicted to love. True it is, the Chinefe and Tartars are not abfolutely beardlefs. When they are about thirty, a fmall penciled kind of whifker grows on the upper lip, and fome fcattered hairs at the end of the chin.

Exclufive of the Eïquimaux, who differ in gait, form, features, and manners, from other favages of North-America, we may likewife call the Akanfans a variety, whom the French have generally named the handfome men. They are tall and ftraight, have good features, without the leaft appearance of beard, have regular eyelids, blue eyes, and fine fair hair ; while the neighbouring people are low of ftature, have abject countenances, black eyes, the hair of the head black as ebony, and of the body thick and rough.

Though the Peruvians are not very tall, and generally thick fet, yet they are tolerably well made. There are many, it is true, who, by being diminutive, are monftrous. Some are deaf, dumb, blind, and idiots ; and others want a limb when born. In all probability, the exceffive labour to which they have been fubjected by the barbarity of the Spaniards, has produced fuch numbers of defective men. Tyranny has an influence on the very phyfical temperament of flaves. Their nofe is aquiline, their forehead narrow, their hair black, ftrong, fmooth, and plentiful ; their complexion an olive red, the apple of the eye black, and the white not very clear. They never have any beard, for we cannot beftow that name on fome fhort ftraggling hairs which fprout in old age ; nor have either men or women the downy hair which generally appears after the age of puberty. In this they are diftinguifhed from all people on earth, even from the Tartars and Chinefe. As in eunuchs, it is the character of their degeneracy.

Judging by the rage which the Americans have to mutilate and disfigure themfelves, we fhould fuppofe they were all difcontented with the proportions of their limbs and bodies. Not a fingle nation has been difcovered in this fourth quarter of the globe, which has not adopted the cuftom of artificially changing, either the form of the lips, the hollow of the ear, or the fhape of the head, by forcing it to affume an extraordinary and ridiculous figure.

K 3

There are favages whofe heads are pyramidal, or conical, with the top terminating in a point. Others have flat heads, with large foreheads, and the back part flattened. This caprice feems to have been the moft fafhionable, at leaft it was the moft common. Some Canadians had their heads perfectly fpherical. Though the natural form of the head really approaches the circular, thefe favages, who, by being thus diftorted, acquired the appellation of bowl or bullet-head, do not appear lefs difgufting, for having made the head too round, and perverted the original purpofe of nature, to which nothing can be added, from which nothing can be taken away, without fome effential error being the refult, which is deftructive to the animal.

In fine, we have feen, on the banks of the Maragnon, Americans with fquare or cubical heads ; that is to fay, flattened on the face, the top, the temples, and the occiput, which appears to be the laft ftage of human extravagance.

It is not eafy to conceive how it was poffible to comprefs and mould the bones of the fcull into fo many various forms, without moft effentially injuring the feat of fenfe, and the organs of reafon, or occafioning either madnefs or idiotifm, fince we fo often have examples, that violent contufions in the region of the temples have occafioned lunacy, and deprived the fufferers of intellectual capacity. For it is not true, as ancient narratives have affirmed, that all Indians with flat or fugar-loaf heads were really idiots. Had this been the cafe, there muft have been whole nations in America either foolifh or frantic, which is impoffible even in fuppofition.

Obfervation by Lintz.

To me it appears very remarkable, that the Jews fhould have taken with them the marks of their

country and race to all parts of the world ; I mean
their fhort, black, curly hair, and brown complexion. Their quicknefs of fpeech, hafte and abrupt-
nefs in all their actions, appear to proceed from the
fame caufes. I imagine the Jews have more gall
than other men.

Extract from a Letter written by M. Fuefsli, *dated*
at Prefburg.

My obfervations have been directed (fays this
great defigner and phyfiognomift) not to the countenance of nations only; being convinced, from
numberlefs experiments, that the general form of
the human body, its attitude and manner, the
funken or raifed pofition of the head between or
above the fhoulders, the firm, the tottering, the
hafty, or flow walk, may frequently be lefs deceitful figns of this or that character, than the countenance feparately confidered. I believe it poffible
fo accurately to characterize man, from the calmeft
ftate of reft, to the higheft gradation of rage, terror, and pain, that, from the carriage of the body,
the turn of the head, and geftures in general, we
fhall be able to diftinguifh the Hungarian, the Scla-
vonian, the Illyrian, the Wallachian ; and to obtain a full and clear conception of the actual, and
in general, the prominent characteriftics of this or
that nation.

Extract of a Letter from Profeffor Camper.

It would be very difficult, if not impoffible, to
give you my particular rules for delineating various
nations and ages with mathematical certainty,
efpecially if I would add all that I have had occafion to remark concerning the beauty of the antiques. Thefe rules I have obtained by conftant
obfervations on the fculls of different nations, of

which I have a large collection, and by a long study of the antiques.

To draw any head accurately in profile, takes
me much time. I have diffected the fculls of people lately dead, that I might be able to define the
lines of the countenance, and the angle of thefe
lines with the horizon. I was thus led to the difcovery of the maximum and minimum of this
angle. I began with the monkey, proceeded to
the Negro and the European, till I afcended to the
countenances of antiquity, and examined a Me-
dufa, an Apollo, or a Venus de Medicis. This
concerns only the profile. There is another difference, in the breadth of the cheeks, which I have
found to be largeft among the Calmucs, and much
fmaller among the Afiatic Negroes. The Chinefe,
and inhabitants of the Molucca and other Afiatic
iflands, appear to me to have broad cheeks, with
projecting jaw-bones ; the under jaw-bone, in particular, very high, and almoft forming a right angle,
which, among Europeans, is very obtufe, and ftill
more fo among the African Negroes.

I have not hitherto been able to procure a real
fcull of an American, and therefore can fay nothing
on that fubject.

I am almoft afhamed to confefs that I have not
yet been able accurately to draw the countenance
of a Jew, although they are fo very remarkable in
their features ; nor have I yet obtained precifion in
delineating the Italian face. It is generally true,
that the upper and under jaw of the European is
lefs broad than the breadth of the fcull, and that
among the Afiatics they are much broader ; but I
have not been able to determine the fpecific differences between European nations.

I have very frequently, by phyfiognomonical fenfations, been able to diftinguifh the foldiers of different nations ; the Scotchman, the Irifhman, and
the native of England ; yet have I never been able

to delineate the diftinguifhing traits. The people
of our provinces are a mixture of all nations ; but,
in the remote and feparated cantons, I find the
countenance to be more flat, and extraordinarily
high from the eyes upward.

CHAPTER XXI.

*Extracts from the Manufcript of a Man of Literature
at Darmftadt, on National Phyfiognomy.*

ALL tribes of people who dwell on uncultivated countries, and confequently are paftoral,
not affembled in towns, would never be capable of
an equal degree of cultivation with Europeans,
though they did not live thus fcattered. Were the
fhackles of flavery fhaken off, ftill their minds
would eternally flumber ; therefore whatever remarks we can make upon them, muft be pathognomonical (I fufpect phyfiognomonical), and we muft
confine ourfelves to their receptive powers of mind,
not being able to fay much of their expreffion.

People who do not bear our badges of fervitude,
are not fo miferable as we fufpect. Their fpecies
of flavery is verv fupportable in their mode of
exiftence. They are incomparably better fed than
German peafants, and have neither to contend
with the cares of providing, nor the exceffes of labour. As their race of horfes exceeds ours in
ftrength and fize, fo do their people thofe among
us who have, or fuppofe they have, property.
Their wants are few, and their underftanding fufficient to fupply the wants they have. The Ruffi-
an or Polifh peafant is, of neceffity, carpenter,
tailor, fhoemaker, mafon, thatcher, &c. and, when

when we examine their performances, we may easily judge of their capacities. Hence their aptitude at mechanical and handicraft profeſſions, as soon as they are taught their principles. Invention of what is great they have no pretenſions to; their mind, like a machine, is at reſt, when the neceſſity that ſet it in motion ceaſes.

Of the numerous nations ſubjeＣt to the Ruſſian ſceptre, I ſhall omit thoſe of the extenſive Siberian diſtriＣts, and confine myſelf to the Ruſſians, properly ſo called, whoſe countries are bounded by Finland, Eaſtland, Livonia, and the borders of Aſia. Theſe are diſtinguiſhable by prodigious ſtrength, firm ſinews, broad breaſt, and coloſſal neck, which, in a whole ſhip's crew, will be the ſame, reſembling the Farneſian Hercules; by their black, broad, thick, rough, ſtrong hair, head and beard; their ſunken eyes, black as pitch; their ſhort forehead, compreſſed to the noſe, with an arch. We often find thin lips, though in general they are pouting, wide, and thick. The women have high cheek-bones, hollow temples, ſnub noſes, and retreating arched foreheads, with very few traits of ideal beauty. At a certain period of life both ſexes frequently become corpulent. Their power of propagation almoſt exceeds belief.

In the centre dwell the Ukranians, of whom moſt of the regiments of Coſſacs are formed. They are diſtinguiſhed among the Ruſſians almoſt as the Jews are among Europeans. They generally have aquiline noſes; are nobly formed; amorous, yielding, crafty, and without ſtrong paſſions; probably becauſe, for ſome thouſands of years, they have followed agriculture, have lived in ſociety, had a form of government, and inhabit a moſt fruitful country, in a moderate climate, reſembling that of France. Among all theſe people, the greateſt aＣtivity and ſtrength of body are united. They are as different from the German boor, as quickſilver is from lead ; and how our anceſtors could ſuppoſe them to be ſtupid, is inconceivable.

Thus too the Turks reſemble the Ruſſians. They are a mixture of the nobleſt blood of Aſia Minor with the more material and groſs Tartar. The Natolian, of a ſpiritual nature, feeds on meditation ; will for days contemplate a ſingle object, ſeat himſelf at the cheſs-board, or wrap himſelf up in the mantle of taciturnity. The eye, void of paſſion or great enterpriſe, abounds in all the penetration of benevolent cunning ; the mouth eloquent ; the hair of the head and beard, and the ſmall neck, declare the flexibility of the man.

The Engliſhman is erect in his gait, and generally ſtands as if a ſtake were driven through his body. His nerves are ſtrong, and he is the beſt runner. He is diſtinguiſhed from all other men by the roundneſs and ſmoothneſs of the muſcles of his face. If he neither ſpeak nor move, he ſeldom declares the capability and mind he poſſeſſes in ſo ſuperior a degree. His ſilent eye ſeeks not to pleaſe. His hair, coat, and character, are alike ſmooth. Not cunning, but on his guard ; and, perhaps, but little colouring is neceſſary to deceive him on any occaſion. Like the bull-dog, he does not bark ; but, if irritated, rages. As he wiſhes not for more eſteem than he merits, ſo he deteſts the falſe pretenſions of his neighbours, who would arrogate excellence they do not poſſeſs. Deſirous of private happineſs, he diſregards public opinion, and obtains a character of ſingularity. His imagination, like a ſea-coal fire, is not the ſplendour that enlightens a region, but expands genial warmth. Perſeverance in ſtudy, and pertinacity, for centuries, in fixed principles, have raiſed and maintained the Britiſh ſpirit as well as the Britiſh government, trade, manufactures, and marine. He has punctuality and probity, not trifling away his time to eſtabliſh falſe

principles, or making a parade with a vicious hypothefis.

In the temperament of nations, the French clafs
is that of the fanguine. Frivolous, benevolent,
and oftentatious, the Frenchman forgets not his
inoffenfive parade till old age has made him wife.
At all times difpofed to enjoy life, he is the beft of
companions. He pardons himfelf much ; and
therefore pardons others, if they will but grant that
they are foreigners, and he is a Frenchman. His
gait is dancing, his fpeech without accent, and his
ear incurable. His imagination purfues the confequences of fmall things with the rapidity of the
fecond-hand of a ftop-watch, but feldom gives
thofe loud, ftrong, reverberating ftrokes which
proclaim new difcoveries to the world. Wit is his
inheritance. His countenance is open, and, at
firft fight, fpeaks a thoufand pleafant, amiable
things. Silent he cannot be, either with eye,
tongue or feature. His eloquence is often deafen-
ing ; but his good humour cafts a veil over all his
failings. His form is equally diftinct from that
of other nations, and difficult to defcribe in words.
No other man has fo little of the firm or deep
traits, or fo much motion. He is all appearance,
all gefture ; therefore the firft impreffion feldom
deceives, but declares who and what he is. His
imagination is incapable of high flights, and the
fublime in all arts is to him offence. Hence his
diflike of whatever is antique in art or literature,
his deafnefs to true mufic, his blindnefs to the
higher beauties of painting. His laft, moft marking trait is, that he is aftonifhed at every thing,
and cannot comprehend how it is poffible men
fhould be other than they are at Paris.

The countenance of the Italian is foul, his
fpeech exclamation, his motion gefticulation. His
form is the nobleft, and his country the true feat
of beauty. His fhort forehead, his ftrong, marked

eyebones, the fine contour of his mouth, give a
kindred claim to the antiquities of Greece. The
ardour of his eyes denotes, that the beneficent fun
brings forth fruit more perfect in Italy than beyond the Alps. His imagination is ever in motion,
ever fympathifing with furrounding objects, and,
as in the poem of Arioſto the whole works of creation are reflected, fo are they generally in the national ſpirit. That power which could bring forth
fuch a work, appears to me the general reprefen-
tative of genius. It fings all, and from it all things
are fung. The fublime in arts is the birthright of
the Italian. Modern religion and politics may
have degraded and falfified his character, may have
rendered the vulgar faithlefs and crafty, but the
fuperior part of the nation abounds in the nobleſt
and beſt of men.

The Dutchman is tranquil, patient, confined, and
appears to will nothing. His walk and eye are
long filent, and an hour of his company will fcarcely produce a thought. He is little troubled by the
tide of paffions, and he will contemplate unmoved
the parading ſtreamers of all nations failing before
his eyes. Quiet and competence are his gods ;
therefore thofe arts alone which can procure thefe
bleffings, employ his faculties. His laws, political
and commercial, have originated in that fpirit of
fecurity which maintains him in the poffeffion of
what he has gained. He is tolerant in all that relates to opinion, if he be but left peaceably to enjoy
his property, and to affemble at the meeting-houfe
of his fect. The character of the ant is fo applicable to the Dutch, that to this literature itfelf con-
forms in Holland. All poetical powers, exerted in
great works or fmall, are foreign to this nation.
They endure pleafure from the perufal of, but produce no poetry. I fpeak of the United Provinces,
and not of the Flemings, whofe jovial character is

L

in the midway between the Italian and French. A high forehead, half-open eyes, full nofe, hanging cheeks, wide open mouth, flefhy lips, broad chin, and large ears, I believe to be characteriftic of the Dutchman.

A German thinks it difgraceful not to know every thing, and dreads nothing fo much as to be thought a fool. Probity often makes him appear a blockhead. Of nothing is he fo proud as of honeft, moral underftanding. According to modern tactics, he is certainly the beft foldier, and the teacher of all Europe. He is allowed to be the greateft inventor, and often with fo little oftentation, that foreigners have, for centuries, unknown to him, robbed him of his glory. From the age of Tacitus, a willing dependant, he has exerted faculties for the fervice of his mafters, which others only exert for freedom and property. His countenance does not, like a painting in frefco, fpeak at a diftance ; but he muft be fought and ftudied. His good nature and benevolence are often concealed under apparent morofenefs, and a third perfon is always neceffary to draw off the veil, and fhow him as he is. He is difficult to move, and, without the aid of old wine, is filent. He does not fufpeft his own worth, and wonders when it is difcovered by others. Fidelity, induftry, and fecrecy, are his principal characteriftics. Not having wit, he indulges his fenfibility. Moral good is the colouring which he requires in all arts. His epic and lyric fpirit walk in unfrequented paths. Hence his great, and frequently gigantic fenfe, which feldom permits him the clear afpeft of enthufiafm, or the glow of fplendour. Moderate in the ufe of this world's delights, he has little propenfity to fenfuality and extravagance ; but he is therefore formal, and lefs focial than his neighbour.

Plate IV.

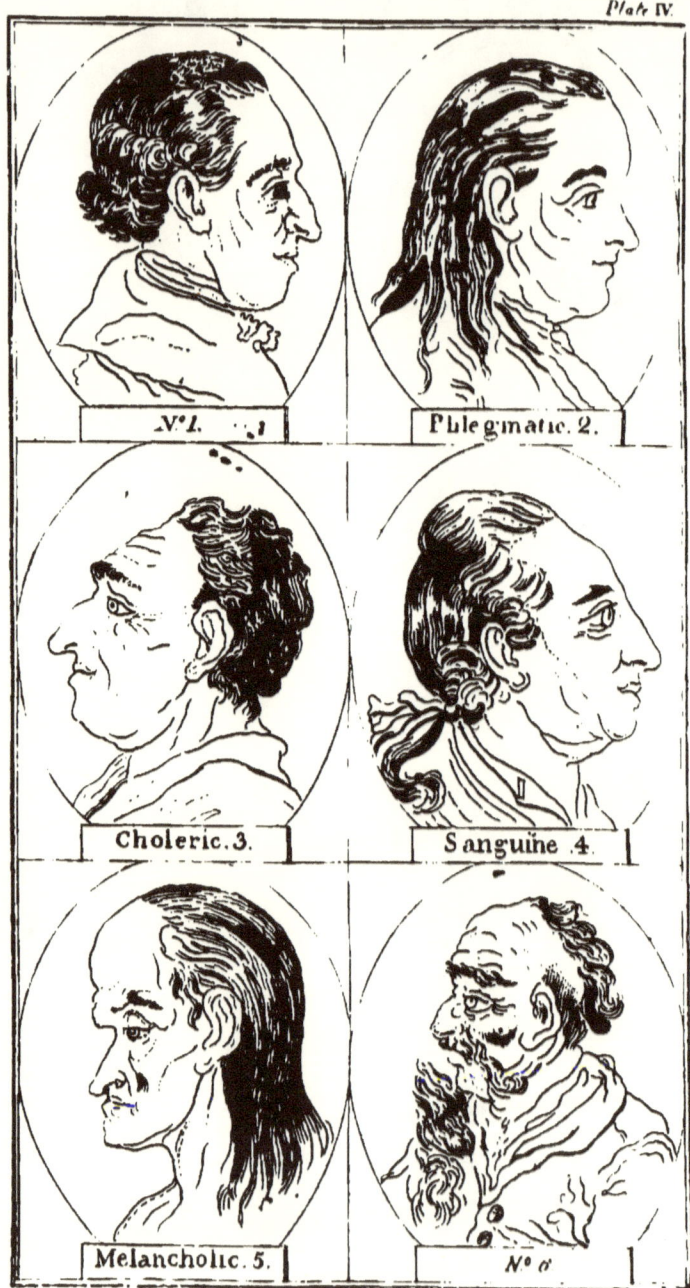

No. 1.

Phlegmatic. 2.

Choleric. 3.

Sanguine. 4.

Melancholic. 5.

No. 6.

CHAPTER XXII.

Description of Plate IV.

Number 1.

WE may certainly call nofes arched and pointed like this, witty ; but the wit is reftrained and moderated by the acute underftanding of
the forehead, the fincere religion of the eye, and
the phlegm of the chin.

Number 2.

The defcent from the nofe to the lips in the
phlegmatic countenance is unphlegmatic, and heterogeneous ; nor does the curvature of the upper
eyelid fufficiently agree with the temperament.
The outlines of the phlegmatic are relaxed, obtufe,
and hanging ; the outline of the eyes, oblique.
Be it underftood, there are other tokens, and that
all phlegmatic perfons have not thefe figns, although whoever has them is certainly phlegmatic.
If the projecting under lip, which is itfelf a fign of
phlegm, fince it is evidently a fuperabundance and
not a want of matter, be angular, and fharply delineated, then it is a fign of choloric phlegm ; that
is to fay, of the ebullition of humidity. If it be
flexible, obtufe, powerlefs, and drooping, it is then
pure phlegm. The forehead, nofe, chin, and hair,
are here very phlegmatic.

Number 3.

The choleric ought to have a more angularly
pointed nofe, and lips more fharply delineated.
The character of choler is much contained in the
drawing of the eyes, either when the pupil pro-

jects, and much of the under part of the white is visible, or when the upper eyelid retreats so that it scarcely can be perceived ; when the eyes open, or when the eye is funken, and the outlines are very definite and firm, without much curvature. In this example, the forehead, eyebrows, nose, chin, and hair, are very choleric ; but the upper part of the countenance more so than the under.

Number 4.

The sanguine needs but little correction, except that the nose ought to be a little farther from the mouth and the eye not so choleric. The levity of the sanguine temperament waves, flutters upon the lip, which, however, at the bottom, is too phlegmatic.

Number 5.

There ought to be a deeper cavity above the nose, and also of the jaw-bone, beside the ear, in this melancholic countenance. I have observed, in many melancholic persons, that the nose declines towards the lips ; nor have I seen this in any who were not sometimes inclined to the melancholic, who likewise have projecting under lips, and small, but not very round, nor very flefhy chins.

There are melancholy persons with very sanguine temperaments ; men of fine irratibility, and moral feelings, who are hurried into vices which they deeply abhor, and which they have not the power to withstand. The gloomy and dispirited character of such is perceptible in the eye that shuns examination, and the wrinkles of the forehead standing opposite to each other. Persons of a real melancholic temperament generally have their mouths shut, but the lips are always somewhat open in the middle. Many melancholic persons have small noſtrils, and ſeldom well arranged, clean, white teeth.

Number 6.

Strength and ardour, enterpriſe, courage, contempt of danger, fortitude of the irritated and irritable. This ſtrength is rather oppreſſive than patient and enduring ; it proclaims its own qualities, reſpectable in a ſtate of reſt, terrible when rouſed.

CHAPTER XXIII.

Reſemblance between Parents and Children.

THE reſemblance between parents and children is very commonly remarkable. Family phyſiognomy is as undeniable as national. To doubt this, is to doubt what is ſelf-evident ; to wiſh to interpret it, is to wiſh to explore the inexplicable ſecret of exiſtence. Striking and frequent as the reſemblance between parents and children is, yet have the relations between the characters and countenances of families never been inquired into. No one has, to my knowledge, made any regular obſervations on this ſubject. I muſt alſo confeſs, that I have myſelf made but few with that circumſtantial attention which is neceſſary. All I have to remark is as follows :

When the father is conſiderably ſtupid, and the mother exceedingly the reverſe, then will moſt of the children be endued with extraordinary underſtanding.

When the father is good, truly good, the chil-

dren will in general be well-difpofed; at leaft moft
of them will be benevolent.

The fon generally appears to inherit moral goodnefs from the good father, and intelligence from
the intelligent mother; the daughter partakes of
the character of the mother.

If we wifh to find the moft certain marks of refemblance between parents and children, they
fhould be obferved within an hour or two after
birth. We may then perceive whom the child moft
refembles in its formation. The moft effential
refemblance is ufually afterwards loft, and does
not perhaps appear for many years; or not till
after death.

When children, as they increafe in years, vifibly
increafe in the refemblance of form and features to
their parents, we cannot doubt but there is an increafing refemblance of character. How much foever the characters of children may appear unlike
that of the parents they refemble, yet will this diffimilarity be found to originate in external circumftances; and the variety of thefe muft be great indeed, if the difference of character is not at length
overpowered by the refemblance of form.

I believe, that from the ftrongly delineated father, the firmnefs and the kind (I do not fay the
form, but the kind) of bones and mufcles are derived; and from the ftrongly delineated mother,
the kind of nerves and form of the countenance;
if the imagination and love of the mother have not
fixed themfelves too deeply in the countenance of
the man.

Certain forms of countenance, in children, appear for a time undecided whether they fhall take
the refemblance of the father or of the mother; in
which cafe I will grant, that external circumftances,
preponderating love for the father or mother, or a
greater degree of intercourfe with either, may influence the form.

We fometimes fee children who long retain a remarkable refemblance to the father, but at length
change, and become more like the mother. I undertake not to expound the leaft of the difficulties
that occur on this fubject; but the moft modeft
philofophy may be permitted to compare uncommon cafes with thofe which are known, even though
they were inexplicable; and this, I believe, is all
that philofophy can and ought to do.

We know that all longings, or mothers' marks,
and whatever may be confidered as of the fame nature, which is much, do not proceed from the father, but from the imagination of the mother. We
alfo know that children moft refemble the father
only when the mother has a very lively imagination, and love for, or fear of the hufband. Therefore, as has been before obferved, it appears that
the matter and *quantum* of the power and of the
life, proceed from the father; and from the imagination of the mother, fenfibility, the kind of
nerves, the form, and the appearance.

There are certain forms and features of countenance which are long propagated, and others which
as fuddenly difappear. The beautiful and the deformed (I do not fay forms of countenances, but
what is generally fuppofed to be beauty and deformity) are not the moft eafily propagated; neither are the middling and infignificant; but the
great and the minute are eafily inherited, and of
long duration.

Parents with fmall nofes may have children with
the largeft and ftrongeft defined; but the father or
mother feldom, on the contrary, have a very ftrong,
that is to fay, large-boned nofe, which is not communicated at leaft to one of their children, and
which does not remain in the family, efpecially
when it is in the female line. It may feem to have
been loft for many years, but foon or late will again
make its appearance, and its refemblance to the

original will be particularly vifible a day or two after death.

Where any extraordinary vivacity appears in the eyes of the mother, there is almoft a certainty that thefe eyes will become hereditary ; for the imagination of the mother is delighted with nothing fo much as with the beauty of her own eyes. Phyfiognomonical fenfation has been hitherto more generally directed to the eyes, than to the nofe and form of the face ; but if women fhould once be induced to examine the nofe, and form of the face, as affiduoufly as they have done their eyes, it is to be expected that the former will be no lefs ftrikingly hereditary than the latter.

Well-arched and fhort foreheads are eafy of inheritance, but not of long duration ; and here the proverb is applicable, *Quod cito fit, cito perit.* (Soon got, foon gone.)

It is equally certain and inexplicable, that fome remarkable phyfiognomies, of the moft fruitful perfons, have been wholly loft to their pofterity ; and it is as certain and inexplicable, that others are never loft. Nor is it lefs remarkable, that certain ftrong countenances, of the father or mother, difappear in the children, and perfectly revive in the grand-children.

As a proof of the powers of the imagination of the mother, we fometimes fee, that a woman fhall have children by the fecond hufband, which fhall refemble the firft, at leaft in the general appearance. The Italians, however, are manifeftly too extravagant, when they fuppofe children, who ftrongly refemble their father, are bafe born. They fay that the mother, during the commiffion of a crime fo fhameful, wholly employs her imagination concerning the poffibility of furprife by, and the image of, her hufband But, were this fear fo to act, the form of the children muft not only have the very image of the hufband, but alfo

his appearance of rage and revenge, without which
the adulterous wife could not imagine the being
furprifed by, or image of, her hufband. It is
this appearance, this rage, that fhe fears, and not
the man.

Natural children generally refemble one of their
parents more than the legitimate.

The more there is of individual love, of pure,
faithful, mild affection, the more this love is reciprocal and unconftrained between the father and
mother, which reciprocal love and affection imply
a certain degree of imagination, and the capacity
of receiving impreffions, the more will the countenances of the children appear to be compofed of
the features of the parents.

The fanguine of all the temperaments is the moft
eafily inherited, and with it volatility ; and, being
once introduced, much induftry and fuffering will
be neceffary to extirminate this volatility.

The natural timidity of the mother may eafily
communicate the melancholy temperament of the
father. Be it underftood that this is eafy, if, in
the decifive moment, the mother be fuddenly feized
by fome predominant fear ; and that it is lefs communicable when the fear is lefs hafty and more re-
flective. Thus we find thofe mothers, who, during the whole time of their pregnancy, are moft in
dread of producing monftrous or marked children,
becaufe they remember to have feen objects that
excited abhorrence, generally have the beft formed, and freeft from marks ; for the fear, though
real, was the fear of reafon, and not the fudden
effect of an object exciting abhorrence rifing in-
ftantaneoufly to fight.

When both parents have given a deep root to
the choleric temperament in a family, it may probably be fome centuries before it be again moderated. Phlegm is not fo eafily inherited, even though
both father and mother fhould be phlegmatic ; for

there are certain moments of life when the phlegmatic acts with its whole power, though it acts thus
but rarely, and thefe moments may and muft have
their effects ; but nothing appears more eafy of
inheritance than activity and induftry, when thefe
have their origin in organization, and the neceffity
of producing alteration. It will be long before an
induftrious couple, to whom not only a livelihood,
but bufinefs, is in itfelf neceffary, fhall not have a
fingle defcendant with the like qualities, as fuch
mothers are generally prolific.

CHAPTER XXIV.

*Remarks on the Opinions of Buffon, Haller, and Bonnet,
concerning the refemblance between Parents and
Children.*

THE theory or hypothefis of Buffon, concerning the caufe of the human form, is well
known, which Haller has abridged and more clearly
explained in the following manner :

" Both fexes have their femen, in which are
active particles of a certain form. From the union
of thefe the fruit of the womb arifes. Thefe particles contain the refemblance of all the parts of
the father or mother. They are, by nature, feparated from the rude and unformed particles of the
human juices, and are impreffed with the form of
all the parts of the body of the father or mother.
Hence arifes the refemblance of children to their
parents. This will account for the mixture of the
features of father and mother in the children—for
fpots in animals, when the male and female are
of different colours—for the Mulatto produced by

a Negro and a White—and for many other phenomena difficult to be refolved.

" It may be afked, how thefe particles can affume
the internal ftructure of the body of the father,
fince they can properly be only the images of the
hollow veffels ? To which it is anfwered, that we
know not all the powers of Nature, and that fhe
may have preferved to herfelf, though fhe has concealed it from her fcholar, Man, the art of making
internally models and impreffions, which fhall exprefs the whole folidity of the model."

Haller, in his preface to Buffon's Natural Hiftory, has, in my opinion, indifputably confuted this
fyftem. But he has not only forborne to elucidate
the refemblance between fathers and children, but
while oppofing Buffon, he has fpoken fo much
on the natural, phyfiological diffimilarity of the
human body, that he appears to have denied this
refemblance. Buffon's hypothefis offended all philofophy ; and though we cannot entirely approve
the theory of Bonnet, yet he has very effectually
oppofed the incongruities of Buffon, to which Buffon himfelf could fcarcely give any ferious faith.
But he, as we fhall foon fee, has either avoided the
queftion of refemblance between parents and children, or, in order to ftrengthen his own fyftem, has
rather fought to palliate than to anfwer difficulties.

BONNET, *concerning organized Bodies.*

" Are the germs of one and the fame fpecies of
organized bodies perfectly like each other, or individually diftinct ? Are they only diftinct in the organs which characterize fex, or have they a refembling difference to each other, fuch as we obferve in individual fubftances of the fame fpecies
of plants or animals ?

" Anfwer.—If we confider the infinite variety
to be obferved in all the products of nature, the

latter will appear moſt probable. The differences which are obſerved in the individuals of the ſame ſpecies, probably depend more on the primitive form of the germs, than on the connexion of the ſexes."

On the R.ſemblance between Children and their Parents.

" I muſt own, that, by the foregoing hypotheſis, I have not been ſuccefsful in explaining the reſemblance of features found between parents and children. But are not theſe features very ambiguous ? Do we not ſuppoſe that to be the cauſe, which probably is not ſo ? The father is deformed, the ſon is deformed after the ſame manner, and it is therefore concluded that deformity is inherited. This may be true ; but it may be falſe. The deformity of each may ariſe from very different cauſes, and theſe cauſes may be infinitely varied.

" It is leſs difficult to explain hereditary diſeaſes. We can eaſily conceive, that defective juices may produce defective germs ; and when the ſame parts of the body are affected by diſeaſe in father or mother, and in child, this ariſes from the ſimilar conformation of the parts, by which they are ſubject to like inconveniencies. Beſides, the miſhapen body often originates in diſeaſe being hereditary, which much diminiſhes the firſt difficulty. For, ſince the juices conducted to thoſe parts are of a bad quality, the parts muſt be more or leſs ill formed, according as they are more or leſs capable of being affected by theſe juices."

R E F L E X I O N.

Bonnet cannot find the origin of family likeneſs in his ſyſtem. But let us take this his ſyſtem in the part where he finds the origin of hereditary

difeafe. Shall the defective juices of father or
mother very much alter the germ, and produce, in
the very parts where the father or mother is injured, important changes of bad formation, more or
lefs, according to the capability of the germ, and
its power of refiftance ? And fhall the healthy
juices of the parent in no manner affect the germ ?
Why fhould not the healthy juices be as active as
the unhealthy ? Why fhould they not introduce
the fame qualities in miniature, which the father
and mother have in the grofs, fince the father and
mother affimilate the nutriment they receive to
their own nature, and fince the feminal juices are
the fpiritual extract of all their juices and powers,
as we have juft reafon to conclude from the moft
continued and accurate obfervations ? Why fhould
they not as naturally, and as powerfully, act upon
the germ, to produce all poffible refemblance ? But
which refemblance is infinitely varied, by differently changeable and changed circumftances; fo
that the germ continually preferves fufficient of its
own original nature and properties, yet is always
very diftinct from the parents, and fometimes even
feems to have derived very little from them, which
may happen from a thoufand accidental caufes or
changes.

Hence family refemblance and diffimilarity being fummarily confidered, we fhall find that nature, wholly employed to propagate, appears to be
entirely directed to produce an equilibrium between the individual power of the germ, in its firft
formation, and the refembling power of the parents; that the originality of the firft form of the
germ may not wholly difappear before the too great
power of refemblance to the parents, but that they
may mutually concur, and both be fubject to numberlefs circumftances, which may increafe or diminifh their refpective powers, in order that the
M

riches of variety, and the utility of the creature, and its dependence on the whole, and the general Creator, may be the greater and more predominant.

From all obfervations on the refemblance between parents and children which I have been enabled to make, it appears to me evident, that neither the theories of Bonnet nor Buffon give any fyftematic explanation of phenomena, the exiftence of which cannot be denied by the fophiftry of hypothefis. Diminifh the difficulties as much as we will, facts will ftill ftare us in the face. If the germ exift preformed in the mother, can this germ, at that time, have phyfiognomy? Can it, at that time, refemble the future, promifcuous, firft, or fecond father? Is it not perfectly indifferent to either? or, if the phyfiognomonical germ exift in the father, how can it fometimes refemble the mother, fometimes the father, often both, and often neither?

To me it appears, that fomething germ-like, or a whole capable of receiving the human form, muft previoufly exift in the mother; but which is nothing more than the foundation of the future fatherly or motherly I know not what, and is the efficient caufe of the future living fruit. This germ-like fomething, which, moft efpecially conftituted agreeable to the human form, is analagous to the nature and temperature of the mother, receives a peculiar individual perfonal phyfiognomy, according to the propenfities of the father or mother, the difpofition of the moment of conception, and probably of many other future decifive moments.

Still much remains to the freedom and predifpofition of man. He may deprave or improve the ftate of the juices, he may calm or agitate his mind, may awaken every fenfation of love, and by various modes increafe or relax them. Yet I think, that neither the nature of the bones, nor the mufcles and nerves, confequently the character, depends on the phyfiognomonical preformation preceding generation ; at leaft, they are far from depending on thefe alone, though I allow the or- ganizable, the primitive form, always has a pecu- liar individuality, which is only capable of receiv- ing certain fubtile influences, and which muft re- ject others.

CHAPTER XXV.

Obfervations on the New-born, the Dying, and the Dead.

I HAVE remarked in fome children, about an hour after a not difficult birth, a ftriking, though infantine refemblance, in the profile, to the profile of the father. In a few days, this refemblance had nearly difappeared. The impreffion of the open air, nutriment, and perhaps of pofition, had fo far altered the outlines, that the child feemed entire- ly different.

Two of thefe children I faw dead, the one about fix weeks, and the other about four years old ; and nearly twelve hours after death, I obferved the fame profile which I had before remarked an hour after birth, with this difference, that the profile of the dead child, as is natural, was fomething more tenfe and fixed than the living. A part of this refemblance, however, on the third day, was re- markably gone.

One man of fifty, and another of feventy years of age, who fell under my obfervation while they were living, and after death, appeared, while liv-

M 2

ing, not to have the leaft refemblance to their
fons, and whofe countenances feemed to be of a
quite different clafs : yet, the fecond day after
death, the profile of one had a ftriking refemblance to that of his eldeft, and, of the other, to
the profile of his third fon ; as much fo as the profile of the dead children before mentioned refembled the living profile an hour after birth, ftronger
indeed, and, as a painter would fay, harder. On
the third day, here alfo a part of the refemblance
difappeared.

I have uniformly obferved among the many
dead perfons I have feen, that fixteen, eighteen,
or twenty-four hours after death, according to the
difeafe, they have had a more beautiful form, better defined, more proportionate, harmonized, ho-
mogeneous, more noble, more exalted, than they
ever had during life.

May there not be, thought I, in all men, an
original phyfiognomy, fubject to be difturbed by
the ebb and flow of accident and paffion ? and is
not this reftored by the calm of death, like as
troubled waters, being again left at reft, become
clear ?

I have obferved fome among the dying, who had
been the reverfe of noble or great during life, and
who, fome hours before their death, or perhaps
fome moments (one was in a delirium), have had an
inexpreffible ennobling of the countenance. Every
body faw a new man ; colouring, drawing, and
grace, all was new, all bright as the morning ;
beyond expreffion, noble and exalted ; the moft
inattentive muft fee, the moft infenfible feel, the
image of God, I faw it break forth and fhine
through the ruins of corruption, was obliged to
turn afide, and adore in filence. Yes, glorious
God ! ftill art thou there, in the weakeft, moft fal-
lible men !

CHAPTER XXVI.

Of the Influence of Countenance on Countenance.

AS the geftures of our friends and intimates become our own, fo, in like manner, does their
appearance. Whatever we love, we would affimilate to ourfelves; and whatever, in the circle of
affection, does not change us into itfelf, that we
change, as far as may be, into ourfelves.

All things act upon us, and we act upon all
things; but nothing has fo much influence as what
we love; and among all objects of affection, nothing acts fo forcibly as the countenance of man.
Its conformity to our countenance makes it moft
worthy our affection. How might it act upon,
how attract our attention, had it not fome marks,
difcoverable or indifcoverable, fimilar to, at leaft of
the fame kind with, the form and features of our
own countenance!

Without, however, wifhing farther to penetrate
into what is impenetrable, or to define what is in-
fcrutable, the fact is indubitable, that countenances
attract countenances, and alfo that countenances
repel countenances; that fimilarity of features
betweeen two fympathetic and affectionate men,
increafe with the developement and mutual communication of their peculiar, individual fenfations,
The reflexion, if I may fo fay, of the perfon beloved, remains upon the countenance of the affectionate.

The refemblance frequently exifts only in a fingle point—in the character of mind and countenance. A refemblance in the fyftem of the bones
prefuppofes a refemblance of the nerves and
mufcles.

M 3

Diffimilar education may affect the latter fo much, that the point of attraction may be invifible to unphyfiognomonical eyes. Suffer the two refembling forms to approach, and they will reciprocally attract and repel each other; remove every intervening obftacle, and nature will foon prevail. They will recongnize each other, and rejoice in the flefh of their flefh, and the bone of their bone : with hafty fteps will proceed to affimilate. Such countenances alfo, which are very different from each other, may communicate, attract, and acquire refemblance ; nay, their likenefs may become more ftriking than that of the former, if they happen to be more flexible, more capable, and to have greater fenfibility.

This refemblance of features, in confequence of mutual affection, is ever the refult of internal nature and organization, and, therefore, of the character of the perfons. It ever has its foundation in a preceding, perhaps, imperceptible refemblance, which might never have been animated, or fufpected, had it not been fet in motion by the prefence of the fympathetic being.

It would be of infinite importance to give the character of thofe countenances which moft eafily receive and communicate refemblance. It cannot but be known, that there are countenances that attract all, others that repel all, and a third kind which are indifferent. The all-repelling render the ignoble countenances over which they have continued influence, more ignoble. The indifferent allows no change. The all-attracting either receive, give, or reciprocally give and receive. The firft change a little, the fecond more, the third moft. " Thefe are the fouls (fays Hemfterhuys the younger) which happily, or unhappily, add the moft exquifite difcernment to that exceffive internal clafticity which occafions them to wifh and feel immoderately ; that is to fay, the souls, which are so modified, or situated, that their attractive force meets the fewest obstacles in its progress."

To study the influence of countenance, this intercourse of mind would be of the utmost importance. I have found the progress of resemblance most remarkable, when two persons, the one richly communicative, the other apt to receive, have lived a considerable time together, without foreign intervention ; when he who gave had given all, or he who received could receive no more, physiognomonical resemblance had attained its *punct m saturationis*. It was incapable of farther increase.

A word here to thee, youth, irritable, and easy to be won. Oh ! pause, consider ; throw not thyself too hastily into the arms of an untried friend. A gleam of sympathy and resemblance may easily deceive thee. If the man, who is thy second self, have not yet appeared, be not rash, thou shalt find him at the appointed hour. Being found, he will attract thee to himself, will give and receive whatever is communicable. The ardour of his eyes will nurture thine, and the gentleness of his voice temper thy too-piercing tones. His love will shine in thy countenance, and his image will appear in thee. Thou wilt become what he is, and yet remain what thou art. Affection will make qualities in him visible to thee, which never could be seen by an uninterested eye. This capability of remarking, of feeling what there is of divine in him, is a power which will make thy countenance assume his resemblance.

CHAPTER XXVII.

On the Influence of the Imagination on the Counte-nance.

A Word only on a fubject concerning which volumes might be written ; for it is a fubject I muft not leave wholly in filence. The little, the nothing I have to fay upon it, can only act as an inducement to deeper meditations on a theme fo profound.

Imagination acts upon our own countenance, rendering it in fome meafure refembling the belov-ed or hated image which is living, prefent, and fleeting before us, and is within the circle of our immediate activity. If a man deeply in love, and fuppofing himfelf alone, were ruminating on his beloved miftrefs, to whom his imagination might lend charms, which, if prefent, he would be unable to difcover : were fuch a perfon obferved by a man of penetration, it is probable that traits of the miftrefs might be feen in the countenance of this meditating lover. So might, in the cruel features of revenge, the features of the enemy be read, whom imagination reprefents as prefent. And thus is the countenance a picture of the cha-racteriftic features of all perfons exceedingly loved or hated.

It is poffible, that an eye lefs penetrating than that of an angel, may read the image of the Creator in the countenance of a truly pious perfon. He who languifhes after Chrift, the more lively, the more diftinctly, the more fublimely, he reprefents to himfelf the very prefence and image of Chrift, the greater refemblance will his own countenance take of this image. The image of imagination often acts more effectually than the real prefence ;

and whoever has feen him of whom we fpeak, the great *HIM*, though it were but an inftantaneous glimpfe, oh ! how inceffantly will the imagination reproduce his image in the countenance !

Our imagination alfo acts upon other countenances. The imagination of the mother acts upon the child ; and hence men long have attempted to influence the imagination for the production of beautiful children. In my opinion, however, it is not fo much the beauty of furrounding forms, as the intereft taken concerning forms in certain moments : and here again, it is not fo much the imagination that acts, as the fpirit ; that being only the organ of the fpirit. Thus it is true, that it is *the fpirit that quickeneth the flefh*, and the image of the flefh (merely confidered as fuch) *profiteth nothing*.

A look of love, from the fanctuary of the foul, has certainly greater forming power than hours of deliberate contemplation of the moft beautiful images. This forming look, if fo I may call it, can as little be premeditatedly given, as any other naturally beautiful form can be imparted by a ftudious contemplation in the looking-glafs. All that creates, and is profoundly active, in the inner man, muft be internal, and be communicated from above ; as I believe it fuffers itfelf not to be occafioned, at leaft not by forethought, circumfpection, or wifdom in the agent, to produce fuch effects. Beautiful forms, or abortions, are neither of them the work of art or ftudy, but of intervening caufes, of the quick-guiding Providence, the predetermining God.

Endeavour to act upon affection, inftead of the fenfes If thou canft but incite love, it will of itfelf feek and find the powers of creation ; but this very love muft itfelf be innate before it can be awakened. Perhaps, however, the moment of this awakening is not in our power ; and therefore, to thofe who would, by plan and method, effect that which is in itfelf fo extraordinary, and imagine they have had I know not what wife and phyfiological circumfpection when they firft awaken love, I might exclaim, in the words of the enraptured fongfter : " I charge you, O ye daughters of " Jerufalem ! by the roes and the hinds of the " field, that ye ftir not up nor awake my love " till he pleafe." Here behold the forming genius :—" Behold he cometh, leaping upon the " mountains, fkipping upon the hills, like a young " hart !"

Unforefeen moments, rapid as the lightning, in my opinion, form and deform. Creation of every kind is momentaneous ; the developement, nutriment, change, improving, injuring, is the work of time, art, induftry, and education. Creative power fuffers itfelf not to be ftudied ; creation cannot be premeditated. Marks may be moulded ; but living effence, within and without refembling itfelf, the image of God, muft be created, born, " not of the will of the flefh, nor of the will of " man, but of God."

CHAPTER XXVIII.

The Effects of the Imagination on the Human Form.

IT is equally true and incomprehenfible, that, by the ftrength of imagination, there are marks communicated by mothers to children during pregnancy ; that there are images, animals, fruit, or other fubftances, on the body of the child ; marks of the hand on the very parts where the pregnant perfon has been fuddenly touched ; averfion to things which have occafioned difguft in the mother ; and a continued fcurvy communicated to the child, by the unexpected fight of a putrid animal. So many marks on the bodies of children, arifing not from imaginary but real accidents, muft oblige us to own, that there is truth in that which is inconceivable : therefore the imagination of the mother acts upon the child.

Of the innumerable examples that might be produced, I fhall cite the two following :

A woman during the time of her pregnancy, was engaged in a card party, and only wanted the ace of fpades to win all that was ftaked; and as it happened, in the change of cards, the fo much wifhed-for ace was given her. Her joy at this fuccefs had fuch an effect upon her imagination, that the child of which fhe was pregnant, when born, had the ace of fpades depicted in the apple of the eye, and without injury to the organ of fight.

The following anecdote is certainly true, and ftill more aftonifhing :

A lady of Rheinthal had, during her pregnancy, a defire to fee the execution of a man, who was fentenced to have his right hand cut off before he was beheaded. She faw the hand fevered from the body, and inftantly turned away and went home, without waiting to fee the death that was to follow. This lady bore a daughter who was living at the time this fragment was written, and who had only one hand. The right-hand came away with the after-birth.

Moral marks, as well as phyfical, are alfo poffible. I have heard of a phyfician, who never failed to fteal fomething from all the chambers through which he paffed, which he would afterwards forget ; and, in the evening, his wife, who fearched his pockets, would find keys, fnuff-boxes, etuis-cafes, fciffars, thimbles, fpectacles, buckles, fpoons and other trinkets, which fhe reftored to

the owners. I have been likewife told of a child,
who, at two years of age, was adopted when beg-
ging at the door of a noble family, received an excellent education, and became a moft worthy man,
except that he could not forbear to fteal. The
mothers of thefe two extraordinary thieves muft,
during pregnancy, have had an extraordinary defire to pilfer. It will be felf evident, that however infufferable fuch men are in a ftate of fociety,
they are rather unfortunate than wicked. Their
actions may be as involuntary as mechanical,
and, in the fight of God, probably as innocent as
the cuftomary motions of our fingers when we tear
bits of paper, or do any other indifferent, thoughtlefs action.

The moral worth of an action muft be eftimated
by its intention, as the political worth muft by
its confequences. As little injury as the ace of
fpades, if the ftory be true, did to the countenance
of the child, as little probably did this thievifh propenfity to the heart. Such a perfon certainly had
no roguifh look, no avaricious, downcaft, fly, pilfering afpect, like one who is both foul and body
a thief. I have not yet feen any man of fuch an
extraordinary character, and therefore cannot judge
of his phyfiognomy by experience; yet we have
reafon ferioufly to conclude, that men fo uncommon muft bear fome marks of fuch deviation of
character in their countenance.

Thofe extraordinary large or fmall perfons, by
which giants and dwarfs, fhould perhaps be
claffed among thefe active and paffive effects of the
imagination. Though giants and dwarfs are not
properly born fuch, yet it is poffible, however incomprehenfible, that Nature may firft, at a certain
age, fuddenly enlarge or contract herfelf.

We have a variety of examples, that the imagination appears not only to act upon the prefent,
but on abfence, diftance, and futurity. Perhaps

apparitions of the dying and the dead may be attributed to this kind of effect. Be it granted that thefe facts, which are fo numerous, are true, and including not only the apparitions of the dead, but of the living, who have appeared to diftant friends, after collecting fuch anecdotes, and adding others on the fubject of prefage and prediction, many philofophical conjectures will thence arife, which may probably confirm my following propofition.

The imagination, incited by the defire and languifhing of love, or inflamed by paffion, may act in diftant places and times. The fick or dying perfon, for example, fighs after an abfent friend, who knows not of his ficknefs, nor thinks of him at the time. The pining of the imagination penetrates, as I may fay, walls, and appears in the form of the dying perfon, or gives figns of his prefence, fimilar to thofe which his actual prefence gives. Is there any real corporeal appearance ? No. The fick or dying perfon is languifhing in his bed, and has never been a moment abfent ; therefore, there is no actual appearance of him whofe form has appeared. What then has produced this appearance ? What is it that has acted thus at a diftance on another's fenfes or imagination ?—Imagination ; but the imagination through the focus of paffion.—How ?—It is inexplicable. But who can doubt fuch facts, who does not mean to laugh at all hiftorical facts ?

May there not be fimilar moments of mind, when the imagination fhall act alike inexplicably on the unborn child ? That the inexplicable difgufts, I will grant ; I feel it perfectly. But is it not the fame in the foregoing examples, and in every example of the kind ? Like as cripples firft become fo many years after birth, which daily experience proves ; may not, after the fame inconceivable manner, the feeds of what is gigantic or dwarfifh be the effects of the imagination on the

N

fruit, which does not make its appearance till years after the child is born?

Could a woman keep an accurate regifter of what happened in all the powerful moments of imagination, during her ftate of pregnancy, fhe then might probably be able to foretell the chief incidents, philofophical, moral, intellectual, and phyfiognomonical, which fhould happen to her child. Imagination actuated by defire, love, or hatred, may, with more than lightning fwiftnefs, kill or enliven, enlarge, diminifh, or impregnate, the organized fœtus with the germ of enlarging or diminifhing wifdom or folly, death or life, which fhall firft be unfolded at a certain time, and under certain circumftances. This hitherto unexplored, but fometimes decifive and revealed creative and changing power of the foul, may be, in its effence, identically the fame with what is called faith working miracles, which latter may be developed and increafed by external caufes, wherever it exifts, but cannot be communicated where it is not. A clofer examination of the foregoing conjectures, which I wifh not to be held for any thing more than conjectures, may perhaps lead to the profoundeft fecrets of phyfiognomy.

CHAPTER XXIX.

Effay, by a late learned man of Oldenburg, (M. Sturtz), on Phyfiognomy, interfperfed with fhort Remarks, by the Author.

"I AM as clearly convinced of the truth of phyfiognomy as Lavater, and of the all-fignificance of each limb and feature. True it is that the mind may be read in the lineaments of the body, and its motions in the features, and their shades.

" Connexion and harmony, caufe and effect, exift through all nature ; therefore between the external and internal of man. Our form is influenced by our parents, by the earth on which we walk, the fun that warms us with its rays, the food that affimilates itfelf with our fubftance, the incidents that determine the fortunes of our lives. Thefe all modify, repair, and chiffel forth the body, and the marks of the tool are apparent both in body and in mind. Each arching, each finuofity of the external, adapts itfelf to the individuality of the internal. It is adherent and pliable, like wet drapery. Were the nofe but a little altered, Cæfar would not be the Cæfar with whom we are acquainted.

" When the foul is in motion, it shines through the body, as the moon through the ghofts of Offian, each paffion throughout the human race has ever the fame language."

From east * to west, envy no where looks with the fatisfied air of magnanimity, nor will difcontent appear like patience. Wherever patience is, there is it expreffed by the fame figns ; as likewife are anger, envy, and every other paffion.

" Philoctetes certainly expreffes not the fenfation of pain like a fcourged flave. The angels of Raphael muft fmile more nobly than the angels of Reinbrandt ; but joy and pain ftill have each their peculiar expreffion. They act according to peculiar laws upon peculiar mufcles and nerves, however various may be the fhades of their expreffion ;

---

* Thofe paffages, which are not marked with inverted commas, are the obfervations of M. Lavater, on the different parts of M. Sturtz's Effay.

and the oftener the paſſion is repeated, or ſet in motion, the more it becomes a propenſity, a favourite habit, the deeper will be the furrows it ploughs.

" But inclination, capacity, modes and gradations of capacity, talents, and an ability for buſineſs, lie much more concealed. A good obſerver will diſcover the wrathful, the voluptuous, the proud, the diſcontented, the malignant, the benevolent, and the compaſſionate, with little difficulty. But the philoſopher, the poet, the artiſt, and their various partitions of genius, he will be unable to determine with equal accuracy. And it will be ſtill more difficult to aſſign the feature or trait in which the token of each quality is ſeaten, whether underſtanding be in the eyebone, wit in the chin, and poetical genius in the mouth."

Yet I hope, I believe, nay, I know, that the preſent century ſhall render this poſſible. The penetrating author of this eſſay would not only have found it poſſible, but would have performed it himſelf, had he only ſet apart a ſingle day to compare and examine a well-arranged collection of characters, either in nature, or well-painted portraits.

" Our attention is always excited whenever we meet with a remarkable man, and we all are more or leſs empirical phyſiognomiſts. We perceive in the aſpect, the mien, the ſmile, mechaniſm of the forehead, ſometimes malice, ſometimes wit, at others penetration. We expect and preſage, from the impulſe of latent ſenſation, very determined qualities, from the form of each new acquaintance ; and, when this faculty of judging is improved by an intercourſe with the world, we often ſucceed to admiration in our judgment on ſtrangers.

" Can we call this feeling, internal unacquired ſenſation, which is inexplicable, or is it compariſon, indication, conclusion from a character we have examined to another which we have not, and occasioned by some external resemblance? Feeling is the ægis of enthusiasts and fools, and, though it may often be conformable to truth, is still neither demonstration nor confirmation of truth; but induction is judgment founded on experience, and this way only will I study physiognomy.

" I meet many strangers, with an air of friendship, I recede from others with cool politeness, though there is no expression of passion to attract, or to disgust. On farther examination, I always found, that I have seen in them some trait either of a worthy or worthless person, with whom I was before acquainted.

" A child, in my opinion acts from like motives, when he evades, or is pleased with, the caresses of strangers, except that he is actuated by more trifling signs, perhaps by the colour of the clothes, the tone of the voice, or often by some motion, which he has observed in the parent, the nurse, or the acquaintance."

This cannot be denied to be often the case, and indeed much more often than is commonly supposed; yet I make no doubt of being able to prove, that there are, in nature and art, a multitude of traits, especially of the extremes of passionate as well as dispassionate faculties, which, of themselves, and without comparison with former experiments, are, with certainty, intelligible to the most unpractised observer. I believe it to be incorporated in the nature of man, in the organization of our eyes and ears, that he should be attracted or repulsed by certain countenances, as well as by certain tones. Let a child, who has seen but a few men, view but the open jaws of a lion, or a tyger, and the smile of a benevolent person, and his nature will infallibly shrink from the one, and meet the smile

N 3

of benevolence with a smile ; not from reason and
comparison, but from the original feelings of nature. For the same reason, we listen with plea-
sure to a delightful melody, and shudder at dis-
cordant shrieks. As little as there is of comparison or consideration on such an occasion, so is
there equally little on the first sight of an extremely pleasing, or an extremely disgusting countenance.

" It is not therefore mere sensation, since I have
good reason, when I meet a person who resembles
Turenne, to expect sagacity, cool resolution, and
ardent enterprize. If, in three men, I find one
possessed of the eyes of Turenne, and the same
marks of prudence ; another with his nose, and
high courage ; the third with his mouth and activity ; I then have ascertained the seat where each
quality expresses itself, and am justified in expect-
ing similar qualities wherever I meet similar features.

" Had we, for centuries past, examined the human form, arranged characteristic features, compared traits, and exemplified inflexions, lines, and
proportions, and had we added explanations to
each, then would our Chinese alphabet of the race
of man be complete, and we need but open it to
find the interpretation of any countenance.
Whenever I indulge the supposition, that such an
elementary work is not absolutely impossible, I expect more from it than even Lavater. I imagine
we may obtain a language so rich, and so determinate, that it shall be possible, from description only,
to restore the living figure ; and that an accurate
description of the mind shall give the outline of
the body, so that the physiognomist, studying some
future Plutarch, shall regenerate great men, and
the ideal form shall, with facility, take birth from
the given definition."

This is excellent ; and, be the author in jest or
earnest ; this is what I entirely, without dreaming,

and moſt abſolutely, expect from the following
century, for which purpoſe, with God's pleaſure, I
will hereafter hazard ſome eſſays.

" With theſe ideal forms ſhall the chambers of
future princes be hung, and he who comes to ſo-
licit employment, ſhall retire without murmuring,
when it is proved to him that he is excluded by
his noſe."

Laugh or laugh not, friends or enemies of truth,
this will, this muſt happen.

" By degrees, I imagine to myſelf a new, and
another world, whence error and deceit ſhall be
baniſhed."

Baniſhed they would be were phyſiognomy the
univerſal religion, were all men accurate obſervers,
and were not diſſimulation obliged to recur to new
arts, by which phyſiognomy, at leaſt for a time,
may be rendered erroneous.

" We have to inquire, whether we ſhould therefore be happier ?"

Happier we ſhould certainly be, although the
preſent conteſt between virtue and vice, ſincerity
and diſſimulation, which ſo contributes to the developement of the grand faculties of man, renders,
as I may ſay, human virtue divine, exalting it to
heaven.

" Truth is ever found in the medium : we will
not hope too little from phyſiognomy, nor will we
expect too much.   Here torrents of objections
break in upon me, ſome of which I am unable to
anſwer.   Do ſo many men in reality reſemble
each other ? Is not the reſemblance general ; and
when particularly examined, does it not vaniſh,
eſpecially if the reſembling perſons be compared
feature by feature ? Does it not happen, that one
feature is in direct contradiction to another ; that
a fearful noſe is placed between eyes which betoken
courage ?"

In the firm parts, or thoſe capable of ſharp out-

lines, accidents excepted, I have never yet found
contradictory features, but often have between the
firm and the flexible, or the ground-form of the
flexible and their apparent fituation. By ground-
form I mean to fay that which is preferved after
death, unlefs diftorted by violent difeafe.

" It is far from being proved, that refemblance
of form univerfally denotes refemblance of mind.
In families where there is moft refemblance, there
are often the greateft varieties of mind. I have
known twins, not to be diftinguifhed from each
other, between whofe minds there was not the
leaft fimilarity."

If this be literally true, I will renounce phyfiognomy, and to whoever fhall convince me of it, I
will give him my copy of thefe fragments, and an
hundred phyfiognomonical drawings. Nor will I
be my own judge, I leave it to the worthy author
of this remark to choofe three arbitrators. Let
them examine the fact accurately, and, if they confirm it, I will own my error. Shades, however, of
thefe twin brothers will firft be neceffary. In all
the experiments I have made, I declare upon my
honour, I have never made any fuch remark.

" And how fhall we be able to explain the innumerable exceptions which almoft overwhelm
rule ? I will only produce fome from my own
obfervation. Dr. Johnfon had the appearance of
a porter ; not the glance of the eye, not any trait
of the mouth, fpeak the man of penetration or
of fcience."

When a perfon of our author's penetration and
judgment thus affirms, I muft hefitate and fay,
he has obferved this, I have not. But how does
it happen, that, in more than ten years obfervation, I have never met any fuch example ? I have
feen many men, efpecially in the beginning of my
phyfiognomonical ftudies, whom I fuppofed to be
men of fenfe, and who were not fo ; but never, to

the beſt of my knowledge, did I meet a wiſe man whom I ſuppoſed a fool. In the frontiſpiece is an engraving of Johnſon. Can a countenance more tranquilly fine be imagined, one that more poſſeſſes the ſenſibility of underſtanding, planning, ſcrutinizing ? In the eyebrows only, and their horizontal poſition, how great is the expreſſion of profound, exquiſite, penetrating underſtanding !

" The countenance of Hume, was that of a common man."

So ſays common report. I have no anſwer but that I ſuſpect the aſpect, or flexible features, on which moſt obſervers found their phyſiognomonical judgment, have, as I may ſay, effaced the phyſiognomy of the bones ; as, for example, the outline and arching of the forehead, to which ſcarcely one in a hundred direct their attention.

" Churchill had the look of a drover; Goldſmith of a ſimpleton ; and the cold eyes of Strange do not betray the artiſt."

The greateſt artiſts have often the coldeſt eyes. The man of genius and the artiſt are two perſons. Phlegm is the inheritance of the mere artiſt.

" Who would ſay, that the apparent ardour of Wille ſpeaks the man who paſſed his life in drawing parallel lines ?"

Ardour and phlegm are not incompatible ; the moſt ardent men are the cooleſt. Scarcely any obſervation has been ſo much verified as this : it appears contradictory, but it is not. Ardent, quickly determining, reſolute, laborious, and boldly enterprizing men, the moments of ardour excepted, have the cooleſt of minds. The ſtyle and countenance of Wille, if the profile portrait of him in my poſſeſſion be a likeneſs, have this character in perfection.

" It appears to me, that Boucher the painter of the graces, has the aſpect of an executioner."

Truly ſo. Such was the portrait I received.

But then, my good M. Sturtz, let us underſtand what is meant by theſe painters of the graces. I find as little in his works, as in his countenance. None of the paintings of Boucher were at all to my taſte. I could not contemplate one of them with pleaſure, and his countenance had the ſame effect. I can now comprehend, ſaid I, on the firſt ſight of his portrait, why I have never been pleaſed with the works of Boucher.

" I once happened to ſee a criminal condemned to the wheel, who, with ſatanic wickedneſs, had murdered his benefactor, and who yet had the benevolent and open countenance of an angel of Guido. It is not impoſſible to diſcover the head of a Regulus among guilty criminals, or of a veſtal in the houſe of correction."

I can confirm this from experience. Far be contradiction from me on this ſubject. But ſuch vicious perſons, however hateful with reſpect to the appearance and effect of their actions, or even to their internal motives, were not originally wicked. Where is the pure, the noble, finely formed, eaſily irritated man, with angelic ſenſibility, who has not his deviliſh moments, in which, were not opportunity happily wanting, he might, in one hour, be guilty of ſome two or three vices, which would exhibit him, apparently at leaſt, as the moſt deteſtable of men ; yet may he be a thouſand times better and nobler than numerous men of ſubaltern minds, held to be good, who never were capable of committing acts ſo wicked, for the commiſſion of which they ſo loudly condemn him, and, for the good of ſociety, are in duty bound to condemn ?

" Lavater will anſwer, ſhow me theſe men, and I will comment upon them, as I have done upon Socrates. Some ſmall, often unremarked trait, will probably explain what appears to you ſo enigmatical. But will not fomething creep into the commentary, which never was in the text ?"

Though this may be, yet it ought not to be the cafe. I will alfo gïant, that a man with a good countenance may act like a rogue ; but, in the firft place, at fuch a moment, his countenance will not appear good ; and, in the next, he will infinitely oftener act like a man of worth.

" Have we any right, from a known character, to draw conclufions concerning one unknown ? or, is it eafy to difcover what that being is, who wanders in darknefs, and dwells in the houfe of contradiction ; who is one creature to-day, and to-morrow the very reverfe ?"

How true, how important is this ! How neceffary a beacon to warn and terrify the phyfiognomift !

" What judgment could we form of Auguftus, if we were only acquainted with his conduct to Cinna ? or of Cicero, if we knew him only from his confulate ? How gigantic rifes Elizabeth among queens, yet how little, how mean, was the fuperannuated coquette ! James II, a bold general, and a cowardly king ! Monk, the revenger of monarchs, the flave of his wife : Algernon Sydney and Ruffel, patriots worthy of Rome, fold to France ! Bacon, the father of wifdom, a bribed judge ! Such difcoveries make us fhudder at the afpect of man, and fhake off friends and intimates like coals of fire from the hand. When fuch cameleon minds can be at one moment great, at another contemptible, and alter their form, what can that form fay ?"

Their form fhows what they may, what they ought to be, and their afpect, in the moment of action, what they are. Their countenance fhows their power, and their afpect the application of their power. The expreffion of their littlenefs

may probably be like the fpots of the fun, invifible
to the naked eye.

" Does not that medium, through which we
are accuftomed to look, tinge our judgment ?
Smellfungus views all objects through a blackened
glafs ; another through a prifm.   Many contemplate virtue through a diminifhing, and vice
through a magnifying medium."

How excellently expreffed !

" A book written by Swift on phyfiognomy,
would certainly have been very different from that
of Lavater.   National phyfiognomy is ftill a large
uncultivated field.   The families of the four clafles
of the race of Adam, from the Efquimaux to the
Greeks, in Europe, and in Germany alone, what
varieties are there which can efcape no obferver !
Heads bearing the ftamp of the form of government, which ever will influence education ; re-
publican haughtinefs, proud of its laws ; the pride
of the flave, who feels pride becaufe he has the
power of inflicting the fcourges he has received ;
Greeks under Pericles, and under Haffan Pacha ;
Romans, in a ftate of freedom, governed by em-
perors, and governed by popes : Englifhmen under Henry the Eighth, and Cromwell.   How have
I been ftruck by the portraits of Hampden, Pym,
and Vane ! All produced varieties of beauty, according to the different nations."

I cannot exprefs how much I am indebted to
the author of this fpirited and energetic effay.
How worthy an act was it in him, whom I had
unintentionally offended, concerning whom I had
publifhed a judgment far from fufficiently noble,
to fend me this effay, with liberty to make what
ufe of it I pleafed ! in fuch a manner, in fuch a
fpirit, may informations, corrections, or doubts
be ever conveyed to me ! Shall I need to apologize
for having inferted it ? or rather, will not moft of
my readers fay, give us more fuch ?

CHAPTER XXX

Quotations from Huart, with Remarks.

1.

SOME are wife and appear not to be fo ; others appear wife and are not fo ; fome again are not, and appear not to be wife ; and others are wife, and alfo appear to be wife.

A touchftone for many countenances.

2. " The fon is often brought in debtor to the great underftanding of the father.

3. " Wifdom in infancy denotes folly in manhood.

" 4. No aid can make thofe bring forth who are not pregnant."

We muft not expect fruit where feed has not been fown. How advantageous, how important, would phyfiognomy become, were it, by being acquainted with every fign of intellectual and moral pregnancy enabled to render aid to all the pregnant and to the pregnant only !

5. The external form of the head is what it ought to be, when it refembles a hollow globe flightly compreffed at the fides with a fmall protuberance at the forehead and back of the head. A very flat forehead, or a fudden defcent at the back of the head, are no good tokens of underftanding."

The profile of fuch a head, notwithftanding the compreffure, would be more circular than oval. The profile of a good head ought to form a circle combined only when with the nofe ; therefore, without the nofe it approaches much more to the oval than the circular. " A very flat forehead, (fays our author) is no fign of good underftanding." True, if the flatnefs refemble that of the ox ; but

O

I have feen perfectly flat foreheads, let me be
rightly underftood, I mean flat only between and
above the eyebrows, in men of great wifdom.
Much indeed, depends upon the pofition and curve
of the outlines of the forehead.

6. Man has more brain than any animal. Were
the quantity of the brain in two of the largeft ox-
en compared to the quantity found in the fmalleft
man, it would prove to be lefs."

7. " Large oranges have thick fkins and little
juice. Heads of much bone and flefh have little
brain. Large bones, with abundance of flefh and
fat, are impediments to the mind."

8. " The heads of wife perfons are very weak,
and fufceptible of the moft minute impreffions."

Often, not always. And how wife ? Wife to
plan, but not to execute. Active wifdom muft
have harder bones. One of the greateft of this
earth's wonders is a man in whom the two qualities
are united, who has fenfibility even to painful excefs, and coloffal courage to refift the impetuous
torrent, the whirlpool, by which he fhall be affail-
ed. Such characters poffefs fenfibility from the
tendernefs of bodily feeling ; and ftrength, not fo
much in the bones as in the nerves.

9. " A thick belly, fays Galen, a thick underftanding."

With equal truth or falfehood, I may add, a thin
belly, a thin underftanding. Remarks fo general,
which would prove fo many able and wife men
to be fools, I value but little. A thick belly certainly is no pofitive token of underftanding, it
is rather pofitive for fenfuality, which is detrimental to the underftanding ; but abftractedly, and
unconnected with other indubitable marks, I cannot
receive this as a general propofition.

10. " Ariftotle holds the fmalleft heads to be
the wifeft."

But this, with all reverence for fo great a man,

I think was fpoken without reflexion. Let a fmall head be imagined on a great body, or a great head on a fmall body, each of which may be found in confequence of accidents that excite or retard growth ; and it will be perceived that, without fome more definite diftinction, neither the large nor the fmall head is, in itfelf, wife or foolifh. It is true, that large heads with fhort triangular foreheads, are foolifh ; as are thofe large heads which are fat, and incumbered with flefh ; but fmall, particularly round heads, with the like incumbrance, are intolerably foolifh, and generally poffefs that, which renders their intolerable folly more intolerable, a pretenfion to wifdom.

11. " It is a good fign, when a fmall perfon has a head fomewhat large, and a large perfon has the head fomewhat fmall."

Provided this extends no farther than *fomewhat*, it may be fuffered ; but it is certainly beft, when the head is in fuch proportion to the body, that it is not remarkable either for its largenefs or fmallnefs.

12. " Memory and imagination refemble the underftanding as a monkey does a man."

13. " It is if no confequence to the genius, whether the flefh be hard or tender, if the brain do not partake of the fame quality ; for experience tells us, that the latter is very often of a different temperament to the other parts of the body. But when both the brain and the flefh are tender, they betoken ill to the underftanding, and equally ill to the imagination."

14. " The fluids which render the flefh tender, are phlegm and blood ; and thefe being moift, according to Galen, render men fimple and ftupid. The fluids, on the contrary, which harden the flefh, are choler and melancholy, (or bile) and thefe generate wifdom and underftanding. It is therefore

O 2

a much worfe fign to have tender flefh than rough ; and tender fignifies a bad memory, with weaknefs of underftanding and imagination."

If I may fo fay, there is an intelligent tendernefs of flefh, which announces much more underftanding than do the oppofite qualities of rough and hard. I can no more clafs coriaceous flefh as the characteriftic of underftanding, than I can tendernefs of flefh, without being more accurately defined, as the characteriftic of folly. It will be proper to diftinguifh between tender and porous, or fpongy, and between rough and firm without hardnefs.

15. " To difcover whether the quality of the brain correfponds with the flefh, we muft examine the hair. If the hair be black, ftrong, rough, and thick, it betokens ftrength of imagination and underftanding."

I am of a different opinion. Let not this be expreffed in fuch general terms. At this moment, I recollect a very weak man, by nature weak, with exactly fuch hair. This roughnefs *(fprodigkeit)* is a fatal word, which, taken in what fenfe it will, never fignifies any thing good.

" But if the hair be tender and weak, it denotes nothing more than goodnefs of memory."

Once more too little : it denotes a finer organization, which receives the impreffion of images at leaft as ftrongly as the figns of images.

16. " When the hair is of the firft quality, and we would farther diftinguifh, whether it betokens goodnefs of underftanding or imagination, we muft pay attention to the laugh. Laughter betrays the quality of the imagination."

And I add, of the underftanding, of the heart, of power, love, hatred, pride, humility, truth, and falfehood. Would I had artifts, who would watch for and defign the outlines of laughter ! The phyfiognomy of laughter would be the beft of elementary books for the knowledge of man. If the laugh be good, fo is the perfon. It is faid of Chrift, that he never laughed. I believe it ; but, had he never fmiled, he would not have been human. The fmile of Chrift muft have contained the precife outline of brotherly love.

17. " Heraclitus fays, a dry eye, a wife mind."

18. " We fhall difcover few men of great underftanding who write a fine hand."

It might have been faid with more accuracy, a fchoolmafter's hand.

CHAPTER XXXI.

Remarks on an Effay on Phyfiognomy, by Profeffor Litchtenberg.

THIS effay is written with much intelligence, much ornament, and a mild diffufive eloquence. It is the work of a very learned, penetrating, and, in many refpects, highly meritorious perfon, who appears to poffefs much knowledge of men, and a large portion of the prompt fpirit of obfervation. This effay merits the utmoft attention and inveftigation. It is fo interefting, fo comprehenfive, affords fo much opportunity of remark for the phyfiognomift, and of remarks which I have yet to make, that I cannot avoid citing the moft important paffages, and fubmitting them to an unprejudiced and accurate examination.

It is far from my intention or wifh to compare myfelf with the excellent author, to make any pretenfion to his fanciful and brilliant wit, and ftill lefs to his learning and penetration. Though I could with, I dare not hope, to meet and

O 3

anfwer him with the fame elegance as his polifhed mind and fine tafte feem to demand. I am
fenfibie of thofe wants which are peculiar to myfelf, and which muft remain mine, even when I
have truth on my fide. Yet, worthy Sir, be affured that I fhall never be unjuft, and that, even
where I cannot affent to your obfervations, I fhall
never forget the efteem I owe your talents, learning, and merits.

Let us in fuppofition, fit down in friendfhip with
your effay before us, and, with that benevolence
which is moft becoming men, philofophers in particular, explain our mutual fentiments concerning
nature and truth.

ON PHYSIOGNOMY.

" Certainly (fays our author) the freedom of
thought, and the very receffes of the heart, were
never more feverely fcrutinized than in the prefent
age."

It appears to me that, at the very beginning,
an improper point of view is taken, which may
probably lead the author and reader aftray through
the whole effay. For my own part, at leaft, I
know of no attacks on the freedom of thought, or
the fecret receffes of the heart. It is univerfally
known, that my labours have been lefs directed to
this than to the knowledge of predominant character, capacities, talents, powers, inclinations, activity, genius, religion, fenfibility, irritability,
and clafticity, of men in general, and not to the
difcovery of actual and prefent thought. As far
as I am concerned, the foul may, and can, in our
witty author's own words, " brood as fecretly over
its treafures as it might have done centuries ago ;
may as tranquilly fmile at the progrefs of all Ba-
bylonian works, at all proud affailants of heaven,
convinced that, long before the completion of

their work, there shall be a confusion of tongues, and the master and the labourers shall be scattered."

Nobody would laugh more than I at the arrogance of that physiognomist, who should pretend to read in the countenance the most secret thoughts and motions of the soul, at any given moment, although there are moments, in which they are legible to the most unpractised physiognomist.

I am of opinion, likewise, the secrets of the heart belong to pathognomy, to which I direct my attention much less than to physiognomy; on which the author says, more wittily than truly, "it is as unnecessary to write on as the art of love.

The author is very right in reminding us, "that we ought to seek physiognomonical instruction from known characters with great caution, and even diffidence."

Our author then says, "Whether physiognomy, in its utmost perfection would promote philanthropy, is at least questionable."

I confidently answer unquestionable, and I hope immediately to induce the reasonable and philanthropic author to say the same. Physiognomy, in its utmost perfection, must mean the knowledge of man in its utmost perfection. And shall not this promote the love of man? or, in other words, shall it not discover innumerable perfections, which the half physiognomist, or the unphysiognomist, are unable to discover? Noble and penetrating friend of man, while writing this, you had forgotten what you had so truly, so beautifully said, "that the most hateful deformity might, by the aid of virtue, acquire irresistible charms." And to whom more irresistible, more legible, than to the perfect physiognomist? irresistible charms certainly promote not hatred, but love. From my own experience, I can sincerely declare, that the improvement of my physiognomonical knowledge

has extended and increafed the power of love in
my heart.

Though this knowledge may fometimes occafion
affliction, ftill it is ever true, that the affliction occafioned by certain countenances, endears, fancti-
fies, and renders enchanting whatever is noble and
lovely, which often glows in the human countenance, like embers among afhes. My attention to
the difcovery of this fecret goodnefs is increafed,
and the object of my labours is its increafe and
improvement; and how do efteem and love extend
themfelves, wherever I perceive a preponderance
of goodnefs! On a more accurate obfervation, the
very countenances that afflict me, and which, for
fome moments, incenfe me againft humanity, do
but increafe a tolerant and benevolent fpirit; for
I then difcern the load, and the nature of that
fenfuality, againft which they have to combat.

All truth, all knowledge of what is, of what
acts upon us, and on which we act, promotes general and individual happinefs. Whoever denies
this is incapable of inveftigation. The more perfect this knowledge is, the greater are its advantages. Whatever profits, whatever promotes happinefs, promotes philanthropy. Where are happy
men to be found without philanthropy? Are fuch
beings poffible? Were happinefs and philanthropy
to be deftroyed or leffened, by any perfect fcience,
truth would war with truth, and eternal wifdom
with itfelf.

The man who can ferioufly maintain, "that a
perfect fcience may be detrimental to human fociety, or may not promote philanthropy, (without
which happinefs among men cannot be fuppofed)
is certainly not a man, in whofe company our author would wilhto philofophize, as certainly will he,
with me affume it as an axiom, that "the nearer
truth, the nearer happinefs." The more our
knowledge and judgment refemble the knowledge

and judgment of the Deity, the more will our philanthropy refemble the philanthropy of the Deity. He who knows how man is formed, who remembers that he is but duft, is the moft tolerant friend of man.

Angels I believe to be better phyfiognomifts, and more philanthropic, than men, although they may perceive in us a thoufand failings and imperfections, which may efcape the moft penetrating eye of man. God, having the moft knowledge of fpirit, is the moft tolerant of fpirits. And who was more tolerant, more affectionate, more lenient, more merciful than thou, who *needeft not that any fhould teftify of man, for thou kneweft what was in man* ?

" It is certain, that the induftrious, the infinuating, and active blockheads in phyfiognomy may do much injury to fociety."

And as certainly worthy Sir, it is my earneft defire, my known endeavour, to deter fuch blockheads from ftudying phyfiognomy. This evil can be prevented only by accurate obfervation. True it is, that every fcience may become dangerous, when ftudied by the fuperficial and the foolifh, and the very reverfe, when ftudied by the accurate and the wife. According to your own principles, therefore, we muft agree in this, that none but the fuperficial, the blockhead, the fanatical enemy of knowledge and learning in general, can wifh to prevent "all inveftigation of phyfiognomonical principles ;" none but fuch a perfon " can oppofe phyfiognomonical labours ; none but a blockhead will fuppofe it unworthy and impracticable, in thefe degenerate days, to awaken fenfibility, and the fpirit of obfervation, or to improve the arts, and the knowledge of men." To grant all this, as you, Sir, do, and yet to fpeak with bitternefs againft phyfiognomy and phyfiognomifts, I call fowing tares among the good feed.

Our author next proceeds to diftinguifh between
phyfiognomy and pathognomy. " Phyfiognomy
(he defines to be) a capability of difcovering the
qualities of the mind and heart from the form and
qualities of the external parts of the body, efpecially the countenance, exclufive of all tranfitory
figns of the motions of the mind; and pathognomy,
the whole femeiotica of the paffions, or the knowledge of the natural figns of the motions of the
mind, according to all their gradations and com-
binations."

I entirely agree with this diftinction, and likewife fubfcribe to thefe given difinitions.

It is next afked, is there phyfiognomy? Is there
pathognomy? To the latter the author juftly re-
plies, "This no man ever yet denied, for what
would all theatrical reprefentations be without it?
The languages of all ages and nations abounds
with pathognomonical remarks, and with which
they are infeparable interwoven."

However, after reading the work feveral times,
I cannot difcover whether the author does or does
not grant the reality of phyfiognomy. In one paffage, the author very excellently fays, "No one
will deny, that in a world where all things are
caufe and effect, and where miracles are not to be
found, each part is a mirror of the whole. We
are often able to conclude, from what is near to
what is diftant, from what is vifible to what is invifible, from the prefent to the paft and the future.
Thus the hiftory of the earth is written, in nature's
characters, in the form of each tract of country,
of its fands, hills, and rocks. Thus each fhell on
the fea-fhore proclaims the once included mind,
connected, like the mind of man, with this fhell.
Thus also might the internal of man be exprefled,
by the external, on the countenance, concerning
which we particularly mean to fpeak. Signs and
traces of thought, inclination, and capacity muft

be perceptible. How vifible are the tokens impreſſed upon the body by trade and climate ! Yet what are trade and climate compared to the ever active foul, created in every fibre, of whofe abfolute legibility from all and to all no one doubts ?"

From all mankind, rather than from the writer of this very excellent paſſage, ſhould I have expected the following : " What ! the phyſiognomiſt will exclaim, can the foul of a Newton refide in the head of a Negro, or an angelic mind in a fiendlike form ?"

As little could I have expected this paſſage :— " Talents and the endowments of the mind, in general, are not expreſſed by any ſigns in the firm parts of the head."

I have never in my life met with any thing more contradictory to nature, and to each other, than the foregoing and the following paragraphs :

" If a pea were thrown into the Mediterranean, an eye more piercing than ours, though infinitely leſs penetrating than the eye of him who fees all things, might perceive the effects produced on the coaſt of China." Thefe are our author's very words.

And ſhall the whole living powers of the foul, " creative in every fibre," have no determinate influence on the firm parts, thofe boundaries of its activity, which firſt were yielding, and acted upon, impreſſed, by every mufcle ; which refemble each other in no human body, which are as various as characters and talents, and are as certainly different as the moſt flexible parts of man ? Shall the whole powers of the foul, I fay, have no determinate influence on thefe, or not by thefe be defined ?

In order to avoid the future imputation of indulging the ſhallow ſtream of youthful declamation, inſtead of producing facts, and principles deduced from experience, let us oppofe experience to declamation, and facts to fubtleties. But firſt a word, that we may perfectly remove a degree of ambiguity, which I should not have expected from the accuracy of a mathematician.

" Why not, (asks our author) why not the soul of Newton in the head of a Negro? Why not an angel mind in a fiend-like form ? Who, reptile! empowered thee to judge of the works of God ?"

Let us be rightly understood. We do not speak here of what God can do, but of what is to be expected from the knowledge we have of his works. We ask what the Author of order actually does, and not whether the soul of Newton can exist in the body of a Negro, or an angelic soul in a fiend-like form. The physiognomonical question is, can an angel's soul act the same in a fiend-like body as in an angelic body ? or, in other words, could the mind of Newton have invented the theory of light, residing in the head of a Negro, thus and thus defined ? Such is the question.

Will you, Sir, who are the friend of truth, will you answer, it might ? You, who have previously said of the world, " all things in it are cause and effect, and miracles are not to be found."

I should indeed be a reptile, judging the works of God, did I maintain its possibility by miracle ; but the question, at present, is not concerning miracles ; it is concerning natural cause and effect.

Having thus clearly stated the argument, permit me, Sir, to decide it, by quoting your own words : " Judas scarcely could be that dirty, deformed mendicant painted by Holbein. No hypocrite, who associates with the good, betrays with a kiss, and afterwards hangs himself, has the look of Holbein's Judas. My experience leads me to suppose Judas must have been distinguished by an insinuating countenance, and an ever-ready smile."

How true ! how excellent ! yet what if I were to exclaim, " Who empowered thee, reptile ! to judge of the work of God ?" What if I were to retort the following juft remark, " Tell me firft, why a virtuous mind is fo often doomed to exift in an infirm body ? Might not alfo, were it God's good pleafure, a virtuous man have a countenance like the beggarly Jew of Holbein, or any other that can be imagined ?"

Can this, however, be called wife or manly reafoning ? How wide is the difference between fuffering and difgufting virtue ? or, is it logical to deduce that, becaufe virtue may fuffer, virtue may be difguftful ? Is not fuffering effential to virtue ? To afk why virtue muft fuffer, is equivalent to afking why God has decreed that virtue fhould exift. Is it alike incongruous to admit that virtue fuffers, and that virtue looks like vice ? Virtue void of conflict, of fuffering, or of felf-denial, is not virtue accurately confidered ; therefore it is folly to afk, why muft the virtuous fuffer ? It is in the nature of things ; but it is not in the nature of things, not in the relation of caufe and effect, that virtues fhould look like vice, or wifdom like foolifhnefs. How, good Sir, could you forget what you have fo expreffively faid, " There is no durable beauty .without virtue, and the moft hateful deformity may, by the aid of virtue, acquire the moft irrefiftible charms ? The author is acquainted with feveral women, whofe example might infpire the moft ugly with hope."

What may be the infirmities of the virtuous we do not inquire, nor whether a man of genius may not become a fool ; we afk, whether virtue, while exifting, can look like prefent vice, or actual folly, like actual wifdom ? You Sir, who are fo profound an inquirer into the nature of man, will certainly never grant, (who, indeed, will ?) that the foul of the beloved difciple of Chrift, could, without a miracle, refide in the dirty, deformed mendicant, the beggarly Jew of Holbein, and act as freely in that

P

as in any other body.   Will you, Sir, continue to
rank yourfelf, in your philofophical refearches,
with thofe, who having maintained fuch fenfelefs
propofitions, rid themfelves of all difficulties by
afking, " Who impowered thee, reptile ! to judge
of the works of God ?"

Let us proceed to examine a few more paffages.

" Our fenfes acquaint us only with the fuperficies, from which all deductions are made. This
is not very favourable to phyfiognomy, for which
fomething more definite is requifite, fince this reading of the fuperficies is the fource of all our errors,
and frequently of our ignorance."

So it is with us in nature ; we abfolutely can read
nothing more than the fuperficies.   In a world de-
void of miracles, the external ever muft have a relation to the internal ; and, could we prove all reading of the fuperficies to be falfe, what fhould we
effect but the deftruction of all human knowledge.
All our inquiries produce only new fuperficies.
All our truth muft be the truth of the fuperficies.
It is not the reading of the fuperficies that is the
fource of all our error ; for, if fo, we fhould have
no truth ; but the not reading, or which is the
fame in effect, the not rightly reading.

If " a pea thrown into the Mediterranean fea
would effect a change in the fuperficies, which
fhould extend to the coaft of China," any error that
we might commit, in our conclufions concerning
the action of this pea, would not be becaufe we
read only the fuperficies, but becaufe we cannot
read the fuperficies.

" That we can only read the fuperficies is not
very favourable to phyfiognomy, for which fomething more definite is requifite."   Something more
definite we have continually endeavoured to give,
and wifh to hear the objections of acute inquirers.
But let facts be oppofed to facts.   Does not our
author, by the expreflion, " fince the internal is

impreffed upon the external," feem to grant the poffibility of this impreffion ? And if fo, does not the fuperficies become the index of the internal ? Does he not thereby grant the phyfiognomy of the firm parts ?

He proceeds to afk, " If the internal be impreffed upon the external, is the impreffion to be difcovered by the eyes of men ?" Dare I truft my eyes, that I have read fuch a paffage in the writings of a philofopher !

We certainly fee what we fee. Be the object there, or be it not, the queftion ever muft be, do we or do we not fee ? That we do fee, and that the author, whenever he pleafes, fees alfo, his effay is a proof, as are his other works. Be this as it may, I know not what would become of all our philofophers and philofophy, were we, at every new difcovery of things, or the relation of things, to afk, was this thing placed there to be difcovered ? With what degree of ridicule would our witty author treat the man who fhould endeavour to render aftronomy contemptible by afking, " Though the wifdom of God is manifeft in the ftars, were the ftars placed there to be difcovered ?" " Muft not figns and effects, which we do not feek, conceal and render thofe erroneous of which we are in fearch ?"

The figns we feek are manifeft, and may be known : they are the terminations of caufes, therefore effects, therefore phyfiognomonical expreffions. The philofopher is an obferver, an obferver of that which is fought, or not fought. He fees, and muft fee, that which prefents itfelf to his eyes; and that which prefents itfelf is the fymbol of fomething that does not prefent itfelf. What he fees can only miflead him when he does not fee rightly. If the conclufion be true, " that figns and effects which we do not feek muft conceal, and render erroneous thofe of which we are in fearch," then ought we to feek no figns and effects, and thus all fciences vanifh.

I have reafon to hope, that a perfon of fo much learning as is our author, would not facrifice all human fciences for the fole purpofe of heaping phyfiognomy on the pile. I grant the poffibility and facility of error is there ; and this fhould teach us circumfpection, fhould teach us to fee the thing that is, without the addition of any thing that is not. But to wifh, by any pretence, to divert us from feeing and obferving, and to render inquiry contemptible, whether with rude or refined wit, would be the moft ridiculous of all fanaticifm. Such ridicule, in the mouth of a profeffed enemy of falfe philofophers, would be as vapid as falfe. I am indeed perfuaded that my antagonift is only in jeft.

" Were the growth of the body (fays the author) in the moft pure of atmofpheres, and modified only by the emotions of the mind, undifturbed by any external power, the ruling paffion, and the pre-vailing talent, I allow, might produce, according to their different gradations, different forms of coun-tenance, like as different falts cryftalize in differ-ent forms, when obftructed by no impediment. But is the body influenced by the mind alone, or is it not rather expofed to all the impulfes of various contradictory powers, the laws of which it is obli-ged to obey ? Thus each mineral, in its pureft ftate, has its peculiar form ; but the anomalies which its combination with others occafions, and the acci-dents to which it is fubjected, often caufe the moft experienced to err, when they would diftinguifh it by its form."

What a fimile ! Salts and minerals compared to an organized body, internally animate ! A grain of falt, which the leaft particle of water will inftan-taneoufly melt, to the human fcull, which has de-fied misfortunes, and millions of external impreffi-

ons for centuries ? Doft not thou blufh, Philofophy ? Not to confine ourfelves to the organization
of the fculls of men and other animals, do we find
that even plants, which have not the internal refiftance, the elafticity of men, and which are expofed
to millions of counteracting impreflions from light,
air, and other bodies, ever change their form, in
in confequence of fuch caufes ? Which of them is
ever miftaken for another by the botanift. The
moft violent accidents fcarcely could effect fuch
a change, fo long as they fhould preferve their organization.

"Thus is the body mutually acted upon by the
mind and external caufes, and manifefts not only
our inclinations and capacities, but alfo the effects
of misfortune, climate, difeafes, food, and thoufands
of inconveniences to which we are fubjected, not
always in confequence of our vice, but often by accidents, and fometimes by our virtues."

Who would, who can, deny this ? But is the
foregoing queftion hereby anfwered ? We are to
attend to that. Does not our eflayeft himfelf fay,
" the body is acted upon by the mind and external caufes ?" Therefore not by external caufes
alone. May it not equally be affected by the internal energy, or inactivity of the mind ? What are
we contending for ? Has it not (if indeed the author be in earneft) the appearance of fophiftry to
oppofe external to internal effects, and yet own the
body is acted upon by both ? And will you, Sir,
acute and wife as you are, maintain that misfortune
can change a wife, a round, and an arched, into a
cylindrical forehead ; one that is lengthened into
one that is fquare ; or the projecting into the fhort
retreating chin ? Who can ferioufly believe and
affirm, that Charles XIV. Henry IV. and Charles
V. men who were undoubtedly fubject to misfortunes, if ever men were, thereby acquired another

P 3

form of countenance, (we fpeak of the firm parts, not of fcars) and which forms denoted a different character to what each poffeffed previous to fuch misfortunes ? Who will maintain, that the nofes of Charles XII. or Henry IV. denoting power of mind, previous to their reverfe of fortune, the one at Pultawa, the other by the hand of Ravaillac, fuffered any change, and were debafed to the infignificant pointed nofe of a girl ? Nature acts from within upon the bones ; accident and fuffering act on the nerves, mufcles, and fkin. If any accident attack the bones ; who is fo blind as not to remark fuch phyfical violence ? The figns of misfortune are either ftrong or feeble : when they are feeble, they are effaced by the fuperior ftrength and power of nature ; when ftrong, they are too vifible to deceive, and by their ftrength and vifibility warn the phyfiognomift not to fuppofe them the features of nature. By the phyfiognomift I mean the unprejudiced obferver, who alone is the real phyfiognomift, and has a right to decide ; not the man of fubtlety, who is wilfully blind to experience.

" Are the defects, which I remark in an image of wax, always the defects of the artift, or are they not the confequences of unfkilful handling, the fun's heat or the warmth of the room."

Nothing, dear friend of truth, is more eafy to remark, in an image of wax, than the original hand of the mafter, although it fhould, by improper handling, accidental preffure, or melting, be injured. This example, Sir, militates againft yourfelf. If the hand of the mafter be vifible in an image of wax, where it is fo eafily defaced, how much more perceptible muft accident be in an organized body, fo individually permanent ? Inftead of an image of . wax, the fimile, in my opinion, would be improved were we to fubftitute a ftatue ; and in this every connoiffeur can diftinguifh what has been broken, chopped, or filed off, as well as what has been added by a later hand. And why fhould not this be known in man ? Why fhould not the original form of man be more diftinguifhable, in defpite of accident, than the beauty and workmanfhip of an excellent ftatue which has been defaced ?

" Does the mind, like an elaftic fluid, always affume the form of the body ? And if a flat nofe were the fign of envy, muft a man, whofe nofe by accident fhould be flattened, confequently become envious ?"

The inquirer will gain but little, be this queftion anfwered in the negative or affirmative. What is gained were we to anfwer, " Yes ; the foul is an elaftic fluid, which always takes the form of the body ?" Would it thence follow that the flattened nofe has loft fo much of its elafticity, as would be neceffary to propel the nofe ? or where would be the advantage fhould we reply, " No ; all fuch comparifons are infignificant, except to elucidate certain cafes : we muft appeal only to facts."

But what would be anfwered to a lefs fubtle and more fimple queftion ? Is there no example of the mind being injured by the maiming of the body ? Has not a fractured fcull, by compreffing the brain, injured the underftanding ? Does not caftration render the male half female ?—But to anfwer wit with reafon, fays a witty writer, is like endeavouring to hold an eel by the tail.

We wholly fubfcribe to the affirmation, that " it is abfurd to fuppofe the moft beautiful mind is to be found in the moft beautiful body, and the moft deformed mind in the moft deformed body."

We have already explained ourfelves fo amply on this fubject, that being fuppofed to hold a contrary opinion appears incomprehenfible. We only fay, there is a proportion and beauty of body, which is more capable of fuperior virtue, fenfibility, and action, than the difproportionate. We fay with the author, " Virtue beautifies, vice deforms." We moſt cordially grant, that honeſty may be found in the moſt ugly, and vice in men of the moſt beautiful forms.

We however, differ from him, concerning the following affertion : " Our languages are exceedingly barren of phyſiognomonical terms. Were it a true ſcience, the language of the vulgar would have been proverbially rich in its terms. The noſe occurs in a *hundred* proverbs and phraſes, but always pathognoſhonically, denoting paſt action, but never phyſiognomonically, betokening character or diſpoſition."

Inſtead of a *hundred*, I am acquainted with only one ſuch phraſe, *naſen rumfe*, to turn up the noſe. *Homo obeſæ, obtuſæ naris*, ſaid the ancients ; and had they not ſaid it, what could thence have been adduced, ſince we can prove *à poſteriori*, that the noſe is a phyſiognomonical ſign of character ?

I have neither the learning nor the inclination to cite ſufficient proofs of the contrary from Homer, Suetonius, Marſhal, and an hundred others. That which is, is, whether perceived by the ancients or not. Such duſt might blind a ſchool-boy, but not the eyes of a ſage, who ſees for himſelf, and who knows that each age has its meaſure of diſcovery, and that there are thoſe who fail not to exclaim againſt all diſcoveries which were not made by the ancients.

" I ſhould be glad to know (ſays our author) not what man may become, but what he is ?"

I muſt confeſs that I wiſh to know both. Many vicious men reſemble valuable paintings, which have been deſtroyed by varniſh. Would you pay no attention to ſuch a painting ! Is it wholly unworthy of you, though a connoiſſeur ſhould aſſure you, the picture is damaged ; but there is a poſſibility of clearing away the varniſh, as this maſter's colours are ſo ſtrongly laid on, and ſo eſſentially good, that no varniſh can penetrate deep enough,

if we are but careful in bringing it away not to in-
jure the picture ? Is this of no importance ? You
obferve the fmalleft change of pofition in the polar
ftar. Days are dedicated to examine how many
ages fhall elapfe before it will arrive at the neareft
point of approach. I do not defpife your labours.
But is it of no importance to you, to fathers, mothers, guardians, teachers, friends, and ftatefmen,
to inquire what a man may become, or what muft
be expected from this or that youth, thus and thus
formed and educated ? Many foolifh people are
like excellent watches, which would go well, were
the regulator but rectified.

Is the goodnefs of the mechanifm of no confequence to you, although a fkilful watchmaker
fhould tell you, this was, and is, an excellent piece
of workmanfhip, infinitely better than that which
you fee fet with brilliants, which, I grant, will go
well for a quarter of a year, but will then ftop !
Clean this, repair it, and ftraighten the teeth of this
fmall wheel. Is this advice of no importance ?
Will you not be informed what it might have been,
what it may yet probably be ? Will you not hear
of a treafure that lies buried, and, while buried, I
own ufelefs ; but will you content yourfelf with
the trifling intereft arifing from this, or that fmall
fum ?

Do you pay attention only to the fruit of the
prefent year, and which is perhaps forced ? And
do you neglect the goodnefs of a tree, which, with
attention may bring forth a thoufand fold, though,
under certain circumftances, it may yet have
brought forth none ! Have the hot blafts of the
fouth parched up its black leaves, or has the ftorm
blown down its half-ripened fruit, and will you
therefore not inquire whether the root does not
ftill remain undeftroyed ?

 I feel I grow weary, and perhaps weary others,
efpecially as I am more and more convinced, that

our pleafant author, at leaft hitherto, meant only
to amufe himfelf.   I fhall therefore only produce
two more contradictions, which ought not to have
efcaped the author, and fcarcely can efcape any
thinking reader.   ·

In one place, he very excellently fays, " Pathognomonical figns, often repeated, are not always entirely effaced, but leave phyfiognomonical impreffions.   Hence originate the lines of folly, ever gap-
ing, ever admiring, nothing underftanding ; hence
the traits of hypocrify ; hence the hollowed cheek,
the wrinkles of obftinacy, and heaven knows how
many other wrinkles.   Pathognomonical diftortion,
which accompanies the practice of vice, will likewife, in confequence of the difeafe it produces, become more diftorted and hateful.   Thus may the
pathognomonical expreffion of friendfhip, compaffion, fincerity, piety, and other moral beauties, become bodily beauty to fuch as can perceive and admire thefe qualities.   On this is founded the phyfiognomy of Gellert, which is the only true part of
phyfiognomy.   This is of infinite advantage to virtue, and is comprehended in a few words, " virtue
beautifies, vice deforms."

The branch therefore hath effect, the root none :
the fruit has phyfiognomy, the tree none ; the
laugh of felf-fufficient vanity may, therefore, arife
from the moft humble of hearts, and the appearance of folly from the perfection of wifdom.   The
wrinkles of hypocrify, therefore, are not the refult
of any internal power or weaknefs.   The author
will always fix our attention on the dial-plate, and
will never fpeak of the power of the watch itfelf.
But take away the dial-plate, and ftill the hand will
go.   Take away thofe pathognomonical traits,
which diffimulation fometimes can effect, and the
internal power of impulfe will remain.   How contradictory therefore is it to fay, the traits of folly

are there, but not the character of folly, the drop of water is vifible, but the fountain, the ocean, is not!

Again.   It is certainly incongruous to fay, "There is pathognomy, but this is as unneceffary (to be written) as an act of love.   It chiefly confifts in the motion of the mufcles of the countenance and the eyes, and is learned by all men.   To teach this would be like an attempt to number the fands of the fea !"

Yet the author, in the very next page, with great acutenefs, begins to teach pathognomy, by explaining twelve of the countenances of Chodowiecki, in which how much is there included of the fcience of phyfiognomy !

Permit me now, my worthy antagonift, yet no longer antagonift, but friend, convinced by truth and the love of truth, I fay, permit me to tranfcribe, in one continued quotation, fome of your excellent thoughts and remarks from your effay, and elucidations on the countenances of Chodowiecki, part of which have been already cited in this fragment, and part not.   I am convinced they will be agreeable to my readers.

"Our judgment concerning countenances frequently acquires certainty, not from phyfiognomonical nor pathognomonical figns, but from the traces of recent actions, which men cannot fhake off. Debauchery, avarice, beggary, have each their livery, by which they are as well known as the foldier by his uniform, or the chimney-fweeper by his footy jacket.   The addition of a trifling expletive in difcourfe will betray the badnefs of education ; and the manner of putting on the hat what is the company we keep, and what the degree of our folly."

Suffer me here to add, fhall not then the whole form of man difcover any thing of his talents and difpofition !   Can the moft milky candour here forget the ftraining at a gnat and fwallowing a camel !

" Maniacs will often not be known to be difor-
dered in their fenfes, if not in action. More will
often be difcovered, concerning what a man really
is, by his drefs, behaviour, and mode of paying his
compliments at his firft vifit and introduction, in a
fingle quarter of an hour, than in all the time he
fhall remain.—(By unphyfiognomonical eyes, permit me to add.) Cleanlinefs and fimplicity of
manner will often conceal paffions.

" Nothing, often, is to be furmifed from the
countenances of the moft dangerous men. Their
thoughts are all concealed under an appearance of
melancholy. Whoever has not remarked this, is
unacquainted with mankind. The heart of the vicious man is always lefs eafy to be read, the better
his education has been, the more ambition he has,
and the better the company he has been accuftomed to keep.

" Cowardice and vanity, governed by an inclination to pleafure and indolence, are not—(fometimes) marked with ftrength equivalent to the mifchief they occafion ; while, on the contrary, fortitude in defence of juftice, againft all opponents
whatever, be their rank and influence what it may,
and the confcious feelings of real felf-worth often,
look very dangerous, efpecially when unaccompani-
ed by a fmiling mouth.

" Specious as the objections brought by the fophiftry of the fenfual may be, it is notwithftanding
certain that there is no poffible durable beauty without virtue, and the moft hateful deformity may, by
the aid of virtue, acquire irrefiftible charms. Examples of fuch perfections, among perfons of both
fexes, I own are uncommon, but not more fo than
heavenly fincerity, modeft compliance, without felf-
degradation, univerfal philanthropy, without bufy
intrufion, a love of order without being minute,
or neatnefs without foppery, which are the virtues
that produce fuch irrefiftible charms.

" Vice, in like manner, in perfons yielding to its influence, may highly deform ; efpecially when, in confequence of bad education, and want of knowledge of the traits of moral beauty, or of will to affume them, the vicious may find no day, no hour, in which to repair the ravages of vice.

" Who will not liften to the mouth, in which no trait, no fhade of falfehood is difcoverable ? Let it preach the experience of what wifdom, what fcience it may, comfort will ever be the harbinger of fuch a phyfician, and confidence haften to welcome his approach.

" One of the moft hateful objects in the creation, fays a certain writer, is a vicious and deformed old woman. We may alfo fay, that the virtuous matron, in whofe countenance goodnefs and the ardour of benevolence are confpicuous, is an object moft worthy our reverence. Age never deforms the countenance, when the mind dares appear unmafked : it only wears off the frefh varnifh, under which coquetry, vanity, and vice were concealed. Wherever age is excedingly deformed, the fame deformity would have been vifible in youth, to the attentive obferver.

" This is not difficult, and were men to act from conviction, inftead of flattering themfelves with the hope of fortunate accidents, happy marriages would be more frequent ; and as Shakefpeare fays, the bonds which fhould unite hearts would not fo often ftrangle temporal happinefs."

This is fpeaking to the heart. Oh ! that I could have written my fragments in company with fuch an obferver ! Who could have rendered greater fervices to phyfiognomy than the man who, with the genius of a mathematician, poffeffes fo accurate a fpirit of obfervation ?

Q

CHAPTER XXXII.

Description of Plate V.

Number 1.

WILLIAM HONDIUS, a Dutch engraver, after Vandyck. We here see mild, languid, flow induſtry, with enterprizing, daring, conſcious heroiſm. This forehead is rounded, not indeed common nor ignoble. The eyebrows are curved, the eyes languid and ſinking, and the whole countenance oval, ductile, and maidenly.

Number 2.

This head, if not ſtupid, is at leaſt common ; if not rude, clumſy. I grant it is a caricature, yet, however, there is ſomething ſharp and fine in the eye and mouth, which a connoiſſeur will diſcover.

Number 3.

This is manifeſtly a Turk, by the arching and poſition of the forehead, the hind part of the head, the eyebrows, and particularly the noſe. The aſpect is that of obſervation, with a degree of curioſity. The open mouth denotes remarking, with ſome reflexion.

Number 4.

It muſt be a depraved taſte which can call this graceful, and therefore it muſt be far from majeſtic. I ſhould neither wiſh a wife, mother, ſiſter, friend, relation, or goddeſs, to poſſeſs a countenance ſo cold, inſipid, affected, ſtony, unimpaſſioned, or ſo perfectly a ſtatue.

Number 5.

The ſtrong grimace of an impotent madman,

Plate.V.

N.º1.

N.º2.

N.º3

N.º4.

N.º5.

N.º6.

who diftorts himfelf without meaning. In the eye is neither attention, fury, littlenefs, nor greatnefs.

Number 6.

The eyes in this head are benevolently ftupid. Wherefoever fo much white is feen as in the left eye, if in company with fuch a mouth, there is feldom much wifdom.

CHAPTER XXXIII.

General Remarks on Women.

I Muft premife, that I am but little acquainted with the female part of the human race. Any man of the world muft know more of them than I can pretend to know. My opportunities of feeing them at the theatre, at balls, or at the card-table, where they beft may be ftudied, have been exceedingly few. In my youth, I almoft avoided women, and was never in love.

Perhaps I ought, for this very reafon, to have left this very important part of phyfiognomy to one much better informed, having myfelf fo little knowledge of the fair fex. Yet might not fuch neglect have been dangerous ? Might another have treated the fubject in the manner which I could wifh ? or, would he have faid the little I have to fay, and which, though little, I efteem to be neceffary and important ?

I frequently fhudder while I think how exceffively, how contrary to my intention, the ftudy of phyfiognomy may be abufed, when applied to women. Phyfiognomy will perhaps fare no better

Q 2

than philofophy, poetry, phyfic, or whatever may
be termed art or fcience.   A little philofophy leads
to atheifm, and much to Chriftianity.   Thus muft
it be with phyfiognomy.   But I will not be difcouraged ; the half precedes the whole.   We learn to
walk by falling, and fhall we forbear to walk left
we fhould fall ?

I can with certainty fay, that true pure phyfiognomonical fenfation, in refpect to the female fex,
beft can feafon and improve life, and is the moft
effectual prefervative againft the degradation of ourfelves or others.

Beft can feafon and improve human life.—What better can temper manly rudenefs, or ftrengthen and
fupport the weaknefs of man, what fo foon can af-
fuage the rapid blaze of wrath, what more charm
mafculine power, what fo quickly diffipate peevifh-
nefs and ill temper, what fo well can wile away the
infipid tedious hours of life, as the near and affectionate look of a noble, beautiful woman ? What
is fo ftrong as her foft delicate hand ? What fo
perfuafive as her tears reftrained ? Who but beholding her muft ceafe to fin ? How can the fpirit
of God act more omnipotently upon the heart,
than by the extending and increafing phyfiognomonical fenfation for fuch an eloquent countenance?
What fo well can feafon daily infipididity ? I
fcarcely can conceive a gift of more paternal and
divine benevolence !

This has fweetened every bitter of my life, this
alone has fupported me under the moft corroding
cares, when the forrows of a burfting heart wanted
vent.   My eyes fwam in tears, and my fpirit groan-
ed with anguifh.   Then when men have daily afked, " where is now thy God ?" when they rejected
the fympathy, the affection of my foul, with rude
contemptuous fcorn ; when acts of honeft fimplicity were calumniated, and the facred impulfe of
confcious truth was ridiculed, hiffed at, and defpi-

fed ; in thofe burning moments, when the world
afforded no comfort, even then did the Almighty
open mine eyes, even then did he give me an un-
failing fource of joy, contained in a gentle, tender,
but internally firm, female mind ; an afpect like
that of unpractifed, cloiftered virginity, which felt,
and was able to efface each motion, each paffion,
in the moft concealed feature of her hufband's
countenance, and who, by thofe means, without
any thing of what the world calls beauty, fhone
forth beauteous as an angel. Can there be a more
noble or important practice than that of a phyfiognomonical fenfation for beauties fo captivating, fo
excellent as thefe.

*This phyfiognomonical fenfation is the moft effectual
prefervative againft the degradation of ourfelves and
others.* What can more readily difcover the boundary between appetite and affection, or cunning
under the mafk of fenfibility ? What fooner can
diftinguifh defire from love, or love from friendfhip ? What can more reverently, internally, and
profoundly feel the fanctity of innocence, the divinity of maiden purity, or fooner detect coquetry
unbleffed, with wiles affecting every look of modefty ? How often will fuch a phyfiognomift turn
contemptuous from the beauties moft adored, from
the wretched pride of their filence, their meafured
affectation of fpeech, the infipidity of their eyes,
arrogantly overlooking mifery and poverty, their
authoritative nofe, their languid, unmeaning lips,
relaxed by contempt, blue with envy, and half bit-
ten through by artifice and malice ! The obviouf-
nefs of thefe and many others will preferve him,
who can fee from the dangerous charms of their
fhamelefs bofom ! How fully convinced is the man
of pure phyfiognomonical fenfation, that he cannot
be more degraded than by fuffering himfelf to be
enfnared by fuch a countenance ! Be this one
proof among a thoufand.

Q 3

But if a noble, fpotlefs maiden but appear ; all innocence and all foul ; all love, and of love all worthy, which muft as fuddenly be felt as fhe manifeftly feels ; if in her large arched forehead all the capacity of immeafurable intelligence which wifdom can communicate be vifible ; if her compreffed but not frowning eyebrows fpeak an unexplored mine of underftanding, or her gentle outlined or fharpened nofe, refined tafte, with fympathetic goodnefs of heart, which flows through the clear teeth, over her pure and efficient lips ; if fhe breathe humility and complacency ; if condefcenfion and mildnefs be in each motion of her mouth, dignified wifdom in each tone of her voice ; if her eyes, neither too open nor too clofe, but looking ftraight forward, or gently turned, fpeak the foul that feeks a fifterly embrace ; if fhe be fuperior to all the powers of defcription ; if all the glories of her angelic form be imbibed like the mild and golden rays of an autumnal evening fun ; may not then thefe fo highly prized phyfiognomonical fenfations be a deftructive fnare or fin, or both ?

" If thine eye be fingle, thy whole body fhall be full of light, as when the bright fhining of a candle doth give thee light." And what is phyfiognomonical fenfations but this finglenefs of eye ? The foul is not to be feen without the body, but in the body ; and the more it is thus feen, the more facred to thee will the body be. What ! man having this fenfation, which God has beftowed, wouldft thou violate the fanctuary of God ? Would thou degrade, defame, debilitate and deprive it of fenfibility ? Shall he whom a good or great countenance does not infpire with reverence and love, incapable of offence, fpeak of phyfiognomonical fenfation ; of that which is the revelation of the fpirit ? Nothing maintains chaftity fo entire, nothing fo truly preferves the thoughts from brutal paffion, nothing fo reciprocally exalts fouls, when they are mutually

held in facred purity. The contemplation of power awakens reverence, and the picture of love in-
fpires love ; not felfifh gratification, but that pure
paffion with which fpirits of heaven embrace.

CHAPTER XXXIV.

General Remarks on Male and Female —A Word
on the Phyfiognomonical Relation of the Sexes.

GENERALLY fpeaking, how much more pure,
tender, delicate, irritable, affectionate, flexible, and patient, is woman than man ! The primary matter of which they are conftituted appears to
be more flexible, irritable, and elaitic, than that of
man They are formed to maternal mildnefs and
affection. All their organs are tender, yielding,
eafily wounded, fenfible, and receptible.

Among a thoufand females there is fcarcely one
without the generic feminine figns, the flexible, the
circular, and the irritable. They are the counter-
part of man, taken out of man, to be fubject to
man ; to comfort him like angels, and to lighten
his cares. " She fhall be faved in child bearing,
if they continue in faith, and charity, and holinefs,
with fobriety." (1 Tim. ii. 15.)

This tendernefs and fenfibility, this light texture
of their fibres and organs, this volatility of feeling
render them fo eafy to conduct and to tempt ; fo
ready of fubmiffion to the enterprize and power of
the man ; but more powerful through the aid of
their charms than man, with all his ftrength. The
man was not firft tempted, but the woman, afterwards the man by the woman. And not only eafily to be tempted, fhe is capable of being formed to

the pureſt, nobleſt, moſt ſeraphic virtue ; to every thing which deſerve praiſe or affection.

Highly fenſible of purity, beauty and ſymmetry, ſhe does not always take time to reflect on internal life, internal death, internal corruption. " The woman ſaw that the tree was good for food, and that it was pleaſant to the eyes and a tree to be deſired to make one wiſe, and ſhe took of the fruit thereof."

The female thinks not profoundly ; profound thought is the power of the man. Women feel more : fenſibility is the power of the woman. They often rule more effectually, more ſovereignly than man. They rule with tender looks, tears, and ſighs, but not with paſſion and threats ; for, if they fo rule, they are no longer women, but abortions.

They are capable of the fweeteſt fenſibility, the moſt profound emotion, the utmoſt humility, and the exceſs of enthuſiaſm. In their countenance are the ſigns of fanctity and inviolability, which every feeling man honours, and the effects of which are often miraculous. Therefore, by the irritabi-lity of their nerves, their incapacity for deep inqui-ry and firm deciſion, they may eaſily, from their extreme fenſibility, become the moſt irreclaimable, the moſt rapturous enthuſiaſts.

The love of woman, ſtrong and rooted as it is, is very changeable ; their hatred almoſt incurable, and only to be effaced by continued and artful flat-tery. Men are moſt profound, women are more ſublime. Men moſt embrace the whole ; women remark individually, and take more delight in fe-lecting the minutiæ which form the whole. Man hears the burſting thunders, views the deſtructive bolt with ſerene aſpect, and ſtands erect amidſt the fearful majeſty of the ſtreaming clouds. Woman trembles at the lightning and the voice of diſtant thunder, and ſhrinks into herſelf, or ſinks into the arms of man.

A ray of light is fingly received by man, woman delights to view it through a prifm, in all its dazzling colours. She contemplates the rainbow as the promife of peace ; he extends his inquiring eye over the whole horizon.

Woman laughs, man fmiles ; woman weeps, man remains filent. Woman is in anguifh when man weeps, and in defpair when man is in anguifh ; yet has fhe often more faith than man. Without religion, man is a difeafed creature, who would perfuade himfelf he is well, and needs not a phyfician : but woman, without religion, is raging and monftrous. A woman with a beard is not fo difgufting as a woman who acts the free-thinker ; her fex is formed to piety and religion. To them Chrift firft appeared ; but he was obliged to prevent them from too ardently and too haftily embracing him.— *Touch me not.* They are prompt to receive and feize novelty, and become its enthufiafts.

In the prefence and proximity of him they love, the whole world is forgotten. They fink into the moft incurable melancholy, as they rife to the moft enraptured heights.

There is more imagination in male fenfation, in the female more heart. When communicative, they are more communicative than man ; when fecret, more fecret. In general they are more patient, long-fuffering, credulous, benevolent, and modeft.

Woman is not a foundation on which to build. She is the gold, filver, precious ftones, wood, hay, ftubble ; (1 Cor. iii. 12.) the materials for building on the male foundation. She is the leaven, or, more expreffively the oil to the vinegar of man ; the fecond part to the book of man. Man fingly, is but half a man, at leaft but half human ; a king without a kingdom. Woman, who feels properly what fhe is, whether ftill or in motion, refts upon the man ; nor is man what he may and ought to be but in conjunction with woman. Therefore " it is not good that man should be alone, but that he should leave father and mother and cleave to his wife, and that they two shall be one flesh."

A Word on the physiognomonical Relation of the Sexes.

Man is the most firm, woman the most flexible.
Man is the straightest, woman the most bending.
Man stands stedfast, woman gently retreats.
Man surveys and observes, woman glances and feels.
Man is serious, woman is gay.
Man is the tallest and broadest, woman the smallest and weakest.
Man is rough and hard, woman is smooth and soft.
Man is brown, woman is fair.
Man is wrinkly, woman is not.
The hair of man is strong and short, of woman more long and pliant.
The eyebrows of man are compressed, of woman less frowning.
Man has most convex lines, woman most concave.
Man has most straight lines, woman most curved.
The countenance of man, taken in profile, is not so often perpendicular as that of the woman.
Man is most angular, woman most round.

CHAPTER XXXV.

On the Physiognomy of Youth.

Extracts from Zimmermann's Life of Haller.

" THE first years of the youth include the history of the man. They develope the qualities of the foul, the materials of future conduct, and the true features of temperament. In riper years diffimulation prevails, or, at leaft, that modification of our thoughts, which is the confequence of experience and knowledge.

" The characteriftics of the paffions, which are undeniably difcovered to us by the peculiar art denominated phyfiognomy, are effaced in the countenance by age ; while, on the contary, their true figns are vifible in youth. The original materials of man are unchangeable ; he is drawn in colours that have no deceit. The boy is the work of nature, the man of art."

How much of the true, how much of the falfe, worthy Zimmermann, at leaft of the indefinite, is there in this paffage ! According to my conception, I fee the clay, the mafs, in the youthful countenance; but not the form of the future man. There are paffions and powers of youth, and paffions and powers of age. Thefe often are contradictory in the fame man, yet are they contained one within the other. Time produces the expreffion of latent traits. A man is but a boy feen through a magnifying glafs, I always, therefore, perceive more in the countenance of a man than of a boy. Diffimulation may indeed conceal the moral materials, but not alter their form. The growth, of powers and paffions, imparts to the firft undefined fketch of what is called a boy's countenance, the firm traits, fhading, and colouring, of manhood.

Thefe are youthful countenances, which declare whether they ever fhall, or fhall not, ripen into man. This they declare, but they only declare it to the great phyfiognomift. I will acknowledge, when, which feldom happens, the form of the head is beautiful, confpicuous, proportionate, greatly featured, well defined, and not too feebly coloured, it will be difficult that the refult fhould be common or vulgar. I likewife know, that where the form is diftorted, efpecially when it is tranfverfe, extended, undefined, or too harfhly defined, much can rarely be expected. But how much do the forms of youthful countenances change, even in the fyftem of the bones ?

Much has been faid of the opennefs, undegeneracy, fimplicity, and ingenuoufnefs of a childifh and youthful countenance. It may be fo, but for my own part, I muft own, I am not fo fortunate as to be able to read a youthful countenance with the fame degree of quicknefs and precifion, however fmall that degree, as one that is manly. The more I converfe with and confider children, the more difficult do I find it to pronounce, with certainty, concerning their character. Not that I do not meet countenances, among children and boys, moft ftrikingly and pofitively fignificant ; yet feldom is the great outline of the youth fo definite. as for us to be able to read in it the man. The moft remarkably advantageous young countenances may eafily, through accident, terror, hurt, or feverity in parents or tutors, be internally injured, without any apparent injury to the whole. The beautiful, the eloquent form, the firm forehead, the deep, fharp eye, the cheerful, open, free, quick-moving mouth remain ; there will only be a drop of troubled water in what elfe appears fo clear ; only an uncommon, fcarcely remarkable, perhaps convulfive motion of the mouth. Thus is hope overthrown, and beauty rendered indiftinct.

As fimplicity is the foil for variety, fo is innocence for the products of vice. Simplicity, not of a youth, but of a child, in thee the Omnifcient only views the progrefs of fleeping paffion ; the gentle wrinkles of youth, the deep of manhood, and the manifold and relaxed of age. Oh ! how different was my infantine countenance to the prefent, in form and fpeech ! But as tranfgreffion follows innocence, fo doth virtue tranfgreffion.

Doth the veſſel ſay to the potter, " wherefore haſt thou made me thus ?—*I am little, but I am I.*" He who created me, did not create me to be a child but a man. Wherefore ſhould I ruminate on the pleaſures of childhood, unburthened with cares? I am what I am. I will forget the paſt, nor weep that I am no longer a child, when I contemplate children in all their lovelineſs. To join the powers of man with the ſimplicity of the child is the height of all my hopes. God grant they may be accompliſhed !

———————————

C H A P T E R　XXXVI.

Phyſiognomical Extracts from an Eſſay inſerted in the Deutſchen Muſeum, a German Journal or Review.

FROM this eſſay I ſhall extract only ſelect thoughts, and chiefly none but thoſe which I ſuppoſe to be importantly true, importantly falſe, or ill defined.

1. " Men with arched and pointed noſes are ſaid to be witty, and that the blunt noſed are not ſo."

A more accurate definition is neceſſary, which, without drawing, is almoſt impoſſible. Is it meant by arched noſes, arched in length or in breadth ? How arched ? This is almoſt as indeterminate as when we ſpeak of arched foreheads. All foreheads are arched. Innumerable noſes are arched, the moſt witty and the moſt ſtupid. Where is the higheſt point of arching ? Where does it begin ? What is its extent ? What is its ſtrength ?

It is true, that people with tender, thin, ſharply defined, angular noſes, pointed below, and ſome-

R

thing inclined towards the lip, are witty, when no other features contradict thefe tokens ; but that people with blunt nofes are not fo, is not entirely true. It can only be faid of certain blunt nofes, for there are others of this kind extremely witty, though their wit is certainly of a different kind to that of the pointed nofe.

2. " It is afked, (fuppofing for a moment, that the arched and the blunt nofe denote the prefence or abfence of wit) is the arched nofe the mere fign that a man is witty, which fuppofes his wit to originate in fome occult caufe, or is the nofe itfelf the caufe of wit ?"

I anfwer, fign, caufe, and effect, combined. Sign ; for it betokens the wit, and is an involuntary expreffion of wit. Caufe ; at leaft caufe that the wit is not greater, lefs, or of a different quality, boundary caufe. Effect ; produced by the quantity, meafure, or activity of the mind, which fuffers not the nofe to alter its form to be greater or lefs. We are not only to confider the form as form, but the matter of which it is moulded, the conformability of which is determined by the nature and ingredients of this matter, which is probably the origin of the form.

True indeed it is, that there are blunt nofes, which are incapable of receiving a certain quantity of wit ; therefore it may be faid with more fubtlety than philofophy, they form an infuperable barrier.

3. " The correfpondence of external figures with internal qualities is not the confequence of external circumftances, but rather of phyfical combination. They are related like caufe and effect, or, in other words, phyfiognomy is not the mere image of internal man, but the efficient caufe."— (I fhould rather fay the limiting caufe)—The form and arrangement of the mufcles determine the mode of thought, and fenfibility of the man."

I add, thefe are alfo determined by the mind of man.

4. " A broad confpicuous forehead is faid to denote penetration. This is natural. The mufcle of the forehead is neceffary to deep thought. If it be narrow and contracted, it cannot render the fame fervice as if fpread out like a fail."

Without contradicting the general propofition of the author, I fhall here more definitely add, it is, if you pleafe generally true, that the more brain, the more mind and capacity. The moft ftupid animals are thofe with leaft brain, and thofe with moft the wifeft. Man, generally wifer, has more brain than other animals ; and it appears juft, to conclude from analogy, that wife men have more brain than the foolifh. But accurate obfervation teaches, that this propofition, to be true, requires much definition and limitation.

Where the matter and form of the brain are fimilar, there the greater fpace for the refidence of the brain is, certainly the fign, caufe and effect of more and deeper comprehenfion ; therefore, *cæteris paribus*, a larger quantity of brain, and confequently a fpacious forehead, is more intelligent than the reverfe. But as we frequently live more conveniently in a fmall well-contrived chamber than in more magnificent apartments, fo do we find, that in many fmall, fhort foreheads, with lefs, or apparently lefs brain than others, the wife mind refides at its eafe.

I have known many fhort, oblique, ftraight-lined (when compared with others apparently arched, or really well-arched) foreheads, which were much wifer, more intelligent, and penetrating, than the moft broad and confpicuous ; many of which latter I have feen in extremely weak men. It feems to me, indeed, a much more general propofition, that fhort compreffed foreheads are wife and underftand-

ing ; though this, likewife, without being more accurately defined, is far from being generally true.

But is it true, that large fpacious foreheads
which, if I do not miſtake, Galen, and after him
Huart, have fuppofed the moſt propitious to deep
thinking, which form a half fphere, are ufually the
moſt ſtupid. The more any forehead (I do not
fpeak of the whole fcull) approaches a femifpherical
form, the more is it weak, effeminate, and incapable of reflexion, and this I fpeak from repeated
experience.

The more ſtraight lines a forehead has, the lefs
capacious it muſt be ; for the more it is arched, the
more muſt it be roomy, and the more ſtraight lines
it has, the more muſt it be contracted. This greater quantity of ſtraight lines, when the forehead is
not flat like a board, for fuch flatnefs takes away
all underſtanding, denotes an increafe of judgment,
but a diminution of fenfibility. There undoubtedly are, however, broad, capacious foreheads, without ſtraight lines, particularly adapted to profound
thinking ; but thefe are confpicuous by their oblique outlines.

5. What the author has faid concerning enthufiaſts, requires much greater precifion, before it
ought to be received as true.

" Enthufiaſts are faid commonly to have flat,
perpendicular foreheads."

Oval, cylindrical, or pointed at top, fhould have
been faid, of thofe enthufiaſts who are calm, cold-
blooded, and always continue the fame. Other
enthufiaſts, that is to fay, fuch as are fubject to a
variety of fenfation, illufion, and fenfual experience, feldom have cylindrical or fugar-loaf heads.
The latter, when enthufiaſts, heat their imagination concerning words and types, the fignification of
which they do not underſtand, and are philofophical, unpoetical enthufiaſts. Enthufiaſts of imagination, or of fenfibility, feldom have flat forms of
the countenance.

6. " Obftinate, like enthufiaftic perfons, have perpendicular foreheads."

The perpendicular always denotes coldnefs, inactivity, narrownefs ; hence firmnefs, fortitude, pertinacity, obftinacy, and enthufiafm, may be there. Abfolute perpendicularity, and abfolute folly, are the fame.

7. " Each difpofition of mind is accompanied by a certain appearance, or motion of the mufcles ; confequently the appearance of man, which is natural to, and ever prefent with him, will be accompanied by, and denote, his natural difpofition of mind. Countenances are fo formed originally, that to one this, and to another that appearance is the eafieft. It is abfolutely impoffible for folly to affume the appearance of wifdom, otherwife it would no longer be folly. The worthy man cannot affume the appearance of difhonefty, or he would be difhoneft."

This is all excellent, the laft excepted. No man is fo good as not, under certain circumftances, to be liable to become difhoneft. He is fo organized, that he may be overtaken by the pleafure of ftealing, when accompanied by the temptation. The poffibility of the appearance muft be there as well as the poffibility of the act. He muft alfo be able to affume the appearance of difhonefty, when he obferves it in a thief, without neceffarily becoming a thief. The poffibility of affuming the appearance of goodnefs is, in my opinion, very different. The appearance of vice is always more eafily affumed by the virtuous, than the appearance of virtue by the vicious ; as it is evidently much eafier to become bad when we are good, than good when we are bad. Underftanding, fenfibility, talents, genius, virtue, or religion, may with much greater facility be loft than acquired. The beft may defcend as low as they pleafe, but the worft cannot afcend to the

R 3

height they might wifh. The wife man may phy-
fically, without a miracle, become a fool, and the
moft virtuous vicious ; but the idiot-born cannot,
without a miracle, become a philofopher, nor the
diftorted villain noble and pure of heart. The moft
beautiful complexion may become jaundiced, may
be loft ; but the negro cannot be wafhed white. I
fhall not become a negro becaufe, to imitate him I
blacken my face, nor a thief, becaufe I affume the
appearance of a thief.

8 " The phyfiognomift ought to inquire, what
is the appearance the countenance can moft eafily
affume, and he will thence learn what is the difpofition of mind. Not that phyfiognomy is therefore
an eafy fcience. On the contrary, this rather fhows
how much ability, imagination, and genius, are neceffary to the phyfiognomift. Attention muft not
only be paid to what is vifible, but what would be
vifible under various other circumftances."

Excellent ; and I add, that as a phyfician can prefage what alteration of colour, appearance, or form
fhall be the confequence of a known difeafe, of the
exiftence of which he is certain, fo can the accurate
phyfiognomift what appearances or expreffions are
eafy or difficult to each kind of mufcle, and form
of forehead, what action is or is not permitted, and
what wrinkles may or may not take place, under
any given circumftances.

9. " When a learner draws a countenance, we
fhall commonly find it is foolifh, and never malici-
ous, fatirical, and the like. May not the effence of
a foolifh countenance hence be abftracted ? Certainly ; or what is the caufe of this appearance ?
The learner is incapable of preferving proportion,
and the ftrokes are unconnected. What is the ftupid countenance ? It is one, the parts of which are
defectively connected, and the mufcles improperly
formed and arranged. Thought and fenfation,
therefore, of which thefe are the infeparable in-
ftruments, muft be alike feeble and dormant.

10. " Exclufive of the mufcles ; there is another fubftance in the body, that is to fay, the fcull,
or bones in general, to which the phyfiognomift at-
tends. The pofition of the mufcles depends on
thefe. How might the mufcle of the forehead
have the pofition proper for thought, if the forehead bones, over which it is extended, had not the
neceffary arches and fuperficies ? The figure of the
fcull, therefore, defines the figure and pofition of
the mufcles, which define thought and fenfation.

11. " The fame may be obferved of the hair,
from the parts and pofition of which conclufions
may be drawn. Why has the Negro woolly hair ?
The thicknefs of the fkin prevents the efcape of
certain of the particles of perfpiration, and thefe
render the fkin opaque and black. Hence the hair
fhoots with difficulty, and fcarcely has it penetrated
before it curls, and its growth ceafes. The hair
fpreads according to the form of the fcull, and the
pofition of the mufcles, and gives occafion to the
phyfiognomift to draw conclufions from the hair to
the pofition of the mufcles, and to deduce other
confequences."

In my opinion our author is certainly in the right
road. He is the firft who, to my knowledge, has
perceived and felt the totality, the combination, the
uniformity of the various parts of the human body.
What he has affirmed, efpecially concerning the
hair, that we may from that make deductions
concerning the nature of the body, and ftill farther
of the mind, the leaft accurate obferver may convince himfeif is truth, by daily experience. White,
tender, clear, weak hair, always denotes weak, delicate, irritable, or rather a timid and eafily oppreffed organization. The black and curly will never
be found on the delicate, tender, medullary head.

As is the hair, fo the mufcles ; as the mufcles, fo
the nerves ; as the nerves, fo the bones ; their powers are mutual, and the powers of the mind to act,

suffer, receive, and give, proportionate. Leaft irritability always accompanies fhort, hard, curly, black hair, and the moft the flaxen and the tender; that is to fay, irritability without elafticity. The one is oppreflive without elafticity, and the other oppreffed without refiftance.

" Much hair, much fat, therefore no part of the human body is more confpicuoufly covered with hair than the head and armpits. From the elafticity of the hair, deduftions may with certainty be made to the elafticity of the charafter. The hair naturally betokens moifture, and may properly determine the quantity of moifture. The inhabitants of cold countries have hair more white, and, on the contrary, thofe of hot countries, black. Lional Wafer obferves, that the inhabitants of the ifthmus of Darien have milk-white hair. Few, if any, have green hair, except thofe who work in copper mines. We feldom find white hair betokening difhonefty, but often dark brown or black, with light-coloured eyebrows. Women have longer hair than men. Men with long hair are always rather effeminate than manly. Dark hair is harfher than light, as is the hair of a man than that of a boy.

12. " As all depends on the quality of the mufcles, it is evident, that in thefe mufcles, which are employed for certain modes of thought and fenfation, ought to be fought the expreffion of fimilar thoughts and fenfations."

Let not the fearch be neglefted, though probably it will be difficult to find them; and they certainly will there be defined with greater difficulty than in the forehead.

13. " The mufcle of the forehead, is the moft important inftrument to the abftraft thinker, for which reafon we always feek for abftraft thought in the forehead."

Rather near and between the eyebrows. It is of confequence to remark the particular moment when the thinker is liftening, or when he is preparing fome acute anfwer. Seize the moment, and another of the important tokens of phyfiognomy is obtained.

14. " Among people who do not abftract, and whofe powers of mind are all in action, men of wit, exquifite tafte, and genius, all the mufcles muft be advantageoufly formed and arranged. Expreffion, therefore, in fuch, muft be fought in the whole countenance."

Yet may it be found in the forehead alone, which is lefs fharp, ftraight-lined, perpendicular, and forked. The fkin is lefs rigid, more eafily moved, more flexible.

15. " How great has been the trouble to convince people, that phyfiognomy is only generally ufeful !"

It is at this very moment difputed by men of the ftongeft minds. How long fhall it continue fo to be ? Yet I fhould fuppofe, that he who curfes the fun, while expofed to its fcorching rays, would, when in the fhade, acknowledge its univerfal utility.

" How afflicting is it to hear, from perfons of the greateft learning, and who might be expected to enlarge the boundaries of human underftanding, the moft fuperficial judgments ? How much is that great æra to be wifhed, when the knowledge of man fhall become a part of natural hiftory ; when pfychology, phyfiology, and phyfiognomy, fhall go hand in hand, and lead us towards the confines of more general, more fublime illumination ?"

CHAPTER XXXVII.

Extracts from Maximus Tyrius.

SINCE the foul of man is the neareft approach to the Deity, it was not proper that God fhould

clothe that which moft refembled himfelf in difho-
nourable garments ; but with a body befitting an
immortal mind, and endowed with a proper capability of motion. This is the only body on earth that
ftands erect. It is magnificent, fuperb, and formed
according to the beft proportion of its moft delicate
parts. Its ftature is not terrific, nor is its ftrength
formidable. The coldnefs of its juices occafions it
not to creep, nor their heat to fly. Man eats not
raw flefh, from the favagenefs of his nature, nor
does he graze like the ox ; but he is framed and
adapted for the executions of his functions. To
the wicked he is formidable ; mild and friendly to
the good. By nature he walks the earth, fwims by
art, and flies by imagination. He tills the earth,
and enjoys its fruits. His complexion is beautiful,
his limbs firm, his countenance is comely, and
beard ornamental. By imitating his body, the
Greeks have thought proper to honour their de-
ities.

Oh ! that I could fpeak with fufficient force !
Oh ! that I could find faith enough with my readers, to convince them how frequently my foul feems
exalted above itfelf, while I contemplate the un-
fpeakably miraculous nature of the human body !
Oh ! that all the languages of the earth would lend
me words, that I might turn the thoughts of men,
not only to the contemplation of others, but, by
the aid of thefe, to the contemplation of themfelves ! No anti-phyfiognomift can more defpife
my work than I myfelf fhall, if I am unable to ac-
complifh this purpofe. How might I confcienti-
oufly write fuch a work were not fuch my views ?
If this be not impulfe, no writer has impulfe. I
cannot behold the fmalleft trait, nor the inflexion
of any outline, without reading wifdom and benevolence, or without waking, as if from a fweet dream
into rapturous, and actual'exiftence, and congratu-
lating myfelf that I alfo am a man.

In each the fmalleft outline of the human body, and how much more in all together, in each member feparately, and how much more in the whole body, however old and runinous the building may appear, or be, how much is there contained of the ftudy of God, the genius of God, the poetry of God ! My trembling and agitated breaft frequently pants after leifure to look into the revelations of God.

2.

" Imagine to thyfelf the moft tranflucent water flowing over a furface, on which grow beauteous flowers, whofe bloom, though beneath, is feen through the pellucid waves ; even fo it is with the fair flower of the foul, planted in a beauteous body, through which its beauteous bloom is feen. The good formation of a youthful body is no other than the bloom of ripening virtue, and as I may fay, the prefage of far higher perfection ; for, as before the rifing of the fun, the mountain tops are gilded by his rays, enlivening the pleafing profpects, and promifing the full approach of day, fo alfo the future maturity of an illuftrious foul fhines through the body, and is to the philofopher the pleafing fign of approaching happinefs."

CHAPTER XXXVIII.

Extracts from a Manufcript by Th——.

" THE relation between the male and female countenance is fimilar to that between youth and manhood. Our experience, that the deep, or fcarcely vifible outline is in proportion to the depth or fhallownefs of thought, is one of the

many proofs that nature has impreffed fuch forms
upon her creatures as fhall teftify their qualities.
That thefe forms or figns are legible to the highly
perceptive foul is vifible in children, who cannot
endure the deceitful, the tell-tale, or the revenge-
ful ; but run with open arms to the benevolent
ftranger.

"We may properly divide our remarks on this
fubject into complexion, lines, and pantomime.
That white, generally fpeaking, is cheerful, and
black, gloomy and terrific, is the confequence of
our love of light, which act fo degenerately, as it
were, upon fome animals, that they will throw
themfelves into the fire ; and of our abhorrence of
darknefs.   The reafon of this our love of light, is,
that it makes us acquainted with things, provides
for the foul hungry after knowledge, and enables
us to find what is neceffary, and avoid what is dangerous.   I only mention this to intimate, that in
this our love of light originates our inclination for
every thing that is perfpicuous.   Certain colours
are, to certain animals, particularly agreeable or
difagreeable.".

What is the reafon of this ? Becaufe they are
the expreffion of fomething which has a relation to
their character, that harmonizes with it, or is difcordant.   Colours are the effect of certain qualities
of object and fubject ; they are therefore characteriftic in each, and become more fo by the manner in
which they are mutually received and repelled.
This would be another immenfe field of inquiry,
another ray of the fun of truth.   All is phyfiognomy !

"Our diflike is no lefs for every thing which is
clothed in dark colours ; and nature has warned
animals, not only againft feeding on earth, but alfo
on dark-green plants ; for the one is as detrimental
as the other.   Thus the man of dark complexion
terrifies an infant that is incapable of judging of his
character.

" So ftrikingly fignificant are the members of
the body, that the afpect of the whole attacks our
feelings, and induces judgments as fudden as they
are juft. Thus, to mention two extremes, all will
acknowledge, at the firft afpect, the elephant to be
the wifeft, and the fifh the moft ftupid of creatures.

" The upper part of the countenance, to the
root of the nofe, is the feat of internal labour,
thought, and refolution ; the under, of thefe in action. Animals, with very retreating foreheads,
have little brain, and the reverfe.

" Projecting nofe and mouth (the latter certainly not always) betoken perfuafion, felf-confidence,
rafhnefs, fhameleffnefs, want of thought, difhonefty, and all fuch feelings as are affembled in hafty
expreffion."
This is a decifion after the manner of the old
phyfiognomifts condemning, and indefinite.

" The nofe is the feat of derifion, its wrinkles
contemn. The upper lip, when projecting, fpeaks
arrogance, threats, and want of fhame ; the part-
ing under-lip, oftentation and folly. Thefe figns
are confirmed by the manner and attitude of the
head, when drawn back, toffed or turned round.
The firft expreffes contempt, during which the nofe
is active ; the latter is a proof of extreme arrogance, during which the projection of the under-
lip is the ftrongeft.

" The in drawn lower part of the countenance,
on the contrary, denotes difcretion, modefty, feri-
oufnefs, diffidence, and its failings are thofe of
malice and obftinacy."
Not fo pofitive. The projecting chin is much
oftener the fign of craft than the retreating. The
latter is feldom fcheming and enterprifing.

" The ftraight formation of the nofe betokens
gravity ; inbent and crooked, noble thoughts. The
flat, pouting upper lip (when it does not clofe well
S

with the under,) fignifies timidity ; the lips refembling each other, circumfpection of fpeech.

" We may divide the face into two principal
kinds. The firft is that in which the cheeks prefent a flat furface, the nofe projecting like a hill,
and the mouth has the appearance of a fabre-
wound, prolonged on an even furface, while the
line of the jaw-bone has but little inflection. Such
a form makes the countenance more broad than
long, and exceedingly rude, inexpreffive, ftupid,
and in every fenfe confined. The principal characteriftics are obftinacy and inflexibility.

" The fecond kind is, when the nofe has a fharp
ridge, and the parts on both fides make acute an-
gles with each other. The cheek bones are not
feen, confequently the mufcular parts between
them and the nofe are full and prominent. The
lips retreat on each fide of the mouth, affume or
open into an oval, and the jaw-bones come to a
point at the chin."

This face denotes a mind more fubtle, active, and
intelligent.

" The better to explain myfelf, I muft here employ the fimile of two fhips. The firft a merchant
veffel, built for deep loading, has a broad bottom,
and her ribs long and flat. This refembles the
broad, flat countenance. The frigate, built for
fwift failing, has a fharp keel or bottom, her ribs
forming acute angles. Such is the fecond countenance. Of thefe two extremes, the firft prefents to
me the image of the meaneft, moft contracted felf-
love ; the fecond of the moft zealous, the nobleft
philanthropy.

" I am fenfible, that nature does not delight in
extremes. Still the underftanding muft take its
departure from thefe as from a light-houfe, efpecially when failing in unknown feas. The defects
and exceffes which are in all works of nature will
then be difcovered, and one or both the boundaries
afcertained.

" On farther examination and application of the
above hypothefis, it will I believe extend through
all nature. A broad countenance is accompanied
by a fhort neck, broad fhoulders and back, and
their known character is felfifhnefs and obtufe fenfation. The long, fmall countenance, has a long
neck, fmall, or low fhoulders and fmall back.
From fuch I fhould expect more juftice, difintereft-
ednefs, and a general fuperiority of focial feelings.

" The features and character of men are effentially altered by education, fituation, intercourfe,
and incidents ; therefore we are juftified in main-
taining, that phyfiognomy cannot look back to the
origin of the features, nor prefage the changes of
futurity ; but from the countenance only, abftracted from all external accidents by which it may be
affected, it may read what any given man may be,
with the following addition at moft : fuch fhall be
the empire of reafon, or fuch the power of fenfuality. This man is too ftubborn to be inftructed ;
that fo flexible he may be led to good or ill.

" From this formation we may in part explain
why fo many men appear to be born for certain
fituations, although they may have rather been
placed in them by accident than by choice. Why
the prince, the nobleman, the overfeer of the poor,
have a lordly, a ftern, or a pedantic manner ; why
the fubject, the fervant, the flave, are pufillanimous
and fpiritlefs ; or the courtezan affected, conftrain-
ed, or infipid. The conftant influence of circumftances on the mind, far exceeds the influence of
nature." Far the contrary.

" Although it is certain, that *innate* fervility is
very diftinct from the fervility of one whom mif-
fortune has rendered a fervant ; like as he whom
chance has made a ruler over his brother, is very
different from one who is by nature fuperior to
vulgar fouls."

There is no such thing as *innate* servility. It is true that, under certain circumstances, some are much more disposed than others to become servile.

" The unfeeling mind of the slave has vacuity more complete, or, if a master, more self-complacency and arrogance, in the open mouth, the projecting lip, and the turned-up nose. The noble mind rules by the comprehensive respect, while, in the closed lips, moderation is expressed. He will serve with sullenness, with downcast eye, and his shut mouth will disdain to complain.

" As the foregoing causes will make durable impressions, so will the adventitious occasion transitory ones, while their power remains. The latter are more apparent than the signs of the countenance at rest, but may be well defined by the principal characteristics of the agitated features; and, by comparison with countenances subject to similar agitations, the nature of the mind may be fully displayed. Anger in the unreasonable ridiculously struggles; in the self-conceited it is fearful rage; in the noble minded, it yields and brings opponents to shame; in the benevolent, it has a mixture of compassion for the offender, moving him to repentance.

" The affliction of the ignorant is outrageous, and of the vain ridiculous; of the compassionate, abundant in tears and communicative; of the resolute, serious, internal, the muscles of the cheeks scarcely drawn upwards, the forehead little wrinkled.

" The love of the ignorant is violent and eager; of the vain, disgusting, which is seen in the sparkling eyes, and the forced smile of the forked cheeks, and the indrawn mouth; of the tender, languishing, with the mouth contracted to intreat; of the man of sense, serious, stedfastly surveying the object, the forehead open, and the mouth prepared to plead.

" On the whole, the fenfations of a man of fortitude are reftrained, while thofe of the ignorant
degenerate into grimace. The latter, therefore,
are not the proper ftudy of the artift, though they
are of the phyfiognomift, and the moral teacher,
that youth may be warned againft too ftrong an expreffion of the emotions of the mind, and of their
ridiculous effects.

" Thus do the communicative and moving fenfations of the benevolent infpire reverence ; but
thofe of the vicious, fear, hatred, or contempt.

" The repetition of paffions engrave their figns
fo deeply, that they refemble the original ftamp of
nature. Hence certainly may be deduced, that the
mind is addicted to fuch paffions. Thus are poetry
and the dramatic art highly beneficial, and thus
may be feen the advantage of conducting youth to
fcenes of mifery and of death.

" Frequent intercourfe forms fuch a fimilarity
between men, that they not only affume a mental
likenefs, but frequently contract fome refemblance
of voice and features. Of this I know feveral examples.

" Each man has his favourite gefture, which
might decypher his whole character, might he be
obferved with fufficient accuracy to be drawn in
that precife pofture. The collection of fuch portraits would be excellent for the firft ftudies of the
phyfiognomift, and would increafe the utility of the
fragments of Lavater tenfold.

" Of equal utility would be a feries of drawings
of the motions peculiar to individuals. The number of thefe in lively men is great, and they are
tranfitory. In the more fedate they are lefs numerous and more grave.

" As a collection of idealized individuals would
promote an extenfive knowledge of various kinds
of men, fo would a collection of the motions of a

fingle countenance promote a hiftory of the human heart, and demonftrate what an arrogant, yet pufillanimous thing the unformed heart is, and the perfeétion it is capable of, from the efforts of reafon and experience.

" It would be an excellent fchool for youth to fee Chrift teaching in the Temple ; afking, Whom feek you ? agonizing in the Garden ; expiring on the Crofs. Ever the fame Godman ! Ever difplaying, in thefe various fituations, the fame miraculous mind, the fame ftedfaft reafon, the fame gentle benevolence. Cæfar jefting with the pirates when their prifoner, weeping over the head of Pompey, finking beneath his affaffins, and cafting an expiring look of affliction and reproach, while he exclaims, *Et tu Brute ?* Belfhazar feafting with his nobles, turning pale at the hand-writing on the wall. The tyrant enraged, butchering his flaves ; and furrounded by condemned wretches entreating mercy from the uplifted fword, pronouncing a general pardon ideal.

" Since fenfation has a relative influence on the voice, muft not there be one principal tone or key, by which all the others are governed, and will not this be the key, in which he fpeaks when unimpaffioned, like as the countenance at reft contains the propenfities to all fuch traits as it is capable of receiving ? Thefe keys of voice, a good mufician, with a fine ear, fhould collect, clafs, and learn to define, fo that he might place the key of the voice befide any given countenance, making proper allowances for changes, occafioned by the form of the lungs, exclufive of difeafe. Tall people, with a flatnefs of breaft, have weak voices.

" This idea, which is more difficult to execute than conceive, was infpired by the various tones in which I have heard *yes* and *no* pronounced. The various emotions under which thefe words are uttered, whether of affurance, decifion, joy, grief, ridicule, or laughter, will give birth to tones as various. Yet each man has his peculiar manner, respondent to his character, of faying yes, no, or any other word. It will be open, hefitating, grave, trifling, fympathizing, cold, peevish, mild, fearlefs, or timid. What a guide for the man of the world, and how do fuch tones difplay or betray the mind !

" Since we are taught by experience, that at certain times, the man of underftanding appears foolith, the courageous cowardly, the benevolent perverfe, and the cheerful difcontented, we might, by the affiftance of thefe accidental traits, draw an ideal of each emotion ; and this would be a moft valuable addition, and an important ftep in the progrefs of phyfiognomy."

CHAPTER XXXIX.

Extracts from NICOLAI *and* WINKELMANN.

Extracts from Nicolai.

1.

" THE diftorted or disfigured form may originate as well from external as from internal caufes ; but the confiftency of the whole is the confequence of conformity between internal and external caufes ; for which reafon moral goodnefs is much more vifible in the countenace than moral evil."

This is true, thofe moments excepted when moral evil is in act.

2. " The end of phyfiognomy ought to be, not conjectures on individual, but the difcovery of general character."

That is to fay, the difcovery of general figns of
powers and fenfations, which certainly are ufelefs,
unlefs they can be individually applied, fince our
intercourfe is with individuals.

3. " Were numerous portraits of the fame man
annually drawn, and the original, by that means,
well known, it would be of great utility to phyfiognomy.

It is poffible, and perhaps only poffible, to procure accurate fhades, or plafter cafts. Minute
changes are feldom accurately enough attended to
by the painter, for the purpofe of phyfiognomy.

4. " The grand queftion of the phyfiognomift in
his refearches will ever be, in what manner is a man
confidered capable of the impreffions of fenfe?
Through what kind of perfpective does he view the
world? What can he give? What receive?

5. " That very vivacity of imagination, that
quicknefs of conception, without which no man can
be a phyfiognomift, is probably almoft infeparable
from other qualities which render the higheft caution neceffary, if the refult of his obfervations is
to be applied to living perfons."

This I readily grant; but the danger will be
much lefs if he endeavours to employ his quick fenfations in determinate figns; if he be able to pourtray the general token of certain powers, fenfations,
and paffions; and if his rapid imagination be only
bufied to difcover and draw refemblances.

Extracts from Winklemann.

1. " Internal fenfation is the characteriftic of
truth and the defigner, who would prefent fuch
natural fenfation to his academy, would not obtain
a fhade of the true, without a particular addition
of fomething, which an ordinary and unimpaffioned
mind cannot read in any model, being ignorant of
the action peculiar to each fenfation and paffion."

The phyfiognomift is formed by internal fenfation, which if the defigner be not, he will give but
the fhadow, and only an indefinite and confufed
fhadow, of the true character of nature.

2. " The forehead and nofe of the Greek god and
goddefs form almoft a ftrait line. The heads of
famous women, on Greek coins, have fimilar profiles, where the fancy might not be indulged in
ideal beauties. Hence we may conjecture, that this
form was as common to the ancient Greeks as the
flat nofe to the Calmuc, or the fmall eye to the
Chinefe. The large eyes of Grecian heads, in gems
and coins, fupport this conjecture."

This ought not to be abfolutely general, and
probably was not, fince numerous medals fhow the
contrary, though in certain ages and countries fuch
might have been the moft common form. Had only
one fuch countenance, however, prefented itfelf
to the genius of art, it would have been fufficient
for its propagation and continuance. This is lefs
our concern than the fignification of fuch a form.
The nearer the approach to the perpendicular, the
lefs is there characteriftic of the wife and graceful;
and the higher the character of worth and greatnefs,
the more obliquely the lines retreat. The more
ftraight and perpendicular the profile of the forehead and nofe is, the more does the profile of the
upper part of the head approach a right angle, from
which wifdom and beauty will fly with equally rapid
fteps. In the ufual copies of thefe famous ancient
lines of beauty, I generally find the expreffion of
meannefs, and, if I dare fo fay, of vague infipidity.
I repeat, in the copies ; in the Sophonifba of An-
gelica Kauffman, for inftance, where probably the
fhading under the hair has been neglected, and
where the gentle arching of the lines, apparently,
was fcarcely attainable.

3. " The line which feparates the repletion from
the excefs of nature is very fmall."

Not to be meafured by induftry or inftrument, yet all powerful, as every thing unattainable is.

4. " A mind as beautiful as was that of Raphael, in an equally beautiful body, is neceffary, firft to feel, and afterwards to difplay, in thefe modern times, the true character of the ancients.

5. " Conftraint is unnatural, and violence difor-der."

Where conftraint is remarked, there let fecret, profound, flowly deftructive paffion be feared; where violence, there open and quick deftroying.

6. " Greatnefs will be expreffed by the ftraight and replete, and tendernefs by the gently curving."

All greatnefs has fomething of ftraight and re-plete, but all the ftraight and replete is not great-nefs. The ftraight and replete muft be in a certain pofition, and muft have a determinate relation to the horizontal, on which the obferver ftands to view it.

" It may be proved, that no principle of beauty exifts in this profile ; for the ftronger the arching of the nofe is, the lefs does it contain of the beau-tiful; and if any countenance feen in profile is bad, any fearch after beauty will there be vain.

The nobleft, pureft, wifeft, moft fpiritual and benevolent countenance, may be beautiful to the phyfiognomift, who, in the extended fenfe of the word beauty, underftands all moral expreffions of good as beautiful; yet the form may not, therefore, accurately fpeaking, deferve the appellation of beautiful.

7. " Nothing is more difficult than to demon-. ftrate a felf-evident truth."

CHAPTER XL.

WHAT Ariftotle has written on phyfiognomy appears to me very fuperficial, ufelefs, and often felf-contradictory, efpecially his general reafoning. Still, however, we fometimes meet an occafional thought which deferves to be felected. The following are fome of thefe :

" A monfter has never been feen which had the form of another creature, and, at the fame time, totally different powers of thinking and acting. Thus for example, the groom judges from the mere appearance of the horfe ; the huntfman, from the appearance of the hound. We find no man entirely like a beaft, although there are fome features in man which remind us of beafts.

" If any one would endeavour to difcover the figns of bravery in man, he would act wifely to collect all the figns of bravery in animated nature, by which courageous animals are diftinguifhed from others. The phyfiognomift fhould then examine all fuch animated beings, which are the reverfe of the former, with refpect to internal character, and, from the comparifon of thefe oppofites, the expreffions or figns of courage would be manifeft.

" As weak hair betokens of fear, fo does ftrong hair courage. This obfervation is applicable not only to men but to beafts. The moft fearful of beafts are the deer, the hare, and the fheep, and the hair of thefe is weaker than that of other beafts. The lion and wild boar, on the contrary, are the moft courageous, which property is confpicuous in their extremely ftrong hair. The fame alfo may be remarked of birds; for, in general, thofe among them which have coarfe feathers are courageous, and thofe that have foft and weak feathers are fearful. This may eafily be applied to men. The people of the north are generally courageous, and have ftrong hair; while thofe of the weft are more fearful, and have more flexible hair.

" Such beafts as are remarkable for their courage, fimply give their voices vent, without any great conftraint, while fearful beafts utter vehement founds. Compare the lion, ox, the barking-dog, and cock, which are courageous to the deer and the hare. The lion appears to have a more mafculine character, than any other beaft. He has a large mouth, a four-cornered not too bony vifage. The upper jaw does not project, but exactly fits the under ; the nofe is rather hard than foft, the eyes are neither funken nor prominent, the forehead is fquare, and fometimes flattened in the middle.

" Thofe who have thick and firm lips, with the upper hung over the under, are fimple perfons, according to the analogy of the ape and monkey."

This is moft indeterminately fpoken. He would have been much more accurate had he faid, thofe whofe under lips are weak, extended, and projecting, beyond the upper, are fimple people.

" Thofe who have the tip of the nofe hard and firm, love to employ themfelves on fubjects that give them little trouble, fimilar to the cow and the ox."

Infupportable ! The few men, who have the tip of the nofe firm, are the moft wearied in their refearches. I fhall tranfcribe no farther. His phyfiognomonical remarks, and his fimilarities to beafts, are generally unfounded in experience.

Porta, next to Ariftotle, has moft obferved the refemblance between the countenances of men and beafts, and has extended this inquiry the fartheft. He, as far as I know, was the firft to render this fimilarity apparent, by placing the countenances of men and beafts befide each other. Nothing can be more true than this fact ; and, while we continue to follow nature, and do not endeavour to make fuch fimilarities greater than they are, it is a fubject that cannot be too accurately examined. But, in this refpect, the fanciful Porta appears to me to have been often mifled, and to have found refemblances which the eye of truth never could difcover. I could difcover no refemblance between the hound and Plato, at leaft from which cool reafon could draw any conclufions. It is fingular enough, that he has alfo compared the heads of men and birds. He might more effectually have examined the exceffive diffimilarity, than the very fmall and almoft imperceptible refemblance which can exift. He fpeaks little concerning the horfe, elephant, and monkey, though it is certain that thefe animals have moft refemblance to man.

A generic difference between man and beaft is particularly confpicuous in the ftructure of the bones. The head of man is placed erect on the fpinal bone. His whole form is as the foundation pillar for that arch in which heaven fhould be reflected, fupporting that fcull by which, like the firmament it is encircled. This cavity for the brain conftitutes the greater part of the head. All our fenfations, as I may fay, afcend and defcend above the jaw-bone, and collect themfelves upon the lips. How do the eyes, that moft eloquent of organs, ftand in need, if not of words, at leaft of the angry conftraint of the cheeks, and all the intervening fhades, to exprefs, or rather to ftammer, the ftrong internal fenfations of man.

How directly the reverfe of this is the formation of beafts ! The head is only attached to the fpine. The brain, the extremity of the fpinal marrow, has no greater extent than is neceffary for animal life,

T

and the conducting of a creature wholly fenfual, and formed but for temporary exiftence. For although we cannot deny, that beafts have the faculty of memory, and act from reflexion, yet the former, as I may fay, is the effect of primary fenfation, and the latter originates in the conftraint of the moment, and the preponderance of this or that object.

In the difference of the fcull which defines the character of animals, we may perceive, in the moft convincing manner, how the bones determine the form, and denote the properties of the creature.

As the characters of animals are diftinct, fo are their forms, bones, and outlines. From the fmalleft winged infect to the eagle that foars and gazes at the fun ; from the weakeft worm, impotently crawling beneath our feet, to the elephant, or the majeftic lion, the gradations of phyfiognomonical expreffion cannot be miftaken. It would be more than ridiculous to expect from the worm, the butterfly, and the lamb, the power of the rattlefnake, the eagle, and the lion. Were the lion and lamb, for the firft time, placed before us, had we never known fuch animals, never heard their names, ftill we could not refift the impreffion of the courage and ftrength of the one, or of the weaknefs and fufferance of the other.

Let me afk the queftion, which are, in general, the weakeft animals, and the moft remote from humanity, the moft incapable of human ideas and fenfations ? Beyond all doubt, thofe which in their form leaft refemble man. To prove this, let us, in imagination, confider the various degrees of animal life, from the fmalleft animalcula to the ape, lion, and elephant ; and the more to fimplify, and give facility to fuch comparifon, let us only compare head to head ; as for example, the lobfter to the elephant, the elephant to the man.

Permit me here juft to obferve, how worthy

would fuch a work be of the united abilities of a
Buffon, a Camper, and a Euler, could they be
found united, that the forms of heads might be
enumerated and defcribed, philofophically and ma-
thematically ; that it might be demonftrated, that
univerfal brutality, in all its various kinds, is cir-
cumfcribed by a determinate line ; and that, among
the innumerable lines of brutality, there is not one
which is not internally and effentially different from
the line of humanity, which is peculiar and unique.

Thoughts of a Friend on brutal and human Phyfieg-
nomy.

" Each brute animal has fome principal quality
by which it is diftinguifhed from all others. As
the make of each is diftinct from all others, fo alfo
is the character. This principal character is denoted by a peculiar and vifible form. Each fpecies of
beaft has certainly a peculiar character, as it has a
peculiar form. May we not hence, by analogy, infer, that predominant qualities of the mind are as
certainly expreffed by predominant forms of the
body, as that the peculiar qualities of a fpecies are
expreffed in the general form of that fpecies ?
" The principal character of the fpecies in animals remains fuch as it was given by nature ; it
neither can be obfcured by acceffory qualities, nor
concealed by art. The effential of the character
can as little be changed as the peculiarity of the
form. May we not therefore, with the greateft degree of certainty, affirm fuch a form is only expreffive of fuch a character ?
" Let us now inquire whether this be applicable
to man, and whether the form, which denotes individual character in a beaft is fignificant of fimilar
character in man, granting that, in man, it may
continually be more delicate, hidden, and compli-

T 2

cated. If, on examination, this queſtion be definitely anſwered in the affirmative, how much is
thereby gained ! But it is conſpicuouſly evident
that, in man, the mind is not one charaċter or quality, but a world of qualities interwoven with and
obſcuring each other. If each quality be expreſſed
by its peculiar form, then muſt variety of qualities
be attended with variety of forms ; and theſe forms,
combining and harmonizing together, muſt become more difficult to ſeleċt and decypher.

  " May not ſouls differ from each other merely
according to their relative connexion with bodies ?
May not ſouls alſo have a determinate capacity,
proportionate to the form and organization of the
body ? Hence each objeċt may make a different
impreſſion on each individual ; hence one may bear
greater burthens and more misfortunes than another. May not the body be conſidered as a veſſel
with various compartments, cavities, pipes, into
which the ſoul is poured, and in conſequence of
which motion and ſenſation begin to aċt ? And
thus may not the form of the body define the capacity of the mind ?"

  Thus far my unknown friend.—Figurative language is dangerous when diſcourſing on the ſoul ;
yet how can we diſcourſe on it otherwiſe ? I pronounce no judgment, but rely on ſenſation and experience, not on words and metaphors. What is,
is, be your language what it will. Whether effeċts
all aċt from the external to the internal, or the reverſe, I know not, cannot, need not know. Experience convinces us that, both in man and beaſt,
power and form are in an unchangeable, harmonized proportion ; but whether the form be determined by the power, or the power by the form, is a
queſtion wholly inſignificant to the phyſiognomiſt.

Obſervations on ſome Animals, and particularly the Horſe.

  The dog has more forehead above the eyes than

most other beasts ; but as much as he appears to
gain in the forehead, he loses in the excels of brutal nose, which has every token of acute scent.
Man too, in the act of smelling, elevates the nostrils.
The dog is also defective in the distance of the
mouth from the nose, and in the meanness, or rather nullity of chin.

Whether the hanging ears of a dog are characteristic of slavish subjection as Buffon has affirmed,
who has written much more reasonably on brute
than on human physiognomy, I cannot determine.

The camel and the dromedary are a mixture of
the horse, sheep, and ass, without what is noble in
the first. They also appear to have something of
the monkey, at least in the nose. Not made to
suffer the bit in the mouth, the power of jaw is
wanting. The determining marks concerning the
bit are found between the eyes and the nose. No
traces of courage or daring are found in these parts.
The threatening snort of the ox and horse is not
perceptible in these ape-like nostrils ; none of the
powers of plunder and prey, in the feeble upper and
under jaw. Nothing but burden-bearing patience
in the eyes.

Wild cruelty, the menacing power of rending,
appear in the bear, abhorring man the friend of
ancient savage nature.

The *unau ai*, or sloth, is the most indolent, help-
less, wretched creature, and of the most imperfect
formation, how extraordinary is the feebleness of
the outline of the head, body, and feet ! No sole
of the feet, no toes small or great, which move in-
dependently, having but two or three long, inbent
claws, which can only move together. Its sluggish-
ness, stupidity, and self-neglect are indescribable.

Who does not read ferocity in the wild boar ; a
want of all that is noble, greediness, stupidity, blunt
feeling, gross appetite ; and in the badger, ignoble,
faithless, malignant, savage gluttony ?

T 3

The profile of the lion is remarkable, efpecially the outline of the forehead and nofe. A man, whofe profile of forehead and nofe fhould refemble that of the lion, would certainly be no common man, but fuch I have never feen. I own, the nofe of the lion is much lefs prominent than that of man, but much more than that of any other quadruped. Royal, brutal ftrength, and arrogant ufurpation are evident, partly in the arching of the nofe, partly in its breadth and parallel lines, and efpecially in the almoft right angle, which the outline of the eyelid forms with the fide of the nofe.

In the eye and fnout of the tyger, what bloodthirfty cruelty, what infidious craft ! Can the laugh of Satan himfelf, at a fallen faint, be more fiendlike than the head of the triumphant tyger ? Cats are tygers in miniature, with the advantage of domeftic education. Little better in character, inferior in power. Unmerciful to birds and mice as the tyger to the lamb. They delight in prolonging torture before they devour, and in this they exceed the tyger.

The more violent qualities of the elephant are difcoverable in the number and fize of his bones ; his intelligence in the roundnefs of his form ; and his docility in the maffinefs of his mufcles ; his art and difcretion in the flexibility of his trunk; his retentive memory in the fize and arching of his forehead, which approaches nearer to the outline of the human forehead than that of any other beaft. Yet how effentially different is it from the human forehead, in the pofition of the eye and mouth, fince the latter generally makes nearly a right angle with the axis of the eye and the middle line of the mouth.

The crocodile proves how very phyfiognomonical teeth are. This, like other creatures, but more vifibly and infallibly than others, in all its parts, outlines and points, has phyfiognomy that cannot

be miſtaken. Thus debaſed, thus deſpicable, thus
knotty, obſtinate, and wicked, thus ſunken below
the noble horſe, terrific, and void of all love and
affection, is this fiend incarnate.

I am but little acquainted with horſes, yet it
ſeems to me indubitable, that there is as great a
difference in the phyſiognomy of horſes as in that
of men. The horſe deſerves to be particularly conſidered by the phyſiognomiſt, becauſe it is one of
thoſe animals whoſe phyſiognomy, at leaſt in profile, is ſo much more prominent, ſharp, and characteriſtic, than that of moſt other beaſts.

" Of all animals the horſe is that, which to
largeneſs of ſize unites moſt. proportion and elegance in the parts of his body ; for, comparing him
to thoſe which are immediately above or below
him, we ſhall perceive that the aſs is ill made, the
head of the lion is too large, the legs of the ox too
ſmall, the camel is deformed, and the rhinoceros
and elephant too unwieldy. There is ſcarcely any
beaſt has ſo various, ſo generally marking, ſo ſpeak-
ing a countenance, as a beautiful horſe.

" In a well made horſe, the upper part of the
neck, from which the mane flows, ought to riſe at
firſt in a right line ; and, as it approaches the head,
to form a curve ſomewhat ſimilar to the neck of
the ſwan. The lower part of the neck ought to be
rectilinear, in its direction from the cheſt to the
nether jaw, but a little inclined forward ; for, were
it perpendicular, the ſhape of the neck would be
defective. The upper part of the neck ſhould be
thin and not fleſhy ; nor the mane, which ought to
be tolerably full, and the hair long and ſtraight.
A fine neck ought to be long and elevated, yet proportionate to the ſize of the horſe. If too long and
ſmall, the horſe would ſtrike the rider with his
head ; if too ſhort and fleſhy, he would bear heavy
on the hand. The head is advantageouſly placed
when the forehead is perpendicular to the horizon.

The head ought to be bony and fmall, not too long;
the ears near each other, fmall, erect, firm, ftraight,
free, and fituated on the top of the head. The
forehead fhould be narrow and fomewhat convex,
the hollows filled up ; the eyelids thin ; the eyes
clear, penetrating, full of ardour, tolerably large, as
I may fay, and projecting from the head ; the pupil large, the under jaw bony, and rather thick ;
the nofe fomewhat arched, the noftrils open, and
well flit, the partition thin ; the lips fine, the mouth
tolerably large, the withers high and fharp." I
muft beg pardon for this quotation from the *Ency-
clopedie*, and for inferting thus much of the defcription of a beautiful horfe, in a phyfiognomonical
effay intended to promote the knowledge and the
love of man.

The more accurately we obferve horfes, the more
fhall we be convinced, that a feparate treatife of
phyfiognomy might be written on them. I have
fomewhere heard a general remark, that horfes are
divided into three claffes, the fwan-necked, the ftag-
necked and the hog-necked. Each of thefe claffes
has its peculiar countenance and character, and
from the blending of which various others originate.

The heads of fwan-necked horfes are commonly
even, the forehead fmall, and almoft flat ; the nofe
extends, arching from the eyes to the mouth ; the
noftrils are wide and open ; the mouth fmall ; the
ears little, pointed, and projecting ; the eyes large
and round ; the jaw below, fmall ; above, fomething
broader ; the whole body well proportioned, and
the horfe beautiful. This kind is cheerful, tractable, and high fpirited. They are very fenfible of
pain, which, when dreffing, they fometimes exprefs
by the voice. Flattery greatly excites their joy, and
they will exprefs their pride of heart by parading
and prancing. I will venture to affert, that a man
with a fwan-neck, or what is much more determin-

ate, with a smooth, projecting profile, and flaxen hair, would have similar sensibility and pride.

The stag-necked has something, in the make of his body, much resembling the stag itself. The neck is small, large, and scarcely bowed in the middle. He carries his head high. I have seen none of these. They are racers and hunters, being particularly adapted for swiftness by the make of the body.

The hog-necked. The neck above and below is alike broad ; the head hanging downwards ; the middle of the nose is concave, in profile ; the ears are long, thick, and hanging ; the eyes small and ugly ; the nostrils small, the mouth large, the whole body round, and the coat long and rough. These horses are intractable, flow, and vicious ; and will run the rider against a wall, stone, or tree. When held in, they rear, and endeavour to throw the rider. Blows or coaxing are frequently alike ineffectual, they continue obstinate and restif.

If we examine the different heads of horses, we shall find, that all cheerful, high-spirited, capricious, courageous horses, have the nose-bone of the profile convex ; and that most of the vicious, restif, and idle, have the same bone flat or concave. In the eyes, mouth, and especially in the nostrils and jaw-bones, are remarkable varieties, concerning which I shall say nothing. I shall here add some remarks on the horse, communicated by a friend.

The grey is the tenderest of horses, and we may here add, that people with light hair, if not effeminate, are yet, it is well known, of tender formation and constitution. The chesnut and iron-grey, the black, and bay, are hardy ; the sorrel are the most hardy, and yet the most subject to disease. The sorrel, whether well or ill-formed, is treacherous. All treacherous horses lay their ears in the neck. They stare and stop, and lay down their ears alternately.

The following paſſage, on the ſame ſubject, is cited from another writer : " When a horſe has broad, long, widely ſeparated, hanging ears, we are well aſſured he is bad and ſluggiſh If he lays down his ears alternately, he is fearful, and apt to ſtart. Thin, pointed, and projecting ears, on the contrary, denote a horſe of good diſpoſition."

We never find that the thick, hog-necked horſe is ſufficiently tractable for the riding-houſe, or that he is of a ſtrong nature when the tail ſhakes, like the tail of a dog. We may be certain, that a horſe with large cheerful eyes, and a fine ſhining coat, if we have no other tokens, is of a good conſtitution and underſtanding.

Theſe remarks are equally applicable to oxen and ſheep, and probably to all other animals. The white ox is not ſo long ſerviceable, for draught or labour, as the black or red : he is more weak or ſickly than theſe. A ſheep with ſhort legs, ſtrong neck, broad back, and cheerful eyes, is a good breeder, and remains peaceably with the flock. And I am of opinion, that if we may judge of the internal by the external of beaſts, men may be judged of in the ſame manner.

C H A P T E R XLI.

Of Birds, Fiſhes, Serpents, and Inſects.

Birds.

BIRDS, whether compared to each other, or to other creatures, have their diſtinct characters. The ſtructure of birds throughout, is lighter than that of quadrupeds. Nature, ever ſtedfaſt to truth,

thus manifefts herfelf in the form of birds. Their
necks are more pliant, their heads fmaller, their
mouths more pointed, and their garb more bright
and fhining than thofe of quadrupeds.

Their diftinction of character, or gradation of
paffive and active power, is expreffed by the following phyfiognomonical varieties :

1. By the form of the fcull. The more flat the
fcull, the more weak, flexible, tender, and fenfible
is the character of the animal. This flatnefs contains lefs, and refifts lefs.

2. By the length, breadth, and arching, or obli-
quity of their beaks ; and here again we find, when
there is arching, there is a greater extent of docility and capacity.

3. By the eyes which appear to have an exact
correfpondence with the arching of the beak.

4. Particularly by the middle line, I cannot fay
of the mouth, but what is analagous to the mouth,
the beak ; the obliquity of which is ever in a remarkable proportion with the outline of the profile
of the head.

Who can behold the eagle hovering in the air,
the powerful lord of fo many creatures, without
perceiving the feal, the native ftar of royalty in his
piercing round eye, the form of his head, his ftrong
wings, his talons of brafs, and, in his whole form,
his victorious ftrength, his contemptuous arrogance,
his fearful cruelty, and his ravenous propenfity ?

Confider the eyes of all living creatures from the
eagle to the mole ; where elfe can be found that
lightning glance, which defies the rays of the fun ?
Where that capacity for the reception of light ?
How truly, emphatically, to all who will hear and
underftand, is the majefty of his kingly character
vifible, not alone in his burning eye, but in the outline of what is analagous to the eyebone, and in the
fkin of the head, where anger and courage are
feated ? But, throughout his whole form, where
are they not ?

Compare the vulture with the eagle, and who does not obferve, in his lengthened neck and beak, and in his more extended form, lefs power and nobility than in the eagle ? In the head of the owl, the ignoble greedy prey; in the dove, mild, humble timidity; and in the fwan, more nobility than in the goofe, with lefs power than in the eagle, and tendernefs than in the dove ; more pliability than in the oftrich; and, in the wild duck, a more favage animal than in the fwan, without the force of the eagle ?

Fifh.

How different is the profile of a fifh from that of a man ! How much the reverfe of human perpendicularity ! How little is there of countenance when compared to the lion ! How vifible is the want of mind, reflexion, and cunning. What little or no analogy to forehead ! What an impoffibility of covering, of half, or entirely clofing the eyes ? The eye itfelf is merely circular and prominent, has nothing of the lengthened form of the eye of the fox or elephant.

Serpents.

I will allow phyfiognomy, when applied to man to be a falfe fcience, if any being throughout nature can be difcovered void of phyfiognomy, or a countenance which does not exprefs its charaćter. What has lefs, yet more phyfiognomy than the ferpent ? May we not perceive in it decifive tokens of cunning and treachery ? Certainly not a trace of underftanding or deliberate plan. No memory, no comprehenfion, but the moft unbounded craft and falfehood. How are thefe reprobate qualities diftinguifhed in their forms ? The very play of their colours, and wonderful meandering of their fpots, appear to announce and to warn us of their deceit.

All men poſſeſſed of real power are upright and honeſt; craft is but the ſubſtitute of power. I do not here ſpeak of the power contained in the folds of the ſerpent ; they all want the power to act immediately, without the aid of cunning. They are formed to " bruiſe the heel, and to have the head bruiſed." The judgment which God has pronounced againſt them is written on their flat, impotent forehead, mouth, and eyes.

Inſects.

How inexpreſſibly various are the characteriſtics impreſſed by the eternal Creator on all living beings ! How has he ſtamped on each its legible and peculiar properties ! How eſpecially viſible is this in the loweſt claſſes of animal life ! The world of infects is a world of itſelf. The diſtance between this and the world of men I own is great ; yet were it ſufficiently known, how uſeful would it be to human phyſiognomy ! What certain proofs of the phyſiognomy of men muſt be obtained from infect phyſiognomy !

How viſible are their powers of deſtruction, of ſuffering and refiſting, of ſenſibility and infenſibility, through all their forms and gradations ! Are not all the compact, hard-winged infects phyſiognomonically and characteriſtically more capable and retentive than various light and tender ſpecies of the butterfly ? Is not the ſofteſt fleſh the weakeſt, the moſt ſuffering, the eaſieſt to deſtroy ? Are not the infects of leaſt brain the beings moſt removed from man, who has the moſt brain ? Is it not perceptible in each ſpecies whether it be warlike, defenſive, enduring, weak, enjoying, deſtructive, eaſy to be cruſhed, or cruſhing ? How diſtinct in the external character are their degrees of ſtrength, of defence, of ſtinging, or of appetite.

U

The great dragon fly fhows its agility and fwiftnefs in the ftructure of its wings; perpetually on
flight in fearch of fmall flies. How fluggifh, on the
contrary, is the crawling caterpillar! How carefully
does he fet his feet as he afcends a leaf! How yielding his fubftance, incapable of refiftance! How
peaceable, harmlefs, and indolent is the moth! How
full of motion, bravery, and hardinefs, is the induftrious ant! How loath to remove, on the contrary, is the harneffed lady-bird!

CHAPTER XLII.

On Shades.

THOUGH fhades are the weakeft and moft vapid, yet they are at the fame time, when the
light is at a proper diftance, and falls properly on
the countenance to take the profile accurately, the
trueft reprefentation that can be given of man.
The weakeft, for it is not pofitive, it is only fomething negative, only the boundary line of half the
countenance. The trueft, becaufe it is the immediate expreffion of nature, fuch as not the ableft
painter is capable of drawing by hand after nature.
What can be lefs the image of a living man than a
fhade? Yet how full of fpeech! Little gold, but
the pureft.

The fhade contains but one line; no motion,
light, colour, height, or depth; no eye, ear, noftril,
or cheek; but a very fmall part of the lip; yet how
decifively it is fignificant! Drawing and painting,
it is probable, originated in fhades. They exprefs,
as I have faid, but little, but the little they do exprefs is exact. No art can attain to the truth of the

shade taken with precision. Let a shade be taken after nature with the greatest accuracy, and with equal accuracy be afterwards reduced upon fine transparent oil paper. Let a profile, of the same size, be taken, by the greatest master, in his happiest moment; then let the two be laid upon each other, and the difference will be immediately evident.

I never found, after repeated experiments, that the best efforts of art could equal nature, either in freedom or in precision, but that there was always something more or less than nature. Nature is sharp and free: whoever studies sharpness more than freedom will be hard, and whosoever studies freedom more than sharpness will become diffuse and indeterminate. I can admire him only, who, equally studious of her sharpness and freedom, acquires equal certainty and impartiality.

To attain this, artist, imitator of humanity! first exercise yourself in drawing shades; afterwards copy them by hand, and next compare and correct. Without this you will with difficulty discover the grand secret of uniting precision and freedom.

I have collected more physiognomonical knowledge from shades alone than from every other kind of portrait; have improved physiognomonical sensation more by the sight of them than by the contemplation of ever mutable nature. Shades collect the distracted attention, confine it to an outline, and thus render the observation more simple, easy, and precise. Physiognomy has no greater, more incontrovertable certainty of the truth of its object than that imparted by shade. If the shade, according to the general sense and decision of all men, can decide so much concerning character, how much more must the living body, the whole appearance, and action of the man! If the shade be oracular, the voice of truth, the word of God, what muſt the living original be illuminated by the ſpirit of God !

Hundreds have aſked, and hundreds will continue to aſk, " What can be expected from mere ſhades ?" Yet no ſhade can be viewed by any one of theſe hundred, who will not form ſome judgment on it, often accurately, more accurately than I could have judged.

In order to make the aſtoniſhing ſignificance of ſhades conſpicuous, we ought either to compare oppoſite characters of men taken in ſhade, or, which may be more convincing, to cut out of black paper, or draw, imaginary countenances widely diſſimilar. Or, again, when we have acquired ſome proficiency in obſervation, to double black paper, and cut two countenances ; and, afterwards, by cutting with the ſciſſars, to make ſlight alterations, appealing to our eye, or phyſiognomonical feeling, at each alteration ; or, laſtly, only to take various ſhades of the ſame countenance, and compare them together. Such experiments would aſtoniſh us, to perceive what great effects are produced by ſlight alterations.

The common method of taking ſhades is accompanied with many inconveniences. It is hardly poſſible the perſon drawn ſhould ſit ſufficiently ſtill ; the deſigner is obliged to change his place, he muſt approach ſo near to the perſon that motion is almoſt inevitable, and the deſigner is in the moſt inconvenient poſition ; neither are the preparatory ſteps every where poſſible, nor ſimple enough. A ſeat purpoſely contrived would be more convenient. The ſhade ſhould be taken on poſt paper, or rather on thin oiled paper, well dried. Let the head and ·back be ſupported by a chair and the ſhade fall on the oil-paper behind a clear flat poliſhed glaſs. Let the drawer ſit behind the glaſs, holding the frame with his left hand, and, having a ſharp black lead pencil, draw with the right. The glaſs, in a de-

Plate VI.

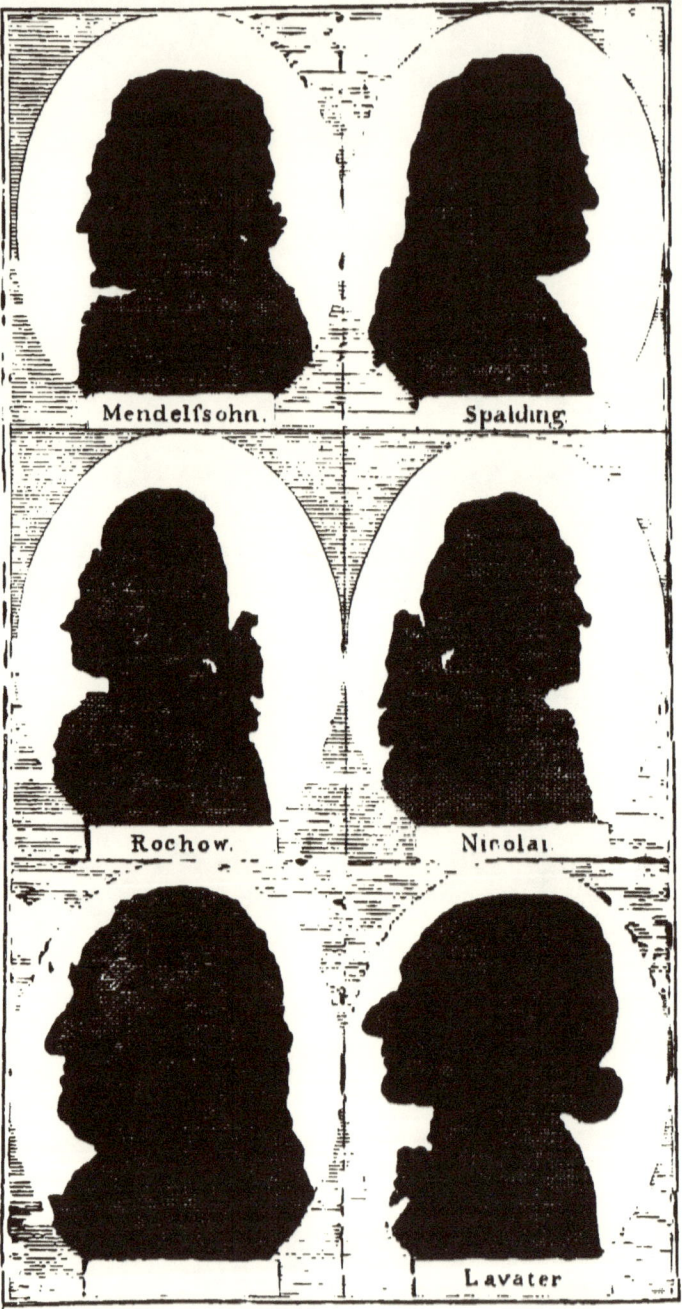

Mendelſsohn.   Spalding.

Rochow.   Nicolai.

Lavater.

tached sliding-frame, may be raised or lowered, according to the height of the person. The bottom of the glass frame, being thin, will be best of iron, and should be raised so as to rest steadily upon the shoulder. In the centre, upon the glass, should be a small piece of wood or iron, to which fasten a small round cushion, supported by a short pin, scarcely half an inch long, which also may be raised or lowered, and against which the person drawn may lean.

CHAPTER XLIII.

Description of Plate VI.

Number I. MENDELSOHN.

IN the forehead and nose, penetration and found understanding are evident. The mouth is much more delicate than the mouth of 2.

Number II. SPALDING.

Clear ideas, love of elegance, purity, accuracy of thought and action ; does not easily admit the unnatural.—The forehead not sufficiently characteristic, but fine taste in the nose.

Number III. ROCHOW.

Has more good sense ; prompt, accurate perception of truth, and delicacy, than 4 : but I suspect less acutenefs.

Number IV. MENDELSOHN.

Whoever hesitates concerning the character of this head, never can have observed the forehead.—

U 3

This arch, abftractedly confidered, efpecially in the
upper part, has more capacity than Nos. 2 and 3.
In the upper outline, alfo, of the under part, underftanding and exquifite penetration cannot be
overlooked.

Number V.

One of thofe mafculine profiles which generally
pleafe. Conceal the under chin, and an approach
to greatnefs is perceptible ; except that greater variation in the outline is wanting, efpecially in the
nofe and forehead. The choleric phlegmatic man
is vifible in the whole ; efpecially in the eyebrows,
nofe, and bottom part of the chin ; as likewife arc
integrity, fidelity, goodnefs, and complaifance.

Number VI. LAVATER.

This fhade, though imperfect may eafily be
known. It muft pafs without comment, or rather
the commentary is before the world, is in this book.
Let that fpeak ; I am filent.

CHAPTER XLIV.

A Word to Travellers.

THERE appear to me to be the three things indifpenfable to travellers, health, money, and
phyfiognomy. Therefore, a phyfiognomonical
word to travellers. I could wifh, indeed, that, inftead of a word, *a traveller's phyfiognomonical companion*
were written ; but this muft be done by an experienced traveller. In the mean time I fhall bid him
farewel, with the following fhort advice :

What do you feek, travellers ? What is your
wifh ? What would you fee more remarkable, more

fingular, more rare, more worthy to be examined,
than the varieties of humanity ? This indeed is
fafhionable.   You inquire after men ; you feek
the wifeft, beft, and greateft men, efpecially the
moft famous.   Why is your curiofity limited to
feeing only ? Would it not be better you fhould
illuminate your own minds by the light of others,
and animate yourfelves by their ardour ?

His curiofity is childifh, which is merely confined
to feeing, whofe ambition defires only to fay, I have
beheld that man.   He who would difregard views
fo confined,   muft ftudy fuch men phyfiognomonically ; if he would learn wifdom, he muft be able
to compare and judge of the relation between their
works, their fame and their form.   By this only
may much be learned.   By this may the ftream be
compared to the fountain, the quality of the waters examined, their courfe, their gentle murmurs,
or more boifterous war.   The inquirer may afk,
what is the degree of originality of thofe men, what
is borrowed, what is internal, what external ? This
forehead, and thefe eyebrows, will thus verfify, thus
tranflate, thus criticife ; therefore, on this eye depends the fate of the writer, the blockhead, or the
man of genius.   This nofe thus eftimates the mortal and the immortal, in human performances.   As
are the features, fo will be the mind.

Yes, fcholars of nature, you have much to learn
from the countenances of famous men.   In them
you will read, that the wafp will dare to alight on
the nofe of the hero.   To me it will be pleafure
when you have acquired this phyfiognomonical fenfation ; for, without this, you will but travel in the
dark ; you will but be led through a picture-galle-
ry blindfold, only that you might fay, I too have
been in that gallery.

Could I travel unknown, I would alfo vifit artifts,
men of learning, and philofophers, men famous in
their refpective countries ; but it fhould either be

my adieu, as the thing leaft important, or as a re-
creation on my arrival. Pardon me, men of re-
nown, I have been credulous in your favour, but I
daily become more circumfpect. Far be it from
me to depreciate your worth. I know many, whofe
prefence does not diminifh but increafe fame ; yet
will I be careful, that remorfe fhall neither dazzle
nor cloud my reafon.

I would rather mix unknown with the multitude,
vifit churches, public walks, hofpitals, orphan-hou-
fes, and affemblies of ecclefiaftics and men of the
law. I would firft confider the general form of the
inhabitants, their height, proportion, ftrength,
weaknefs, motion, complexion, attitude, gefture,
and gait. I would obferve them individually, fee,
compare, clofe my eyes, trace in imagination all I
had feen, open them again, correct my memory,
and clofe and open them alternately. I would ftudy for words, write, and draw with a few determinate traits, the general form, fo eafy to be difcovered. I would compare my drawings with the
known general form of the people. How eafily
might a fummary, an index of the people be obtained.

Having made thefe familiar to me, I would defcend to the particular, would fearch for the general form of the head, would afk, Is it moft confined
to the cylindrical, the fpherical, the fquare, the
convex, or the concave ? Is the countenance open,
is it writhed, is it free, or forked ? I would next
examine the forehead, then the eyebrows, the outline and colour of the eyes, the nofe, and efpecially
the mouth when it is open ; and the teeth, with
their appearances, to difcover the national characteriftic.

Could I but define the line of the opening of the
lips, in feven promifcuous countenances, I imagine
I fhould have found the general phyfiognomonical
character of the nation or place. I almoft dare to

eſtabliſh it as an axiom, that what is common to ſix or ſeven perſons of any place, taken promiſcuouſly, is more or leſs common to the whole. Exceptions there may be, but they will be rare.

I next would plant myſelf in a public walk, or at the croſſing of ſtreets. There I would wait patiently for the unknown noble countenance, uncorrupted by fame and adulation, which certainly, moſt certainly, I ſhould find : for in all countries on earth, wherever a hundred common men are aſſembled, one not common may be found ; and out of a thouſand, ten ; and I muſt have, indeed, little eye, little ſenſibility for noble humanity, little faith in Providence, which ſeeks its adorers, if I did not find this one in a hundred, or at leaſt in the ten among the thouſand. He that ſeeketh ſhall find. I waited not in vain. He came, I found him, he paſſed by me. And what were the tokens by which I diſcovered him, in every town, every nation, under every cope of heaven, and among all people, kindred, and tongues ?—By the general combination of the countenance, by the upper outline of the forehead, the eyebrows, the baſis of the noſe, and the mouth, ſo conformable to each other, ſo parallel and horizontal, at the firſt glance. By the wrinkleſs, compreſſed, yet open forehead, the powerful eyebrows ; the eaſily diſcerned, eaſily delineated ſpace between the eyebrows, which extends itſelf to the back of the noſe, like the great ſtreet from the market-place to the chief gate of a city. By the ſhut but freely breathing mouth ; the chin, neither haggard nor fleſhy ; the deep and ſhining attraction of the eye ; which all, uncautiouſly and unintentionally betrayed themſelves to my reſearch : or, I diſcovered him even in his foreign and diſtorted form, from which the arrogant, ſelf-ſuppoſed handſome, would turn with contempt. I ſee through his diſguiſe, as I ſhould the hand of a great maſter through the ſmear of varniſh.

I approach the favourite of heaven. I queftion him concerning what I do, and what I do not wifh to know, that I may hear the voice of the foul proceeding from the mouth ; and, viewing him nearer, I fee all the obliquities of diftortion vanifh. I afk him concerning his occupation, his family, his place of refidence. I inquire the road thither. I come unexpectedly upon him into his houfe, into his workfhop ; he rifes, I oblige him to be feated, to continue his labour. I fee his children, his wife, and am delighted. He knows not what I want, nor do I know myfelf, yet I am pleafed with him, and he with me. I purchafe fomething or nothing, as it happens. I inquire particularly after his friends. " You have but few, but thofe few are faithful." He ftands aftonifhed, fmiles or weeps, in the innocence and goodnefs of his heart, which he wifhes to conceal, but which is open as day. He gains my affection ; our emotions are reciprocally expanded and ftrengthened ; we feparate reluctantly, and I know I have entered a houfe which is entered by the angels of God.

Oh ! how gratefully, how highly is he rewarded for his labours who travels, interefted in behalf of humanity, and with the eyes of a man, to collect, in the fpirit, the children of God, who are fcattered over the world ! This appears to me to be the fupreme blifs of man, as it muft be of angels.

If I meet him not, I have no refource but in fociety. Here I hear him moft who fpeaks leaft, mildeft, and moft unaffectedly. Wherever I meet the fmile of felf-fufficiency, or the oblique look of envy, I turn away, and feek him who remains opprefled by the loud voice of confidence. I fet myfelf rather befide the anfwerer than the man of clamorous loquacity ; and ftill rather befide the humble inquirer than the voluble folver of all difficulties.

He who haftens too faft, or lags behind, is no

companion of mine. I rather feek him who walks with a free, firm, and even ftep ; who looks but little about him ; who neither carries his head aloft, nor contemplates his legs and feet. If the hand of affliction be heavy on him, I fet myfelf by his fide, take his hand, and, with a glance, infufe conviction to his foul, that God is love.

I fix in my memory the fimple outlines of the loud and the violent, the laugher and the fmiler, of him who gives the key, and him who takes. I then commit them to paper ; my collection increafes. I compare, arrange, judge, and am aftonifhed. I every where find fimilarity of traits, fimilarity of character ; the fame humanity every where, and every where the fame tokens.

CHAPTER XLV.

A Word to Princes and Judges.

FOR your ufe, moft important of men, how will- ingly would I write a treatife. Who fo much as you need a perfect knowledge of man, free from cabal, or the intervention of felf-intereft ! Suffer me to approach your throne, and prefent my pe- tition.

In your moft fecret common place-book keep an index to each clafs of character among men, taken from at leaft ten of the moft accurate proofs ; not at a diftance, not among foreigners, but feek at home for the wifeft and beft of your own fubjects. Wherever a wife and good prince governs, there are excellent fubjects. Such a prince believes that he has fuch fubjects, although at the moment he fhould be unacquainted with them ; or at leaft, that he has fubjects capable of wifdom and goodnefs. Wherever one good perfon is, there certainly are two, as certainly as where the female is, there will the male be.

Suffer me, princes, confecrated as you are among men, to entreat you, for the honour of humanity, principally to ftudy, to feek for, and to feize on excellence. Judge not too fuddenly, nor by mere appearances. That which a prince once approves, it may afterwards be difficult or dangerous to reject. Depend not on the teftimony of others, which, to princes efpecially, is ever exaggerated either in praife or blame; but examine the countenance, which, though it may diffemble to a prince, or rather to the dignity of a prince, cannot deceive him as a man. Having once difcovered wifdom and goodnefs in a fubject, honour fuch a fubject as the beft bleffing which heaven can, in this world, beftow upon its favourites. Seek features that are ftrong, but not forbidding; gentle, yet not effeminate; pofitive, without turbulence; natural, not arrogant; with open eyes, clear afpects, ftrong nofes near the forehead, and with fuch let your thrones be furrounded.

Entruft your fecrets to proportionate and parallel drawn countenances: to horizontal, firm, compreffed eyebrows; channelled, not too rigoroufly clofed, red, active, but not relaxed or withered lips. Yet I will forbear to delineate, and again only entreat, that the countenance may be facred to you for the fake of goodnefs and wifdom.

And you, judges, judge not indeed by appearances, but examine according to appearances, Juftice blindfold without phyfiognomy is as unnatural as blindfold love. There are countenances which cannot have committed a multitude of vices. Study the traits of each vice, and the forms in which vice naturally or unwillingly refides. There are capabilities and incapabilities in the countenance, things which it can will, others which it cannot. Each paffion, open or concealed, has its peculiar language. The appearance of innocence is as determinate to the experienced eye as the appearance of health.

Bring guilt and innocence face to face, and examine them ; in your prefence, and when they fuppofe you do not obferve them ; in the prefence and in the abfence of witneffes ; with juftice fee, with juftice hear and obey, the determined voice of unprejudiced conviction. Remark their walk when they enter, and when they leave the judgment-hall. Let the light fall upon their countenances, be yourfelf in the fhade. Phyfiognomy will render the torture* unneceffary, will deliver innocence, will make the moft obdurate vice turn pale, will teach us how we may act upon the moft hardened. Every thing human muft be imperfect, yet will it be evident that the torture, more difgraceful to man than the halter, the axe, and the wheel, is infinitely more uncertain and dangerous than phyfiognomy. The pain of torture is more horrible even than the fucceeding death, yet it is only to prove, to difcover truth. Phyfiognomy fhall not execute, and yet it fhall prove ; and by its proof, vice alone, and not innocence, fhall fuffer. O ye judges of men, be men, and humanity fhall teach you, with more open eyes, to fee and abhor all that is human !

---

* A few years fince one philofopher wrote to another, the *torture* will foon be abolifhed in Auftria. It was afked, What fhall be its fubftitute ? The penetrating look of the judge, replied Sonnenfels. Phyfiognomy will, in twenty-five years, become a part of jurifprudence, inftead of the torture, and lectures will be read in the univerfities on the *Phyfiognomice forence*, inftead of the *Medicina forenfis*.

V

CHAPTER XLVI.

A Word to the Clergy.

YOU alfo my brethren, need a certain degree of phyfiognomy, and perhaps, princes except-ed, no men more. You ought to know whom you have before you, that you may difcern fpirits, and portion out the word of truth to each, according to his need and capacity. To whom can a know-ledge of the degree of actual and poffible virtue, in all who appear before you, be more advantageous than to you ?

To me phyfiognomy is more indifpenfable than the liturgy. It is to me alike profitable for doctrine, exhortation, comfort, correction, examination ; with the healthy, with the fick, the dying, the ma-lefactor ; in judicial examinations, and the educa-tion of youth. Without it, I fhould be as the blind leading the blind.

A fingle countenance might rob me of ardour or infpire me with enthufiafm. Whenever I preach, I generally feek the moft noble countenance, on which I endeavour to act, and the weakeft when teaching children. It is generally our own fault if our hearers are inattentive ; if they do not them-felves give the key, in which it is neceffary they fhould be addreffed.

Every teacher poffeffed of phyfiognomonical fen-fation, will eafily difcern and arrange the principal claffes among his hearers, and what each clafs can and cannot receive. Let fix or feven claffes, of va-rious capacities, be felected ; let a chief, reprefen-tative, a characteriftic countenance, of each clafs be chofen : let thefe countenances be fixed in the memory, and let the preacher accommodate himfelf to each ; fpeaking thus to one, and thus to ano-ther, and in fuch a manner to a third.

There cannot be a more natural, effective, or definite incitement to eloquence, than suppoling some characteristic countenance present of the capacity of which almoft mathematical certainty may be obtained. Having fix or feven, I have nearly my whole audience before me. I do not then fpeak to the winds. God teaches us by phyliognomy to act upon the beft of men according to the beft of means.

CHAPTER XLVII.

Phyfiognomonical Elucidations of Countenances.

A REGULAR *well formed count nance,* is where all the parts are remarkable for their fymmetry. The principal features, as the eyes, nofe, and mouth, neither fmall nor bloated ; yet diftinct and well-defined. In which the pofition of the parts, taken together, and viewed at a diftance, appears nearly horizontal and parallel.

A beautiful countenance is that in which, befides the proportion and pofition of the parts, harmony, uniformity, and mind, are vifible ; in which nothing is fuperfluous, nothing deficient, nothing difproportionate, nothing fuperadded, but all is conformity and concord.

A pleafant countenance does not neceffarily require perfect fymmetry and harmony, yet nothing muft be wanting, nothing burthenfome. Its pleafantry will principally exift in the eye and lips, which muft have nothing commanding, arrogant, contemptuous, but muft generally fpeak complacency, affability and benevolence.

V 2

A gracious countenance arifes out of the pleafant, when, far from any thing affuming, to the mildeſt benevolence are added affability and purity.

A charming countenance muſt not fimply confiſt either of the beautiful, the pleafant, or the gracious ; but when to thefe is added a rapid propriety of motion, which renders it charming.

An infinuating countenance leaves no power to active or paffive fufpicion. It has fomething more than the pleafant, by infufing that into the heart, which the pleafant only manifeſts.

Other fpecies of thefe delightful countenances are, the attracting, the winning, the irrfiſtible.

Very diſtinct from all thefe are the amufing, the divertingly loquacious, the merely mild, and alfo the tender and delicate.

Superior, and more lovely ſtill, is the purely innocent, where no diſtorted, oblique mufcle, whether in motion, or at reſt, is ever feen.

This is ſtill more exalted, when it is full of foul, of natural fympathy and power to excite fympathy.

When in a pure countenance good power is accompanied by a fpirit of order, I may call it an attic countenance.

Spiritually beautiful may be faid of a countenance where nothing thoughtlefs, inconfiderate, rude, or fevere, is to be expected ; and the afpect of which immediately and mildly incites emotion in the principal powers of the mind.

Noble is when we have not the leaſt indiſcretion to fear, and when the countenance is exalted above us, without a poffibility of envy, while it is lefs fenfible of its own fuperiority than of the pleafure we receive in its prefence.

A great countenance will have few fmall fecondary traits ; will be in grand divifions, without wrinkles; muſt exalt, muſt affect us, in fleep, in plaiſter of Paris, in every kind of caricature ; as, for example, that of Philip de Comines.

A sublime countenance can neither be painted nor described ; that by which it is distinguished from all others can only be felt. It must not only move, it must exalt the spectator. We must at once feel ourselves greater and less in its presence than in the presence of all others. Whoever is conscious of its excellence, and can despise or offend it, may, as hath been before said, blaspheme against the Holy Ghost.

CHAPTER XLVIII.

Physiognomonical Anecdotes.

I.

I REQUIRE nothing of thee, said a father to his innocent son, when bidding him farewel, but that you will bring me back your present countenance.

2. A noble, amiable, and innocent young lady, who had been educated principally in the country, saw her face in the glass as she passed it with a candle in her hand, retiring from evening prayers, and having just laid down her Bible. Her eyes were cast to the ground, with inexpressible modesty, at the sight of her own image. She passed the winter in town, surrounded by adorers, hurried away by dissipation, and plunged in trifling amusements. She forgot her Bible and her devotion. In the beginning of spring she returned to her country seat, her chamber, and the table on which the Bible lay. Again she had the candle in her hand, and again saw herself in the glass. She turned pale, put down the candle, retreated to a sofa, and fell on her

knees : " O God ! I no longer know my own face.
How am I degraded ! My follies and vanities are
all written in my countenance. Wherefore have
they been neglected, illegible, to this inftant ? O
come and expel, come and utterly efface them,
mild tranquillity, fweet devotion, and ye gentle
cares of benevolent love !"

3. " I will forfeit my life, (faid Titus of the
prieft Tacitus) if this man be not an arch knave.
I have three times obferved him figh and weep
without caufe ; and ten times turn afide to conceal a laugh he could not reftrain, when vice or
misfortune were mentioned."

4. A ftranger faid to a phyfiognomift, " How
many dollars is my face worth ?"—" It is hard to
determine," replied the latter. " It is worth fifteen hundred, (continued the queftioner) for fo
many has a perfon lent me upon it, to whom I was
a total ftranger."

5. A poor man afked alms. " How much do
you want ?" faid the perfon of whom he afked,
aftonifhed at the peculiar honefty of his countenance. " How fhall I dare to fix a fum ?" anfwered the needy perfon. " Give me what you pleafe,
Sir, I fhall be contented and thankful."—" Not fo,"
replied the phyfiognomift, " as God lives I will give
you what you want, be it little or much."—" Then,
Sir, be pleafed to give me eight fhillings."—" Here
they are ; had you afked a hundred guineas you
fhould have had them."

CHAPTER XLIX.

*Mifcellaneous Extracts from Kæmpf's Effay on the
Temperaments, with Remarks.*

I.

WILL not phyfiognomy be to man what the
looking-glafs is to an ugly woman ?

Let me alfo add to the handfome woman. The wife looks in the glafs, and wafhes away fpots; the fool looks, turns back, and remains as he was.

2. " Each tempeiament, each charaɗer, has its good and bad. The one has inclinations of which the other is incapable. The one has more than the other. The ingot is of more worth than the guineas individually, into which it is coined ; yet the latter are moſt ufeful. The tulip delights by its beauty, the carnation by its fmell. The unfeemly wormwood difpleafes both taſte and fmell, yet, in medical virtue, is fuperior to both. There it is that each contributes to the perfeɗion of the whole."

The carnation fhould not wifh to be a tulip, the finger an eye, nor the weak defire to aɗ within the circle of the ſtrong. Each has its peculiar circle, as it has its peculiar form. To wifh to depart from this circle, is like wifhing to be tranfported into another body.

3. " Within the courfe of a year, we are affured, that the aɗivity of nature changes the body, yet we are fenfible of no change of mind, although our body has been fubjeɗed to the greateſt changes, in confequence of meat, drink, air, and other accidents ; the difference of air and manner of life does not change the temperament."

The foundation of charaɗer lies deeper, and is, in a certain degree, independent of all accidents. It is probably the fpiritual and immortal texture, into which all that is vifible, corruptible and tranfitory, is interwoven.

4. " A block of wood may be carved by the ſtatuary into what form he fhall pleafe ; he may make it an Æfop or an Antinous, but he will never change the inherent nature of the wood."

To know and diſtinguifh the materials and form of men, fo far as knowledge contributes to their proper application, is the higheſt and moſt effectual wiſdom of which human nature is capable.

5. " In the eyes of certain perſons there is ſome-thing ſublime, which beams and exacts reverence. This ſublimity is the concealed power of raiſing themſelves above others, which is not the wretched effect of conſtraint, but primitive eſſence. Each finds himſelf obliged to ſubmit to this ſecret pow-er, without knowing why, as ſoon as he perceives that look, implanted by nature to inſpire reverence, ſhining in the eyes. Thoſe who poſſeſs this natu-ral, ſovereign eſſence, rule as lords, or lions, among men by native privilege, with heart and tongue conquering all.

6. " There are only four principal aſpects, all different from each other, the ardent, the dull, the fixed, and the fluctuating."

The proof of all general propoſitions is their ap-plication. Let phyſiognomonical axioms be applied to known individuals, friends or enemies, and their truth or falſehood, preciſion or inaccuracy, will eaſily be determined. Let us make the experiment with the above, and we ſhall certainly find there are numerous aſpects which are not included within theſe four : ſuch as the luminous aſpect, very dif-ferent from the ardent, and neither fixed like the melancholic, nor fluctuating like the ſanguine.

There is the look or aſpect, which is at once rapid and fixed, and, as I may ſay, penetrates and attach-es at the ſame moment. There is the tranquilly ac-tive look, neither choloric nor phlegmatic. I think it would be better to arrange them into the giving, the receiving, and the giving and receiving combi-ned ; or into intentive and extenſive ; or into the attracting, repelling, and unparticipating ; into the contracted, the relaxed, the ſtrained, the attaining, the unattaining, the tranquil, the ſteady, the ſlow, the open, the cloſe, the cold, the amorous, the com-plying, the firm, the courageous, the faithful, &c.

CHAPTER L.

Upon Portrait Painting.

PORTRAIT painting, is the moſt natural, man-ly, uſeful, noble, and, however apparently eaſy, the moſt difficult of arts. Love firſt diſcov-ered this heavenly art. Without love what could it perform ?

Since a great part of this preſent work, and the ſcience on which it treats, depend on this art, it is proper that ſomething ſhould be ſaid on the ſubjeʧt. Something ; for how new, how important, and great a work might be written on this art ! For the honour of man, and of the art, I hope ſuch a work will be written. I do not think it ought to be the work of a painter, however great in his profeſſion, but of the underſtanding friend of phyſiognomy, the man of taſte, the daily confidential obſerver of the great Portrait painter.

Sultzer, that philoſopher of taſte and diſcernment, has an excellent article, in his dictionary, on this ſubjeʧt, under the word Portrait. But what can be ſaid in a work ſo confined, on a ſubjeʧt ſo exten-five ? Again, whoever will employ his thoughts on this art, will find that it is ſufficient to exerciſe all the ſearching, all the active powers of man ; that it never can be entirely learned, nor ever can arrive at ideal perfeʧtion.

I ſhall now attempt to recapitulate ſome of the avoidable and unavoidable difficulties attendant on this art ; the knowledge of which, in my opinion, is as neceſſary to the painter as to the phyſiognomiſt.

Let us firſt inquire, What is portrait painting ? It is the communication, the preſervation of the image of ſome individual ; the art of ſuddenly de-picting all that can be depicted of that half of man, which is rendered apparent, and which never can be conveyed in words. If what Göthe has somewhere said, be true, and in my opinion nothing can be more true, that the beft text for a commentary on man, is his prefence, his countenance, his form. How important then is the art of portrait painting !

To this obfervation of Göthe's, I will add a paffage on the fubject from Sultzer's excellent dictionary : " Since no object of knowledge whatever can be more important to us than a thinking and feeling foul, it cannot be denied but that man, confidered according to his form, even though we fhould neglect what is wonderful in him, is the moft important of vifible objects."

The portrait painter fhould know, feel, and be penetrated with this; penetrated with reverence for the greateft work of the greateft mafter. Were fuch the fubject of his meditation, not from conftraint, but native fenfation ; were it as natural to him as the love of life, how important, how facred to him would his art become ! Sacred to him fhould be the living countenance as the text of holy fcripture to the tranflator. As careful fhould the one be not to falfify the work, as fhould be the other not to falfify the word of God.

How great is the contempt which an excellent tranflator of an excellent work deferves, whofe mind is wholly inferior to the mind of his original. And is it not the fame with the portrait painter ? The countenance is the theatre on which the foul exhibits itfelf : here muft its emanations be ftudied and caught. Whoever cannot feize thefe emanations, cannot paint ; and whoever cannot paint thefe, is no portrait painter.

Each perfect portrait is an important painting, fince it difplays the human mind with the peculiarities of perfonal character. In fuch we contemplate a being where underftanding, inclinations, sensations, passions, good and bad qualities of mind and heart are mingled in a manner peculiar to itself. We here frequently see them better than in nature herself, since in nature nothing is fixed, all is swift, all is transient. In nature also we seldom behold the features under that propitious aspect in which they will be transmitted by the able painter.

Could we indeed seize the fleeting transitions of nature, or had she her moments of stability, it would then be much more advantageous to contemplate nature than her likeness; but this being impossible, and since likewise few people will suffer themselves to be observed, sufficiently to deserve the name of observation, it is to me indisputable, that a better knowledge of man may be obtained from portraits than from nature, she being thus uncertain, thus fugitive.

Hence the rank of the portrait painter may easily be determined; he stands next to the historical painter. Nay history painting itself derives a part of its value from its portraits; for expression, one of the important requisites in historical painting, will be the more estimable, natural, and strong, the more of actual physiognomy is expressed in the countenances, and copied after nature. A collection of excellent portraits is highly advantageous to the historical painter for the study of expression.

Where shall we find the historical painter, who can represent real beings with all the decorations of fiction? Do we not see them all copying copies? True it is, they frequently copy from imagination; but this imagination is only stored with the fashionable figures of their own or former times.

This premised, let us now enumerate some of the surmountable difficulties of portrait painting. I am conscious the freedom with which I shall speak my thoughts will offend, yet to give offence is far from my intention. I wish to aid, to teach that art, which is the imitation of the works of God : I wish improvement. And how is improvement poſſible without a frank and undiſguiſed diſcovery of de-fects ?

In all the works of portrait painters which I have ſeen, I have remarked the want of a more philoſo-phical, that is to ſay, a more juſt, intelligible, and univerſal knowledge of men. The inſect painter, who has no accurate knowledge of inſects, the form, the general, the particular, which is appropriated to each inſect, however good a copyiſt he may be, will certainly be a bad painter of inſects. The por-trait painter, however excellent a copyiſt, (a thing much leſs general than is imagined by connoiſſeurs) will paint portraits ill, if he have not the moſt ac-curate knowledge of the form, proportion, connex-ion, and dependance of the great and minute parts of the human body, as far as they have a remark-able influence on the ſuperficies; if he has not moſt accurately inveſtigated each individual member and feature. For my own part, be my knowledge what it may, it is far from accurate in what relates to the minute ſpecific traits of each ſenſation, each member, each feature ; yet I daily remark that this acute, this indiſpenſable knowledge, is at preſent every where uncultivated, unknown, and difficult to convey to the moſt intelligent painters.

Whoever will be at the trouble of conſidering a number of men promiſcuouſly taken, feature by fea-ture, will find that each ear, each mouth, notwith-ſtanding their infinite diverſity, have yet their ſmall curves, corners, characters, which are common to all, and which are found ſtronger or weaker, more or leſs marking, in all men who are not monſters born, at leaſt in theſe parts.

Of what advantage is all our knowledge of the great proportions of the body and countenance ? (Yet even that part of knowledge is, by far, not ſufficiently ſtudied, nor ſufficiently accurate. Some future phyſiognomonical painter will juſtify this aſfertion, till when be it confidered as nothing more than cavil.) Of what advantage, I fay, is all our knowledge of the great proportions, when the knowledge of the finer traits, which are equally true, general, determinate, and no lefs fignificant, is wanting ? And this want is fo great, that I appeal to thofe who are belt informed, whether many of the ableft painters, who have painted numercus portraits, have any tolerably accurate or general theory of the mouth only. I do not mean the ana-tomical mouth, but the mouth of the painter, which he ought to fee and may fee, without any anatomi-cal knowledge.

I have examined volume after volume of engra-vings of portraits, after the greateft mafters, and am therefore intitled to fpeak. But let us confine obfervations to the mouth. Having previoufly ftudied infants, boys, youth, manhood, old age, maidens, wives, matrons, with refpect to the gene-ral properties of the mouth ; and having difcover-ed thefe, let us compare, and we fhall find that al-moft all painters have failed in the general theory of the mouth ; that it feldom happens, and feems only to happen by accident, that any mafter has underftood thefe general properties. Yet how in-defcribably much depends on them ! What is the particular, what the characteriftic, but fhades of the general ! As it is with the mouth, fo it is with the eyes, eyebrows, nofe, and each part of the counte-nance.

The fame proportion exifts between the great features of the face ; and as there is this general proportion in all countenances, however various, fo is there a fimilar proportion between the fmall traits of thefe parts. Infinitely varied are the great features, in their general combination and propor-tion. As infinitely varied are the fhades of the fmall traits, in thefe features, however great their

W

general refemblance. Without an accurate knowledge of the proportion of the principal features, as
for example, of the eyes and mouth, to each other,
it muft ever be mere accident, and accident that indeed rarely happens, when fuch proportion exifls
in the works of the painter. Without an accurate
knowledge of the particular conftituent parts, and
traits of each principal feature, I once again repeat,
it muft be accident, miraculous accident, fhould any
.one of them be juftly delineated.

This remark may induce the reflecting artift to
ftudy nature intimately by principle, and to fhow
him, if he be in fearch of permanent fame, that,
though he ought to behold and ftudy the works of
the greateft mafters with .efteem and reverence, he
yet ought to examine and judge for himfelf. Let
him not make the virtue modefly his plea, for under this does omniprefent mediocrity fhelter itfelf.
Modefty, indeed, is not fo properly virtue as the
garb and ornament of virtue, and of exifting pofitive power. Let him, I fay, examine for himfelf,
and ftudy nature in whole and in part, as if no man
ever had obferved, or ever fhould obferve, but himfelf. Deprived of this, young artift, thy glory,
will but refemble a meteor's blaze ; it will only be
.founded on the ignorance of thy cotemporaries.

By far the greateft part of the beft portrait painters, when moft fuccefsful, like the majority of
phyfiognomifts, content themfelves with expreffing
the character of the paffions in the moveable, the
mufcular features of the face. They do not underftand, they laugh at, rules which prefcribe the
grand outline of the countenance as indifpenfable
to portrait painting, independent of the effects produced by the action of the mufcles.

Till inftitutions fhall be formed for the improvement of portrait painting, perhaps till a phyfiognomonical fociety or academy fhall produce phyfiognomonical portrait painters, we fhall at beft but

creep in the regions of phyſiognomy, where we might otherwiſe ſoar. One of the greateſt obſtacles to phyſiognomy is the actual, incredible imperfection of this art. There is generally a defect of eye, or hand of the painter, or the object is defective which is to be delineated, or, perhaps, all three. The artiſt cannot diſcover what *is*, or cannot draw it when he diſcovers it. The object continually alters its poſition, which ought to be ſo exact, ſo continually the ſame ; or ſhould it not, and ſhould the painter be endowed with an all-obſerving eye, an all-imitative hand, ſtill there is the laſt inſuperable difficulty, that of the poſition of the body, which can but be momentary, which is conſtrained, falſe, and unnatural, when more than momentary.

What I have ſaid is trifling, indeed, to what might be ſaid. According to the knowledge I have of it, this is yet uncultivated ground. How little has Sulzer himſelf ſaid on the ſubject! But what could he ſay in a dictionary ? A work wholly dedicated to this is neceſſary to examine and decide on the works of the beſt portrait painters, and to inſert all the cautions and rules neceſſary for the young artiſt, in conſequence of the infinite variety, yet incredible uniformity, of the human countenance.

The artiſt who wiſhes to paint portraits perfectly, muſt ſo paint, that each ſpectator may, with truth exclaim, " This is indeed to paint ! this is true, living likeneſs ; perfect nature ; it is not painting ! Outline, form, proportion, poſition, attitude, complexion, light and ſhade, freedom, eaſe, nature ! Nature in every characteriſtic diſpoſition ! Nature in the complexion, in each trait, in her moſt beauteous, happieſt moments, her moſt ſelect, moſt propitious ſtate of mind ; near at a diſtance, on every ſide Truth and Nature ! Evident to all men, all ages, the ignorant and the connoiſſeur ; moſt cor-

ſpicuous to him who has moſt knowledge ; no ſuſ-
picion of art ; a countenance in a mirror, to which
we would ſpeak, that ſpeaks to us ; that contemplates more than it is contemplated ; we ruſh to it,
we embrace it, we are enchanted !"

Emulate ſuch excellence, young artiſts, and the
leaſt of your attainments in this age will be riches
and honour, and fame in futurity. With tears
you will receive the thanks of father, friend, and
huſband, and your work will honour that Being,
whoſe creations it is the nobleſt gift of man to imitate, only in their ſuperficies, and during a ſingle
inſtant of their exiſtence.

CHAPTER LI.

Deſcription of Plate VII.

Number 1.   *The late* KING *of* PRUSSIA.

HOW much yet how little is there of the royal
countenance in this copy ! The covered forehead, may be ſuſpected from this noſe, this ſovereign feature. The forked deſcending wrinkles of
the noſe are expreſſive of killing contempt. The
great eyes, with a noſe ſo bony, denotes a firmneſs
and fire not eaſily to be withſtood   Wit and ſatirical fancy are apparent in the mouth though defectively drawn. There is ſomething minute ſeen in
the chin which cannot well be in nature.

Number 2.   *The* EMPRESS *of* RUSSIA.

Except the ſmallneſs of the noſtril, and the diſtance of the eyebrow from the outline of the forehead, no one can miſtake the princely, the ſuperior,

Plate VII

Late K. of Prufsia.

Emp.: of Rufsia.

Voltaire.

Malherbe.

Voifin

Lavater.

the mafculine firmnefs of this, neverthelefs feminine, but fortunate and kind countenance.

Number 3. **V**OLTAIRE.

Precifion is wanting to the outline of the eye, power to the eyebrows, the fting, the fcourge of fatire to the forehead. The under part of the profile, on the contrary, fpeaks a flow of wit, acute, exuberant, exalted, ironical, never deficient in reply.

Number 4. MALHERBE.

Here is a high, comprehenfive, powerful, firm, retentive, French forehead, that appears to want the open, free, noble effence of the former; has fomething rude and productive; is more choleric; and its firmnefs appears to border on harfhnefs.

Number 5. VOISIN.

The delicate conftruction of the forehead, the afpect of the man of the world,' the beauty of the nofe, in particular, the fomewhat rafh, fatirical mouth, the pleafure loving chin, all fhow the Frenchman of a fuperior clafs.—The excellent companion, the fanciful wit, the fupple courtier, are every where apparent.

Number 6. LAVATER.

A bad likenefs of the author of thefe fragments, yet not to be abfolutely miftaken. The whole afpect, efpecially the mouth, fpeaks inoffenfive tranquillity, and benevolence bordering on weaknefs; —More underftanding and lefs fenfibility in the nofe than the author fuppofes himfelf to poffefs— Some talent for obfervation in the eye and eyebrows.

W 3

CHAPTER LII.

Miscellaneous Quotations.

1.

"CAMPANELLA has not only made very accurate obfervations on human faces, but was very expert in mimicking fuch as were any way remarkable. Whenever he thought proper to penetrate into the inclinations of thofe he had to deal with, he compofed his face, his geftures, and his whole body, as nearly as he could into the exact fimilitude of the perfon he intended to examine, and then carefully obferved what turn of mind he feemed to acquire by his change. So that, fays my author, he was able to enter into the difpotition and thoughts of people, as effectually as if he had been changed into the very man. I have often obferved that, on mimicking the geftures and looks of angry, or placid, or frightened, or daring men, I have involuntarily found my mind turned into that paffion, whofe appearance I endeavoured to imitate. Nay, I am convinced, it is hard to avoid it, though one ftrove to feparate the paffion from its correfpondent geftures. Our minds and bodies are fo clofely and intimately connected, that one is incapable of pain or pleafure without the other. Campanella, of whom we have been fpeaking, could fo abftract his attention from any fufferings of his body, that he was able to endure the rack itfelf without much pain; and, in leffer pains, every body muft have obferved, that, when we can employ our attention on any thing elfe, the pain has been for a time fufpended. On the other hand, if by any means the body is indifpofed to perform fuch geftures, or to be ftimulated into fuch emotions as any paffion ufually produces in it, that paffion itfelf never can arife, though it fhould be merely mental, and immediately affecting none of the senses. As an opiate or spiritous liquor shall suspend the operation of grief, fear, or anger, in spite of all our efforts to the contrary; and this by inducing in the body a disposition contrary to that which it receives from these passions." This passage is extracted from Burke on the Sublime and Beautiful.

2. "Who can explain wherein consists the difference of organization between an ideot and another man?"

The naturalist, whether Buffon or any other, who is become famous, and who can ask this question, will never be satisfied with any given answer, even though it were the most formal demonstration.

3. "Diet and exercise would be in vain recommended to the dying."

There are countenances which no human wisdom or power can rectify; but that which is impossible to man, is not so to God.

4. "The appearance without must be deformity and shame, when the worm gnaws within."

Let the hypocrite, devoured by conscience, assume whatever artful appearance he will, of severity, tranquillity, or vague solemnity, his distortion will ever be apparent to the physiognomist.

5. "Take a tree from its native soil, its free air, and mountainous situation, and plant it in the confined circulation of a hot-house : there it may vegetate, but in a weak and sickly condition. Feed the foreign animal in a den; you will find it in vain. It starves in the midst of plenty, or grows fat and feeble."

This, alas! is the mournful history of many a man.

6. "A portrait is the ideal of an individual, not of men in general."

A perfect portrait is neither more nor less than the circular form of a man reduced to a flat surface, and which shall have the exact appearance of the perfon for whom it was painted, feen in a ca-mera obfcura.

7. I once afked a friend, " How does it happen, that artful and fubtle people always have one or both eyes rather clofed ?"—" Becaufe they are fee-ble, (anfwered he.) Who ever faw ftrength and fubtlety united ? The miftruft of others is mean-nefs towards ourfelves."

8. This fame friend, who to me is a man of ten thoufand for whatever relates to mind, wrote two valuable letters on phyfiognomy to me, from which I am allowed to make the following extracts :

" It appears to me to be an eternal law, that the firft is the only true impreflion. Of this I offer no proof, except by afferting fuch is my belief, and by appealing to the fenfations of others. The ftran-ger affects me by his appearance, and is, to my fen-fitive being, what the fun would be to a man born blind reftored to fight.

" Rouffeau was right when he faid of D. that man does not pleafe me though he has never done me any injury; but I muft break with him before it comes to that.

" Phyfiognomy is as neceffary to man as lan-guage." I may add, as natural.

CHAPTER LIII.

Mifcellaneous Thoughts.

I.

ALL is good. All good may, and muft be mif-ufed. Phyfiognomonical fenfation is in itfelf as truly good as godlike, as expreffive of the exalt-ed worth of human nature as moral fenfation, perhaps they are both the fame. The fuppreffing, the deftroying a fenfation fo deferving of honour, where it begins to act, is finning againft ourfelves, and in reality equal to refifting the good fpirit. Indeed, good impulfes and actions muft have their limits, in order that they may not impede other good impulfes and actions.

2. Each man is a man of genius in his large or fmall fphere. He has a certain circle in which he can act with inconceivable force. The lefs his kingdom, the more concentrated is his power, confequently the more irrefiftible is his form of government. Thus the bee is the greateft of mathematicians, as far as its wants extend. Having difcovered the genius of a man, how inconfiderable foever the circle of his activity may be, having caught him in the moment when his genius is in its higheft exertions, the characteriftic token of that genius will alfo be eafily difcovered.

3. The approach of the Godhead cannot be nearer, in the vifible world, and in what we denominate nature, than in the countenance of a great and noble man. Chrift could not but truly fay, " He who feeth me feeth Him that fent me." God cannot, without a miracle, be feen any where fo fully as in the countenance of a good man. Thus the effence of any man is more prefent, more certain to me, by having obtained his fhade.

4. Great countenances awaken and ftimulate each other, excite all that can be excited. Any nation, having once produced a Spencer, a Shakefpeare, and a Milton, may be certain that a Steele, a Pope, and an Addifon will follow. A great countenance has the credentials of its high original in itfelf. With calm reverence and fimplicity nourifh the mind with the prefence of a great countenance ; its emanations fhall attract and exalt thee. A great countenance, in a ftate of reft, acts more powerfully than a common countenance impaffioned ; its ef-

fects, though unrefembling, are general. The fortunate difciples, though they knew Him not, yet did their hearts burn within them, while he talked with them by the way, and opened to them the fcriptures. The buyers and fellers whom he diove out of the Temple, durft not oppofe him.

It may from hence be conceived how certain perfons, by their mere prefence, have brought a feditious multitude back to their duty, although the latter had acquired the full power. That natural, unborrowed, indwelling power, which is confequently fuperior to any which can be affumed, is as evident to all eyes as the thunder of heaven is to all ears.

5. Great phyfiognomonical wifdom not only confifts in difcovering the general character of, and being highly affected by the prefent countenance, or this or that particular propenfity, but in difcriminating the individual character of each kind of mind, and its capacity, and being able to define the circle beyond which it cannot pafs ; to fay what fenfation, actions, and judgments, are, or are not, to be expected from the man under confideration, that we may not idly wafte power, but difpenfe juft fufficient to actuate, and put him in motion.

No man is more liable to the error of thoughtlefs hafte than I was.. Four or five years of phyfiognomonical obfervation were requifite to cure me of this too hafty wafte of power. It is a part of benevolence to give, intruft, and participate ; but phyfiognomy teaches when, how, and to whom to give. It therefore teaches true benevolence to affift where affiftance is wanted, and will be accepted. Oh ! that I could call at the proper moment, and with proper effect, to the feeling and benevolent heart. Wafte not, caft not thy feed upon the waters, or upon a rock. Speak only to the hearer ; unbofom thyfelf but to thofe who can underftand thee ; philofophize with none but philofophers ; fpi-

ritualize only with the fpiritual. It requires greater
power to bridle ftrength than to give it the rein.
To withhold is often better than to give. What is
not enjoyed will be caft back with acrimony, or
trodden to wafte, and thus will become ufelefs to
all.

6. To the good be good ; refift not the irrefiftible countenance. Give the eye that afks, that comes
recommended to thee by Providence, or by God
himfelf, and which to rejeᴄt is to rejeᴄt God, who
cannot afk thee more powerfully than when entreating in a cheerful, open, innocent countenance.
Thou canft not more immediately glorify God than
by wifhing and aᴄting well to a countenance replete
with the fpirit of God ; nor more certainly, and
abhorrently, offend and wound the majefty of God,
than by defpifing, ridiculing, and turning from
fuch a countenance. God cannot more effeᴄtually
move man than by man. Whoever rejeᴄts the man
of God, rejeᴄts God. To difcover the radiance of
the Creator in the vifage of man is the pre-eminent
quality of man ; it is the fummit of wifdom and
benevolence to feel how much of this radiance is
there, to difcern this ray of Divinity through the
clouds of the moft debafed countenances, and dig
out this fmall gem of heaven from amid the ruins
and rubbifh by which it is encumbered.

7. Shouldeft thou, friend of man, efteem phyfiognomy as highly as I do, to whom it daily becomes
of greater worth, the more I difcover its truth ; if
thou haft an eye to feleᴄt the few noble, or that
which is noble in the ignoble, that which is divine
in all men, the immortal in what is mortal, then
fpeak little, but obferve much ; difpute not, but
exercife thy feufation ; for thou wilt convince no
one to whom this fenfation is wanting.

When noble poverty prefents to you a face, in
which humility, patience, faith, and love, fhine
confpicuoufly, how fuperior will thy joy be in his

words who has told thee, "inafmuch as thou haft done it unto one of the leaft of thefe my brethren, thou haft done it unto me!"

With a figh of hope you will exclaim, when youth and diffipation prefent themfelves, this forehead was delineated by God for the fearch and the difcovery of truth. In this eye refts wifdom yet unripened.

CHAPTER LIV.

Of the Union between the Knowledge of the Heart and Philanthropy.—Mifcellaneous phyfiognomical Thoughts from Holy Writ.

MAY the union between the knowledge of the heart and philanthropy be obtained by the fame means? Does not a knowledge of the heart deftroy or weaken philanthropy? Does not our good opinion of any man diminifh when he is perfectly known? And if fo, how may philanthropy be increafed by this knowledge?

What is here alledged is truth; but it is partial truth. And how fruitful a fource of error is partial truth! It is a certain truth, that the majority of men are lofers, by being accurately known. But it is no lefs true, that the majority of men gain as much on one fide, as they lofe on the other by being thus accurately known. Who is fo wife as never to act foolifhly? Where is the virtue wholly unpolluted by vice; with thoughts, at all moments, fimple, direct, and pure? I dare undertake to maintain, that all men, with fome very rare exceptions, lofe by being known. But it may alfo be proved, by the moſt irrefragable arguments, that all men gain by being known ; confequently a knowledge of the heart is not detrimental to the love of mankind, but promotes it.

Phyſiognomy diſcovers actual and poſſible perfections, which, without its aid, muſt ever have remained hidden. The more man is ſtudied, the more power and poſitive goodneſs he will be diſcovered to poſſeſs. As the experienced eye of the painter, perceives a thouſand ſmall ſhades and colours, which are unremarked by common ſpectators, ſo the phyſiognomiſt views a multitude of actual or poſſible perfections, which eſcape the general eye of the deſpiſer, the ſlanderer, or even the more benevolent judge of mankind.

I ſpeak from experience the good which I, as a phyſiognomiſt, have obſerved in people round me, has more than compenſated that maſs of evil, which, though I appeared blind, I could not avoid ſeeing.

The more I have ſtudied man, the more have I been convinced of the general influence of his faculties ; the more have I remarked, that the origin of all evil is good, that thoſe very powers which made him evil, thoſe abilities, forces, irritability, elaſticity, were all in themſelves actual, poſitive good. The abſence of theſe, indeed, would have occaſioned the abſence of an infinity of evil, but ſo would they likewiſe of an infinity of good. The eſſence of good has given birth to much evil ; but it contains in itſelf the poſſibility of a ſtill infinite increaſe of good.

The leaſt failing of an individual incites a general outcry, and his character is at once darkened, trampled on, and deſtroyed. The phyſiognomiſt views and praiſes the man whom the whole world condemns. What, does he praiſe vice ?—No—Does he excuſe the vicious ?—No : he whiſpers, or loudly affirms, "Treat this man after ſuch a manner, and you will be aſtoniſhed at what he is able,

X

what he may be made willing to perform. He is not fo wicked as he appears; his countenance is better than his actions. His actions, it is true, are legible in his countenance; but not more legible than his great powers, his fenfibility, the pliability of that heart which has had an improper bent. Give but thefe powers, which have rendered him vicious, another direction, and other objects, and he will perform miracles of virtue."

Yes, the phyfiognomift will pardon where the moft benevolent philanthropift muft condemn. For myfelf, fince I have become a phyfiognomift, I have gained knowledge, fo much more accurate, of fo many excellent men, and have had fuch frequent occafions to rejoice my heart in the difcoveries I made concerning fuch men, that this, as I may fay, has reconciled me to the whole human race. What I here mention as having happened to myfelf, each phyfiognomift being himfelf, a man, muft have undoubtedly felt.

Mifcellaneous Phyfiognomonical Thoughts from Holy Writ.

" Thou haft fet our iniquities before thee, our fecret fins in the light of our countenance." Pfalm xc. 8.—No man believes in the omnifcience, or has fo ftrong a conviction of the prefence of God and his angels, or reads the hand of heaven fo vifible in the human countenance, as the phyfiognomift.

" Which of you by taking thought can add one cubit unto his ftature ?—And why take ye thought for raiment ?—Seek ye firft the kingdom of God, and his righteoufnefs, and all thefe things fhall be added unto you." Matt. vi. 27, 28, 33.—No man, therefore, can alter his form. The improvement of the internal will alfo be the improvement of the external. Let men take care of the internal, and a fufficient care of the external will be the refult.

" When ye faft, be not as the hypocrites, of a

fad countenance; for they disfigure their faces that they may appear unto men to faft. Verily I fay unto you, they have their reward. But thou, when thou fafteft, anoint thine head and walh thy face, that thou appear not unto men to faft, but unto thy Father which is in fecret, and thy Father, which feeth in fecret, fhall reward thee openly." Matt. vi. 16, 17, 18 —Virtue, like vice, may be concealed from men, but not from the Father in fecret, nor from him in whom his fpirit is, who fathoms not only the depths of humanity but of divinity. He is rewarded, who means that the good he has fhould be feen in his countenance.

"Some feeds fell by the way fide, and the fowls came and devoured them up; fome fell upon ftony places, where they had not much earth, and forthwith they fprung up, becaufe they had no deepnefs of earth; and when the fun was up they were fcorched, and becaufe they had not car h they withered away; and fome fell among thorns, and the thorns fprung up and choaked them; but others fell into good ground, and brought forth fruit, fome an hundred fold, fome fixty fold, fome thirty fold." Matt. xiii. 4, 5, 6, 7, 8 —There are many men, many countenances, in whom nothing can be planted, each fowl devours the feed; or they are hard like ftone, with little earth, (or flefh) have habits which ftifle all that is good. There are others that have good bones, good flefh, with a happy proportion of each, and no ftifling habits.

"For whofoever hath to him fhall be given, and he fhall have more abundance; but whofoever hath not, from him fhall be taken away even that he hath." Matt. xiii. 12.—True again of the good and bad countenance. He who is faithful to the propenfities of nature, he hath, he enjoys, he will manifeftly be ennobled. The bad will lofe even the good traits he hath received.

"Take heed that you defpife not one of thefe

X 2

little ones ; for I fay unto you, that in heaven their angels do always behold the face of my father which is in heaven." Matt. xviii. 10.—Probably the angels fee the countenance of the father in the countenance of the children.

"If any man have ears to hear let him hear. Do you not perceive, that whatever thing from without entereth into the man it cannot defile him, becaufe it entereth not into his heart, but into the belly, and goeth out into the draught, purging all meats? And he faid, that which cometh out of the man, that defileth the man." Mark vii. 16, 18, 19, 20.—This is phyfiognomonically true. Not external accidents, nor fpots which may be wafhed away, not wounds which may be healed, nor even fcars which remain, will defile the countenance in the eye of the phyfiognomift, neither can paint beautify it to him.

" A little leaven leaveneth the whole lump." Galat. v. o.—A little vice often deforms the whole countenance. One fingle falfe trait makes the whole a caricature.

" Ye are our epiftle, written in our hearts, known and read of all men. Forafmuch as ye are manifeftly declared to be the epiftle of Chrift miniftered by us, written not with ink, but with the fpirit of the living God." 2 Cor. iii. 2, 3.—What need have the good of letters of recommendation to the good? The open countenance recommends itfelf to the open countenance. No letters of recommendation can recommend the perfidious countenance, nor can any flanderer deprive the countenance, beaming with the divine fpirit, of its letters of recommendation. A good countenance is the beft letter of recommendation.

I fhall conclude with the important paffage from the epiftle to the Romans:

" God hath concluded them all in unbelief, that he might have mercy upon all. Oh! the depth of the riches, both of the wifdom and knowledge of God! How unfearchable are his judgments, and his ways paſt finding out! For who hath known the mind of the Lord? or who hath been his counfellor? or who hath firſt given to him, and it ſhall be recompenfed unto him again? For of him, and through him, and to him, are all things. To whom be glory for ever. Amen."

CHAPTER LV.

Of the apparently falfe decifions of Phyſiognomy—Of the general Objections made to Phyſiognomy—Particular objections anſwered.

ONE of the ftrongeſt objections to the certainty of phyfiognomy is, that the beſt phyfiognomiſts often judge very erroneouſly.

It may be proper to make fome remarks on this objection.

Be it granted the phyfiognomiſt often errs; that is to fay, his difcernment errs, not the countenance —But to conclude there is no fuch fcience as phyfiognomy, becaufe phyfiognomiſts err, is the fame thing as to conclude there is no reafon, becaufe there is much falfe reafoning.

To fuppofe that, becaufe the phyfiognomiſt has made fome falfe decifions, he has no phyfiognomonical difcernment, is equal to fuppofing that a man, who had committed fome miſtakes of memory, has no memory; or, at beſt, that his memory is very weak —We muſt be lefs haſty. We muſt firſt inquire in what proportion his memory is faithful, how often it has failed, how often been accurate. The mifer may perform ten acts of charity: muſt

X 3

we therefore affirm he is charitable ? Should we
not rather inquire how much he might have given,
and how often it has been his duty to give ?—The
virtuous man may have ten times been guilty, but
before he is condemned, it ought to be afked, in
how many hundred inftances he has acted uprightly ?
He who games muft oftener lofe than he who re-
frains from gaming. He who flides or fkaits upon
the ice is in danger of many a fall, and of being
laughed at by the lefs adventurous fpectator. Whoever frequently gives alms, is liable, occafionally,
to diftribute his bounties to the unworthy. He,
indeed, who never gives cannot commit the fame
miftake, and may truly vaunt of his prudence, fince
he never furnifhes opportunities for deceit. In
like manner, he who never judges never can judge
falfely. The phyfiognomift judges oftener than
the man who ridicules phyfiognomy, confequently
muft oftener err than he who never rifks a phyfiognomonical decifion.

Which of the favourable judgments of the benevolent phyfiognomift may not be decried as falfe ?
Is he not himfelf a mere man, however circumfpect,
upright, honourable and exalted he may be ; a man
who has in himfelf the root of all evil, the germe
of every vice ; or, in other words, a man whofe
moft worthy propenfities, qualities, and inclinations, may occafionally be overftrained, wrefted,
and warped ?

You behold a meek man, who, after repeated
and continued provocations to wrath, perfifts in
filence ; who, probably, never is overtaken by anger, when he himfelf alone is injured. The phyfiognomift can read his heart, fortified to bear and
forbear, and immediately exclaims, behold the
moft amiable, the moft unconquerable, gentlenefs.
—You are filent—You laugh—You leave the place,
and fay, " Fye on fuch a phyfiognomift ! How full
of wrath have I feen this man !"—When was it

that you faw him in wrath?—Was it not when fome one had miftreated his friend?—" Yes, and he behaved like a frantic man in defence of this friend, which is proof fufficient that the fcience of phyfiognomy is a dream, and the phyfiognomift a dreamer."—But who is in an error, the phyfiognomift or his cenfurer?—The wifeft man may fometimes utter folly—This the phyfiognomift knows, but, regarding it not, reveres and pronounces him a wife man.—You ridicule the decifion, for you have heard this wife man fay a foolifh thing.—Once, more, who is in an error?—The phyfiognomift does not judge from a fingle incident, and often not from feveral combining incidents.—Nor does he, as a phyfiognomift, judge only by actions. He obferves the propenfities, the character, the effential qualities and powers, which often, are apparently contradicted by individual actions.

Again—He who feems ftupid or vicious may yet probably poffefs indications of a good underftanding, and propenfities to every virtue. Should the beneficent eye of the phyfiognomift, who is in fearch of good, perceive thefe qualities, and announce them; fhould he not pronounce a decided, judgment againft the man, he immediately becomes a fubject of laughter. Yet how often may difpofitions to the moft heroic virtue be there buried! How often may the fire of genius lay deeply fmothered beneath the embers!—Wherefore do you fo anxioufly, fo attentively, rake among thefe afhes?—Becaufe here is warmth—Notwithftanding that at the firft, fecond, third, fourth raking, duft only will fly in the eyes of the phyfiognomift and fpectator. The latter retires laughing, relates the attempt, and makes others laugh alfo. The former may perhaps patiently wait and warm himfelf by the flame he has excited. Innumerable are the inftances where the moft excellent qualities are evergrown and ftifled by the weeds of error. Fu-

turity fhall difcover why, and the difcovery fhall
not be in vain. The common unpractifed eye be-
holds only a defolate wildernefs. Education, circumftances, neceffities, ftifle every effort toward
perfection. The phyfiognomift infpects, becomes
attentive, and waits. He fees and obferves a thoufand contending contradictory qualities; he hears
a multitude of voices exclaiming, What a man !
But he hears too the voice of the Deity exclaim,
What a man ! He prays, while thofe revile who
cannot comprehend, or, if they can, will not, that
in the countenance, under the form they view,
lie concealed beauty, power, wifdom, and a divine
nature.

Still further, the phyfiognomift, or obferver of
man, who is a man, a Chriftian, that is to fay a wife
and good man, will a thoufand times act contrary to
his own phyfiognomonical fenfations, I do not exprefs myfelf accurately—He appears to act contrary
to his internal judgment of the man. He fpeaks
not all he thinks—This is an additional reafon why
the phyfiognomift fo often appears to err ; and
why the true obferver, obfervation and truth are in
him, is fo often miftaken, and ridiculed. He reads
the villain in the countenance of the beggar at his
door, yet does not turn away, but fpeaks friendly
to him, fearches his heart, and difcovers ;—Oh
God, what does he difcover !—An immeafurable
abyf, a chaos of vice !—But does he difcover nothing more, nothing good ?—Be it granted he finds
nothing good, yet he there contemplates clay which
muft not fay to the potter, why haft thou made me
thus ? He fees, prays, turns away his face, and
hides a tear which fpeaks, with eloquence inexpreffible, not to man, but to God alone. He ftretches
out his friendly hand, not only in pity to a haplefs
w.fe, whom he has rendered unfortunate, not only
for the fake of his helplefs innocent children, but
in compaffion to himfelf, for the fake of God, who.

has made all things, even the wicked themfelves, for his own glory. He gives, perhaps, to kindle a fpark which he yet perceives, and this is what is called (in fcripture) giving his heart.—Whether the unworthy man mifufes the gift, or mifufes it not, the judgment of , the donor will alike be arraigned. Whoever hears of the gift will fay, How has this good man again fuffered himfelf to be deceived !

Man is not to be the judge of man, and who feels this truth more coercively than the phyfiognomift ? The mightieft of men, the Ruler of man, came not to judge the world, but to fave. Not that he did not fee the vices of the vicious, nor that he concealed them from himfelf or others, when philanthropy required they fhould be remarked and detected. Yet he judged not, punifhed not.—He forgave— " Go thy way fin no more."—Judas he received as one of his difciples, protected him, embraced him— Him in whom he beheld his future betrayer.

Good men are moft apt to difcover good —Thine eye cannot be chriftian if thou givest me not thy heart. Wifdom without goodnefs is folly, I will judge juftly and act benevolently.

Once more—A profligate man, an abandoned woman, who have ten times been to blame when they affirmed they were not, on the eleventh are condemned when they are not to blame. They apply to the phyfiognomift. He inquires, and finds that, this time they are innocent. Difcretion loudly tells him he will be cenfured fhould he fuffer it to be known that he believes them innocent ; but his heart more loudly commands him to fpeak, to bear witnefs for the prefent innocence of fuch rejected perfons. A word efcapes him and a multitude of reviling voices are at once heard—" Such a judgment ought not to have been made by a phyfiognomift !"—Yet who has decided erroneoufly ?

The above are a few hints and reafons to the difcerning, to induce them to judge as cautioufly con-

cerning the phyfiognomift, as they would wifh him
to judge concerning themfelves, or others.

Of the general Objections made to Phyfiognomy.

Innumerable are the objections which may be
raifed againft the certainty of judgments drawn from,
the lines and features of the human countenance.
Many of thefe appear to me to be eafy, many difficult, and fome impoffible to be anfwered.

Before I felect any of them, I will firft ftate fome
general remarks, the accurate confideration, and
proof of which will remove many difficulties.

It appears to me that, in all refearches, we ought
firft to inquire what can be faid in defence of any
propofition. One irrefragable proof of the actual
exiftence and certainty of a thing will overbalance
ten thoufand objections. One pofitive witnefs, who
has all poffible certainty that knowledge and reafon
can give, will preponderate againft innumerable
others who who arc only negative. All objections
againft a certain truth are in reality only negative
evidence. " We never obferved this : we never
experienced that."—Though ten thoufand fhould
make this affertion, what would it prove againft one
man of underftanding, and found reafon, who
fhould anfwer, " But I have obferved, and you,
alfo, may obferve, if you pleafe." No well founded objection can be made againft the exiftence of a
thing vifible to fenfe. Argument cannot difprove
fact. No two oppofing pofitive facts can be adduced ; all objections, to a fact, therefore, mutt be
negative.

Let this be applied to phyfiognomy. Pofitive
proofs of the true and acknowleged fignification of
the face and its features, againft the clearnefs and
certainty of which nothing can be alledged, render
innumerable objections, although they cannot probably be anfwered, perfectly infignificant. Let us

therefore endeavour to inform ourfelves of thofe pofitive arguments which phyfiognomy affords. Let us fiift make ourfelves ftedfaft in what is certainly true, and we fhall foon be enabled to anfwer many objections, or to reject them as unworthy any anfwer.

It appears to me that in the fame proportion as a man remarks and adheres to the pofitive, will be the ftrength and perfeverance of his mind. He whofe talents do not furpafs mediocrity is accuftomed to overlook the pofitive, and to maintain the negative with invincible obftinacy.

Thou fhouldeft firft confider what thou art, what is thy knowledge, and what are thy qualities and powers, before thou inquireft what thou art not, knoweft not, and what the qualities and powers are that thou haft not ? This is a rule which every man who wifhes to be wife, virtuous and happy ought, not only to prefcribe to himfelf, but, if I may ufe fo bold a figure, to incorporate with, and make a part of, his very foul. The truly wife always firft directs his inquiries concerning what is ; the man of weak intellect, the pedant, firft fearches for that which is wanting. The true philofopher looks firft for the pofitive proofs of the propofition. I fay firft—I am very defirous that my meaning fhould not be mifunderftood, and, therefore, repeat, *firft*. The fuperficial mind firft examines the negative objections.—This has been the method purfued by infidels, the opponents of Chriftianity. Were it granted that Chriftianity were falfe, ftill this method would neither be logical, true, nor conclufive. Therefore fuch modes of reafoning muft be fet afide, as neither logical nor conclufive, before we can proceed to anfwer objections.

To return once more to phyfiognomy, the queftion will be reduced to this.—" Whether there are any proofs fufficiently pofitive and decifive, in favour of phyfiognomy, to induce us to difregard the moſt plauſible objections ?"—Of this I am as much convinced as I am of my own exiſtence ; and every unprejudiced reader will be the ſame, who ſhall read this work through, if he only poſſefs ſo much diſcernment and knowledge as not to deny that eyes are given us to ſee! although there are innumerable eyes in the world that look and do not ſee.

It may happen that learned men, of a certain deſcription, will endeavour to perplex me by argument. They, for example, may cite the female buterfly of Reaumur, and the large winged ant, in order to prove how much we may be miſtaken, with reſpect to final cauſes, in the products of nature—They may aſſert, " wings, undoubtedly ap-" pear to be given for the purpoſe of flight, yet " theſe inſects never fly ; therefore wings are not " given for that purpoſe.—And by a parity of rea-" ſoning, ſince there are wiſe men, who, probably " do not ſee, eyes are not given for the purpoſe of " ſight."—To ſuch objections I ſhall make no reply, for never, in my whole life, have I been able to anſwer a ſophiſm. I appeal only to common ſenſe. I view a certain number of men, who all have the gift of ſight, when they open their eyes, and there is light, and who do not ſee when their eyes are ſhut. As this certain number are not ſelect, but taken promiſcuouſly, among millions of exiſting men, it is the higheſt poſſible degree of probability that all men, whoſe formation is ſimilar, that have lived, do live, or ſhall live, being alike provided with thoſe organs we call eyes, muſt ſee. This at leaſt, has been the mode of arguing and concluding among all nations, and in all ages. In the ſame degree as this mode of reaſoning is convincing, when applied to other ſubjects, ſo it is when applied to phyſiognomy, and is equally applicable ; and, if untrue in phyſiognomy, it is equally untrue in every other inſtance.

I am therefore of opinion, that the defender of

phyfiognomy may reft the truth of the fcience on
this propofition, " That it is univerfally confeffed
" that, among ten, twenty, or thirty men, indif-
" criminately felected, there as certainly exifts a
" phyfiognomonical expreffion, or demonftrable
" correfpondence of internal power and fenfation,
" with external form and figure, as that, among
" the like number of men, in the like manner fe-
" lected, they have eyes and can fee." Having
proved this, he has as fufficiently proved the uni-
verfality and truth of phyfiognomy as the univer-
fality of fight by the aid of eyes, having fhown'that
ten, twenty, or thirty men, by the aid of eyes,
are all capable of feeing. From a part I draw a conclufion to the whole; whether thofe I have feen
or thofe I have not.

But it will be anfwered, though this may be
proved of certain features, does it therefore, follow that it may be proved of all ?—I am perfuaded
it may : if I am wrong fhow me my error.

Having remarked that men who have eyes and
ears fee and hear, and being convinced that eyes
were given him for the purpofe of fight, and ears
for that of hearing; being unable longer to doubt
that eyes and ears have their deftined office, I think
I draw no improper conclufion, when I fuppofe
that every other fenfe, and member, of this fame
human body, which fo wonderfully form a whole,
has each a particular purpofe; although it fhould
happen that I am unable to difcover what the particular purpofes of fo many fenfes, members, and
integuments may be. Thus do I reafon alfo, concerning the fignification of the countenance of man,
the formation of his body, and the difpofition of
his members.

If it can be proved that any two or three features
have a certain determinate fignification, as determinate as that the eye is the expreffion of the countenance, is it not accurate to conclude, according

Y

to the mode of reasoning above cited, universally acknowledged to be just, that those features are also significant, with the signification of which I am unacquainted.—I think myself able to prove, to every person of the commonest understanding, that all men without exception, at least under certain circumstances, and in some particular feature, may, indeed, have more than one feature, of a certain determinate signification ; as surely as I can render it comprehensible, to the simplest person, that certain determinate members of the human body are to answer certain determinate purposes.

Twenty or thirty men, taken promiscuously, when they laugh, or weep, will, in the expression of their joy or grief, possess something in common with, or similar to, each other. Certain features will bear a greater resemblance to each other among them than they otherwise do, when not in the like sympathetic state of mind.

To me it appears evident that, since excessive joy and grief are universally acknowledged to have their peculiar expressions, and that the expression of each is as different as the different passions of joy and grief, it must, therefore, be allowed that the state of rest, the medium between joy and grief, shall likewise have its peculiar expression; or, in other words, that the muscles which surround the eyes and lips, will indubitably be found to be in a different state.

If this be granted concerning the state of the mind in joy, grief, or tranquillity ; why should not the same be true concerning pride, humility, patience, magnanimity, and other affections ?

According to certain laws the stone flies upward, when thrown with sufficient force ; by other laws, equally certain, it afterwards falls to the earth ; and will it not remain unmoved according to laws equally fixed if suffered to be at rest ? Joy according to certain laws expressed in one manner, grief in another, and tranquillity in a third. Wherefore then fhall not anger, gentlenefs, pride, humility, and other paffions, be fubject to certain laws; that is, to certain fixed laws?

All things in nature are or are not fubjected to certain laws. There is a caufe for all things or there is not. All things are caufe and effect, or are not. Ought we not hence to derive one of the firft axioms of philofophy? And, if this be granted, how immediately is phyfiognomy relieved from all objections, even from thofe which we know not how to anfwer; that is, as foon as it fhall be granted there are certain characteriftic features, in all men, as characteriftic as the eyes are to the countenance!

But, it will be faid, how different are the expreffions of joy and grief, of the thoughtful and the thoughtlefs! And how may thefe expreffions be reduced to rule?

How different from each other are the eyes of men, and of all creatures; the eye of an eagle from the eye of a mole, an elephant, and a fly! and yet we believe of all who have no evident figns of infirmity, or death, that they may fee.

The feet and ears are as various as are the eyes; yet we univerfally conclude of them all, they were given us for the purpofes of hearing and walking.

Thefe varieties by no means prevent our believing that the eyes, ears, and feet, are the expreffions, the organs of feeing, hearing, and walking; and why fhould we not draw the fame conclufions concerning all features and lineaments of the human body? The expreffions of fimilar difpofitions of mind cannot have greater variety than have the eyes, ears and feet, of all beings that fee, hear, and walk; yet may we as eafily obferve and determine what they have in common, as we can obferve and determine what the eyes, ears, and feet, which are

Y 2

ſo various, among all beings that ſee, hear, and walk,
have alſo in common. This well conſidered, how
many objections will be anſwered or, become inſignificant !

Various Objections to Phyſiognomy Anſwered.

Objection 1. " It is ſaid, we find perſons who,
from youth to old age, without ſickneſs, without
debauchery, have continually a pale, death-like aſpect; who, neverthelefs, enjoy an uninterrupted
and confirmed ſtate of health."

Anſwer. Theſe are uncommon caſes. A thouſand men will ſhow their ſtate of health by the complexion and roundneſs of the countenance, to one
in whom theſe appearances will differ from the
truth.—I ſuſpect that theſe uncommon caſes are the
effects of impreſſions, made on the mother, during
her ſtate of pregnancy.—Such caſes may be confidered as exceptions, the accidental cauſes of which
may, perhaps, not be difficult to diſcover.

To me it ſeems we have as little juſt cauſe hence
to draw concluſions againſt the ſcience of phyſiognomy, as we have againſt the proportion of the
human body, becauſe there are dwarfs, giants, and
monſtrous births.

Objection 2. A friend writes me word, " He is
acquainted with a man of prodigious ſtrength, who,
the hands excepted, has every appearance of weakneſs, and would be ſuppoſed weak by all to whom
he ſhould be unknown."

Anſwer. I could wiſh to ſee this man. I much
doubt whether his ſtrength be only expreſſed in his
hands, or, if it were, ſtill it is expreſſed, in the
hands; and, were no exterior ſigns of ſtrength to
be found, ſtill he muſt be conſidered as an exception, an example unexampled. But, as I have ſaid,
I much doubt the fact. I have never yet ſeen a
ſtrong man whoſe ſtrength was not diſcoverable in
various parts.

Objection 3. " We perceive the signs of bravery and heroism in the countenances of men who are, notwithstanding, the first to run away."

Answer. The less the man is the greater he wishes to appear.

But what were these signs of heroism ? Did they resemble those found in the Farnesian Hercules ?— Of this I doubt : let them be drawn, let them be produced ; the physiognomist will probably say, at the second, if not at the first, glance, *quanta species !* Sickness, accident, melancholy, likewise, deprive the bravest men of courage. This contradiction, however ought to be apparent, to the physiognomist.

Objection 4. " We find persons whose exterior appearance denotes extreme pride, and who, in their actions, never betray the least symptom of pride."

Answer. A man may be proud, and affect humility.

Education and habit may give an appearance of pride, although the heart be humble ; but this humility of heart will shine through an appearance of pride, as sunbeams through transparent clouds. It is true that this apparently proud man would have more humility had he less of the appearance of pride.

Objection 5. " We see mechanics who, with incredible ingenuity, produce the most curious works of art, and bring them to the greatest perfection ; yet who, in their hands and bodies, resemble the rudest peasants and wood-cutters ; while the hands of fine ladies are totally incapable of such minute and curious performances."

Answer. I should desire these rude and delicate frames to be brought together and compared.— Most naturalists describe the elephant as gross and stupid in appearance ; and, according to this apparent stupidity, or rather according to that stupidity which they afcribe to him, wonder at his addrefs. Let the elephant and the tender lamb be placed fide by fide, and the fuperiority of addrefs will be vifible from the formation and flexibility of the body without farther trial.

Ingenuity and addrefs do not fo much depend upon the mafs as upon the nature, mobility, internal fenfation, nerves, conftruction, and fupplenefs of the body and its parts.

Delicacy is not power, power is not minutenefs. Apelles would have drawn better with charcoal than many miniature painters wi. 1 the fineft pencil. The tools of a mechanic may be rude, and his mind the very reverfe. Genius will work better with a clumfy hand, than ftupidity with a hand the moft pliable.—I will indeed allow your objection to be well founded, if nothing of the character of an artift is difcoverable in his countenance ; but, before you come to a decifion, it is neceffary you fhould be acquainted with the various marks that denote mechanical genius, in the face. Have you confidered the luftre, the acutenefs, the penetration, of his eyes ; his rapid, his decifive, his firm afpect ; the projecting bones of his brow, his arched forehead, the fupplenefs, the delicacy, or the maffinefs of his limbs ? Have you well confidered thefe particulars ? "I could not fee it in him," is eafily faid. More confideration is requifite to difcover the character of the man.

Objection 6. "There are perfons of peculiar penetration who have very unmeaning countenances."

Anfwer. The affertion requires proof.

For my own part, after many hundred miftakes, I have continually found the fault was in my want of proper obfervation.—At firft, for example, I looked for the tokens of any particular quality, too much in one place ; I fought and found it not, although I knew the perfon poffeffed extraordinary powers. I have been long before I could difcover the feat of character. I was deceived, fometimes by feeking too partially, at others, too generally. To this I was particularly liable in examining thofe who had only diftinguifhed themfelves in fome particular purfuit ; and, in other refpects, appeared to be perfons of very common abilities, men whofe powers were all concentrated to a point, to the examination of one fubject ; or men whofe powers were very indeterminate : I exprefs myfelf improperly, powers which had never been excited, brought into action. Many years ago, I was acquainted with a great mathematician, the aftonifhment of Europe ; who, at the firft fight, and even long after, appeared to have a very common countenance. I drew a good likenefs of him, which obliged me to pay a more minute attention, and found a particular trait which was very marking and decifive. A fimilar trait to this, I many years afterwards, difcovered in another perfon, who, though widely different, was alfo a man of great talents ; and who, this trait excepted, had an unmeaning countenance, which feemed to prove the fcience of phyfiognomy all erroneous. Never fince this time have I difcovered that particular trait in any man who did not poffefs fome peculiar merit, however fimple his appearance might be.

This proves how true and falfe, at once, the objection may be which ftates, " Such a perfon appears to be a weak man, yet has great powers of mind."

I have been written to concerning D'Alembert, whofe countenance, contrary to all pohyfiognomonical fcience, was one of the moft common. To this I can make no anfwer, unlefs I had feen D'Alembert. This much is certain, that his profile, by Cochin, which yet muft be very inferior to the original, not to mention other lefs obvious traits, has a forehead, and in part a nofe, which were ne-

ver feen in the countenance of any perfon of moderate, not to fay mean, abilities.

Objection 7. " We find very filly people with
very expreflive countenances."

Who does not daily make this remark ? My only
anfwer, which I have repeatedly given, and which I
think perfectly fatisfactory, is, that the endowments of nature may be excellent ; and yet by want
of ufe, or abufe, may be deftroyed. Power is there,
but it is power mifapplied : the fire wafted in the
purfuit of pleafure can no longer be applied to the
difcovery and difplay of truth.—It is fire without
light, fire that ineffectually burns.

I have the happinefs to be acquainted with fome
of the greateft men in Germany and Switzerland ;
and I can, upon my honour, affert that, of all the
men of genius with whom I am acquainted, there
is not one who does not exprefs the degree of invention and powers of mind he poffeffes in the features of his countenance, and particularly in the
form of his head.

I fhall only felect the following names, from an
innumerable multitude.   Charles XII. Louis XIV.
Turenne, Sully, Polignac, Montefquieu, Voltaire,
Diderot.—Newton, Clarke, Maupertuis, Pope,
Locke, Swift, Leffing, Bodmer, Sultzer, Haller.
I believe the character of greatnefs in thefe heads is
vifible in every well drawn outline.   I could produce numerous fpecimens, among which an experienced eye would fcarcely ever be miftaken.

F I N I S.

www.ingramcontent.com/pod-product-compliance
Lightning Source LLC
Chambersburg PA
CBHW020857020726
47497CB00005B/1446